Restless Spirits

Restless Spirits

Ghost Stories by American Women, 1872–1926

Edited with an introduction by

Catherine A. Lundie

University of Massachusetts Press

AMHERST

LC 96-19250
ISBN 1-55849-055-8 (cloth); 056-6 (pbk.)

Designed by Steve Dyer
Set in Adobe Caslon
Printed and bound by Braun-Brumfield, Inc.

Library of Congress Cataloging-in-Publication Data
Restless spirits : ghost stories by American women, 1872-1926 /
edited with an introduction by Catherine A. Lundie.
p. cm.
Includes bibliographical references.
ISBN 1-55849-055-8 (cloth : alk. paper). —
ISBN 1-55849-056-6 (pbk. : alk. paper)
1. Ghost stories, American. 2. American fiction—Women authors.
3. American fiction—20th century. 4. American fiction—19th century.
5. Supernatural—Fiction. 6. Women—Fiction.
I. Lundie, Catherine A., 1961-   .
PS648.G48R47   1996
813'.08733089287—dc20   96-19250
CIP

British Library Cataloguing in Publication data are available.

*For the women who
penned these splendid tales*

ACKNOWLEDGMENTS

To Mary Nyquist, Dennis Duffy, Linda Hutcheon, and Janet Benton for their advice and encouragement. To my parents and family for their unbounded support. To my friends for their enthusiasm. To Todd for his love and for always listening.

Contents

CONTENTS

Restless Spirits

INTRODUCTION

"You're wondering why I take this so cool, as if it wasn't anything so much out of the common. . . . It appeared to come about so natural, just in the course of things. . . ."
—ANNIE SLOSSON, "A Dissatisfied Soul"

THESE HOMELY WORDS OF EXPLANATION, SPOKEN BY ANNIE SLOS-son's Mrs. Weaver about the day her dead sister-in-law walked through the front door, could stand as a motto for all of the tales collected here. In these ghost stories by turn-of-the-century American women, there is free and easy passage between the natural and supernatural worlds. This does not mean that the appearance of a ghost isn't frightening; even the placid Mrs. Weaver feels "'a swimmy feeling in my head and a choky feeling down my throat, and a sort of trembly feeling all over.'" Yet she sees no point in making a fuss: "'I says, 'Why, good-morning, Maria, you've come back.' And she says, 'Good-morning, Lyddy: yes, I have.'" Mrs. Weaver is not alone in her no-nonsense attitude toward the supernatural. Her emphasis on realism and the everyday—"'we sort of got used to it after a spell, as you do to anything'"—is characteristic of most seers of ghosts in these stories. In the worldview espoused by the authors gathered here, the doors stand wide open between living and dead, present and past, natural and supernatural.

The present collection itself hopes to open a door into a part of America's literary past that has been closed for the better part of a century.[1] Although aficionados of the ghost story will probably recognize the names of Edith Wharton, Mary E. Wilkins Freeman, and Ellen Glasgow, they will not likely be familiar with those of Gertrude Morton, M. E. M. Davis, or Anne Page. Yet these women, and others whose tales appear here, had enormous popular success with the ghost story in the turn-of-the-century United States.[2] These authors contributed a uniquely feminist chapter to the annals of supernatural literature. Unlike most fiction produced during this heyday of the genre, with its male narrators, ghosts, and protagonists, American women's ghost stories revolve very much around a female world. The narrative voice is (almost always) female, the characters are (almost entirely) female, even the ghosts are (almost without exception) female. Male characters are generally peripheral, because they show themselves to be antipathetic to the very possibility of the supernatural. As Mary Heaton Vorse's Beata realizes with resignation in "The Second Wife," her husband "couldn't admit what he had seen. In his man's world such things couldn't be."

But for what reasons do these restless spirits return? And why have their authors brought them into being in the first place? Men's supernatural fiction of the same era is usually discussed as a demonstration of the weighty social concerns and cultural anxieties of an increasingly technologized civilization. Critics conclude that the genre allowed male writers to give voice to their culture's tension between material and spiritual conceptions of the world.[3] In contrast, women's ghost stories, which have received much less critical attention, are most often assessed as less substantial, less worldly. Even critics who champion the stories tend to describe them in terms of the "female fears," "female rage," "female desire," or "female pain" that emerges through their focus on issues of vulnerability and marginality. Although this description is valid on a certain level, authors do not produce texts solely out of private experience. Women's ghost stories are also shaped by their particular intellectual, economic, and political milieu; they too grow out of social concerns and cultural anxieties, albeit some different ones than those experienced by men. If one can detect fear, rage, desire, and pain in these tales, then one must logically ask: what exactly are the authors afraid of? enraged by? desirous of? pained by? In other words, why are these women, like the female characters they raise from the dead, such restless spirits?

When examined in social and cultural terms, ghost stories by turn-of-the-century American women reveal themselves to center on the institutions and ideological issues that shaped their authors' lives. Marriage, motherhood, sexuality, mental and physical health, spinsterhood, widowhood: over and over, with chilling insistence, the stories confront these themes. Through them the authors explore the deeply entrenched ideologies of womanhood—the "angel in the house," the sanctity of motherhood, "passionlessness"—that had evolved over the course of the nineteenth century in the United States. Depicting women of different classes (and, to a lesser degree, races), the tales simultaneously reflect and question the era's cultural discourses on the nature and role of the female.[4] As such, they provide a rich and valuable source of insight into the all-pervasiveness of the ideologies in these women writers' lives. Set in all corners of the United States, from Maine to Louisiana to the Midwest, these are exclusively ghost stories of American women's lives, a fact that makes them additionally unique.

The decision of these authors to employ the ghost story genre is a significant one. The supernatural is intertwined with the American literary mainstream of the nineteenth and early twentieth centuries. Authors as diverse as Washington Irving, Herman Melville, Ambrose Bierce, and Henry James capitalized on the literary possibilities of the supernatural, using it as a forum through which to investigate otherwise unapproachable moral, psychological, and political issues. For the women writers, its function was similar; the ghost story acted as allegory, allowing them to explore issues they felt needed addressing. At the same time, it shielded them from the critical recrimination to which they were more vulnerable. The allegorical nature of the ghost story enabled them to displace their grievances onto supernatural forces, thereby safely giving voice to the political "other" of their messages. Within this process, then, the ghost itself often acts as (speaking) symbol for the writers' dissatisfactions.

For this reason, perhaps, ghosts in American women's stories are unusually likely to retain the personality and in some cases even the physical form that they had while living. By the turn of the century, this type of ghost was seen as more or less passé in men's ghost stories, belonging as it did to the older, "largely decorative" gothic tradition, as Jack Sullivan deprecatingly calls it. Connoisseurs of the ghostly tale preferred a "more actively loathsome, menacing quality." The distinction is captured in more imaginative terms by H. P. Lovecraft: "[W]here the older stock ghosts were pale and stately, and apprehended chiefly through the sense of sight," the newer ghost is "a sluggish, hellish night-abomination midway betwixt beast and man—and usually *touched* before it is *seen.*" But to utilize this type of being would be to defeat the purpose of the supernatural encounter in American women's ghostly fiction. While encounters between living and dead in traditional, male-authored ghost stories occur as "just deserts for past wickedness" or simply "through incautious enthusiasm, folly, or sheer bad luck,"[5] the reason is entirely different in the stories collected here. As Lynette Carpenter and Wendy Kolmar point out, "[W]omen characters realize their commonality with the ghostly women and children they encounter and are often called upon to understand and act upon the messages brought by those who haunt their houses."[6]

The stories in this volume are organized thematically in order to highlight their social and cultural contexts, and a summary of themes follows. There are, naturally, interconnections between each story and a number of themes; these tales can be read in a variety of ways, as their appeal is wide ranging. They should prove both intriguing and entertaining to readers of all sorts.

Until Death Do Us Part . . . and After: Marriage

What the Presence had wrought upon him in the night was
visible in his altered mien. He looked, more than anything else,
to be in need of sleep. He had eaten his sorrow, and that was the
end of it—as it is with men.
— MARY AUSTIN, "The Readjustment"

The institution of marriage, to judge by the frequency with which it is
written about, is the topic that most haunts turn-of-the-century American
women writers. This is not surprising, as the marriage relationship was
considered the primary source of a woman's identity. The rapid industrial-
ization and commercialization of nineteenth-century America resulted in
an ever-widening separation of male and female spheres. While men spent
increasing amounts of time in the workplace, women were relegated more
and more to home and family. Charged with preserving values and creating
a safe haven for husband and children, woman was to be the angel in the
house. Her presumed suitability for such a role was grounded in the assumption that females were morally superior to males, itself a cornerstone
for the ideology of "true womanhood." This popular ideal of womanhood
had by midcentury become firmly established, and although it operated
most powerfully in the lives of middle-class, white women, it was held up
as a model to all females, regardless of class or race. The "true woman"
was expected to be the embodiment of purity, piety, submissiveness, and
domesticity.

The ghost stories on marriage, however, tell the secret, the disallowed
story, of the reality behind "home as haven" and what it really means to be a
true woman or an angel in the house. They provide thought-provoking,
often painful examinations of the marital relationship, exploring infidelity
(of both husband and wife), sexual and psychological abuse, marriages of
convenience, and the less dramatic but also tragic mismatching of partners.

Edith Wharton's "The Lady's Maid's Bell" is a tale about an upper-class
New York couple who are utterly incompatible. The brutal Mr. Brympton
casts responsibility for this on his reserved wife, blaming his alternating
bouts of sexual exploitation and neglect of her on the fact that she makes
their home "'about as lively as the family vault.'" When the ghost of Emma
Saxon, Mrs. Brympton's maid and companion of twenty years, mutely appears to Hartley, the new lady's maid, Hartley is unable to break through
caste to piece together the scattered clues that suggest her mistress has a

secret that needs protecting. Sexual victimization, helplessness, class barriers—these are all untold female stories that the silent Emma symbolizes. Wharton does not tell a simple tale of goodness besieged by evil, yet it is clear that Mrs. Brympton, the "angel" whose servants "worshipped the ground she walked on," is a legitimate Victorian angel in the house nonetheless. Neither she nor the women who serve and love her are able to rescue Mrs. Brympton from her fate as Mr. Brympton's wife.

In Mary Austin's "The Readjustment," a dissatisfied wife returns to haunt her husband, seeking a deeper meaning to the emotionally stunted life they had led together. The communication between husband and dead wife is facilitated by a nameless neighbor woman, who isn't surprised when she finds that Emma Jossylin has returned. In fact, she comments to herself, it would be " '[a] sight stranger if she wouldn't.' " For Emma was a woman who "had always wanted things different, wanted them with a fury of intentness that implied offensiveness in things as they were." But when the neighbor gets the pathetic Sim to finally bare his "small soul" to Emma, revealing that he had loved her, her presence clings close. It becomes apparent that Emma, even with her overwhelming superiority and ambitions, would have cared for him willingly had he once confided in her. Austin shows that marriage, even one of such unequal partners, involves a torturous commitment, the strength of which is demonstrated in this story by its transcendence of death. Yet even as the burden of responsibility fell on Emma in life, it falls on her (and the neighbor) in death, for it is she who tries to achieve peace for this torn couple. Emma Jossylin must "readjust" to her new state by accepting that her marriage could not have been any more fulfilling than it was, that her husband was incapable of giving any more than he does under the pressure of her haunting.

Olivia Howard Dunbar's "The Shell of Sense" also features a wife willing to postpone her heavenly reward to see her husband once again, but Frances returns because she loved Allan and cannot let him go. Frances's posthumous narrative is concerned with the actual state of death, and the victory of the spiritual over the merely human is what allows Frances to deal with her sense of betrayal when she finds that her marriage had been a farce: her husband had been in love not with her, but with her sister. The tale gives the lie to the nineteenth-century marital ideal, for this apparently successful example is proven to have been a charade due to the emotional infidelity of one partner and the duping of another. Significantly, the blame is put on the husband. His primary concern has always been with himself, the narrative points out—first in his emotional desertion of his wife, and then in his hurried willingness to dismiss her claims after her death. The fact that he kept Frances "wrapped in the white cloak of unblemished loyalty" was more a function of necessity than a sign of decency; Theresa did not fall in love with Allan until after her sister's death, and she would never have listened to his protestations before it. It is only Theresa's sympathy, her recognition of Frances's feelings of betrayal, that allows the earthbound spirit of her sister to be freed.

Zora Neale Hurston's "Spunk," set in the autonomous Black community of Eatonville, Florida, displays the incorporation of African beliefs about the spirit world into African American oral and literary traditions. It also demonstrates that the "man-instinct of possession" (to borrow a phrase from Kate Chopin's "Her Letters") is alive and thriving in this Black community. The "object" of whom possession is under dispute is Lena Kanty, a woman who has openly taken a lover in preference to her weak and cowardly husband. The store-porch community, which acts as a kind of ancient chorus, validates her choice: "'Now you know a woman don't want no man like that.'" The statement is telling in another way—while the tale foregrounds the contest of the two men and the prowess of Spunk Banks, it is the supremely desirable Lena who holds the reins of power. Spunk, although not the marrying kind, is ready to settle down with her. Joe's love for Lena is so great that he transcends death to "'have it out wid the man that's got all he ever had.'" Hurston uses the supernatural as a corrective to Spunk for his morally irresponsible behavior. But what about Lena? Two men are dead for love of her; all the bravado about possession takes on great irony when they die and she lives. And although her lamentations at Spunk's wake are "deep and long," she will not mourn forever, as the community implicitly recognizes: "The women ate heartily of the funeral baked meats and wondered who would be Lena's next. The men whispered coarse conjectures between guzzles of whiskey." Ultimately it is Lena who gets what she wants, and this will eventually take the form of a third spouse.

Hildegarde Hawthorne's "A Legend of Sonora" is a triumph of atmosphere and compact horror. Secretly learning of her lover's betrayal and unwilling to live without him, Maria takes matters into her own hands and rewrites the role he has chosen for her. Instead of playing the woman scorned, she decides to play the immortal beloved. She greets him dressed in bridal white, bearing a "loving cup" of wine. Sharing the wine from the chalice-like vessel, they pledge their troth to one another. Then Maria speaks the closing words on what is, unbeknownst to him, a bizarre wedding ceremony: "'Let us never be parted any more.'" With these words of benediction, Maria's lover becomes her partner for eternity, and their spirits perpetually reenact their death scene—in essence, the walk down the aisle. It is surely of significance that the horseman who encounters the ghosts is another young man, riding along jauntily, humming a love song. Maria's life story is transformed before the reader's eyes to a living legend, one that will teach the terrified young man lessons of fidelity and commitment.

The stories in this section provide an honest exploration of the abuses that can be committed in the name of love and marriage, and they reveal a dissatisfaction with, even a bitterness over, the ideology of domesticity. Their seriousness of theme and the fact that they vastly outnumber ghost stories on any other subject suggest the centrality of the institution of marriage in the lives of American women of the time. At their least dramatic, they reveal women's disillusionment with the marital relationship. At their most dramatic, their heroines accept death as a welcome alternative to continuing a loveless partnership.

A sense emerges from these stories that the ideologies of love and marriage in nineteenth- and early twentieth-century America, in all their various articulations, were obviously lacking in something. And that something, according to these stories, was predominantly a failure to allow a woman to be herself. Rather, she was expected to be someone's wife, to act only in relation to him: to fail to do so was a violation of true womanhood. Such a creed of self-effacement did not allow for women's real personalities or needs, but rather rendered them invisible. All this sounds terribly gloomy, yet the tales are anything but, as they offer subversive and empowering alternatives to long-suffering wifehood. Ultimately, the supernatural allows these wives a satisfaction beyond reproach or control.

The Tie that Binds: Motherhood

"Her life was mortgaged to the child. This business of being a parent is something you don't forget nor get away from—not in Heaven or in Hell! It is the tie that holds forever. It is the thing that binds His duties on the shoulders of God Himself!"
—CORNELIA P. COMER, "The Little Gray Ghost"

Motherhood is another subject that appears with almost obsessive frequency in the nineteenth- and early twentieth-century women's ghost stories. As the marriage stories confront the basic conflict of how to be both person and wife, these tales address the issue of how to be both person and mother. This was revolutionary, because American literature, like the culture at large, refused to acknowledge the inexorable demands of motherhood. Where is the discussion of a mother's inevitable confrontations with pain, disease, and death in the fiction of the day? Where is the mention of the sheer physical exhaustion of mothering a child? What about the endless self-sacrifices, the lifelong commitment, the feelings of entrapment? These unspoken but very real aspects of motherhood are glossed over in nineteenth- and early twentieth-century fiction, sentimentalized to the point of innocuousness, and their supposed absence is used as further evidence of woman's innate fitness to be a mother. Society expected women to be fulfilled through motherhood, and any woman who openly questioned the "sacred duty," even in fictional format, would have been vilified.

Seldom in mainstream fiction could a woman show feelings of frustration with or exhaustion from the demands of motherhood, and only by reading against the grain can we see these tensions at all. But in American women's ghost stories, the mother-child bond exerts a stranglehold from beyond the grave, and all of its ramifications can be explored. These tales usually fall into two categories. In the first, a child returns from the dead in order to find a woman to mother it in the afterlife. Although motherhood is occasionally sentimentalized, the sentiment is undercut by the demands of the child ghosts, for these are not childish spirits waiting contentedly to greet their mothers in glory. These are beings earthbound until they can coerce a woman to sacrifice her life to mother them in the next world. The fact that the appearance of the dead child is received not so much with terror or surprise as with a sense of the inevitable is chilling in itself.

"The Children" by Josephine Dodge Daskam Bacon (a story marked by an unfortunate anti-Semitism) provides a good example of this type of tale. It also contains many disturbing implications about wifehood and motherhood, for two young women are devastated by their loss or lack of children more than by their loss or lack of husbands. The drive to seek her fulfilment in motherhood has led Mrs. Childress to a mild insanity. Her maid Sarah, who has lost her own children, corroborates and participates in this insanity. Sarah's unreliable narration emphasizes the weirdness of the situation in which these women live for eight years, and the whisperings of the supernatural act as metaphors for it. The materialization of the female child represents the ultimate fulfilment for Mrs. Childress, yet there is a price to pay for having finally achieved motherhood. Sarah, as surrogate mother to the ghost children, also pays a price, but a lesser one. And in a sinister passing on of the role of mother, she goes on to bear a boy and girl child, named for the ghostly children whom she and her mistress had brought into being.

The second most common category of ghost stories on motherhood are those in which a dead woman is unable to achieve the "peace that passeth understanding" because she has left a child on earth. The woman is forced by the very fact of her motherhood to return from the beyond in order to protect or make provision for the child. Like those in the first category, these stories are almost without exception domestic and undramatic, and there is no terror, only pathos, in the figure of the ghostly mother. Although the stories lack the chill of those featuring the child ghost, it is amply replaced by the feeling, never articulated but made painfully clear, of a tie that binds into eternity.

In "Broken Glass," a tale by the interestingly named Georgia Wood Pangborn, we have a classic portrayal of the tortures suffered by a dead mother for her orphaned child. Pangborn also deals specifically with the institution of motherhood as it is affected by class and culture, which very few ghost stories of the period do. Pangborn examines the pervasiveness of the maternal ideal when she tells the story of Mrs. Waring, a mother who is able through leisure and money to devote herself fully to the nurture of her children. But she has missed the true meaning of motherhood, as she learns when haunted by the ghost of an immigrant working-class mother, one whose own daughter is in Mrs. Waring's service as nursemaid to her children. The story insists that motherhood is a universal vocation, one that rises above the boundaries of class, culture, race, and even time and space.

Cornelia A. P. Comer's "The Little Gray Ghost" is the heavily undercut tale of Carruthers, a fey man of Scottish origin. He is one of the Chosen, people whose mission it is to give advice to the spirits of the newly dead to help them move on. He meets his match in a spirit he calls the Little Gray One, who had in her young life known "lawless passion, mother-love, the agony of separation from her own, jealousy, hatred, the red rage that murders." Earthbound because she has committed suicide and left her child orphaned, Kitty Dundas is on a mother-mission to persuade Carruthers and his childless wife to adopt Teresita. Although Carruthers, through selfishness, stubbornness, and racism, refuses and becomes "hag-ridden," he is finally won over when he realizes the strength of Kitty's responsibility and consequently of her torture—the fact that motherhood " 'is the tie that holds forever.' "

In Katharine H. Brown's "Hunger," Eleanor (who had been orphaned at an early age) remembers, when her own baby babbles about the "gone-away lady," her own childhood vision of a young woman who had haunted her bedside. In a sympathy born of her new motherhood, Eleanor gradually comes to realize that the vision was actually the ghost of her dead mother. Eleanor's self-pity for her own orphaned loneliness vanishes as she realizes that this young mother was the one most truly deprived; Eleanor's lack of comprehension through the years, the frozen way in which she had greeted the nocturnal visitations, had denied the ghost the chance to mother. So now the earthbound spirit has turned to the new baby, her grandson, with her frustrated love, as Eleanor recognizes: "'Oh, you poor little love! You poor little hungry, eager thing! He's yours too, dear. Yours and mine.'" Although the story fulfils the most saccharine requirements of fiction on the mother-child bond, its sentiment is undercut by the agony endured by the unfulfilled mother-spirit. The references to hunger and deprivation throughout the tale leave an overall impression of pain that is only slightly diminished by the tale's "resolution." In fact, nothing is actually resolved; having her daughter's understanding and her grandson's love does not seem to free this restless spirit, who is seemingly condemned to an eternal purgatory of vicarious mothering.

Charlotte Perkins Gilman's "The Giant Wistaria" is a tale within a tale that does not fall into any category, for both its mother and child have died. Grounding her tale in a New England made known by Nathaniel Hawthorne, Gilman, like Hawthorne, gives us a story of a young woman and an illegitimate child. Estrangement from her own mother, separation from her infant, and imprisonment—privations forced on her by her father—drove her to desperation. Even if she had managed to escape her prison, the young mother would have been a Hester Prynne, penniless and scorned in a hard land. Like Kitty Dundas, she chooses not to live. But unlike Kitty Dundas, she realizes that death will not release her from responsibility for her child, so she commits both infanticide and suicide. The mother ghost has had to wait a century for the sympathy of three young women to "tell" her tragic story. Their sympathy shows us that Gilman does not intend us to condemn the woman for her actions. So too does the carnelian cross she wears, Gilman's reinterpretation of Hawthorne's scarlet letter. That this young mother wears the symbol of Christ, not the symbol of adultery, implies that she and her innocent child, far from being the "blot," "stain," or "shame" of Samuel Dwining's interpretation, were blessed by God. Yet even blessed motherhood is powerless against patriarchal puritanism, symbolized by the giant wistaria that confines the woman even in death.

In their reworking of the sentimentalized mother-child relationships of nineteenth-century fiction, the ghost stories on motherhood, although a nonrealistic genre, have a distinct quality of realism. In these tales, as in those that explore the marital bond, there is little of gothic drama, of vindictive jealousy or undying passion. They are fairly subdued stories, with a peculiar, creeping horror that lies in their insistence that, dead or alive, you cannot escape the responsibilities of motherhood.

The "Other" Woman: Sexuality

"In heaven's name," I cried irritably, "who is she?" "Don't you know?" She appeared genuinely surprised. "Why, she is the other Mrs. Vanderbridge. She died fifteen years ago, just a year after they were married, and people say a scandal was hushed up about her, which he never knew. She isn't a good sort, that's what I think of her, though they say he almost worshipped her."
—ELLEN GLASGOW, "The Past"

Complex concerns about women's sexuality appear in a large number of ghost stories. Many of these stories are about marriage as well; fictional explorations by women writers of sexuality outside marriage were still quite rare at this time.[7] But these tales focus especially on issues of sexuality and are marked by a strong dichotomy of good and bad, asexual and sexual. In three of the tales included here, two women (one dead, one alive) are bifurcated into categories of the demonic and the divine. In the fourth, the woman is herself bifurcated into separate roles of lover and wife. This duality is a reflection of nineteenth-century American culture's double-edged view of women's sexuality. It had been only within the past century or so that the traditional Anglo-American conception of women as a sexually voracious "daughter of Eve" had been reversed to one of woman as a primarily moral and spiritual being. Americans were busy canonizing Victorian womanhood, but the older notion of woman's sexual nature was only shadowed, never entirely eclipsed. As a result, literature and art was riddled with portrayals of the two-sided nature of woman. These stories are enthralling in their expression of what was clearly a cultural preoccupation.

M. E. M. Davis's "At La Glorieuse," set on a Louisiana plantation and redolent of Southern gothic, is a prime example. As the tale opens, young Richard Keith is wooing the daughter of the house, sweet and innocent Félice Arnault. Yet the old mansion has another inhabitant: its dead young mistress, faithless in life and death, whose posthumous libido is so strong that she must seduce even her daughter's lover. Hélène Pallacier, with her pagan ancestry, her exotic beauty, and her totems, vamps Richard from beyond the grave, and he perversely spurns the gentle charms of the pure (and living) Félice in favor of her dead mother. When Richard is finally freed of Hélène's enthralment and decides to return to Félice, confident that she will be waiting because she "is not the kind of woman who loves more than once," he is, ironically, only too right. And so Hélène of the monstrous sexual appetite still manages to claim victory over her pure rival, "Sister Mary of the Cross, who in the world had been Félicité Arnault."

In a startling number of the ghost stories on sexuality, the two female rivals are the first (now dead) and second wives of the same man. Being a second wife was a common enough phenomenon in those times, when men were frequently widowed by disease or complications arising from child-birth. The anxieties attendant on filling the role of second wife to a husband with previously set expectations and standards, sexual and otherwise, must have been enormous. Living as she did in the first wife's house, sleeping with her husband, and often caring for her children, a second wife was haunted continually by the memory of the woman she had replaced. In the stories here, this metaphorical haunting becomes literal. The second wife's anxieties are justified, for she is not dealing with a benevolent spirit who seeks to ease the path of her successor, but with the restless dead—apparently jealous, competitive, and vengeful. The second wife perceives the first wife as evil, and this evil has its locus in the first wife's beauty, her passion, and her hold over the husband, which the second wife can never achieve.

In Ellen Glasgow's "The Past," the present Mrs. Vanderbridge's health succumbs to the pressure of the first wife's haunting until she discovers a packet of love letters that reveal the first wife's secret: an adulterous affair. The second and morally superior Mrs. Vanderbridge burns the letters rather than revealing their secret to her husband, an action that lays the ghost to rest. So the second wife finally gets her man, but only by being the willing instrument of evil, the concealer of sexual sins. Through her decision not to expose the rival who has been destroying her marriage, Mrs. Vanderbridge suggests that she has guessed the real reason behind the ghost's "animosity and bitterness": the ghost is unable to rest because Mrs. Vanderbridge has the power to change her husband's memories of the first wife. By destroying the letters, the second wife blots out the sins of the past, thus restoring the first wife to her original young and loving self. The dead woman's need to preserve her image as angel in the house is what keeps her from resting in peace, an incredible testimony to the strength of the ideal of female purity and a curiously subversive example of appearance versus reality in the sexual arena.

"Secret Chambers" by Mrs. Wilson Woodrow (née Nancy Mann Waddel) also pivots on the takeover of second wife by first. Although initially the two wives have diametrically opposed personalities, when second wife Sylvia is exposed to the same deprivation of love and companionship as the "feminine Narcissus" Adele, she begins to respond in the same way. Yet even when Sylvia unconsciously reenacts the final scene of Adele's life, Arnold does not realize his responsibility for the fate of his first wife. Arnold distinguishes between the two women on the basis of their relationship to him alone: the first wife was passionate and demanding, and the second is passionless and undemanding. Passion is equated with selfishness and egotism, while passionlessness is seen as altruistic. Of course Arnold does not recognize that his objections to Adele reside in the demands she makes on his own passion and egotism. Even more significant is Sylvia's extreme sympathy for and attraction to Adele. She *likes* living the "more thrilling and intense" life of Adele, and ultimately the two wives seem more like co-conspirators than rivals. This point acts subversively to undermine the seemingly conventional ending, which forecasts a roseate future in which Adele has been laid to rest.

In stories of first and second wives, the second wife perceives herself initially as the perfect wife, a paragon of sense and sensibility. She is calm, self-assured, rational—everything that the first wife apparently was not. She acknowledges that she is not as beautiful or passionate as the first, but with her society's distrust of female beauty and passion, she is able to dismiss these qualities with the faintly smug assurance that her tamer beauty and more temperate personality are better for him. When her marriage begins to fail, however, and her own personality starts to splinter, the first wife's attractions take on increasingly sinister implications and a strange appeal. In these tales, the second wife strives desperately to dismiss the first wife as the one who failed—the one who stifled her husband, sickened into hysteria, committed adultery, went mad, killed herself. Yet in spite of her efforts to dismiss this other—the beautiful one, the brilliant one, the one her husband loved first—the first wife is her most powerful temptation. This point is crucial: the demonic/divine construct in Western patriarchal culture pits women against one another, thus controlling their sexuality and guaranteeing their sexual accessibility to men. Yet here the paradigm is both exposed and critiqued, as the two women join forces, however briefly, against the male power to which they have both been subject.

The unnamed female protagonist of Kate Chopin's "Her Letters" is her own "other woman." One man's lover and another man's wife, she separates the two roles so successfully that her husband has no suspicion that his wife had a sexual side until after her death. "Her Letters" is not a ghost story in any conventional sense, centering as it does on the love letters of this adulterous wife. Yet the tale uses metaphors of the supernatural to describe the power of the wife's letters over her widowed husband. The woman feels no guilt, no regret as she recalls her love affair; although characterized by passion, it was also a mating of souls. In a delightful turning of the tables of nineteenth-century sentimental fiction, the husband in this story is the victim of his wife's infidelity. But is he at all responsible for his victimization? Although this woman gave only a pale version of herself in her role as wife, he was content to believe that a real woman *was* only a patchwork of socially approved, wifely characteristics: "cold and passionless, but true, and watchful of his comfort and his happiness." He gradually becomes obsessed with the letters, until his wife's meaning to him (in spite of her years of devotion and his happiness and satisfaction with her) is reduced to the suspicion that she had been unfaithful. The deliberate absence of authorial comment leaves the reader searching for a clue as to Chopin's intentions. That clue is the package of letters, and the fact that they are *her* letters, not to be shared by husband and wife. Although the letters are a symbol of the wife's dissatisfaction with her sex life and marriage, it is the husband's man-instinct of possession that gives them the power to haunt him.

Ghost stories on the subject of sexuality defy categorization more than any others. While the authors *are* making statements, conscious or not, about the sexual ideology that affects their lives, the tales exhibit a certain ambivalence. Their fascination, even obsession with bad women suggests a fascination with sexuality itself. And their male characters, whose weakness and selfishness in the face of women's passion or need indicates that they are to be condemned, seem to embody society and its restrictive sexual ideology. All of this adds up to a dissatisfaction with and possibly even a confusion over what a "good woman" should be in sexual terms. These tales are unquestionably the most dramatic and exciting in the entire genre.

Madwomen or Mad Women? The Medicalization of the Female

> "If it were true, it were enough to craze me; and if it were not true, I was already crazed. And there it is! I can't make out, sometimes, whether I am really beside myself or not; for it seems that whether I was crazed or sane, if it were true, they would naturally put me out of sight and hearing—bury me alive, as they have done, in this Retreat."
> —HARRIET SPOFFORD, "Her Story"

The influence of a burgeoning medical and psychiatric practice on society's perception and treatment of women also makes its way into the ghost stories. These tales are particularly poignant if one speculates on the medical history of women's nervous illness and its connection with ideologies of the female mind and body. Over the course of the nineteenth century and into the early decades of this one, a widespread belief in woman's susceptibility to illness developed in the United States. Medical literature propagated the theory that the nineteenth-century woman had a greater delicacy of constitution and was more prone to physical and mental debility than her grandmother. When this invalid woman emerged in American society, she also emerged in its fiction. By midcentury she had become a standard feature in much American literature by both male and female writers.

Toward the end of the nineteenth century, the medical profession became increasingly interested in the concept of nervous diseases. The advent of Freud and his school ushered in a new era in the treatment of women's nervous disorders, removing it in large part from the arena of gynecology and into that of psychology. The result was an erosion of the territory that marked the boundaries between mental and physical in the diagnosis of women's illnesses. Nervous illness, although originating in the body, was often manifested in the mind, and so treatments ministered to both. The medical profession became an increasing presence in American society and the American home as time wore on. Extending its voice of authority over behaviors previously not considered in medical terms, it influenced the experience of and cultural response to emotional distress. As a result, lay attitudes toward female behavior began to change. Confusion over medical distinctions between mental and physical in the diagnosis of women's nervous illnesses caused people to start to perceive as aberrant what might have been accepted in earlier times as a passing illness or dismissed as eccentricity.

"The Second Wife" by Mary Heaton Vorse is a case in point. The tale is told from the viewpoint of the tranquil Beata, second wife to Graham Yates. Graham's first wife, Alène, had been a woman of "peculiar loveliness and charm" and a "fascinating personality." Yet several years back she had been stricken with an "illness of the spirit" and had called upon her friend Beata to come and stay with her. But instead of regaining her health under Beata's care, Alène sickens, subjecting both husband and friend to "gathering nerve-storms" and "terrible, meaningless, heart-rending scenes," drawing them into "the hell where she lived" until she finally dies from an overdose of sleeping potion. And six months after her marriage to Alène's husband,

Beata finds her personality being invaded by that of his first wife. Beata is aware of what is happening, but she finds an insidious attraction in Alène's life of intense emotion, so unlike her own. Her husband sees the gradual takeover of her personality, yet he dismisses it as nervous illness: "'You've had a lot of odd little streaks lately, Beata.'" When Beata finally confronts Graham with her newfound knowledge that Alène had committed suicide—not because of her poisoned nerves, but because her husband had fallen in love with her friend—he refuses to acknowledge it, even in the face of the metempsychosis he witnesses. Graham, whenever his (current) wife exhibits deep passion and emotion, rejects her as mentally unstable and no longer worthy of him. By forcing Beata to live through her own suffering at having been labeled ill, misunderstood, and condescended to, Alène has achieved a triumph in finally making herself understood. Vorse's story clearly chafes against the medical definitions of women and illness, but it is unable to do *more* than chafe. For Alène loses her husband and then her life. Beata is alive and still has Graham, but his refusal to recognize the intervention of the supernatural means that she will always be mentally suspect in his eyes.

"Her Story" by Harriett Prescott Spofford is another tale in which a husband uses the label of mental illness for his own comfort and convenience. It is a monologue told by a woman who has found her voice only after spending ten years in the insane asylum to which her husband committed her. The delineation of the narrator's "symptoms" is brilliant because they can be interpreted in two ways. The first interpretation, a product of late nineteenth-century thought, is that the story represents the hysterical hallucinations of a jealous wife: it is to this explanation that husband Spencer adheres, with a little persuasion by his evil ward. But Spofford, a member of an old New England family and heir of that region's longstanding preoccupation with women-as-witches, creates another level of meaning by her use of gothic motifs and supernatural suggestions. These indicate that there is more here than just a tale of a woman driven to madness; that the narrator is not the victim of her own failing mind, but of a supernatural force beyond her control. This second interpretation of her symptoms, one of an earlier time in American history, suggests that the story presents the bizarre and sometimes delusional experiences that characterized the various "possession" behaviors of witchcraft victims. Despite the ease with which a hysteric's symptoms could be conflated with possession behaviors, Spofford subtly weights her evidence in favor of the latter. The very specific nature of the narrator's affliction—persecution by the witch/ward's "familiars," the muttering voices, and so on—supports this interpretation.

The popular view of the Victorian era's treatment of women's illnesses is that droves of Victorian women were unjustly labeled mad and packed away. Yet this view is inaccurate, the result of critical discussions that have been isolated from medical or cultural context. More recently, studies of women's nervous disease in the late nineteenth and early twentieth centuries reveal many varieties, even gradations, of both illness and treatment. Although there were mental institutions and hospitals, there were also a plethora of private "retreats" or "asylums" that advertised their services, without stigma, even in the best magazines. These were frequently resort-like places where the rich and famous (largely female) could "get away from it all." The picture of this era's treatment of female nervous illness that still prevails, however, stems largely from writings of the time—from Charlotte Bronte's Bertha Rochester, imprisoned in her attic in *Jane Eyre,* and from Charlotte Perkins Gilman's unnamed narrator in her bar-windowed, yellow wall-papered attic room in *The Yellow Wallpaper.*

Josephine Dodge Daskam Bacon's "The Gospel" implicitly provides a complete refutation of Gilman's fictionalized experience with the rest cure. Bacon takes the reader step by step through a fictional rendering of the rest cure and the ways it prepares the protagonist to return, a wiser and stronger woman, to the domestic duties she has deserted through nervous illness. Bacon also provides this woman (and the reader) with a warning in the form of a ghostly mentor, who discovered "the gospel" of domesticity too late. Following a vow made as she was dying, the spirit spends eternity preaching this gospel to women who have fallen from their destined path of domestic-ity. Bacon's tale reflects some contemporaneous trends in medical thought: while illnesses of both body and mind were still being treated with physical cures, many theories stressed the power of mind over body. Thus Bacon's protagonist is able to get better because she wants to; she simply needs a little ghostly guidance to know what she wants!

Helen R. Hull's "Clay-Shuttered Doors," published in 1926, shows us society's changing expectations of the figure of the female invalid. Thalia Corson is pronounced dead at the scene of an accident caused by her careless husband. Yet when Winchester pleads with her to come back to him, insist-ing, "'You weren't hurt. That was nothing,'" she returns through "clay-shuttered doors," believing that he loves and needs her. Thalia soon realizes her mistake, but decides to remain long enough to play out her social role in his big business merger. Evidence that she repeatedly revivifies herself is ignored by Winchester, who refuses to believe that there is anything wrong with Thalia but her own fragile constitution: "'she's so damned nervous, you know.'" He continues to ignore his wife's bizarre behavior, alternating between the search for a quick fix—sending her to a "nerve specialist" or on a holiday—and the consolation he finds in the arms of a "gaudy lady." Underlying his attitude is the assumption that Thalia's nervous illness is a matter of an intent to be ill, of "'whims.'" Thus when she brings herself back for the last time, serving her final function as hostess, Winchester is "angry rather than concerned" by the odd manner in which she receives a tribute to her part in the deal. And while he storms, "'I'm going to stop this nonsense!'" Thalia lies dead, killed for the second time by his cruel carelessness.

The stories in this section suggest that beliefs about the interconnections between the female mind and body are the most powerful of any imposed upon women. It is as if women, once persuaded by their culture to start thinking of themselves as "nervous," to interpret even the slightest signs of stress as mental illness, begin to doubt themselves, to the point that their power of self-assertion fails entirely: Alène commits suicide; Spofford's unnamed narrator refuses to tell her doctors the true story that will set her free; Dr. Stanchon's patient allows him to browbeat her in the name of medicine; Thalia Corson continues to smooth the way for her husband's business deals and refuses to correct his wilful misconceptions about her "illness."

These are not empowering tales, though many of the ghost stories in this collection are. In these, women are victims, silenced by the voice of patriarchal authority, both medical and marital. Although these tales resist the power of the medical discourse on women's illness, the women in them are ultimately powerless. It is only Bacon's protagonist, who submits and is therefore "cured," who escapes. Although there is a fifty-year span between the tales here (the largest span of any section), there is a frightening sameness about cultural constructions of gender and illness: women continue to be threatened by invalidism and by the interpretation and subsequent dismissal of their actions as evidence of mental illness. It is crucial to understand that these stories pivot as much on the man/woman relation as they do on the mind/body relation. In each, clear gender lines are drawn between those who have the power to define illness and those who must accept being defined as ill. It is only the supernatural that allows the women in these tales to subvert, however temporarily, that power.

Shades of Discontent: Widows and Spinsters

> To her mother Lois's lack of beauty was an unpardonable fault . . . if she had been handsome, like herself, the mother thought, she would have married, but an unmarried woman couldn't look for the consideration that was shown to her married sisters. She, of course, was useful, but not of much account in the world.
>
> —ANNE PAGE, "Lois Benson's Love Story"

The nineteenth century brought a greater freedom of choice for American women in matters of courtship, marriage, and single life. Among women who did not wed, the single lifestyle varied greatly, according to race and class. White, middle-class women often had the means to enjoy their independence or to pursue a career. But for those without social status and financial means, a single life could be one of economic hardship and social marginality. Unmarried women on the whole were considered social failures, and consequently were viewed with condescension or pity. Portrayals of single women in literature of the period range from the comical old maid to the bitter-tongued, frustrated spinster, but none are quite depicted with seriousness. These characters almost always find a "purpose" in life through self-sacrifice and devotion to others. Part yet not part of someone else's family, they are content to stand in the shadows while their lovelier sisters bask in the love of husbands and children. Yet ghost stories that focus on the state of single women speak to the discontent of this way of life. The dissatisfaction felt by these characters arises not simply from the lack of a mate. A constellation of privations and pettinesses afflicts their existence, often as a result of attitudes toward single women, their duties and their worth.

Frequently, a woman such as the title character in Anne Page's "Lois Benson's Love Story" had to give up her ambitions in order to support widowed or aged parents. For these women, spinsterhood meant hard work and self-sacrifice. Lois's self-centered and mean-spirited parents consider her dedication no more than their right; hers "was the service of a faithful slave, and was accepted by both as such." Yet, writes Page, "Lois Benson herself was no saint, and she carried her cross at times with only a wayward spirit": the distinction between love and obligation is often blurred for her. So when the dream visions begin, the physically and emotionally starved

Lois feeds on them in secret, scarcely daring to hope that they may have some meaning in this world. Even when she learns that Reuben is a real man, she still cannot believe they will ever meet, so conditioned is she to disappointment. Only when her dream visions cease and her negative expectations are fulfilled does the full irony of the title become apparent. Lois picks up the cross of her existence, knowing "her life will be a long, unbroken road upon which, wearily and alone, she must journey." Seldom in fiction have the glorified duties of the spinster appeared so shorn of rhetoric. Page paints an unrelieved picture of a stark, purposeless existence.

Many single women who were unable to afford their own homes lived with relatives or friends, an arrangement that presumably provided them with emotional support as well. Yet for Maria Bliven of Annie Trumbull Slosson's "The Dissatisfied Soul," warm welcomes and the affection of a network of family and friends are just not enough. According to the narrator, Mrs. Weaver, Maria " 'was the fittiest, restlessest, changeablest person I ever saw or heard of; and never, never quite satisfied.' " The source of Maria's restlessness is never pinpointed by the less-than-analytical Mrs. Weaver, yet one can deduce that there is a reason why Maria never stayed anywhere " 'long enough at a time for anybody to get tired of her.' " Maria's claim on her various hosts is, after all, quite slender. She is only Mrs. Weaver's first husband's sister, and that good lady repeatedly sings the praises of her second husband for allowing Maria to visit so often. The nearest blood relative she has is just a half-brother. Whatever its genesis, Maria's dissatisfaction with her lot is so great that even when she dies, she is unable to " 'stay put, as you might say.' " But being back in life (and with the Weavers again) does not suit her either, and it is with grim determination that Maria declares, " 'wherever they carry me this time, I guess when I wake up I shall—be—satisfied.' " Dissatisfied with what life had to offer her, she apparently finds peace in the afterlife, for this second time she stays put. Although Slosson's story is humorous (due largely to the deadpan narrative of Mrs. Weaver), the character of Maria Bliven is not.

Contrary to popular belief, the number of women who lived single lives in nineteenth-century America was actually quite small. Studies have shown that, by the turn of the century, more than ninety percent of all women married. Historians posit that, although women had greater lifestyle options than in previous centuries, they were still socially, economically, and sexually vulnerable without husbands. In addition to a desire for the respectability and security that marriage brought, women were attracted by their century's greater emphasis on romantic love as a basis for union. White

Americans were living longer than they had in the past, and thus their marriages lasted longer. Yet for all the gains in life expectancy, death rather than divorce still ended most marriages, in many cases when the marriage partners were relatively young.

Gertrude Morton's "Mistress Marian's Light" belongs to a long tradition of New England fiction in which women are widowed by the sea. When news comes that Mistress Marian's betrothed is lost at sea, she is rendered senseless. But when she arises, with hair "as white as the foam that dashed against the rocks," she is convinced that her lover is not dead. After several years spent happily in the service of others, during which she nightly places a light for her lover in the window, she disappears. Did her lover come to claim her in a phantom ship, as one tipsy old sailor avers? Or did she return, without telling anyone, to the unknown parts from whence she came? On hot summer nights, at the time of year when her lover's ship foundered, a light appears in the untenanted cottage window. Even after the cottage falls to ruins, a light can be seen hovering a few feet above the ground where it had stood. At first glance, this gentle tale would seem to suggest that Marian's love and constancy lived on, distilled to this one ghostly light. But in supernatural fiction, manifestations occur only when spirits are not at rest! This suggests a more chilling meaning to Mistress Marian's tale, a meaning corroborated by the "timid young maiden" in a merry sailing party, who senses the eternal longing behind the fact that "'Mistress Marian's light is still burning.'" Instinctively she seeks protection from Marian's fate by nestling closer to "the skipper at the helm."

While natural disasters accounted for the widowing of many women, others were left alone through the ravages of diseases such as tuberculosis and diphtheria. Even though life expectancy had increased at the end of the century, both women and men died much younger than they do today in the United States. In Mary E. Wilkins Freeman's "Luella Miller," a number of characters die young, but not from natural causes! The title character is at first glance the ideal Victorian woman—beautiful and decorously helpless. But when the people who "do for her," including her husband, start dropping dead, that helplessness takes on vampiric connotations. This overly dependent wife/widow is held up for scrutiny throughout the tale by the narrator, a sharp-eyed, acid-tongued spinster. Luella Miller seduces others into caring for her many and selfish needs, draining the life out of them. She doesn't particularly seem to mind being a widow, as long as someone else takes care of her. Lydia Anderson, on the other hand, is a hard-working, self-denying, self-reliant, God-fearing, law-abiding woman. Yet she has lived a life of bitterness and repression, and her portrayal of Luella as vampiric seems suspect, due to her continued jealousy of the long-dead woman. A large part of the story's power comes from Freeman's dual narrative structure. Lydia's storytelling is skillful, but it is the frame narrative introducing Lydia and her story and later providing details of her death that belies any ambiguity about Luella's vampirism. The conclusion—that Lydia is subject to the same fate as Luella's other victims—is supported by her obsessive retelling of Luella's story, the manner of her own death, and the fact that it is her death, the "sequel," "which has become folklore in the village."

There is no real horror in the stories about widows and spinsters. There is, however, a dread inherent in the details of everyday life for many of these characters, in large part because their daily lives are such a grind. One particularly noteworthy difference between these tales and the others in this volume is that here, women are workers. Whether peeling potatoes or feeding the livestock, they are far from the leisured ladies in the majority of the other tales. This could reflect the fact that, as widows and spinsters, these women were in marginal positions. Alternately, their status as single or widowed women could have become a more noticeable feature when they had to work. Although the nineteenth century idolized the home as a haven, it was in reality a workplace. The protagonists in these tales work for themselves, but in the other stories they employ other women to work for them. This issue is addressed, directly and indirectly, in a number of the tales, from "Broken Glass" or "The Children" to "Secret Chambers" and "At La Glorieuse." In each case, the seeing of spirits causes women to form peculiar bonds across divisions of class, race, and work status.

> "Upon my soul . . . if I *were* superstitious, if I *were* a woman, I
> should probably imagine it to seem—a presence!"
> —OLIVIA HOWARD DUNBAR, "The Shell of Sense"

Women have traditionally been forced by their subordinate position in society to see both sides of things, to maintain an insider/outsider stance. The style and content of these ghost stories by turn-of-the-century American women are in keeping with this stance. They reveal a conscious challenge, not only to the epistemology of traditional ghost stories, which assert that there is a knowable reality, but to dominant notions of reality in a patriarchal culture. The stories, through the narrative strategies of the supernatural, are able to reveal a powerful aspect of women's reality—that continually effacing oneself, putting one's own needs to the side, leads one to the position of ultimate outsider: the ghost.

These women writers were clearly haunted by thoughts and issues deemed unspeakable. As ghost stories, they vary in what Edith Wharton called the "thermometrical quality," the ability to send a shiver down the reader's spine. Many of Wharton's stories and those of her female contemporaries revolve upon the horror that could lie in a woman's everyday life. These women are not dealing with fantastic worlds; they are dealing with their own. Thus, in telling the stories of their lives through the medium of the ghost story, they give us tales that are both uncannily realistic and strange. Ghost stories, as Gillian Beers cleverly points out, are about the "insurrection, not the resurrection of the dead."[8] I would add that the real insurrectionists, the real restless spirits, are the authors. It is very exciting that their still-resonant tales are available once again.

Notes

1. The research that led to the uncovering of this body of fiction was prompted by Alfred Bendixen's *Haunted Women: The Best Supernatural Tales by American Women Writers* (1985), a collection of thirteen stories by eleven authors. In that volume, Bendixen points out that American women's ghost stories suffered from critical neglect, a wrong that has since begun to be redressed. Lynette Carpenter and Wendy Kolmar have edited a volume of critical essays called *Haunting the House of Fiction: Feminist Perspectives on Ghost Stories by American Women.* This excellent anthology includes essays on both nineteenth- and twentieth-century American women writers of ghost stories, from Sarah Orne Jewett to Toni Morrison. I am particularly indebted to Carpenter and Kolmar's introduction and to Kathy Fedorko's "Edith Wharton's Haunted Fiction: 'The Lady's Maid's Bell' and *The House of Mirth.*" Prior to the publication of this anthology, critical discussion had been limited to the occasional article on an individual author who has remained well known, such as Wharton or Freeman. *What Did Miss Darrington See? An Anthology of Feminist Supernatural Fiction,* edited by Jessica Amanda Salmonson and with an introduction by Rosemary Jackson, spans the period from 1850 to 1988 and collects the works of women from the United States, England, and Latin America. Salmonson and Jackson provide an interesting, comprehensive, feminist overview of the field. *Victorian Ghost Stories by Eminent Women Writers* and *The Virago Book of Ghost Stories,* edited by Richard Dalby and introduced by Jennifer Uglow, are important anthologies of British women's ghost stories that include several American women's tales.

2. The tales range from 1872 to 1926, with a high concentration in the 1890s to 1910s. Some appeared in single-author collections, but the majority found a market in the periodical press—not just ladies' magazines, but in family, high-brow, and sensational periodicals too. They were very much a part of mainstream popular fiction.

INTRODUCTION

3. Supernatural fiction, per se, has itself received much less critical attention than other related genres like the gothic. And, as mentioned, the majority of criticism focuses on male authors. See for example Julia Briggs, *Night Visitors: The Rise and Fall of the English Ghost Story* (London: Faber, 1977); Michael Cox and Robert Gilberts, eds., "Introduction" to *The Oxford Book of English Ghost Stories* (Oxford: Oxford UP, 1989); Louis S. Gross, *Redefining the American Gothic from* Wieland *to* Day of the Dead (Ann Arbor: UMI Research Press, 1989); Howard Kerr, *Mediums, and Spirit-Rappers, and Roaring Radicals: Spiritualism in American Literature 1850–1900* (Urbana: U of Illinois P, 1972); Howard Kerr, John W. Crowley, and Charles L. Crow, eds., *The Haunted Dusk: American Supernatural Fiction, 1820–1920* (Athens: U of Georgia P, 1983); Alan Gardner Lloyd-Smith, *Uncanny American Fiction: Medusa's Face* (London: Macmillan, 1989); H. P. Lovecraft, *Supernatural Horror in Literature* (New York: Dover, 1973); Peter Messent, Introduction to *Literature of the Occult: A Collection of Critical Essays* (Englewood Cliffs, N.J.: Prentice-Hall, 1981); Peter Penzoldt, *The Supernatural in Fiction* (London: Peter Nevill, 1952); Donald R. Ringe, *American Gothic: Imagination and Reason in Nineteenth-Century Fiction* (Lexington: UP of Kentucky, 1982); Dorothy Scarborough, *The Supernatural in Modern English Fiction* (New York: G. P. Putnam's Sons, 1917); and Jack Sullivan, *Elegant Nightmares: The English Ghost Story from Le Fanu to Blackwood* (Athens: Ohio UP, 1978).

4. To my regret, the stories in this anthology are limited, with the exception of Hurston's "Spunk," to the productions of white women. The lack of published stories by women of color in the last century was due to a lack of opportunity; that these women were also feeling "haunted," were also expressing themselves in ghost stories, is unquestionable given the rich tradition of the supernatural in non-Western cultures. A glance at the proliferation of supernatural elements in mainstream writing by women of color today supports this claim. See Elizabeth Ammons's *Conflicting Stories: American Women Writers at the Turn into the Twentieth Century* for information about women of color writing in this period. See also her introduction to *Short Fiction by Black Women, 1900–1920*, a volume from the Schomburg Library of Nineteenth-Century Black Women Writers series, for a full discussion of publishing opportunities available to African American women. The stories collected here are also heterosexual in focus. The only ghostly tales I know of from this period that depict lesbian relationships are Elizabeth Stuart Phelps's "Since I Died" and Alice Brown's "There and Here," and are already available in *What Did Miss Darrington See?*

5. Sullivan, 6; Lovecraft, 102; Cox and Gilberts, xv.

6. Introduction, *Haunting the House of Fiction*, 14.

7. One notable exception is Kate Chopin's *The Awakening* (1899), a novel that likewise questioned the ideology of motherhood and that drew much critical revilement.

8. Gillian Beers, "Ghosts," *Essays in Criticism* 28 (1978): 259–64.

⊰ I ⊱

Until Death Do Us Part
. . . and After: Marriage

⟨⦿⟩

"Once I tried to go back; but she turned and looked at me."

Illustration by Walter Appleton Clark for Edith Wharton, "The Lady's Maid's Bell,"
Scribner's Magazine *32 (1902). Photo courtesy Metropolitan Toronto Reference Library.*

EDITH WHARTON
(1862–1936)

The author of novels, novellas, short stories, poetry, and travel books, Edith Wharton achieved both popular and critical acclaim during her lifetime. Born Edith Newbold Jones into the most exclusive New York society, she was educated at home by governesses. At age twenty-three she made a proper society marriage to Edward Wharton, scion of a prominent Boston family. Although she had early displayed writing talent, it had been discouraged, and her career did not get fully underway until she was thirty. Wharton's marriage was never happy, and after her divorce in 1913 she took up permanent residence in France. A devotee of the ghost story, she claimed that "till I was twenty-seven or eight, I could not sleep in the room with a book containing a ghost-story," and that "I have frequently had to burn books of this kind, because it frightened me to know that they were downstairs in the library!" Wharton's ghost stories, among the finest of her time, provide chilling investigations of gender roles and relations. "The Lady's Maid's Bell" made its debut in *Scribner's Magazine* in 1902. It most recently appeared in *The Ghost Stories* of Edith Wharton (New York: Charles Scribner's Sons, 1985).

The Lady's Maid's Bell

I

IT WAS THE AUTUMN AFTER I HAD THE TYPHOID. I'D BEEN three months in hospital, and when I came out I looked so weak and tottery that the two or three ladies I applied to were afraid to engage me. Most of my money was gone, and after I'd boarded for two months, hanging about the employment agencies, and answering any advertisement that looked any way respectable, I pretty nearly lost heart, for fretting hadn't made me fatter, and I didn't see why my luck should ever turn. It did though—or I thought so at the time. A Mrs. Railton, a friend of the lady that first brought me out to the States, met me one day and stopped to speak to me: she was one that had always a friendly way with her. She asked me what ailed me to look so white, and when I told her, "Why, Hartley," says she, "I believe I've got the very place for you. Come in to-morrow and we'll talk about it."

The next day, when I called, she told me the lady she'd in mind was a niece of hers, a Mrs. Brympton, a youngish lady, but something of an invalid, who lived all the year round at her country-place on the Hudson, owing to not being able to stand the fatigue of town life.

"Now, Hartley," Mrs. Railton said, in that cheery way that always made me feel things must be going to take a turn for the better—"now understand me, it's not a cheerful place I'm sending you to. The house is big and gloomy; my niece is nervous, vapourish; her husband—well, he's generally away; and the two children are dead. A year ago I would as soon have thought of shutting a rosy active girl like you into a vault, but you're not particularly brisk yourself just now, are you? and a quiet place, with country air and wholesome food and early hours, ought to be the very thing for you. Don't mistake me," she added, for I suppose I looked a trifle downcast; "you may find it dull but you won't be unhappy. My niece is an angel. Her former maid, who died last spring, had been with her twenty years and worshipped the ground she walked on. She's a kind mistress to all, and where the mistress is kind, as you know, the servants are generally good-humoured, so you'll probably get on well enough with the rest of the household. And you're the very woman I want for my niece: quiet, well-mannered, and educated above your station. You read aloud well, I think? That's a good thing; my niece likes to be read to. She wants a maid that can be something of a companion: her last was, and I can't say how she misses her. It's a lonely life . . . Well, have you decided?"

"Why, ma'am," I said, "I'm not afraid of solitude."

"Well, then, go; my niece will take you on my recommendation. I'll telegraph her at once and you can take the afternoon train. She has no one to wait on her at present, and I don't want you to lose any time."

I was ready enough to start, yet something in me hung back; and to gain time I asked, "And the gentleman, ma'am?"

"The gentleman's almost always away, I tell you," said Mrs. Railton, quick-like—"and when he's there," says she suddenly, "you've only to keep out of his way."

I took the afternoon train and got out at D—— station at about four o'clock. A groom in a dog-cart was waiting, and we drove off at a smart pace.

It was a dull October day, with rain hanging close overhead, but by the time we turned into Brympton Place woods the daylight was almost gone. The drive wound through the woods for a mile or two, and came out on a gravel court shut in with thickets of tall black-looking shrubs. There were no lights in the windows, and the house *did* look a bit gloomy.

I had asked no questions of the groom, for I never was one to get my notion of new masters from their other servants: I prefer to wait and see for myself. But I could tell by the look of everything that I had got into the right kind of house, and that things were done handsomely. A pleasant-faced cook met me at the back door and called the house-maid to show me up to my room. "You'll see madam later," she said. "Mrs. Brympton has a visitor."

I hadn't fancied Mrs. Brympton was a lady to have many visitors, and somehow the words cheered me. I followed the house-maid upstairs, and saw, through a door on the upper landing, that the main part of the house seemed well furnished, with dark panelling and a number of old portraits. Another flight of stairs led us up to the servants' wing. It was almost dark now, and the house-maid excused herself for not having brought a light. "But there's matches in your room," she said, "and if you go careful you'll be all right. Mind the step at the end of the passage. Your room is just beyond."

I looked ahead as she spoke, and half-way down the passage I saw a woman standing. She drew back into a doorway as we passed and the house-maid didn't appear to notice her. She was a thin woman with a white face, and a darkish stuff gown and apron. I took her for the housekeeper and thought it odd that she didn't speak, but just gave me a long look as we went by. My room opened into a square hall at the end of the passage. Facing my door was another which stood open: the house-maid exclaimed when she saw it:

"There—Mrs. Blinder's left that door open again!" said she, closing it.

"Is Mrs. Blinder the housekeeper?"

"There's no housekeeper: Mrs. Blinder's the cook."

"And is that her room?"

"Laws, no," said the house-maid, cross-like. "That's nobody's room. It's empty, I mean, and the door hadn't ought to be open. Mrs. Brympton wants it kept locked."

She opened my door and led me into a neat room, nicely furnished, with a picture or two on the walls; and having lit a candle she took leave, telling me that the servants'-hall tea was at six, and that Mrs. Brympton would see me afterward.

I found them a pleasant-spoken set in the servants' hall, and by what they let fall I gathered that, as Mrs. Railton had said, Mrs. Brympton was the kindest of ladies; but I didn't take much notice of their talk, for I was watching to see the pale woman in the dark gown come in. She didn't show herself, however, and I wondered if she ate apart; but if she wasn't the housekeeper, why should she? Suddenly it struck me that she might be a trained nurse, and in that case her meals would of course be served in her room. If Mrs. Brympton was an invalid it was likely enough she had a nurse. The idea annoyed me, I own, for they're not always the easiest to get on with, and if I'd known I shouldn't have taken the place. But there I was and there was no use pulling a long face over it; and not being one to ask questions I waited to see what would turn up.

When tea was over the house-maid said to the footman: "Has Mr. Ranford gone?" and when he said yes, she told me to come up with her to Mrs. Brympton.

Mrs. Brympton was lying down in her bedroom. Her lounge stood near the fire and beside it was a shaded lamp. She was a delicate-looking lady, but when she smiled I felt there was nothing I wouldn't do for her. She spoke very pleasantly, in a low voice, asking me my name and age and so on, and if I had everything I wanted, and if I wasn't afraid of feeling lonely in the country.

"Not with you I wouldn't be, madam," I said, and the words surprised me when I'd spoken them, for I'm not an impulsive person; but it was just as if I'd thought aloud.

She seemed pleased at that, and said she hoped I'd continue in the same mind; then she gave me a few directions about her toilet, and said Agnes the house-maid should show me next morning where things were kept.

"I am tired tonight, and shall dine upstairs," she said. "Agnes will bring me my tray, that you may have time to unpack and settle yourself; and later you may come and undress me."

"Very well, ma'am," I said. "You'll ring, I suppose?"

I thought she looked odd.

"No—Agnes will fetch you," says she quickly, and took up her book again.

Well—that was certainly strange: a lady's maid having to be fetched by the house-maid whenever her lady wanted her! I wondered if there were no bells in the house; but the next day I satisfied myself that there was one in every room, and a special one ringing from my mistress's room to mine; and after that it did strike me as queer that, whenever Mrs. Brympton wanted anything, she rang for Agnes, who had to walk the whole length of the servants' wing to call me.

But that wasn't the only queer thing in the house. The very next day I found out that Mrs. Brympton had no nurse; and then I asked Agnes about the woman I had seen in the passage the afternoon before. Agnes said she had seen no one, and I saw that she thought I was dreaming. To be sure, it was dusk when we went down the passage, and she had excused herself for not bringing a light; but I had seen the woman plain enough to know her again if we should meet. I decided that she must have been a friend of the cook's, or of one of the other women-servants; perhaps she had come down from town for a night's visit, and the servants wanted it kept secret. Some ladies are very stiff about having their servants' friends in the house over-night. At any rate, I made up my mind to ask no more questions.

In a day or two another odd thing happened. I was chatting one afternoon with Mrs. Blinder, who was a friendly disposed woman, and had been longer in the house than the other servants, and she asked me if I was quite comfortable and had everything I needed. I said I had no fault to find with my place or with my mistress, but I thought it odd that in so large a house there was no sewing-room for the lady's maid.

"Why," says she, "there *is* one: the room you're in is the old sewing-room."

"Oh," said I; "and where did the other lady's maid sleep?"

At that she grew confused, and said hurriedly that the servants' rooms had all been changed about last year, and she didn't rightly remember.

That struck me as peculiar, but I went on as if I hadn't noticed: "Well, there's a vacant room opposite mine, and I mean to ask Mrs. Brympton if I mayn't use that as a sewing-room."

To my astonishment, Mrs. Blinder went white, and gave my hand a kind of squeeze. "Don't do that, my dear," said she, trembling-like. "To tell you the truth, that was Emma Saxon's room, and my mistress has kept it closed ever since her death."

"And who was Emma Saxon?"

"Mrs. Brympton's former maid."

"The one that was with her so many years?" said I, remembering what Mrs. Railton had told me.

Mrs. Blinder nodded.

"What sort of woman was she?"

"No better walked the earth," said Mrs. Blinder. "My mistress loved her like a sister."

"But I mean—what did she look like?"

Mrs. Blinder got up and gave me a kind of angry stare. "I'm no great hand at describing," she said; "and I believe my pastry's rising." And she walked off into the kitchen and shut the door after her.

II

I had been near a week at Brympton before I saw my master. Word came that he was arriving one afternoon, and a change passed over the whole household. It was plain that nobody loved him below stairs. Mrs. Blinder took uncommon care with the dinner that night, but she snapped at the kitchen-maid in a way quite unusual with her; and Mr. Wace, the butler, a serious, slow-spoken man, went about his duties as if he'd been getting ready for a funeral. He was a great Bible-reader, Mr. Wace was, and had a beautiful assortment of texts at his command; but that day he used such dreadful language, that I was about to leave the table, when he assured me it was all out of Isaiah; and I noticed that whenever the master came Mr. Wace took to the prophets.

About seven, Agnes called me to my mistress's room; and there I found Mr. Brympton. He was standing on the hearth; a big fair bull-necked man, with a red face and little bad-tempered blue eyes: the kind of man a young simpleton might have thought handsome, and would have been like to pay dear for thinking it.

He swung about when I came in, and looked me over in a trice. I knew what the look meant, from having experienced it once or twice in my former places. Then he turned his back on me, and went on talking to his wife; and I knew what *that* meant, too. I was not the kind of morsel he was after. The typhoid had served me well enough in one way: it kept that kind of gentleman at arm's-length.

"This is my new maid, Hartley," says Mrs. Brympton in her kind voice; and he nodded and went on with what he was saying.

In a minute or two he went off, and left my mistress to dress for dinner, and I noticed as I waited on her that she was white, and chill to the touch.

Mr. Brympton took himself off the next morning, and the whole house drew a long breath when he drove away. As for my mistress, she put on her hat and furs (for it was a fine winter morning) and went out for a walk in the gardens, coming back quite fresh and rosy, so that for a minute, before her colour faded, I could guess what a pretty young lady she must have been, and not so long ago, either.

She had met Mr. Ranford in the grounds, and the two came back together, I remember, smiling and talking as they walked along the terrace under my window. That was the first time I saw Mr. Ranford, though I had often heard his name mentioned in the hall. He was a neighbour, it appeared, living a mile or two beyond Brympton, at the end of the village; and as he was in the habit of spending his winters in the country he was almost the only company my mistress had at that season. He was a slight tall gentleman of about thirty, and I thought him rather melancholy-looking till I saw his smile, which had a kind of surprise in it, like the first warm day in spring. He was a great reader, I heard, like my mistress, and the two were for ever borrowing books of one another, and sometimes (Mr. Wace told me) he would read aloud to Mrs. Brympton by the hour, in the big dark library where she sat in the winter afternoons. The servants all liked him, and perhaps that's more of a compliment than the masters suspect. He had a friendly word for every one of us, and we were all glad to think that Mrs. Brympton had a pleasant companionable gentleman like that to keep her company when the master was away. Mr. Ranford seemed on excellent terms with Mr. Brympton, too; though I could but wonder that two gentlemen so unlike each other should be so friendly. But then I knew how the real quality can keep their feelings to themselves.

As for Mr. Brympton, he came and went, never staying more than a day or two, cursing the dulness and the solitude, grumbling at everything, and (as I soon found out) drinking a deal more than was good for him. After Mrs. Brympton left the table he would sit half the night over the old Brympton port and madeira, and once, as I was leaving my mistress's room rather later than usual, I met him coming up the stairs in such a state that I turned sick to think of what some ladies have to endure and hold their tongues about.

The servants said very little about their master; but from what they let drop I could see it had been an unhappy match from the beginning. Mr. Brympton was coarse, loud and pleasure-loving; my mistress quiet, retiring, and perhaps a trifle cold. Not that she was not always pleasant-spoken to him: I thought her wonderfully forbearing; but to a gentleman as free as Mr. Brympton I daresay she seemed a little offish.

Well, things went on quietly for several weeks. My mistress was kind, my duties were light, and I got on well with the other servants. In short, I had nothing to complain of; yet there was always a weight on me. I can't say why it was so, but I know it was not the loneliness that I felt. I soon got used to that; and being still languid from the fever, I was thankful for the quiet and the good country air. Nevertheless, I was never quite easy in my mind. My mistress, knowing I had been ill, insisted that I should take my walk regular, and often invented errands for me:—a yard of ribbon to be fetched from the

village, a letter posted, or a book returned to Mr. Ranford. As soon as I was
out of doors my spirits rose, and I looked forward to my walks through the
bare moist-smelling woods; but the moment I caught sight of the house
again my heart dropped down like a stone in a well. It was not a gloomy
house exactly, yet I never entered it but a feeling of gloom came over me.

Mrs. Brympton seldom went out in winter; only on the finest days did she
walk an hour at noon on the south terrace. Excepting Mr. Ranford, we had
no visitors but the doctor, who drove over from D—— about once a week.
He sent for me once or twice to give me some trifling direction about my
mistress, and though he never told me what her illness was, I thought, from
a waxy look she had now and then of a morning, that it might be the heart
that ailed her. The season was soft and unwholesome, and in January we had
a long spell of rain. That was a sore trial to me, I own, for I couldn't go out,
and sitting over my sewing all day, listening to the drip, drip of the eaves, I
grew so nervous that the least sound made me jump. Somehow, the thought
of that locked room across the passage began to weigh on me. Once or twice,
in the long rainy nights, I fancied I heard noises there; but that was nonsense, of course, and the daylight drove such notions out of my head. Well,
one morning Mrs. Brympton gave me quite a start of pleasure by telling me
she wished me to go to town for some shopping. I hadn't known till then
how low my spirits had fallen. I set off in high glee, and my first sight of the
crowded streets and the cheerful-looking shops quite took me out of myself.
Toward afternoon, however, the noise and confusion began to tire me, and I
was actually looking forward to the quiet of Brympton, and thinking how I
should enjoy the drive home through the dark woods, when I ran across an
old acquaintance, a maid I had once been in service with. We had lost sight
of each other for a number of years, and I had to stop and tell her what had
happened to me in the interval. When I mentioned where I was living she
rolled up her eyes and pulled a long face.

"What! The Mrs. Brympton that lives all the year at her place on the
Hudson? My dear, you won't stay there three months."

"Oh, but I don't mind the country," says I, offended somehow at her tone.
"Since the fever I'm glad to be quiet."

She shook her head. "It's not the country I'm thinking of. All I know is
she's had four maids in the last six months, and the last one, who was a friend
of mine, told me nobody could stay in the house."

"Did she say why?" I asked.

"No—she wouldn't give me her reason. But she says to me, *Mrs. Ansey*,
she says, *if ever a young woman as you know of thinks of going there, you tell her
it's not worth while to unpack her boxes.*"

"Is she young and handsome?" said I, thinking of Mr. Brympton.

"Not her! She's the kind that mothers engage when they've gay young gentlemen at college."

Well, though I knew the woman was an idle gossip, the words stuck in my head, and my heart sank lower than ever as I drove up to Brympton in the dusk. There *was* something about the house—I was sure of it now . . .

When I went in to tea I heard that Mr. Brympton had arrived, and I saw at a glance that there had been a disturbance of some kind. Mrs. Blinder's hand shook so that she could hardly pour the tea, and Mr. Wace quoted the most dreadful texts full of brimstone. Nobody said a word to me then, but when I went up to my room Mrs. Blinder followed me.

"Oh, my dear," says she, taking my hand, "I'm so glad and thankful you've come back to us!"

That struck me, as you may imagine. "Why," said I, "did you think I was leaving for good?"

"No, no, to be sure," said she, a little confused, "but I can't a-bear to have madam left alone for a day even." She pressed my hand hard, and, "Oh, Miss Hartley," says she, "be good to your mistress, as you're a Christian woman." And with that she hurried away, and left me staring.

A moment later Agnes called me to Mrs. Brympton. Hearing Mr. Brympton's voice in her room, I went round by the dressing-room, thinking I would lay out her dinner-gown before going in. The dressing-room is a large room with a window over the portico that looks toward the gardens. Mr. Brympton's apartments are beyond. When I went in, the door into the bedroom was ajar, and I heard Mr. Brympton saying angrily:—"One would suppose he was the only person fit for you to talk to."

"I don't have many visitors in winter," Mrs. Brympton answered quietly.

"You have *me!*" he flung at her, sneeringly.

"You are here so seldom," said she.

"Well—whose fault is that? You make a place about as lively as the family vault—"

With that I rattled the toilet-things, to give my mistress warning, and she rose and called me in.

The two dined alone, as usual, and I knew by Mr. Wace's manner at supper that things must be going badly. He quoted the prophets something terrible, and worked on the kitchen-maid so that she declared she wouldn't go down alone to put the cold meat in the ice-box. I felt nervous myself, and after I had put my mistress to bed I was half tempted to go down again and persuade Mrs. Blinder to sit up awhile over a game of cards. But I heard her door closing for the night and so I went on to my own room. The rain had begun again, and the drip, drip, drip seemed to be dropping into my brain. I lay awake listening to it, and turning over what my friend in town had said. What puzzled me was that it was always the maids who left. . .

After a while I slept; but suddenly a loud noise wakened me. My bell had rung. I sat up, terrified by the unusual sound, which seemed to go on jangling through the darkness. My hands shook so that I couldn't find the matches. At length I struck a light and jumped out of bed. I began to think I must have been dreaming; but I looked at the bell against the wall, and there was the little hammer still quivering.

I was just beginning to huddle on my clothes when I heard another sound. This time it was the door of the locked room opposite mine softly opening and closing. I heard the sound distinctly, and it frightened me so that I stood stock still. Then I heard a footstep hurrying down the passage toward the main house. The floor being carpeted, the sound was very faint, but I was quite sure it was a woman's step. I turned cold with the thought of it, and for a minute or two I dursn't breathe or move. Then I came to my senses.

"Alice Hartley," says I to myself, "someone left that room just now and ran down the passage ahead of you. The idea isn't pleasant, but you may as well face it. Your mistress has rung for you, and to answer her bell you've got to go the way that other woman has gone."

Well—I did it. I never walked faster in my life, yet I thought I should never get to the end of the passage or reach Mrs. Brympton's room. On the way I heard nothing and saw nothing: all was dark and quiet as the grave. When I reached my mistress's door the silence was so deep that I began to think I must be dreaming, and was half minded to turn back. Then panic seized me, and I knocked.

There was no answer, and I knocked again, loudly. To my astonishment the door was opened by Mr. Brympton. He started back when he saw me, and in the light of my candle his face looked red and savage.

"*You?*" he said, in a queer voice. "*How many of you are there, in God's name?*"

At that I felt the ground give under me; but I said to myself that he had been drinking, and answered as steadily as I could: "May I go in, sir? Mrs. Brympton has rung for me."

"You may all go in, for what I care," says he, and, pushing by me, walked down the hall to his own bedroom. I looked after him as he went, and to my surprise I saw that he walked as straight as a sober man.

I found my mistress lying very weak and still, but she forced a smile when she saw me, and signed to me to pour out some drops for her. After that she lay without speaking, her breath coming quick, and her eyes closed. Suddenly she groped out with her hand, and "*Emma,*" says she, faintly.

"It's Hartley, madam," I said. "Do you want anything?"

She opened her eyes wide and gave me a startled look.

"I was dreaming," she said. "You may go, now, Hartley, and thank you kindly. I'm quite well again, you see." And she turned her face away from me.

III

There was no more sleep for me that night, and I was thankful when daylight came.

Soon afterward, Agnes called me to Mrs. Brympton. I was afraid she was ill again, for she seldom sent for me before nine, but I found her sitting up in bed, pale and drawn-looking, but quite herself.

"Hartley," says she quickly, "will you put on your things at once and go down to the village for me? I want this prescription made up—" here she hesitated a minute and blushed—"and I should like you to be back again before Mr. Brympton is up."

"Certainly, madam," I said.

"And—stay a moment—" she called me back as if an idea had just struck her—"while you're waiting for the mixture, you'll have time to go on to Mr. Ranford's with this note."

It was a two-mile walk to the village, and on my way I had time to turn things over in my mind. It struck me as peculiar that my mistress should wish the prescription made up without Mr. Brympton's knowledge; and, putting this together with the scene of the night before, and with much else that I had noticed and suspected, I began to wonder if the poor lady was weary of her life, and had come to the mad resolve of ending it. The idea took such hold on me that I reached the village on a run, and dropped breathless into a chair before the chemist's counter. The good man, who was just taking down his shutters, stared at me so hard that it brought me to myself.

"Mr. Limmel," I says, trying to speak indifferent, "will you run your eye over this, and tell me if it's quite right?"

He put on his spectacles and studied the prescription.

"Why, it's one of Dr. Walton's," says he. "What should be wrong with it?"

"Well—is it dangerous to take?"

"Dangerous—how do you mean?"

I could have shaken the man for his stupidity.

"I mean—if a person was to take too much of it—by mistake of course—" says I, my heart in my throat.

"Lord bless you, no. It's only lime-water. You might feed it to a baby by the bottleful."

I gave a great sigh of relief and hurried on to Mr. Ranford's. But on the way another thought struck me. If there was nothing to conceal about my visit to the chemist's, was it my other errand that Mrs. Brympton wished me to keep private? Somehow, that thought frightened me worse than the other. Yet the two gentlemen seemed fast friends, and I would have staked my head on my mistress's goodness. I felt ashamed of my suspicions, and concluded that I was still disturbed by the strange events of the night. I left the note at Mr. Ranford's, and hurrying back to Brympton, slipped in by a side door without being seen, as I thought.

An hour later, however, as I was carrying in my mistress's breakfast, I was stopped in the hall by Mr. Brympton.

"What were you doing out so early?" he says, looking hard at me.

"Early—me, sir?" I said, in a tremble.

"Come, come," he says, an angry red spot coming out on his forehead, "didn't I see you scuttling home through the shrubbery an hour or more ago?"

I'm a truthful woman by nature, but at that a lie popped out ready-made. "No, sir, you didn't," said I and looked straight back at him.

He shrugged his shoulders and gave a sullen laugh. "I suppose you think I was drunk last night?" he asked suddenly.

"No, sir, I don't," I answered, this time truthfully enough.

He turned away with another shrug. "A pretty notion my servants have of me!" I heard him mutter as he walked off.

Not till I had settled down to my afternoon's sewing did I realize how the events of the night had shaken me. I couldn't pass that locked door without a shiver. I knew I had heard someone come out of it, and walk down the passage ahead of me. I thought of speaking to Mrs. Blinder or to Mr. Wace, the only two in the house who appeared to have an inkling of what was going on, but I had a feeling that if I questioned them they would deny everything, and that I might learn more by holding my tongue and keeping my eyes open. The idea of spending another night opposite the locked room sickened me, and once I was seized with the notion of packing my trunk and taking the first train to town; but it wasn't in me to throw over a kind mistress in that manner, and I tried to go on with my sewing as if nothing had happened. I hadn't worked ten minutes before the sewing machine broke down. It was one I had found in the house, a good machine but a trifle out of order: Mrs. Blinder said it had never been used since Emma Saxon's death. I stopped to see what was wrong, and as I was working at the machine a drawer which I had never been able to open slid forward and a photograph fell out. I picked it up and sat looking at it in a maze. It was a woman's likeness, and I knew I had seen the face somewhere—the eyes had an asking look that I had felt on me before. And suddenly I remembered the pale woman in the passage.

I stood up, cold all over, and ran out of the room. My heart seemed to be thumping in the top of my head, and I felt as if I should never get away from the look in those eyes. I went straight to Mrs. Blinder. She was taking her afternoon nap, and sat up with a jump when I came in.

"Mrs. Blinder," said I, "who is that?" And I held out the photograph.

She rubbed her eyes and stared.

"Why, Emma Saxon," says she. "Where did you find it?"

I looked hard at her for a minute. "Mrs. Blinder," I said, "I've seen that face before."

Mrs. Blinder got up and walked over to the looking-glass. "Dear me! I must have been asleep," she says. "My front is all over one ear. And now do run along, Miss Hartley, dear, for I hear the clock striking four, and I must go down this very minute and put on the Virginia ham for Mrs. Brympton's dinner."

IV

To all appearances, things went on as usual for a week or two. The only difference was that Mr. Brympton stayed on, instead of going off as he usually did, and that Mr. Ranford never showed himself. I heard Mr. Brympton remark on this one afternoon when he was sitting in my mistress's room before dinner:

"Where's Ranford?" says he. "He hasn't been near the house for a week. Does he keep away because I'm here?"

Mrs. Brympton spoke so low that I couldn't catch her answer.

"Well," he went on, "two's company and three's trumpery; I'm sorry to be in Ranford's way, and I suppose I shall have to take myself off again in a day or two and give him a show." And he laughed at his own joke.

The very next day, as it happened, Mr. Ranford called. The footman said the three were very merry over their tea in the library, and Mr. Brympton strolled down to the gate with Mr. Ranford when he left.

I have said that things went on as usual; and so they did with the rest of the household; but as for myself, I had never been the same since the night my bell had rung. Night after night I used to lie awake, listening for it to ring again, and for the door of the locked room to open stealthily. But the bell never rang, and I heard no sound across the passage. At last the silence began to be more dreadful to me than the most mysterious sounds. I felt that *someone* was cowering there, behind the locked door, watching and listening as I watched and listened, and I could almost have cried out, "Whoever you are, come out and let me see you face to face, but don't lurk there and spy on me in the darkness!"

Feeling as I did, you may wonder I didn't give warning. Once I very nearly did so; but at the last moment something held me back. Whether it was compassion for my mistress, who had grown more and more dependent on me, or unwillingness to try a new place, or some other feeling that I couldn't put a name to, I lingered on as if spell-bound, though every night was dreadful to me, and the days but little better.

For one thing, I didn't like Mrs. Brympton's looks. She had never been the same since that night, no more than I had. I thought she would brighten up after Mr. Brympton left, but though she seemed easier in her mind, her spirits didn't revive, nor her strength either. She had grown attached to me, and seemed to like to have me about; and Agnes told me one day that, since Emma Saxon's death, I was the only maid her mistress had taken to. This gave me a warm feeling for the poor lady, though after all there was little I could do to help her.

After Mr. Brympton's departure, Mr. Ranford took to coming again, though less often than formerly. I met him once or twice in the grounds, or in the village, and I couldn't but think there was a change in him, too; but I set it down to my disordered fancy.

The weeks passed, and Mr. Brympton had now been a month absent. We heard he was cruising with a friend in the West Indies, and Mr. Wace said that was a long way off, but though you had the wings of a dove and went to the uttermost parts of the earth, you couldn't get away from the Almighty. Agnes said that as long as he stayed away from Brympton the Almighty might have him and welcome; and this raised a laugh, though Mrs. Blinder tried to look shocked, and Mr. Wace said the bears would eat us.

We were all glad to hear that the West Indies were a long way off, and I remember that, in spite of Mr. Wace's solemn looks, we had a very merry dinner that day in the hall. I don't know if it was because of my being in better spirits, but I fancied Mrs. Brympton looked better, too, and seemed more cheerful in her manner. She had been for a walk in the morning, and after luncheon she lay down in her room, and I read aloud to her. When she dismissed me I went to my own room feeling quite bright and happy, and for the first time in weeks walked past the locked door without thinking of it. As I sat down to my work I looked out and saw a few snow-flakes falling. The sight was pleasanter than the eternal rain, and I pictured to myself how pretty the bare gardens would look in their white mantle. It seemed to me as if the snow would cover up all the dreariness, indoors as well as out.

The fancy had hardly crossed my mind when I heard a step at my side. I looked up, thinking it was Agnes.

"Well, Agnes—" said I, and the words froze on my tongue; for there, in the door, stood Emma Saxon.

I don't know how long she stood there. I only know I couldn't stir or take my eyes from her. Afterward I was terribly frightened, but at the time it wasn't fear I felt, but something deeper and quieter. She looked at me long and long, and her face was just one dumb prayer to me—but how in the world was I to help her? Suddenly she turned, and I heard her walk down the passage. This time I wasn't afraid to follow—I felt that I must know what she wanted. I sprang up and ran out. She was at the other end of the passage, and I expected her to take the turn toward my mistress's room; but instead of that she pushed open the door that led to the backstairs. I followed her down the stairs, and across the passageway to the back door. The kitchen and hall were empty at that hour, the servants being off duty, except for the footman, who was in the pantry. At the door she stood still a moment, with another look at me; then she turned the handle, and stepped out. For a minute I hesitated. Where was she leading me to? The door had closed softly after her, and I opened it and looked out, half expecting to find that she had disappeared. But I saw her a few yards off hurrying across the courtyard to the path through the woods. Her figure looked black and lonely in the snow, and for a second my heart failed me and I thought of turning back. But all the while she was drawing me after her; and catching up an old shawl of Mrs. Blinder's I ran out into the open.

Emma Saxon was in the wood-path now. She walked on steadily, and I followed at the same pace, till we passed out of the gates and reached the highroad. Then she struck across the open fields to the village. By this time the ground was white, and as she climbed the slope of a bare hill ahead of me I noticed that she left no foot-prints behind her. At sight of that my heart shrivelled up within me, and my knees were water. Somehow, it was worse here than indoors. She made the whole countryside seem lonely as the grave, with none but us two in it, and no help in the wide world.

Once I tried to go back; but she turned and looked at me, and it was as if she had dragged me with ropes. After that I followed her like a dog. We came to the village and she led me through it, past the church and the blacksmith's shop, and down the lane to Mr. Ranford's. Mr. Ranford's house stands close to the road: a plain old-fashioned building, with a flagged path leading to the door between box-borders. The lane was deserted, and as I turned into it I saw Emma Saxon pause under the old elm by the gate. And now another fear come over me. I saw that we had reached the end of our journey, and that it was my turn to act. All the way from Brympton I had been asking myself what she wanted of me, but I had followed in a trance, as it were, and not till I saw her stop at Mr. Ranford's gate did my brain begin to clear itself. I stood a little way off in the snow, my heart beating fit to strangle me, and my feet frozen to the ground; and she stood under the elm and watched me.

I knew well enough that she hadn't led me there for nothing. I felt there was something I ought to say or do—but how was I to guess what it was? I had never thought harm of my mistress and Mr. Ranford, but I was sure now that, from one cause or another, some dreadful thing hung over them. *She* knew what it was; she would tell me if she could; perhaps she would answer if I questioned her.

It turned me faint to think of speaking to her; but I plucked up heart and dragged myself across the few yards between us. As I did so, I heard the house-door open and saw Mr. Ranford approaching. He looked handsome and cheerful, as my mistress had looked that morning, and at sight of him the blood began to flow again in my veins.

"Why, Hartley," said he, "what's the matter? I saw you coming down the lane just now, and came out to see if you had taken root in the snow." He stopped and stared at me. "What are you looking at?" he says.

I turned toward the elm as he spoke, and his eyes followed me; but there was no one there. The lane was empty as far as the eye could reach.

A sense of helplessness came over me. She was gone, and I had not been able to guess what she wanted. Her last look had pierced me to the marrow; and yet it had not told me! All at once, I felt more desolate than when she had stood there watching me. It seemed as if she had left me all alone to carry the weight of the secret I couldn't guess. The snow went round me in great circles, and the ground fell away from me.

A drop of brandy and the warmth of Mr. Ranford's fire soon brought me to, and I insisted on being driven back at once to Brympton. It was nearly dark, and I was afraid my mistress might be wanting me. I explained to Mr. Ranford that I had been out for a walk and had been taken with a fit of giddiness as I passed his gate. This was true enough; yet I never felt more like a liar than when I said it.

When I dressed Mrs. Brympton for dinner she remarked on my pale looks and asked what ailed me. I told her I had a headache, and she said she would not require me again that evening, and advised me to go to bed.

It was a fact that I could scarcely keep on my feet; yet I had no fancy to spend a solitary evening in my room. I sat downstairs in the hall as long as I could hold my head up; but by nine I crept upstairs, too weary to care what happened if I could but get my head on a pillow. The rest of the household went to bed soon afterward; they kept early hours when the master was away, and before ten I heard Mrs. Blinder's door close, and Mr. Wace's soon after.

It was a very still night, earth and air all muffled in snow. Once in bed I felt easier, and lay quiet, listening to the strange noises that come out in a house after dark. Once I thought I heard a door open and close again below: it might have been the glass door that led to the gardens. I got up and peered out of the window; but it was in the dark of the moon, and nothing visible outside but the streaking of snow against the panes.

I went back to bed and must have dozed, for I jumped awake to the furious ringing of my bell. Before my head was clear I had sprung out of bed, and was dragging on my clothes. *It is going to happen now,* I heard myself saying; but what I meant I had no notion. My hands seemed to be covered with glue—I thought I should never get into my clothes. At last I opened my door and peered down the passage. As far as my candle-flame carried, I could see nothing unusual ahead of me. I hurried on, breathless; but as I pushed open the baize door leading to the main hall my heart stood still, for there at the head of the stairs was Emma Saxon, peering dreadfully down into the darkness.

For a second I couldn't stir; but my hand slipped from the door, and as it swung shut the figure vanished. At the same instant there came another sound from below stairs—a stealthy mysterious sound, as of a latchkey turning in the house-door. I ran to Mrs. Brympton's room and knocked.

There was no answer, and I knocked again. This time I heard someone moving in the room; the bolt slipped back and my mistress stood before me. To my surprise I saw that she had not undressed for the night. She gave me a startled look.

"What is this, Hartley?" she says in a whisper. "Are you ill? What are you doing here at this hour?"

"I am not ill, madam; but my bell rang."

At that she turned pale, and seemed about to fall.

"You are mistaken," she said harshly; "I didn't ring. You must have been dreaming." I had never heard her speak in such a tone. "Go back to bed," she said, closing the door on me.

But as she spoke I heard sounds again in the hall below: a man's step this time; and the truth leaped out on me.

"Madam," I said, pushing past her, "there is someone in the house—"

"Someone—?"

"Mr. Brympton, I think—I hear his step below—"

A dreadful look came over her, and without a word, she dropped flat at my feet. I fell on my knees and tried to lift her: by the way she breathed I saw it was no common faint. But as I raised her head there came quick steps on the stairs and across the hall: the door was flung open, and there stood Mr. Brympton, in his travelling-clothes, the snow dripping from him. He drew back with a start as he saw me kneeling by my mistress.

"What the devil is this?" he shouted. He was less high-coloured than usual, and the red spot came out on his forehead.

"Mrs. Brympton has fainted, sir," said I.

He laughed unsteadily and pushed by me. "It's a pity she didn't choose a more convenient moment. I'm sorry to disturb her, but—"

I raised myself up aghast at the man's action.

"Sir," said I, "are you mad? What are you doing?"

"Going to meet a friend," said he, and seemed to make for the dressing-room.

At that my heart turned over. I don't know what I thought or feared; but I sprang up and caught him by the sleeve.

"Sir, sir," said I, "for pity's sake look at your wife!"

He shook me off furiously.

"It seems that's done for me," says he, and caught hold of the dressing-room door.

At that moment I heard a slight noise inside. Slight as it was, he heard it too, and tore the door open; but as he did so he dropped back. On the threshold stood Emma Saxon. All was dark behind her, but I saw her plainly, and so did he. He threw up his hands as if to hide his face from her; and when I looked again she was gone.

He stood motionless, as if the strength had run out of him; and in the stillness my mistress suddenly raised herself, and opening her eyes fixed a look on him. Then she fell back, and I saw the death-flutter pass over her . . .

We buried her on the third day, in a driving snow-storm. There were few people in the church, for it was bad weather to come from town, and I've a notion my mistress was one that hadn't many near friends. Mr. Ranford was among the last to come, just before they carried her up the aisle. He was in black, of course, being such a friend of the family, and I never saw a gentleman so pale. As he passed me, I noticed that he leaned a trifle on a stick he carried; and I fancy Mr. Brympton noticed it, too, for the red spot came out sharp on his forehead, and all through the service he kept staring across the church at Mr. Ranford, instead of following the prayers as a mourner should.

When it was over and we went out to the graveyard, Mr. Ranford had disappeared, and as soon as my poor mistress's body was underground, Mr. Brympton jumped into the carriage nearest the gate and drove off without a word to any of us. I heard him call out, "To the station," and we servants went back alone to the house.

MARY AUSTIN

(1868–1934)

Mary Hunter Austin's wide-ranging opus is marked by a love of nature and an interest in social and political reform. An advocate of women's and Native American rights, she was a lecturer, journalist, playwright, novelist, poet, essayist, short-story writer, and author of children's books. Born and raised in Illinois, she moved with her family to California after her graduation from Blackburn College. There she formed a lifelong interest in the environment, particularly the American West and its inhabitants. In 1891 she wed Stafford Wallace Austin, a union that ended in divorce in 1914. Much of her fiction focuses on the difficulties facing women in both marriage and career. Elements of the supernatural are occasionally present in the fiction that Austin bases on Native mythology. She also creates a number of narrators who possess mystical and visionary qualities. "The Readjustment" was published in *Harper's* in April 1908.

The Readjustment

EMMA JOSSYLIN HAD BEEN DEAD AND BURIED THREE DAYS. The sister who had come to the funeral had taken Emma's child away with her, and the house was swept and aired; then, when it seemed there was least occasion for it, Emma came back. The neighbor woman who had nursed her was the first to know it. It was about seven of the evening, in a mellow gloom: the neighbor woman was sitting on her own stoop with her arms wrapped in her apron, and all at once she found herself going along the street under an urgent sense that Emma needed her. She was half-way down the block before she recollected that this was impossible, for Mrs. Jossylin was dead and buried, but as soon as she came opposite the house she was aware of what had happened. It was all open to the summer air; except that it was a little neater, not otherwise than the rest of the street. It was quite dark; but the presence of Emma Jossylin streamed from it and betrayed it more than a candle. It streamed out steadily across the garden, and even as it reached her, mixed with the smell of the damp mignonette, the neighbor woman owned to herself that she had always known Emma would come back.

"A sight stranger if she wouldn't," thought the woman who had nursed her. "She wasn't ever one to throw off things easily."

Emma Jossylin had taken death, as she had taken everything in life, hard. She had met it with the same hard, bright, surface competency that she had presented to the squalor of the encompassing desertness, to the insuperable commonness of Sim Jossylin, to the affliction of her crippled child; and the intensity of her wordless struggle against it had caught the attention of the townspeople and held it in a shocked, curious awe. She was so long a-dying, lying there in the little low house, hearing the abhorred footsteps going about her house and the vulgar procedure of the community encroach upon her like the advances of the sand wastes on an unwatered field. For Emma had always wanted things different, wanted them with a fury of intentness that implied offensiveness in things as they were. And the townspeople had taken offence, the more so because she was not to be surprised in any inaptitude for their own kind of success. Do what you could, you could never catch Emma Jossylin in a wrapper after three o'clock in the afternoon. And she would never talk about the child—in a country where so little ever happened that even trouble was a godsend if it gave you something to talk about. It was reported that she did not even talk to Sim. But there the common resentment got back at her. If she had thought to effect anything with Sim Jossylin against the benumbing spirit of the place, the evasive hopefulness, the large sense of leisure that ungirt the loins, if she still hoped somehow to get away with him to some place for which by her dress, by her manner, she seemed forever and unassailably fit, it was foregone that nothing would come of it. They knew Sim Jossylin better than that. Yet so vivid had been the force of her wordless dissatisfaction that when the fever took her and she went down like a pasteboard figure in the damp, the wonder was that nothing toppled with her. And as if she too had felt herself indispensable, Emma Jossylin had come back.

The neighbor woman crossed the street, and as she passed the far corner of the gate, Jossylin spoke to her. He had been standing, she did not know how long a time, behind the syringa bush, and moved even with her along the fence until they came to the gate. She could see in the dusk that before speaking he wet his lips with his tongue.

"She's in there," he said at last.

"Emma?"

He nodded. "I been sleeping at the store since—but I thought I'd be more comfortable—as soon as I opened the door, there she was."

"Did you see her?"

"No."

"How do you know, then?"

"Don't you know?"

The neighbor felt there was nothing to say to that.

"Come in," he whispered, huskily. They slipped by the rose tree and the wistaria and sat down on the porch at the side. A door swung inward behind them. They felt the Presence in the dusk beating like a pulse.

"What do you think she wants?" said Jossylin. "Do you reckon it's the boy?"

"Like enough."

"He's better off with his aunt. There was no one here to take care of him, like his mother wanted." He raised his voice unconsciously with a note of justification, addressing the room behind.

"I am sending fifty dollars a month," he said; "he can go with the best of them." He went on at length to explain all the advantage that was to come to the boy from living at Pasadena, and the neighbor woman bore him out in it.

"He was glad to go," urged Jossylin to the room. "He said it was what his mother would have wanted."

They were silent then a long time, while the Presence seemed to swell upon them and encroached upon the garden. Finally, "I gave Zeigler the order for the monument yesterday," Jossylin threw out, appeasingly. "It's to cost three hundred and fifty." The Presence stirred. The neighbor thought she could fairly see the controlled tolerance with which Emma Jossylin threw off the evidence of Sim's ineptitude.

They sat on helplessly without talking after that, until the woman's husband came to the fence and called her.

"Don't go," begged Jossylin.

"Hush!" she said. "Do you want all the town to know? You had naught but good from Emma living, and no call to expect harm from her now. It's natural she should come back—if—if she was lonesome like—in—the place she's gone to."

"Emma wouldn't come back to this place," Jossylin protested, "without she wanted something."

"Well, then, you've got to find out," said the neighbor woman.

All the next day she saw, whenever she passed the house, that Emma was still there. It was shut and barred, but the Presence lurked behind the folded blinds and fumbled at the doors. When it was night and the moths began in the columbine under the window, It went out and walked in the garden.

Jossylin was waiting at the gate when the neighbor woman came. He sweated with helplessness in the warm dusk, and the Presence brooded upon them like an apprehension that grows by being entertained.

"She wants something," he appealed, "but I can't make out what. Emma knows she is welcome to everything I've got. Everybody knows I've been a good provider."

The neighbor woman remembered suddenly the only time she had ever drawn close to Emma Jossylin touching the child. They had sat up with it together all one night in some childish ailment, and she had ventured a question: "What does his father think?" And Emma had turned her a white, hard face of surpassing dreariness. "I don't know," she admitted; "he never says."

"There's more than providing," suggested the neighbor woman.

"Yes. There's feeling . . . but she had enough to do to put up with me. I had no call to be troubling her with such." He left off to mop his forehead, and began again.

"Feelings," he said; "there's times a man gets so wore out with feelings, he doesn't have them any more."

He talked, and presently it grew clear to the woman that he was voiding all the stuff of his life, as if he had sickened on it and was now done. It was a little soul knowing itself and not good to see. What was singular was that the Presence left off walking in the garden, came and caught like a gossamer on the ivy tree, swayed by the breath of his broken sentences. He talked, and the neighbor woman saw him for once as he saw himself and Emma, snared and floundering in an inexplicable unhappiness. He had been disappointed too. She had never relished the man he was, and it made him ashamed. That was why he had never gone away, lest he should make her ashamed among her own kind. He was her husband; he could not help that, though he was sorry for it. But he could keep the offence where least was made of it. And there was a child—she had wanted a child, but even then he had blundered—begotten a cripple upon her. He blamed himself utterly, searched out the roots of his youth for the answer to that, until the neighbor woman flinched to hear him. But the Presence stayed.

He had never talked to his wife about the child. How should he? There was the fact—the advertisement of his incompetence. And she had never talked to him. That was the one blessed and unassailable memory, that she had spread silence like a balm over his hurt. In return for it he had never gone away. He had resisted her that he might save her from showing among her own kind how poor a man he was. With every word of this ran the fact of his love for her—as he had loved her with all the stripes of clean and uncleanness. He bared himself as a child without knowing; and the Presence stayed. The talk trailed off at last to the commonplaces of consolation between the retchings of his spirit. The Presence lessened and streamed toward them on the wind of the garden. When it touched them like the warm air of noon that lies sometimes in hollow places after nightfall, the neighbor woman rose and went away.

The next night she did not wait for him. When a rod outside the town—it was a very little one—the burrowing owls *whoowhooed*, she hung up her apron and went to talk with Emma Jossylin. The Presence was there, drawn in, lying close. She found the key between the wistaria and the first pillar of the porch; but as soon as she opened the door she felt the chill that might be expected by one intruding on Emma Jossylin in her own house.

" 'The Lord is my shepherd!' " said the neighbor woman; it was the first religious phrase that occurred to her; then she said the whole of the psalm, and after that a hymn. She had come in through the door, and stood with her back to it and her hand upon the knob. Everything was just as Mrs. Jossylin had left it, with the waiting air of a room kept for company.

"Em," she said, boldly, when the chill had abated a little before the sacred words—"Em Jossylin, I've got something to say to you. And you've got to hear," she added with firmness as the white curtains stirred duskily at the window. "You wouldn't be talked to about your troubles when . . . you were here before, and we humored you. But now there is Sim to be thought of. I guess you heard what you came for last night, and got good of it. Maybe it would have been better if Sim had said things all along instead of hoarding them in his heart, but, anyway, he has said them now. And what I want to say is, if you was staying on with the hope of hearing it again, you'd be making a mistake. You was an uncommon woman, Emma Jossylin, and there didn't none of us understand you very well, nor do you justice, maybe; but Sim is only a common man, and I understand him because I'm that way myself. And if you think he'll be opening his heart to you every night, or be any different from what he's always been on account of what's happened, that's a mistake, too . . . and in a little while, if you stay, it will be as bad as it always was . . . men are like that . . . you'd better go now while there's understanding between you." She stood staring into the darkling room that seemed suddenly full of turbulence and denial. It seemed to beat upon her and take her breath, but she held on.

"You've got to go . . . Em . . . and I'm going to stay until you do," she said with finality; and then began again:

" 'The Lord is nigh unto them that are of a broken heart,' " and repeated the passage to the end. Then, as the Presence sank before it, "You better go, Emma," persuasively: and again, after an interval:

" 'He shall deliver thee in six troubles.'

" 'Yea, in seven there shall no evil touch thee.' " The Presence gathered itself and was still; she could make out that it stood over against the opposite corner by the gilt easel with the crayon portrait of the child.

" 'For thou shalt forget thy misery. Thou shalt remember it as waters that are past,' " concluded the neighbor woman, as she heard Jossylin on the gravel outside. What the Presence had wrought upon him in the night was visible in his altered mien. He looked, more than anything else, to be in need of sleep. He had eaten his sorrow, and that was the end of it—as it is with men.

"I came to see if there was anything I could do for you," said the woman, neighborly, with her hand upon the door.

"I don't know as there is," said he. "I'm much obliged, but I don't know as there is."

"You see," whispered the woman, over her shoulder, "not even to me." She felt the tug of her heart as the Presence swept past her. The neighbor went out after that and walked in the ragged street, past the schoolhouse, across the creek below the town, out by the fields, over the headgate, and back by the town again. It was full nine of the clock when she passed the Jossylin house. It looked, except for being a little neater, not other than the rest of the street. The door was open and the lamp was lit; she saw Jossylin black against it. He sat reading in a book like a man at ease in his own house.

———◆———

OLIVIA HOWARD DUNBAR
(1873–1953)

Journalist, short-story writer, and biographer, Olivia Howard Dunbar enjoyed a reputation as a prominent New York writer. Born in Bridgeport, Massachusetts, she graduated from Smith College, then worked as a journalist for the *New York World* until 1902. An active member of the women's suffrage movement, she also wrote feature articles and short stories for the leading magazines of the day. In 1914 she married the poet Ridgeley Torrence, following which she retained both her career and her name. Among Dunbar's many short stories are ghostly tales that explore marriage and women's lives. "The Shell of Sense" appeared in the December 1908 issue of *Harper's*.

The Shell of Sense

IT WAS INTOLERABLY UNCHANGED, THE DIM, DARK-TONED room. In an agony of recognition my glance ran from one to another of the comfortable, familiar things that my earthly life had been passed among. Incredibly distant from it all as I essentially was, I noted sharply that the very gaps that I myself had left in my bookshelves still stood unfilled; that the delicate fingers of the ferns that I had tended were still stretched futilely toward the light; that the soft agreeable chuckle of my own little clock, like some elderly woman with whom conversation has become automatic, was undiminished.

Unchanged—or so it seemed at first. But there were certain trivial differences that shortly smote me. The windows were closed too tightly; for I had always kept the house very cool, although I had known that Theresa preferred warm rooms. And my work-basket was in disorder: it was preposterous that so small a thing should hurt me so. Then, for this was my first experience of the shadow-folded transition, the odd alternation of my emotions bewildered me. For at one moment the place seemed so humanly familiar, so distinctly my own proper envelope, that for love of it I could have laid my cheek against the wall; while in the next I was miserably conscious of strange new shrillnesses. How could they be endured—and had I ever endured them?—those harsh influences that I now perceived at the window; light and color so blinding that they obscured the form of the wind, tumult so discordant that one could scarcely hear the roses open in the garden below?

But Theresa did not seem to mind any of these things. Disorder, it is true, the dear child had never minded. She was sitting all this time at my desk—at *my* desk,—occupied, I could only too easily surmise how. In the light of my own habits of precision it was plain that that sombre correspondence should have been attended to before; but I believe that I did not really reproach Theresa, for I knew that her notes, when she did write them, were perhaps less perfunctory than mine. She finished the last one as I watched her, and added it to the heap of black-bordered envelopes that lay on the desk. Poor girl! I saw now that they had cost her tears. Yet, living beside her day after day, year after year, I had never discovered what deep tenderness my sister possessed. Toward each other it had been our habit to display only a temperate affection, and I remember having always thought it distinctly fortunate for Theresa, since she was denied my happiness, that she could live so easily and pleasantly without emotions of the devastating sort. . . . And now, for the first time, I was really to behold her. . . . Could it be Theresa, after all, this tangle of subdued turbulences? Let no one suppose that it is an easy thing to bear, the relentlessly lucid understanding that I then first exercised; or that, in its first enfranchisement, the timid vision does not yearn for its old screens and mists.

Suddenly, as Theresa sat there, her head, filled with its tender thoughts of me, held in her gentle hands, I felt Allan's step on the carpeted stair outside. Theresa felt it, too,—but how? for it was not audible. She gave a start, swept the black envelopes out of sight, and pretended to be writing in a little book. Then I forgot to watch her any longer in my absorption in Allan's coming. It was he, of course, that I was awaiting. It was for him that I had made this first lonely, frightened effort to return, to recover. . . . It was not that I had supposed he would allow himself to recognize my presence, for I had long been sufficiently familiar with his hard and fast denials of the invisible. He was so reasonable always, so sane—so blindfolded. But I had hoped that because of his very rejection of the ether that now contained me I could perhaps all the more safely, the more secretly, watch him, linger near him. He was near now, very near,—but why did Theresa, sitting there in the room that had never belonged to her, appropriate for herself his coming? It was so manifestly I who had drawn him, I whom he had come to seek.

The door was ajar. He knocked softly at it. "Are you there, Theresa?" he called. He expected to find her, then, there in my room? I shrank back, fearing, almost, to stay.

"I shall have finished in a moment," Theresa told him, and he sat down to wait for her.

No spirit still unreleased can understand the pang that I felt with Allan sitting almost within my touch. Almost irresistibly the wish beset me to let him for an instant feel my nearness. Then I checked myself, remembering— oh, absurd, piteous human fears!—that my too unguarded closeness might alarm him. It was not so remote a time that I myself had known them, those blind, uncouth timidities. I came, therefore, somewhat nearer—but I did not touch him. I merely leaned toward him and with incredible softness whispered his name. That much I could not have forborne; the spell of life was still too strong in me.

But it gave him no comfort, no delight. "Theresa!" he called, in a voice dreadful with alarm—and in that instant the last veil fell, and desperately, scarce believingly, I beheld how it stood between them, those two.

She turned to him that gentle look of hers.

"Forgive me," came from him hoarsely. "But I had suddenly the most— unaccountable sensation. Can there be too many windows open? There is such a—chill—about."

"There are no windows open," Theresa assured him. "I took care to shut out the chill. You are not well, Allan!"

"Perhaps not." He embraced the suggestion. "And yet I feel no illness apart from this abominable sensation that persists—persists. . . . Theresa, you must tell me: do I fancy it, or do you, too, feel—something—strange here?"

"Oh, there is something very strange here," she half sobbed. "There always will be."

"Good heavens, child, I didn't mean that!" He rose and stood looking about him. "I know, of course, that you have your beliefs, and I respect them, but you know equally well that I have nothing of the sort! So—don't let us conjure up anything inexplicable."

I stayed impalpably, imponderably near him. Wretched and bereft though I was, I could not have left him while he stood denying me.

"What I mean," he went on, in his low, distinct voice, "is a special, an almost ominous sense of cold. Upon my soul, Theresa,"—he paused—"if I

were superstitious, if I *were* a woman, I should probably imagine it to seem—
a presence!"

He spoke the last word very faintly, but Theresa shrank from it nevertheless.

"*Don't* say that, Allan!" she cried out. "Don't think it, I beg of you! I've
tried so hard myself not to think it—and you must help me. You know it is
only perturbed, uneasy spirits that wander. With her it is quite different. She
has always been so happy—she must still be."

I listened, stunned, to Theresa's sweet dogmatism. From what blind dis-
tances came her confident misapprehensions, how dense, both for her and
for Allan, was the separating vapor!

Allan frowned. "Don't take me literally, Theresa," he explained; and I,
who a moment before had almost touched him, now held myself aloof and
heard him with a strange untried pity, new born in me. "I'm not speaking of
what you call—spirits. It's something much more terrible." He allowed his
head to sink heavily on his chest. "If I did not positively know that I had
never done her any harm, I should suppose myself to be suffering from guilt,
from remorse. . . . Theresa, you know better than I, perhaps. Was she
content, always? Did she believe in me?"

"Believe in you?—when she knew you to be so good!—when you adored
her!"

"She thought that? She said it? Then what in Heaven's name ails me?—
unless it is all as you believe, Theresa, and she knows now what she didn't
know then, poor dear, and minds—"

"Minds what? What do you mean. Allan?"

I, who with my perhaps illegitimate advantage saw so clear, knew that he
had not meant to tell her: I did him that justice, even in my first jealousy. If I
had not tortured him so by clinging near him, he would not have told her.
But the moment came, and overflowed, and he did tell her—passionate,
tumultuous story that it was. During all our life together, Allan's and mine,
he had spared me, had kept me wrapped in the white cloak of an unblemished loyalty. But it would have been kinder, I now bitterly thought, if,
like many husbands, he had years ago found for the story he now poured
forth some clandestine listener; I should not have known. But he was faithful and good, and so he waited till I, mute and chained, was there to hear
him. So well did I know him, as I thought, so thoroughly had he once been
mine, that I saw it in his eyes, heard it in his voice, before the words came.
And yet, when it came, it lashed me with the whips of an unbearable
humiliation. For I, his wife, had not known how greatly he could love.

And that Theresa, soft little traitor, should, in her still way, have cared too! Where was the iron in her, I moaned within my stricken spirit, where the steadfastness? From the moment he bade her, she turned her soft little petals up to him—and my last delusion was spent. It was intolerable; and none the less so that in another moment she had, prompted by some belated thought of me, renounced him. Allan was hers, yet she put him from her; and it was my part to watch them both.

Then in the anguish of it all I remembered, awkward, untutored spirit that I was, that I now had the Great Recourse. Whatever human things were unbearable, I had no need to bear. I ceased, therefore, to make the effort that kept me with them. The pitiless poignancy was dulled, the sounds and the light ceased, the lovers faded from me, and again I was mercifully drawn into the dim, infinite spaces.

There followed a period whose length I cannot measure and during which I was able to make no progress in the difficult, dizzying experience of release. "Earth-bound" my jealousy relentlessly kept me. Though my two dear ones had forsworn each other, I could not trust them, for theirs seemed to me an affectation of a more than mortal magnanimity. Without a ghostly sentinel to prick them with sharp fears and recollections, who could believe that they would keep to it? Of the efficacy of my own vigilance, so long as I might choose to exercise it, I could have no doubt, for I had by this time come to have a dreadful exultation in the new power that lived in me. Repeated delicate experiment had taught me how a touch or a breath, a wish or a whisper, could control Allan's acts, could keep him from Theresa. I could manifest myself as palely, as transiently, as a thought. I could produce the merest necessary flicker, like the shadow of a just-opened leaf, on his trembling, tortured consciousness. And these unrealized perceptions of me he interpreted, as I had known that he would, as his soul's inevitable penance. He had come to believe that he had done evil in silently loving Theresa all these years, and it was my vengeance to allow him to believe this, to prod him ever to believe it afresh.

I am conscious that this frame of mind was not continuous in me. For I remember, too, that when Allan and Theresa were safely apart and sufficiently miserable I loved them as dearly as I ever had, more dearly perhaps. For it was impossible that I should not perceive, in my new emancipation, that they were, each of them, something more and greater than the two beings I had once ignorantly pictured them. For years they had practised a selflessness of which I could once scarcely have conceived, and which even now I could only admire without entering into its mystery. While I had lived solely for myself, these two divine creatures had lived exquisitely for me. They had granted me everything, themselves nothing. For my undeserving sake their lives had been a constant torment of renunciation—a torment they had not sought to alleviate by the exchange of a single glance of understanding. There were even marvellous moments when, from the depths of my newly informed heart, I pitied them:—poor creatures, who, withheld from the infinite solaces that I had come to know, were still utterly within that

Shell of sense
So frail, so piteously contrived for pain.

Within it, yes; yet exercising qualities that so sublimely transcended it. Yet the shy, hesitating compassion that thus had birth in me was far from being able to defeat the earlier, earthlier emotion. The two, I recognized, were in a sort of conflict; and I, regarding it, assumed that the conflict would never end; that for years, as Allan and Theresa reckoned time, I should be obliged to withhold myself from the great spaces and linger suffering, grudging, shamed, where they lingered.

It can never have been explained, I suppose, what, to devitalized perception such as mine, the contact of mortal beings with each other appears to be. Once to have exercised this sense-freed perception is to realize that the gift of prophecy, although the subject of such frequent marvel, is no longer mysterious. The merest glance of our sensitive and uncloyed vision can detect the strength of the relation between two beings, and therefore instantly calculate its duration. If you see a heavy weight suspended from a slender string, you can know, without any wizardry, that in a few moments the string will snap; well, such, if you admit the analogy, is prophecy, is foreknowledge. And it was thus that I saw it with Theresa and Allan. For it was perfectly visible to me that they would very little longer have the strength to preserve, near each other, the denuded impersonal relation that they, and that I, behind them, insisted on; and that they would have to separate. It was my sister, perhaps the more sensitive, who first realized this. It had now become possible for me to observe them almost constantly, the effort necessary to visit them had so greatly diminished; so that I watched her, poor, anguished girl, prepare to leave him. I saw each reluctant movement that she made. I saw her eyes, worn from self-searching; I heard her step grown timid from inexplicable fears; I entered her very heart and heard its pitiful, wild beating. And still I did not interfere.

For at this time I had a wonderful, almost demoniacal sense of disposing of matters to suit my own selfish will. At any moment I could have checked their miseries, could have restored happiness and peace. Yet it gave me, and I could weep to admit it, a monstrous joy to know that Theresa thought she was leaving Allan of her own free intention, when it was I who was contriving, arranging, insisting. . . . And yet she wretchedly felt my presence near her; I am certain of that.

A few days before the time of her intended departure my sister told Allan that she must speak with him after dinner. Our beautiful old house branched out from a circular hall with great arched doors at either end; and it was through the rear doorway that always in summer, after dinner, we passed out into the garden adjoining. As usual, therefore, when the hour came, Theresa led the way. That dreadful daytime brilliance that in my present state I found so hard to endure was now becoming softer. A delicate, capricious twilight breeze danced inconsequently through languidly whispering leaves. Lovely pale flowers blossomed like little moons in the dusk, and over them the breath of mignonette hung heavily. It was a perfect place—and it had so long been ours, Allan's and mine. It made me restless and a little wicked that those two should be there together now.

For a little they walked about together, speaking of common, daily things. Then suddenly Theresa burst out:

"I am going away, Allan. I have stayed to do everything that needed to be done. Now your mother will be here to care for you, and it is time for me to go."

He stared at her and stood still. Theresa had been there so long, she so definitely, to his mind, belonged there. And she was, as I also had jealously known, so lovely there, the small, dark, dainty creature, in the old hall, on the wide staircases, in the garden. . . . Life there without Theresa, even the intentionally remote, the perpetually renounced Theresa—he had not dreamed of it, he could not, so suddenly, conceive of it.

"Sit here," he said, and drew her down beside him on a bench, "and tell me what it means, why you are going. Is it because of something that I have been—have done?"

She hesitated. I wondered if she would dare tell him. She looked out and away from him, and he waited long for her to speak.

The pale stars were sliding into their places. The whispering of the leaves was almost hushed. All about them it was still and shadowy and sweet. It was that wonderful moment when, for lack of a visible horizon, the not yet darkened world seems infinitely greater—a moment when anything can happen, anything be believed in. To me, watching, listening, hovering, there came a dreadful purpose and a dreadful courage. Suppose, for one moment, Theresa should not only feel, but *see* me—would she dare to tell him then?

There came a brief space of terrible effort, all my fluttering, uncertain forces strained to the utmost. The instant of my struggle was endlessly long and the transition seemed to take place outside me—as one sitting in a train, motionless, sees the leagues of earth float by. And then, in a bright, terrible flash I knew I had achieved it—I had *attained visibility*. Shuddering, insubstantial, but luminously apparent, I stood there before them. And for the instant that I maintained the visible state I looked straight into Theresa's soul.

She gave a cry. And then, thing of silly, cruel impulses that I was, I saw what I had done. The very thing that I wished to avert I had precipitated. For Allan, in his sudden terror and pity, had bent and caught her in his arms. For the first time they were together; and it was I who had brought them.

Then, to his whispered urging to tell the reason of her cry, Theresa said:

"Frances was here. You did not see her, standing there, under the lilacs, with no smile on her face?"

"My dear, my dear!" was all that Allan said. I had so long now lived invisibly with them, he knew that she was right.

"I suppose you know what it means?" she asked him, calmly.

"Dear Theresa," Allan said, slowly, "if you and I should go away somewhere, could we not evade all this ghostliness? And will you come with me?"

"Distance would not banish her," my sister confidently asserted. And then she said, softly: "Have you thought what a lonely, awesome thing it must be to be so newly dead? Pity her, Allan. We who are warm and alive should pity her. She loves you still,—that is the meaning of it all, you know—and she wants us to understand that for that reason we must keep apart. Oh, it was so plain in her white face as she stood there. And you did not see her?"

"It was your face that I saw," Allan solemnly told her—oh, how different he had grown from the Allan that I had known!—"and yours is the only face that I shall ever see." And again he drew her to him.

She sprang from him. "You are defying her, Allan!" she cried. "And you must not. It is her right to keep us apart, if she wishes. It must be as she insists. I shall go, as I told you. And, Allan, I beg of you, leave me the courage to do as she demands!"

They stood facing each other in the deep dusk, and the wounds that I had dealt them gaped red and accusing. "We must pity her," Theresa had said. And as I remembered that extraordinary speech, and saw the agony in her face, and the greater agony in Allan's, there came the great irreparable cleavage between mortality and me. In a swift, merciful flame the last of my mortal emotions—gross and tenacious they must have been—was consumed. My cold grasp of Allan loosened and a new unearthly love of him bloomed in my heart.

I was now, however, in a difficulty with which my experience in the newer state was scarcely sufficient to deal. How could I make it plain to Allan and Theresa that I wished to bring them together, to heal the wounds that I had made?

Pityingly, remorsefully, I lingered near them all that night and the next day. And by that time I had brought myself to the point of a great determination. In the little time that was left, before Theresa should be gone and Allan bereft and desolate, I saw the one way that lay open to me to convince them of my acquiescence in their destiny.

In the deepest darkness and silence of the next night I made a greater effort than it will ever be necessary for me to make again. When they think of me, Allan and Theresa, I pray now that they will recall what I did that night, and that my thousand frustrations and selfishnesses may shrivel and be blown from their indulgent memories.

Yet the following morning, as she had planned, Theresa appeared at breakfast dressed for her journey. Above in her room there were the sounds of departure. They spoke little during the brief meal, but when it was ended Allan said:

"Theresa, there is half an hour before you go. Will you come up-stairs with me? I had a dream that I must tell you of."

"Allan!" She looked at him, frightened, but went with him. "It was of Frances you dreamed," she said, quietly, as they entered the library together.

"Did I say it was a dream? But I was awake—thoroughly awake. I had not been sleeping well, and I heard, twice, the striking of the clock. And as I lay there, looking out at the stars, and thinking—thinking of you, Theresa,—she came to me, stood there before me, in my room. It was no sheeted spectre, you understand; it was Frances, literally she. In some inexplicable fashion I seemed to be aware that she wanted to make me know something, and I waited, watching her face. After a few moments it came. She did not speak, precisely. That is, I am sure I heard no sound. Yet the words that came from her were definite enough. She said: 'Don't let Theresa leave you. Take her and keep her.' Then she went away. Was that a dream?"

"I had not meant to tell you," Theresa eagerly answered, "but now I must. It is too wonderful. What time did your clock strike, Allan?"

"One, the last time."

"Yes; it was then that I awoke. And she had been with me. I had not seen her, but her arm had been about me and her kiss was on my cheek. Oh, I knew; it was unmistakable. And the sound of her voice was with me."

"Then she bade you, too—"

"Yes, to stay with you. I am glad we told each other." She smiled tearfully and began to fasten her wrap.

"But you are not going—*now!*" Allan cried. "You know that you cannot, now that she has asked you to stay."

"Then you believe, as I do, that it was she?" Theresa demanded.

"I can never understand, but I know," he answered her. "And now you will not go?"

I am freed. There will be no further semblance of me in my old home, no sound of my voice, no dimmest echo of my earthly self. They have no further need of me, the two that I have brought together. Theirs is the fullest joy that the dwellers in the shell of sense can know. Mine is the transcendent joy of the unseen spaces.

————◆————

ZORA NEALE HURSTON
(1891–1960)

Novelist, short-story writer, dramatist, anthropologist, and folklorist, Zora Neale Hurston has left behind an invaluable legacy of African American literature and culture. The most acclaimed woman writer of the Harlem Renaissance, she was born and raised in Eatonville, Florida, a self-governed, all-Black town. She studied anthropology with Franz Boas at Barnard College, from which she graduated in 1928. Hurston's dedication to preserving African American culture, evident in "Spunk," can be seen in both her literature and her career. Her other supernatural tales, which appear largely in *Mules and Men* (1935), similarly demonstrate the rich African oral tradition, modified in accord with the Black experience of slavery in America. The story was first published in *Opportunity* in June 1925.

Spunk

I

A GIANT OF A BROWN SKINNED MAN SAUNTERED UP THE ONE street of the Village and out into the palmetto thickets with a small pretty woman clinging lovingly to his arm.

"Looka theah, folkses!" cried Elijah Mosley, slapping his leg gleefully. "Theah they go, big as life an' brassy as tacks."

All the loungers in the store tried to walk to the door with an air of nonchalance but with small success.

"Now pee-eople!" Walter Thomas gasped, "Will you look at 'em!"

"But that's one thing Ah likes about Spunk Banks—he ain't skeered of nothin' on God's green foot-stool—*nothin'!* He rides that log down at saw-mill jus' like he struts 'round wid another man's wife—jus' don't give a kitty. When Tes' Miller got cut to giblets on that circle-saw, Spunk steps right up and starts ridin'. The rest of us was skeered to go near it."

A round shouldered figure in overalls much too large, came nervously in the door and the talking ceased. The men looked at each other and winked.

"Gimme some soda-water. Sass'prilla Ah reckon," the new-comer ordered, and stood far down the counter near the open pickled pig-feet tub to drink it.

Elijah nudged Walter and turned with mock gravity to the new-comer.

"Say Joe, how's everything up yo' way? How's yo' wife?"

Joe started and all but dropped the bottle he held in his hands. He swallowed several times painfully and his lips trembled.

"Aw 'Lige, you oughn't to do nothin' like that," Walter grumbled. Elijah ignored him.

"She jus' passed heah a few minutes ago goin' thata way," with a wave of his hand in the direction of the woods.

Now Joe knew his wife had passed that way. He knew that the men lounging in the general store had seen her, moreover, he knew that the men knew *he* knew. He stood there silent for a long moment staring blankly, with his Adam's apple twitching nervously up and down his throat. One could actually *see* the pain he was suffering, his eyes, his face, his hands and even the dejected slump of his shoulders. He set the bottle down upon the counter. He didn't bang it, just eased it out of his hand silently and fiddled with his suspender buckle.

"Well, Ah'm goin' after her today. Ah'm goin' an' fetch her back. Spunk's done gone too fur."

He reached deep down into his trouser pocket and drew out a hollow ground razor, large and shiny, and passed his moistened thumb back and forth over the edge.

"Talkin' like a man, Joe. Course that's *yo'* fambly affairs, but Ah like to see grit in anybody."

Joe Kanty laid down a nickel and stumbled out into the street.

Dusk crept in from the woods. Ike Clarke lit the swinging oil lamp that was almost immediately surrounded by candle-flies. The men laughed boisterously behind Joe's back as they watched him shamble woodward.

"You oughtn't to said whut you did to him, Lige,—look how it worked him up," Walter chided.

"And Ah hope it did work him up. Tain't even decent for a man to take and take like he do."

"Spunk will sho' kill him."

"Aw, Ah doan' know. You never kin tell. He might turn him up an' spank him fur gettin' in the way, but Spunk wouldn't shoot no unarmed man. Dat razor he carried outa heah ain't gonna run Spunk down an' cut him, an' Joe ain't got the nerve to go up to Spunk with it knowing he totes that Army 45. He makes that break outa heah to bluff us. He's gonna hide that razor behind the first likely palmetto root an' sneak back home to bed. Don't tell me nothin' 'bout that rabbit-foot colored man. Didn't he meet Spunk an' Lena face to face one day las' week an' mumble sumthin' to Spunk 'bout lettin' his wife alone?"

"What did Spunk say?" Walter broke in—"Ah like him fine but tain't right the way he carries on wid Lena Kanty, jus' cause Joe's timid 'bout fightin'."

"You wrong theah, Walter. 'Tain't cause Joe's timid at all, it's cause Spunk wants Lena. If Joe was a passle of wile cats Spunk would tackle the job just the same. He'd go after *anything* he wanted the same way. As Ah wuz sayin' a minute ago, he tole Joe right to his face that Lena was his. 'Call her,' he says to Joe. 'Call her and see if she'll come. A woman knows her boss an' she answers when he calls.' 'Lena, ain't I yo' husband?' Joe sorter whines out. Lena looked at him real disgusted but she don't answer and she don't move outa her tracks. Then Spunk reaches out an' takes hold of her arm an' says: 'Lena, youse mine. From now on Ah works for you an' fights for you an' Ah never wants you to look to nobody for a crumb of bread, a stitch of close or a shingle to go over yo' head, but *me* long as Ah live. Ah'll git the lumber foh owah house tomorrow. Go home an' git yo' things together!'"

"'Thass mah house' Lena speaks up. 'Papa gimme that.'

"Well," says Spunk, "doan give up whut's yours, but when youse inside don't forget youse mine, an' let no other man git outa his place wid you!"

"Lena looked up at him with her eyes so full of love that they wuz runnin' over an' Spunk seen it an' Joe seen it too, and his lip started to tremblin' and his Adam's apple was galloping up and down his neck like a race horse. Ah bet he's wore out half a dozen Adam's apples since Spunk's been on the job with Lena. That's all he'll do. He'll be back heah after while swallowin' an' workin' his lips like he wants to say somethin' an' can't."

"But didn't he do *nothin'* to stop 'em?"

"Nope, not a frazzlin' thing—jus' stood there. Spunk took Lena's arm and walked off jus' like nothin' ain't happened and he stood there gazin' after them till they was outa sight. Now you know a woman don't want no man like that. I'm jus' waitin' to see whut he's goin' to say when he gits back."

II

But Joe Kanty never came back, never. The men in the store heard the sharp report of a pistol somewhere distant in the palmetto thicket and soon Spunk came walking leisurely, with his big black Stetson set at the same rakish angle and Lena clinging to his arm, came walking right into the general store. Lena wept in a frightened manner.

"Well," Spunk announced calmly, "Joe come out there wid a meatax an' made me kill him."

He sent Lena home and led the men back to Joe—Joe crumple and limp with his right hand still clutching his razor.

"See mah back? Mah cloes cut clear through. He sneaked up an' tried to kill me from the back, but Ah got him, an' got him good, first shot," Spunk said.

The men glared at Elijah, accusingly.

"Take him up an' plant him in 'Stoney lonesome'," Spunk said in a careless voice. "Ah didn't wanna shoot him but he made me do it. He's a dirty coward, jumpin' on a man from behind."

Spunk turned on his heel and sauntered away to where he knew his love wept in fear for him and no man stopped him. At the general store later on, they all talked of locking him up until the sheriff should come from Orlando, but no one did anything but talk.

A clear case of self-defense, the trial was a short one, and Spunk walked out of the court house to freedom again. He could work again, ride the dangerous log-carriage that fed the singing, snarling, biting, circle-saw; he could stroll the soft dark lanes with his guitar. He was free to roam the woods again; he was free to return to Lena. He did all of these things.

III

"Whut you reckon, Walt?" Elijah asked one night later. "Spunk's gittin' ready to marry Lena!"

"Naw! Why Joe ain't had time to git cold yit. Nohow Ah didn't figger Spunk was the marryin' kind."

"Well, he is," rejoined Elijah. "He done moved most of Lena's things— and her along wid 'em—over to the Bradley house. He's buying it. Jus' like Ah told yo' all right in heah the night Joe wuz kilt. Spunk's crazy 'bout Lena. He don't want folks to keep on talkin' 'bout her—thass reason he's rushin' so. Funny thing 'bout that bob-cat, wan't it?"

"Whut bob-cat, 'Lige? Ah ain't heered 'bout none."

"Ain't cher? Well, night befo' las' was the fust night Spunk an' Lena moved together an' jus' as they was goin' to bed, a big black bob-cat, black all over, you hear me, *black*, walked round and round that house and howled like forty, an' when Spunk got his gun an' went to the winder to shoot it, he says it stood right still an' looked him in the eye, an' howled right at him. The thing got Spunk so nervoused up he couldn't shoot. But Spunk says twan't no bob-cat nohow. He says it was Joe done sneaked back from Hell!"

"Humph!" sniffed Walter, "he oughter be nervous after what he done. Ah reckon Joe come back to dare him to marry Lena, or to come out an' fight. Ah bet he'll be back time and agin, too. Know what Ah think? Joe wuz a braver man than Spunk."

There was a general shout of derision from the group.

"Thass a fact," went on Walter. "Lookit whut he done; took a razor an' went out to fight a man he knowed toted a gun an' wuz a crack shot, too; 'nother thing Joe wuz skeered of Spunk, skeered plumb stiff! But he went jes' the same. It took him a long time to get his nerve up. 'Tain't nothin' for Spunk to fight when he ain't skeered of nothin'. Now, Joe's done come back to have it out wid the man that's got all he ever had. Y'll know Joe ain't never had nothin' nor wanted nothin' besides Lena. It musta been a h'ant cause ain' nobody never seen no black bob-cat."

"'Nother thing," cut in one of the men, "Spunk waz cussin' a blue streak today 'cause he 'lowed dat saw wuz wobblin'—almos' got 'im once. The machinist come, looked it over an' said it wuz alright. Spunk musta been leanin' t'wards it some. Den he claimed somebody pushed 'im but 'twant nobody close to 'im. Ah wuz glad when knockin' off time come. I'm skeered of dat man when he gits hot. He'd beat you full of button holes as quick as he's look atcher."

IV

The men gathered the next evening in a different mood, no laughter. No badinage this time.

"Look 'Lige, you goin' to set up wid Spunk?"

"Naw, Ah reckon not, Walter. Tell yuh the truth, Ah'm a lil bit skittish. Spunk died too wicket—died cussin' he did. You know he thought he wuz done outa life."

"Good Lawd, who'd he think done it?"

"Joe."

"Joe Kanty? How come?"

"Walter, Ah b'leeve Ah will walk up thata way an' set. Lena would like it Ah reckon."

"But whut did he say, 'Lige?"

Elijah did not answer until they had left the lighted store and were strolling down the dark street.

"Ah wuz loadin' a wagon wid scantlin' right near the saw when Spunk fell on the carriage but 'fore Ah could git to him the saw got him in the body—awful sight. Me an' Skint Miller got him off but it was too late. Anybody could see that. The fust thing he said wuz: 'He pushed me, 'Lige—the dirty

⊰ 66 ⊱

hound pushed me in the back!'—He was spittin' blood at ev'ry breath. We laid him on the sawdust pile with his face to the East so's he could die easy. He helt mah han' till the last, Walter, and said: 'It was Joe, 'Lige—the dirty sneak shoved me . . . he didn't dare come to mah face . . . but Ah'll git the son-of-a-wood louse soon's Ah get there an' make hell too hot for him. . . . Ah felt him shove me. . . .!' Thass how he died."

"If spirits kin fight, there's a powerful tussle goin' on somewhere ovah Jordan 'cause Ah b'leeve Joe's ready for Spunk an' ain't skeered anymore— yas, Ah b'leeve Joe pushed 'im mahself."

They had arrived at the house. Lena's lamentations were deep and loud. She had filled the room with magnolia blossoms that gave off a heavy sweet odor. The keepers of the wake tipped about whispering in frightened tones. Everyone in the Village was there, even old Jeff Kanty, Joe's father, who a few hours before would have been afraid to come within ten feet of him, stood leering triumphantly down upon the fallen giant as if his fingers had been the teeth of steel that laid him low.

The cooling board consisted of three sixteen-inch boards on saw horses, a dingy sheet was his shroud.

The women ate heartily of the funeral baked meats and wondered who would be Lena's next. The men whispered coarse conjectures between guzzles of whiskey.

———◆◆◆———

HILDEGARDE HAWTHORNE
(1871–1952)

Journalist, novelist, short-story writer, poet, biographer, and author of travelogues and histories, Hildegarde Hawthorne pursued a life of letters unlike any other of Nathaniel Hawthorne's descendants. Born in New York City, the daughter of Julian Hawthorne, she received little formal education as her large family migrated from New York to Dresden to England to Long Island to Jamaica. "A Legend of Sonora," which appeared in *Harper's New Monthly Magazine* in October 1891, established her literary reputation at the age of twenty. Hawthorne continued to write fiction and review books until World War I, when she volunteered for war work in France and became a correspondent for the *Herald Tribune* and the *New York Times*. In 1920 she married John Milton Oskison and moved to California. Inspired by the setting, she wrote several Westerns and three books about that state. Hawthorne also wrote a handful of ghost stories, notable for a certain unearthly hush, the product of her economy of style and talent for capturing atmosphere.

A Legend of Sonora

TWO PERSONS, A MAN AND A WOMAN, FACED EACH OTHER under a clump of live-oaks. Hard by were visible the walls of an adobe house crumbling with age. The sun was setting; a slight breeze stirred in the dark branches of the trees, which all through the hot Mexican day had been motionless. The woman was dark and small, with large eyes and a graceful body; the man, a swarthy vaquero, in serape and sombrero.

"And you heard him say—that?" said she.

"Yes, señorita. He said, 'I love you! I love you!' twice, like that. And then he kissed her."

"Ah! he kissed her. Anything else?"

"This!" He handed her a slip of folded paper. It contained a woman's name, a few words of passion, and a signature. As the señorita's eyes perused it, they contracted, and she drew in a long breath. The vaquero watched her keenly. "I found it in the arbor after they had gone," said he.

She looked away dreamily. "Thank you, thank you, Mazeppa," she muttered. "It is late. I must go in now. Adios, Mazeppa!" She turned, and, moving slowly, vanished behind a corner of the adobe house.

The vaquero remained motionless until she was out of sight. Then he pressed his hands to his lips, and flung them out towards her with a passionate gesture. The next moment he had mounted his horse and was gone.

An hour passed. Again the sound of hoofs. A handsome young señor, jauntily attired, galloped up to the door of the house, and springing from the saddle, hitched his rein over a large hook projecting from the wall. "Hola! Maria, little one!" he called out, in a rich, joyous voice. "Where is my little Maria?"

The señorita appeared, smiling. She was in white, with a reboso drawn around her delicate face. She bore a two-handled silver cup, curiously chased. "See," she said, "I have brought you some wine. Such a long ride, just to see me!" She was holding out the cup towards him; but, as he was about to receive it, she drew it back suddenly. She was pale; her eyes glittered. "I too am thirsty," she said. She lifted the cup to her lips and took a deep draught. "Now, you shall finish it," she added, handing it to him.

He nodded to her laughingly. "To our love!" he said, and drained it. "But how strangely you look at me, little one!" he exclaimed, as he set the cup down and caught his breath. "Is anything wrong?"

"All is well," she answered. "I am happy. Are you happy?"

"I? I am with you, am I not?"

She put her hand in his. "Let us never be parted any more," she said. "Come; we'll walk to the hill-top and see the moon rise."

Hand in hand, they sauntered along the path up the bare hill-side. On and on they walked, slowly, slowly. Maria gave a little gasp, and glanced with dilated eyes at her lover. He smiled faintly, and tried to draw her towards him, but, somehow, did not; and still they moved slowly on their way. The hill-top seemed strangely far off. Maria pressed forward, grasping her lover's hand. What made the distance seem so long? Surely it was but a stroll of ten minutes; yet it was as though they had been walking an hour—a year—many years!

Down the hill-side path came a horseman, riding quietly and humming a love song. He was close upon the two figures before he appeared to be aware of them. They half stopped, as if to speak to him. The horse shivered and plunged. The rider stared at the couple but an instant, then, driving home his spurs, sprang past them.

"Mother of God!" he faltered, crossing himself as he threw a backward glance up the path, on which nothing was now visible, "the ghosts! The little girl who, they say down below, poisoned herself and her lover fifty years ago!"

———◦•◆•◦———

⚜ II ⚜

The Tie That Binds:
Motherhood

‿‿◉‿‿

"Isn't he splendid!"

*Illustration by Olive Rush for Katharine Holland Brown, "Hunger," Scribner's
Magazine 41, no. 3 (1907). Photo courtesy Metropolitan Toronto Reference Library.*

JOSEPHINE DASKAM BACON
(1876–1961)

Josephine Dodge Daskam Bacon enjoyed a literary career that spanned more than four decades. Born in Connecticut, she attended Smith College. After graduating in 1898, she launched her reputation with a volume of short stories about that institution. In 1903 she married Selden Bacon and continued to write, publishing thirty-six volumes of poetry and short stories in all. Bacon was also a pioneer in the Girl Scouts Movement and compiled the handbook used by that organization. One chatty biographical dictionary from 1914 listed her interests as "all country sports, farming, stock breeding, amateur dramatics and music." The two ghostly tales that appear in this volume were taken from *The Strange Cases of Dr. Stanchon* (1913), a collection of stories loosely connected by the figure of Dr. Stanchon, a turn-of-the-century alienist.

The Children

IT ALL CAME OVER ME, AS YOU MIGHT SAY, WHEN I BEGAN to tell the new housemaid about the work. Not that I hadn't known before, of course, what a queer sort of life was led in that house; it was hard enough the first months, goodness knows. But then, a body can get used to anything. And there was no harm in it—I'll swear that to my dying day! Although a lie's a lie, any way you put it, and if all I've told—but I'll let you judge for yourself.

As I say, it was when I began to break Margaret in, that it all came over me, and I looked about me, in a way of speaking, for how I should put it to her. She'd been house-parlor-maid in a big establishment in the country and knew what was expected of her well enough, and I saw from the first she'd fit in nicely with us; a steady, quiet girl, like the best of the Scotch, looking to save her wages, and get to be housekeeper herself, some day, perhaps.

But when Hodges brought the tray with the porringers on it and the silver mug, for me to see, and said, "I suppose this young lady'll take these up, Miss Umbleby?" and when Margaret looked surprised and said, "I didn't know there were children in the family—am I supposed to wait on them, too?"—then, as I say, it all came over me, and for the first time in five years I really saw where I stood, like.

I stared at Hodges and then at the girl, and the tray nearly went down amongst us.

"Do you mean to say you haven't told her, Sarah?" says Hodges (and that was the first time that ever he called me by my given name).

"She's told me nothing," Margaret answers rather short, "and if it's invalid children or feeble-minded, I take it most unkind, Miss Umbleby, for I've never cared for that sort of thing, and could have had my twenty-five dollars a month this long time, if I'd wanted to go out as nurse."

"Take the tray up this time, yourself, Mr. Hodges, please," I said, "and I'll have a little talk with Margaret," and I sat down and smoothed my black silk skirt (I always wore black silk of an afternoon) nervously enough, I'll be bound.

The five years rolled away like yesterday—as they do now—as they do now——

I saw myself, in my mind's eye, new to the place, and inclined to feel strange, as I always did when I made a change, though I was twenty-five and no chicken, but rather more settled than most, having had my troubles early and got over them. I'd just left my place—chambermaid and seamstress—in a big city house, and though it was September, I was looking out for the country, for I was mortal tired of the noise and late hours and excitement that I saw ahead of me. It was parties and balls every night and me sitting up to undress the young ladies, for they kept no maid, like so many rich Americans, and yet some one must do for them. There was no housekeeper either, and the mistress was not very strong and we had to use our own responsibility more than I liked—for I wasn't paid for that, do you see, and that's what they forget in this country.

"I think I've got you suited at last, Sarah," the head of the office had said to me, "a nice, quiet place in the country, good pay and light work, but everything as it should be, you understand. Four in help besides the housekeeper and only one in family. Church within a mile and every other Sunday for yourself."

That was just what I wanted, and I packed my box thankfully and left New York for good, I hoped, and I got my wish, for I've never seen the inside of it since.

A middle-aged coachman in good, quiet country livery, met me at the little station, and though he was a still-mouthed fellow and rather reserved, I made out quite a little idea of the place on the way. The mistress, Mrs. Childress, was a young widow, deep in her mourning, so there was no company. The housekeeper was her old nurse, who had brought her up. John, who drove me, was coachman-gardener, and the cook was his wife—both Catholics. Everything went on very quiet and regular and it was hoped that the new upstairs maid wouldn't be one for excitement and gaiety. The inside man had been valet to Mr. Childress and was much trusted and liked by the family. I could see that old John was a bit jealous in that direction.

We drove in through a black iron gate with cut stone posts and old black iron lanterns on top, and the moment we were inside the gates I began to take a fancy to the place. It wasn't kept up like the places at home, but it was neat enough to show that things were taken thought for, and the beds of asters and dahlias and marigolds as we got near the house seemed so home-like and bright to me, I could have cried for comfort. Childerstone was the name of the place; it was carved on a big boulder by the side of the entrance, and just as we drove up to the door John stopped to pick some dahlias for the house (being only me in the wagon) and I took my first good look at my home for twenty years afterward.

There was something about it that went to my heart. It was built of grey cut stone in good-sized blocks, square, with two windows each side the hall door. To some it might have seemed cold-looking, but not to me, for one side was all over ivy, and the thickness of the walls and the deep sills looked solid and comfortable after those nasty brown-stone things all glued to each other in the city. It looked old and respectable and settled, like, and the sun, just at going down, struck the windows like fire and the clean panes shone. There was that yellow light over everything and that stillness, with now and then a leaf or so dropping quietly down, that makes the fall of the year so pleasant, to my mind.

The house stood in beeches and the trunks of them were grey like the house and the leaves all light lemon-coloured, like the sky, and that's the way I always think of Childerstone—grey and yellow and clean and still. Just a few rooks (you call them crows here), went over the house, and except for their cry as they flew, there wasn't a sound about the place. I can see how others might have found it sad, but it never seemed so to me.

John set me down at the servants' entrance and there, before ever I'd got properly into the hall, the strangeness began. The cook in her check apron was kneeling on the floor in front of the big French range with the tears streaming down her face, working over her rosary beads and gabbling to drive you crazy. Over her stood a youngish but severe-appearing man in a white linen coat like a ship's steward, trying to get her up.

"Come, Katey," he was saying, "come, woman, up with you and help— she'll do no harm, the poor soul! Look after her, now, and I'll send for the doctor and see to madam—it's only a fit, most like!"

Then he saw me and ran forward to give a hand to my box.

"You're the chambermaid, Miss, I'm sure," he said. "I'm sorry to say you'll find us a bit upset. The housekeeper's down with a stroke of some sort and the madam's none too strong herself. Are you much of a hand to look after the sick?"

"I'm not so clumsy as some," I said. "Let me see her," and so we left the cook to her prayers and he carried my box to my room.

I got into a print dress and apron and went to the housekeeper's room. She was an elderly person and it looked to me as if she was in her last sickness. She didn't know any one and so I was as good as another, and I had her tidy and comfortable in bed by the time the doctor came. He said she would need watching through the night and left some medicine, but I could see he had little hope for her. I made up a bed in the room and all that night she chattered and muttered and took me for different ones, according as her fever went and came. Towards morning she got quiet, and as I thought, sensible again.

"Are you a nurse?" she says to me.

"Yes, Mrs. Shipman, be still and rest," I told her, to soothe her.

"I'm glad the children are sent away," she went on, after a bit. "'Twould break their mother's heart if they got the fever. Are the toys packed?"

"Yes, yes," I answered, "all packed and sent."

"Be sure there's enough frocks for Master Robertson," she begged me. "He's so hard on them and his aunties are so particular. And my baby must have her woolly rabbit at night or her darling heart will be just broken!"

"The rabbit is packed," I said, "and I saw to the frocks myself."

There's but one way with the sick when they're like that, and that's to humour them, you see. So she slept and I got a little nap for myself. I was glad the children were away by next morning, for she was worse, the cook lost her head, and managed to break the range so that the water-back leaked and John and Hodges were mopping and mending all day. The madam herself had a bad turn and the doctor (a New York doctor for madam, you may be sure!) brought out a handsome, dark woman, the trained hospital nurse, with him. Madam wasn't allowed to know how bad her old nurse was.

So it turned out that I'd been a week in the house without ever seeing my mistress. The nurse and I would meet on the stairs and chat a little, evenings, and once I took a turn in the grounds with her. She was a sensible sort of girl, not a bit above herself, as our English nursing-sisters are, sometimes, but very businesslike, as they say, and a good, brisk way with her. She saw a lot more than she spoke of, Miss Jessop did, I'll warrant!

"It's a good thing the children are sent away," I said. "They always add to the bother when there's sickness."

"Why, are there children?" says she. "Oh, yes, a boy and a girl," I answered, "poor old Mrs. Shipman is forever talking about them. She thinks she's their nurse, it seems, as she was their mother's."

"I wish they were here, then," says she, "for I don't like the looks of my patient at all. She doesn't speak seven words a day, and there's really little or nothing the matter with her, that I can see. She's nervous and she's low and she wants cheering, that's all. I wonder the doctor doesn't see it."

That night, after both patients were settled, she came up to my room and took a glance at the old lady, who was going fast.

"Mrs. Childress will soon have to know about this," she said and then, suddenly, "Are you sure about the children, Sarah?"

"Sure about them?" I repeated after her. "In what way, Miss Jessop?"

"That there are any," says she.

"Why, of course," I answered, "Mrs. Shipman talks of nothing else. They're with their aunty, in New Jersey, somewhere. It's a good thing there are some, for from what she says when she's rambling, the house and all the property would go out of the family otherwise. It's been five generations in the Childress family, but the nearest now is a cousin who married a Jew, and the family hate her for it. But Master Robertson makes it all safe, Mrs. Shipman says."

"That's a queer thing," said she. "I took in a dear little picture of the boy and girl this afternoon, to cheer her up a bit, and told her to try to think they were the real ones, who'd soon be with her, for that matter, and so happy to see their dear mamma, and she went white as a sheet and fainted in my arms. Of course, I didn't refer to it again. She's quiet now, holding the picture, but I feared they were dead and you hadn't known."

"Oh, no," said I. "I'm sure not," and then I remembered that I'd been told there was but one in family. However, that's often said when there's a nurse to take care of small children (though it's not quite fair, perhaps), and I was certain of the children, anyway, for there were toys all about Mrs. Shipman's room and some seed-cookies and "animal-crackers," as they call those odd little biscuits, in a tin on her mantel.

However, we were soon to learn something that made me, at least, all the more curious. The doctor came that morning and told Miss Jessop that her services would be no longer required, after he had seen her patient.

"Mrs. Childress is perfectly recovered," he said, "and she has unfortunately conceived a grudge against you, my dear girl. I need you, anyway, in town. Poor old Shipman can't last the night now, and I want all that business disposed of very quietly. I have decided not to tell Mrs. Childress until it is all over and the funeral done with. She is in a very morbid state, and as I knew her husband well I have taken this step on my own responsibility. Hodges seems perfectly able to run things, and to tell the truth, it would do your mistress far more good to attend to that herself," he said, turning to me.

"It would be a good thing for the poor woman to have some one about her, Dr. Stanchon," the nurse put in quietly. "If there were children in the house, now———"

"Children!" he cried, pulling himself up and staring at her. "Did you speak to her about them? Then that accounts for it! I should have warned you."

"Then they *did* die?" she asked him. "That's what I thought."

"I'm afraid not," he said, shaking his head with a queer sort of sad little smile. "I forgot you were strange here. Why, Miss Jessop, didn't you know that———"

"Excuse me, sir, but there's no sign of your mare about—did you tie her?" says Hodges, coming in in a great hurry, and the doctor swore and ran off and I never heard the end of the sentence.

Well, I'm running on too long with these little odds and ends, as I'm sure Margaret felt when I started telling her all about it. The truth is I dreaded then, just as I dread now, to get at the real story and look our conduct straight in the face. But I'll get on more quickly now.

Old Mrs. Shipman died very quiet in her sleep and madam wasn't told, which I didn't half like. The doctor was called out of those parts to attend on his father, very suddenly, and Hodges managed the funeral and all. It was plain to see he was a very trusty, silent fellow, devoted to the family. I took as much off him as I could, and I was dusting the drawing-room the day of the funeral, when I happened to pick up a photograph in a silver frame of the same little fellow in the picture the nurse had shown me—a dear little boy in short kilts.

"That's Master Robertson, isn't it?" I said, very carelessly, not looking at him—I will own I was curious. He gave a start.

"Yes—yes, certainly, that's Master Robertson—if you choose to put it that way," he said, and I saw him put his hand up to his eyes and his mouth twitched and he left the room.

I didn't question him again, naturally; he was a hard man to cross and very haughty, was William Hodges, and no one in the house but respected him.

That day I saw Mrs. Childress for the first time. She was a sweet, pretty thing, about my own age, but younger looking, fair, with grey eyes. She was in heavy crêpe and her face all fallen and saddened like, with grief and hopelessness—I felt for her from the moment I saw her. And all the more that I'd made up my mind what her trouble was: I thought that the children were idiots, maybe, or feeble-minded, anyhow, and so the property would go to the Jew in the end and that his family were hating her for it! Folly, of course, but women will have fancies, and that seemed to fit in with all I'd heard.

She'd been told that Shipman was away with some light, infectious fever, and she took it very mildly, and said there was no need to get any one in her place, at present.

"Hodges will attend to everything," she said, in her pretty, tired way; "not that there's much to do—for one poor woman."

"Things may mend, ma'am, and you'll feel more like having some friends about you, most likely, later on," I said, to cheer her a bit.

She shook her head sadly.

"No, no, Sarah—if I can't have my own about me, I'll have no others," she said, and I thought I saw what she meant and said no more.

That night the doctor and the legal gentleman that looked after the family affairs were with us and my mistress kept them for dinner. I helped Hodges with the serving and was in the butler's pantry after Mrs. Childress had left them with their coffee and cigars, and as Hodges had left the door ajar I couldn't help catching a bit of the talk now and then.

"The worst of it is this trouble about the children," said the doctor. "She will grieve herself into a decline, I'm afraid."

"I suppose there's no hope?" said the other gentleman.

"No hope?" the doctor burst out. "Why, man, Robertson's been dead six months!"

"To be sure—I'd forgotten it was so long. Well, well, it's too bad, too bad," and Hodges came back and closed the door.

I must say I was thoroughly put out with the doctor. Why should he have told me a lie? And it was mostly from that that I deliberately disobeyed him that night, for I knew from the way he had spoken to the nurse that he didn't wish the children mentioned. But I couldn't help it, for when I came to her room to see if I could help her, she was sitting in her black bedroom gown with her long hair in two braids, crying over the children's picture. "Hush, hush, ma'am," I said, kneeling by her and soothing her head, "if they were here, you may be sure they wouldn't wish it."

"Who? Who?" she answers me, quite wild, but not angry at all. I saw this and spoke it out boldly, for it was plain that she liked me.

"Your children, ma'am," I said, softly but very firm, "and you should control yourself and be cheerful and act as if they *were* here—as if it had pleased God to let you have them and not *Himself!*"

Such a look as she gave me! But soon she seemed to melt, like, and put out her arm over my shoulders.

"What a beautiful way to put it, Sarah!" says she, in a dreamy kind of way. "Do you really think God has them—somewhere?"

"Why, of course, ma'am," said I, shocked in good earnest. "Who else?"

"Then you think I might love them, just as if—just as if——" here she began to sob.

"Why, Mrs. Childress," I said, "where is your belief? That's all that's left to mothers. I know, for I've lost two, and their father to blame for it, which you need never say," I told her.

She patted my shoulder very kindly. "But oh, Sarah, if only they *were* here!" she cried, "really, really here!"

"I know, I know," I said, "it's very hard. But try to think it, ma'am—it helped me for weeks. Think they're in the room next you, here, and you'll sleep better for it."

"Shall I?" she whispered, gripping my hand hard. "I believe I would—how well you understand me, Sarah! And will you help me to believe it?"

I saw she was feverish and I knew what it means to get one good refreshing night without crying, and so I said, "Of course I will, ma'am; see, I'll open the door into the next room and you can fancy them in their cribs, and I'll sleep in there as if it was to look after them, like."

Well, she was naught but a child herself, the poor dear, and she let me get her into bed like a lamb and put her cheek into her hand and went off like a baby. It almost scared me, to see how easy she was to manage, if one did but get hold of the right way. She looked brighter in the morning and as Hodges had told me that Shipman used to do for her, I went in and dressed her—not that I was ever a lady's maid, mind you, but I've always been one to turn my hand easily to anything I had a mind to, and I was growing very fond of my poor lady—and then, I was a little proud, I'll own, of being able to do more for her than her own medical man, who couldn't trust a sensible woman with the truth!

She clung to me all the morning, and after my work was done, I persuaded her to come out for the air. The doctor had ordered it long ago, but she was obstinate, and would scarcely go at all. That day, however, she took a good stroll with me and it brought a bit of colour into her cheeks. Just as we turned toward the house she sat down on a big rock to rest herself, and I saw her lip quiver and her eyes begin to fill. I followed her look and there was a child's swing, hung from two ropes to a low bough. It must have been rotted with the rains, for it looked very old and the board seat was cracked and worn. All around—it hung in a sort of little glade—were small piles of stones and bits of oddments that only children get together, like the little magpies they are.

There's no use to expect any one but a mother or one who's had the constant care of little ones to understand the tears that come to your eyes at a sight like that. What they leave behind is worse than what they take with them; their curls and their fat legs and the kisses they gave you are all shut into the grave, but what they used to play with stays there and mourns them with you.

I saw a wild look come into her eyes, and I determined to quiet her at any cost.

"There, there, ma'am," I said quickly, "'tis only their playthings. Supposing they were there, now, and enjoying them! You go in and take your nap, as the doctor ordered, and leave me behind . . ."

She saw what I meant in a twinkling and the colour jumped into her face again. She turned and hurried in and just as she went out of sight she looked over her shoulder, timid like, and waved her hand—only a bit of a wave, but I saw it.

Under a big stone in front of me, for that part of the grounds was left wild, like a little grove, I saw a rusty tin biscuit box, and as I opened it, curiously, to pass the time, I found it full of little tin platters and cups. Hardly thinking what I did, I arranged them as if laid out for tea, on a flat stone, and left them there. When I went to awaken her for lunch, I started, for some more of those platters were on the table by her bed and a white woolly rabbit and a picture book! She blushed, but I took no notice, and after her luncheon I spied her going quickly back to the little grove.

"Madam's taking a turn for the better, surely," Hodges said to me that afternoon. "She's eating like a Christian now. What have you done to her, Miss Umbleby?" (I went as "Miss" for it's much easier to get a place so.)

"Mr. Hodges," I said, facing him squarely, "the doctors don't know everything. You know as well as I that it's out of nature not to mention children, where they're missed every hour of the day and every day of the month. It's easing the heart that's wanted—not smothering it."

"What d'you mean?" he says, staring at me.

"I mean toys and such like," I answered him, very firm, "and talk of them that's not here to use them, and even pretending that they are, if that will bring peace of mind, Mr. Hodges."

He rubbed his clean shaven chin with his hand.

"Well, well!" he said at last. "Well, well, well! You're a good girl, Miss Umbleby, and a kind one, that's certain. I never thought o' such a thing. Maybe it's all right, though. But who could understand a woman, anyway?"

"That's not much to understand," said I, shortly, and left him staring at me.

She came in late in the afternoon with the rabbit under her arm and there was Mr. Hodges in the drawing-room laying out the tea—we always had everything done as if the master was there, and guests, for the matter of that; she insisted on it. He knew his place as well as any man, but his eye fell on the rabbit and he looked very queer and nearly dropped a cup. She saw it and began to tremble and go white, and it came over me then that now or never was the time to clinch matters or she'd nearly die from shame and I couldn't soothe her any more.

"Perhaps Hodges had better go out and bring in the rest of the toys, ma'am," I says, very careless, not looking at her. "It's coming on for rain. And he can take an umbrella . . . shall he?"

She stiffened up and gave a sort of nod to him.

"Yes, Hodges, go," she said, half in a whisper, and he bit his lip, and swallowed hard and said, "Very good, madam," and went.

Well, after that, you can see how it would be, can't you? One thing led to another, and one time when she was not well for a few days and rather low, I actually got the two little cribs down from the garret and ran up some white draperies for them. She'd hardly let me leave her, and indeed there was not so much work that I couldn't manage very well. She gave all her orders through me and I was well pleased to do for her and let Mr. Hodges manage things, which he did better than poor old Shipman, I'll be bound. By the time we told her about Shipman's death, she took it very easy—indeed, I think, she'd have minded nothing by that time, she had grown so calm and almost healthy.

Mr. Hodges would never catch my eye and I never talked private any more with him, but that was the only sign he didn't approve, and he never spoke for about a month, but joined in with me by little and little and never said a word but to shrug his shoulders when I ordered up a tray with porringers on it for the nursery (she had a bad cold and got restless and grieving). I left her in the nursery with the tray and went out to him, for I saw he wished to speak to me at last.

"Dr. Stanchon would think well of this, if he was here. Is that your idea, Miss Umbleby?" he said to me, very dry. (The doctor had never come back, but gone to be head of a big asylum out in the west.)

"I'm sure I don't know, Mr. Hodges," I answered. "I think any doctor couldn't but be glad to see her gaining every day, and when she feels up to it and guests begin to come again, she'll get willing to see them and forget the loss of the poor little things."

"The loss of *what?*" says he, frowning at me.

"Why, the children," I answered.

"What children?"

"Master Robertson, of course, and Miss Winifred," I said, quite vexed with his obstinacy. (I had asked her once if the baby was named after her and she nodded and went away quickly.)

"See here, my girl," says he, "there's no good keeping this up for my benefit. *I'm* not going into a decline, you know. I know as well as you do that she couldn't lose what she never had!"

"Never had!" I gasped. "She never had any children?"

"Of course not," he said, steadying me, for my knees got weak all of a sudden. "That's what's made all the trouble—that's what's so unfortunate! D'you mean to say you didn't know?"

I sank right down on the stairs. "But the pictures!" I burst out.

"If you mean that picture of Mr. Robertson Childress when he was a little lad and the other one of him and his sister that died when a baby, and chose to fancy they were *hers,*" says he, pointing upstairs, "it's no fault of mine, Miss Umbleby."

And no more it was. What with poor old Shipman's ramblings and the doctor's words that I had twisted into what they never meant, I had got myself into a fine pickle.

"But what shall I do, Mr. Hodges?" I said, stupid-like, with the surprise and the shock of it. "It'd kill her, if I stopped now."

"That's for you to decide," said he, in his reserved, cold way, "I have my silver to do."

Well, I did decide. I lay awake all night at it, and maybe I did wrong, but I hadn't the heart to see the red go out of her cheek and the little shy smile off her pretty mouth. It hurt no one, and the mischief was done, anyway—

there'd be no heir to Childerstone, now. For five generations it had been the same—a son and a daughter to every pair, and the old place about as dear to each son, as I made out, as ever his wife or child could be. General Washington had stopped the night there, and some great French general that helped the Americans had come there for making plans to attack the British, and Colonel Robertson Childress that then was had helped him. They had plenty of English kin and some in the Southern States, but no friends near them, on account of my mistress's husband having to live in Switzerland for his health and his father dying young (as he did) so that his mother couldn't bear the old place. But as soon as Mr. Robertson was told he was cured and could live where he liked, he made for Childerstone and brought his bride there—a stranger from an American family in Switzerland—and lived but three months. If anybody was ever alone, it was that poor lady, I'm sure. There was no big house like theirs anywhere about—no county families, as you might say—and those that had called from the village she wouldn't see, in her mourning. And yet out of that house she would not go, because he had loved it so; it was pitiful.

There's no good argle-bargling over it, as my mother used to say, I'd do the same again! For I began it with the best of motives, and as innocent as a babe, myself, of the real truth, you see.

I can shut my eyes, now, and it all comes back to me as it was in the old garden, of autumn afternoons—I always think of Childerstone in the autumn, somehow. There was an old box hedge there, trimmed into balls and squares, and beds laid out in patterns, with asters and marigolds and those little rusty chrysanthemums that stand the early frosts so well. A wind-break of great evergreens all along two sides kept it warm and close, and from the south and west the sun streamed in onto the stone dial that the Childress of General Washington's time had had brought over from home. It was set for Surrey, Hodges told me once, and no manner of use, consequently, but very settled and homelike to see, if you understand me. In the middle was an old stone basin, all mottled and chipped, and the water ran out from a lion's mouth in some kind of brown metal, and trickled down its mane and jaws and splashed away. We cleaned it out, she and I, one day, *pretending we had help*, and Hodges went to town and got us some gold fish for it. They looked very handsome there. Old John kept the turf clipped and clean and routed out some rustic seats for us—all grey they were and tottery, but he strengthened them, and I smartened them up with yellow chintz cushions I found in the garret—and I myself brought out two tiny arm-chairs, painted wood, from the loft in the coach house. We'd sit there all the afternoon in September, talking a little, me mending and my mistress embroidering on some little frocks I cut out for her. We talked about the children, of course. They got to be as real to me as to her, almost. Of course at first it was all what they *would* have been (for she was no fool, Mrs. Childress, though you may be thinking so) but by little and little it got to be what they *were*. It couldn't be helped.

Hodges would bring her tea out there and she'd eat heartily, for she never was much of a one for a late dinner, me sewing all the time, for I always knew my place, though I believe in her kind heart she'd have been willing for me to eat with her, bless her! Then she'd look at me so wistful-like, and say, "I'll leave you now, Sarah—eat your tea and don't keep out too late. Good-bye—good-bye . . ." Ah, dear me!

I'd sit and think, with the leaves dropping quiet and yellow around me and the water dripping from the lion's mouth and sometimes I'd close my eyes and—I'll swear I could hear them playing quietly beyond me! They were never noisy children. I'll say now something I never mentioned, even to her, and I'd say it if my life hung by it. More than once I've left the metal tea-set shut in the biscuit box and found it spread out of mornings. My mistress slept in the room next me with the door open, and am I to think that William Hodges, or Katey, crippled with rheumatism, or that lazy old John came down and set them out? I've taken a hasty run down to that garden (we called it the children's garden, after a while) because she took an idea, and seen the swing just dying down, and not a breath stirring. That's the plain gospel of it. And I've lain in my bed, just off the two cribs, and held my breath at what I felt and heard. She knew it, too. But never heard so much as I, and often cried for it. I never knew why that should be, nor Hodges, either.

There was one rainy day I went up in the garret and pulled the old rocking-horse out and dusted it and put it out in the middle and set the doors open and went away. It was directly over our heads as we sat sewing, and—ah, well, it's many years ago now, a many and a many, and it's no good raking over too much what's past and gone, I know. And as Hodges said, afterward, the rain on the roof was loud and steady. . . .

I don't know why I should have thought of the rocking-horse, and she not that was always thinking and planning for them. Hodges said it was because I had had children. But I could never have afforded them any such toy as that. Still, perhaps he was right. It was odd his saying that (he knew the facts about me, of course, by that time) being such a dry man, with no fancy about him, you might say, and disliking the whole subject, as he always did, but so it was. Men will often come out with something like that, and quite astonish one.

He never made a hint of objection when I was made housekeeper, and that was like him, too, though I was, to say so, put over him. But he knew my respect for him, black silk afternoons or no black silk, and how we all leaned on him, really.

And then Margaret came, as I said, and it was all to tell, and a fine mess I made of it and William Hodges that settled it, after all.

For Margaret wanted to pack her box directly and get off, and said she'd never heard of such doings and had no liking for people that weren't right.

"Not right?" says Hodges, "not right? Don't you make any such mistake, my girl. Madam attends to all her law business and is at church regularly, and if she's not for much company—why, all the easier for us. Her cheques are as sensible as any one's, I don't care who the man is, and a lady has a right to her fancies. I've lived with very high families at home, and if I'm suited, you may depend upon it the place is a good one. Go or stop, as you like, but don't set up above your elders, young woman."

So she thought it over and the end of it all was that she was with us till the last. And gave me many a black hour, too, poor child, meaning no harm, but she admired Hodges, it was plain, and being younger than I and far handsomer in a dark, Scotch way, it went hard with me, for he made no sign, and I was proud and wouldn't have showed my feelings for my life twice over.

Well, it went on three years more. I made my little frocks longer and the gold fish grew bigger and we set out new marigolds every year, that was all. It was like some quiet dream, when I've gone back and seemed a girl again in the green lanes at home, with mother clear-starching and the rector's daughter hearing my catechism and Master Lawrence sent off to school for bringing me his first partridge. Those dreams seem long and short at one and the same time, and I wake years older, and yet it has not been years that passed but only minutes. So it was at Childerstone. The years went by like the hours went in the children's garden, all hedged in, like, and quiet and leaving no mark. We all seemed the same to each other and one day was like another, full, somehow, and busy and happy, too, in a quiet, gentle way.

When old Katey lay dying she spoke of these days for the first time to me. She'd sent up the porringers and set out glasses of milk and made cookies in heart shapes with her mouth tight shut for all that time, and we never knowing if she sensed it rightly or not. But on her deathbed she told me that she felt the Blessed Mary (as she called her) had given those days to my poor mistress to make up for her for all she'd lost and all she'd never had, and that she'd confessed her part in it and been cleared, long ago. I never loved any time better, looking back, nor Hodges either. One season the Christmas greens would be up, and then before we knew it the ice would be out of the brooks and there would be crocuses and daffodils for Mr. Childress's grave.

She and I took all the care of it and the key to the iron gate of it lay out on her low work table, and one or other of us always passing through, but one afternoon in summer when I went with a basket of June roses, she being not quite up to it that day, there on the flat stone I saw with my own eyes a little crumpled bunch of daisies—all nipped off short, such as children pick, and crushed and wilted in their hot little hands! And on no other tomb but his. But I was used to such as that, by then. . . .

Margaret was handy with her needle, and I remember well the day she made the linen garden hat with a knot of rose-colour under the brim.

"You don't think this will be too old, do you, ma'am?" she said when she showed it to my mistress, and the dear lady was that pleased!

"Not a bit, Margaret," she said and I carried it off to Miss Winifred's closet. Many's the time I missed it after that, and knew too much to hunt. It was hunting that spoiled all, for we tried it. . . .

And yet we didn't half believe. Heaven help us, we knew, but we didn't believe: St. Thomas was nothing to us!

Margaret was with us three years when the new family came. Hodges told us that Hudson River property was looking up and land was worth more every year. Anyway, in one year two families built big houses within a mile of us and we went to call, of course, as in duty bound. John grumbled at getting out the good harness and having the carriage re-lined, but my mistress knew what was right, and he had no choice. I dressed her very carefully, and we watched her off from the door, a thought too pale in her black, but sweet as a flower, and every inch full of breeding, as Hodges said.

I never knew what took place at that visit, but she came back with a bright red circle in each cheek and her head very high, and spent all the evening in the nursery. Alone, of course, for I heard little quick sounds on the piano in the drawing-room, and the fairy books were gone from the children's book-shelves, and Margaret found them in front of the fire and brought them to me. . . .

It was only three days before the new family called on us (a pair of ponies to a basket phaeton—very neat and a nice little groom) and my heart jumped into my mouth when I saw there were two children in with the lady: little girls of eight and twelve, I should say. 'Twas the first carriage callers that ever I'd seen in the place, and Hodges says to me as he goes toward the hall,

"This is something like, eh, Miss Umbleby?"

But I felt odd and uncertain, and when from behind the library door I heard the lady say, "You see I've kept my word and brought my babies, Mrs. Childress—my son is hardly old enough for yours—only four—but Helena and Lou can't wait—they are so impatient to see your little girl!"—when I heard that, I saw what my poor mistress had been at, and the terrible situation we were in (and had been in for years) flashed over me and my hands got cold as ice.

"Where is she?" the lady went on.

At that I went boldly into the library and stood by my mistress's chair—I couldn't desert her then, after all those years.

"Where? where?" my poor lady repeated, vague-like and turning her eyes so piteous at me that I looked the visitor straight in the face and getting between her and my mistress I said very calmly,

"I think Miss Winifred is in the children's garden, madam; shall I take the young ladies there?"

For my thought was to get the children out of the way, before it all came out, you see.

Oh, the look of gratitude she gave me! And yet it was a mad thing to do. But I couldn't desert her—I couldn't.

"There, you see, mamma!" cried the youngest, and the older one said,

"We can find our way, thank you," very civil, to me.

"Children have sharp eyes," said the lady, laughing. "One can't hide them from each other—haven't you found it so?"

"Now what the devil does she mean by that?" Hodges muttered to me as he passed by me with the tray. He always kept the silver perfect, and it did one's heart good to see his tray: urn and sugar and cream just twinkling and the toast in a covered dish—old Chelsea it was—and new cakes and jam and fresh butter, just as they have at home.

I don't know what they talked of, for I couldn't find any excuse to stop in the room, and she wouldn't have had it, anyway. I went around to the front to catch the children when they should come back, and quiet them, but they didn't come, and I was too thankful to think much about it.

After about half an hour I saw the oldest one coming slowly along by herself, looking very sulky.

"Where's your sister, dear?" I said, all in a tremble, for I dreaded how she might put it.

"She's too naughty—I can't get her to leave," she said pettishly, and burst into the library ahead of me. My mistress's face was scarlet and her eyes like two big stars—for the first time I saw that she was a beauty. Her breath came very quick and I knew as well as if I'd been there all the time that she'd been letting herself go, as they say, and talked to her heart's content about what she'd never have a chance to talk again to any guest. She was much excited and the other woman knew it and was puzzled, I could see, from the way she looked at her.

Now the girl burst into the talk.

"Mamma, Lou is so naughty!" she cried. "I saw the ponies coming up the drive, and I told her it was time, but she won't come!"

"Gently, daughter, gently," said the lady, and put her arm around her and smoothed her hair. "Why won't Lou come?"

I can see that room now, as plain as any picture in a frame: the setting sun all yellow on the gilt of the rows of books, the streak of light on the waxed oak floor, the urn shining in the last rays. There was the mother patting the big girl, there was Hodges with his hand on the tray, and there was me standing behind my mistress, with her red cheeks and her poor heaving bosom.

"Why won't Lou come?" she asked the girl again.

"Because," she says, still fretful, and very loud and clear, "because she is taking a pattern of the little girl's hat and trying to twist hers into that shape! I told her you wouldn't like it."

My mistress sprang up and the chair fell down with a crash behind her. I turned (Hodges says) as white as a sheet and moved nearer her.

"Hat!" she gasped. "What hat? *whose hat?*"

There seemed to be a jingling, like sleighbells, all through the air, and I thought I was going crazy till I saw that it came from the tray, where Hodges's hand was shaking so, and yet he couldn't take it off.

"The hat with the rose-coloured ribbon on it," said the girl, "the one we saw as we drove in, you know, mamma. It's so becoming."

"Sarah! Sarah! did you hear? Did you hear?" shrieked my mistress. "She saw, Sarah, *she saw!*"

Then the colour went out of her like when you blow out a candle, and she put her hand to her heart.

"Oh, oh, what pain!" she said very quickly, and Hodges cried, "My God, she's gone!" and I caught her as she fell and we went down together, for my knees were shaking.

When I opened my eyes there was only Margaret there, wetting my forehead, for William had gone for a doctor. Not that it was of any use, for she never breathed. But the smile on her face was lovely.

We got her on her bed and the sight of her there brought the tears to me and I cried out, "Oh, dear, oh, dear! she was all I had in the world, and now——"

"Now you've got me, my girl, and isn't that worth anything to you, Sarah?"

That was William Hodges, and he put his arm over my shoulder, right before Margaret, and looked so kind at me, so kind—I saw in a moment that no one else was anything to him and that he had always cared for me. And that, coming so sudden, when I had given up all hope of it, was too much for me, weak as I was, and I fainted off again and woke up raving hot with fever and half out of my mind, but not quite, for I kept begging them to put off the funeral till I should be able to be up.

But this, of course, was not done, and by the time I was out of hospital the turf was all in place on her dear grave.

William had managed everything and had picked out all the little keep-sakes I should have chosen—the heirs were most kind, though Jews. Indeed, I've felt different to that sort of people ever since, for they not caring for the house on account of its being lonely, to their way of thinking, made it into a children's home for those of their belief as were poor and orphaned, and whatever may have been, the old place will never lack for children now.

I never stepped foot in the grounds again, for William Hodges, though the gentlest and fairest of men, never thwarted me but once, and it was in just that direction. Moreover, he forbade me to speak of what only he and I knew for a certainty, and he was one of that sort that when a command is laid, it's best kept.

We've two fine children—girl and boy—and he never murmured at the names I chose for them. Indeed, considering what my mistress's will left me and what his master had done for him, he was as pleased as I.

"They're named after our two best friends, Sarah," he said, looking hard at me, once.

And I nodded my head, but if she saw me, in heaven, she knew who were in my heart when I named them!

Georgia Wood Pangborn
(1872–1955)

Georgia Wood Pangborn was born in Malone, New York. Like Bacon and Dunbar, she graduated from Smith College, and like the latter, went on to become a member of the New York literati. In 1894 she married H. L. Pangborn and continued to write, becoming an enormously popular contributor to both highbrow and popular magazines. She wrote a large number of supernatural tales, many of which focus on motherhood, as does "Broken Glass." Her children, Edgar and Mary Pangborn, who figure in many of these tales, themselves became well-known fantasy authors. Pangborn's finely crafted ghost stories put her among the top writers of the genre in her day. "Broken Glass" was published by *Scribner's Magazine* in August 1911.

Broken Glass

"I CAN'T STAY BUT A MINUTE," SAID MRS. WARING, SPREAD-ing her long hands above the wood blaze. "I was taking my evening constitutional over the moors. *Did* you see the sunset? And the firelight dancing in your open windows was so dear and sweet and homey I had to come. Babies in bed?"

"Oh, yes. Such perfectly good six-o'clock babies! I can tuck them up myself and still have time to dress safe from sticky fingers. Delia is such a blessing. So big and soft and without any nerves, and really and truly fond of them. When she leaves me for a day I am perfectly wild and lost."

"What is the matter with us women," said Mrs. Waring frowningly, "that we can't take care of our own children and run our own houses, to say nothing of spinning and weaving as our grandmothers did? My grandmother was a Western pioneer and brought up six without help, and— buried three. Think of it! To *lose* a child—" A strong shudder went through her delicate body. "How can a woman live after that? We can gasp through the bearing—you and I know that—but to lose—" She covered her face with her ringed hands.

"But, my dear," said the sleek woman by the fire, "your babies are such little Samsons! That nightmare ought not to bother you now."

"No. It oughtn't. That it does so only shows the more our modern unfitness."

"I suppose our grandmothers must have been more of the Delia type."

"And yet we think the Delia type inferior. It's solid and quiet and stupid—not always honest, but it succeeds with children. You and I are reckoned among the cultured. We read—in three languages—and write magazine verse. Your nocturne is to be given in concert next week—yet I think that Delia and her type rather despise us because we are wrecks after spending an afternoon trying to keep a creeping baby from choking and bumping and burning and taking cold, or reading Peter Rabbit the fiftieth time to Miss Going-on-Three."

"The question is," said Mrs. Waring coiling bonelessly in the Morris chair, "what will our children be? You and I may be inferior, but," she caught her lower lip in her teeth, "my babies came to me after I was thirty, and I know their value, as your Delia type or your grandmother type doesn't for all her motherliness. When women are mothers in the early twenties they don't know. They can't. My music filled in those years. Filled them! It served to express the despair of a barren woman—that was all. Since they came fools have condoled with me because I have had to give up my 'career' for their sake. Career!" She threw back her head with a savage laugh, and stood up with her hands in her coat pocket. "Here," her voice growing very gentle and humorous as she took out the tatters of a little book gay with red and green, "give me some paste. I promised to mend it. She has read it to pieces at last. I though I could rhyme about sunsets and love and death, but nobody ever loved my rhymes as she loves this. Let's write some children's verse, you and I——

"'Goldilocks was naughty, she began to sulk and pout;
She threw aside her playthings—'

That's the way, you see, not——

"'When from the sessions of sweet silent thought.'"

She had seated herself at the big flat-topped desk as she spoke and was deftly pasting and mending.

"I've written one; or Tommy has. We were sitting up with his first double tooth. We had taken a go-cart ride in the early moonlight and I was taking cows as an example of people who chew properly. So we got up a song— (past one o'clock it was and a dark and stormy morning)——

> "'The moon goes sailing through the sky
> The cows are chewing—chewing—'"

"He liked that but when he'd had it fifty times he changed it——

> "'The cows go sailing through the sky
> The moon is chewing—chewing—'"

"And it is better that way; I can recommend it as a lullaby."

"Thanks, but I've some of my own pretty nearly as good. A Norwegian maid left me a legacy——

> "'Go away du Fisker mand
> Catch a pretty fish fish—sh—sh
> Bring it home to baby boy
> Quicker than a wish—wish—shsh.'"

"That's not bad; I'll remember it when the moon's chewing palls. . . .

"As I was saying, you and I know the value of our children even if our type is inferior to the Delia type; and if we were bereft of our Delias and didn't have to dress for dinner and had no time to read we should show up quite as well as the Delias.

"We use the Delias for them because we want them to have everything of the best. Delias *are* best when they're little. We enter later on. We couldn't nurse our babies. All that part of us was metamorphosed into brain—thanks to a mistaken education. Very well; we must nourish them with our brains. We can. And we go and get the best service we can, maids and nurses; we bring them home to our nests like cats bringing mice—for the babies. . . .

"But I'm afraid I've got to let Aileen go. She told Martha a story about Indians carrying off children and nearly scared the child to death. And when I went to find them yesterday afternoon over by the empty Taylor cottage, they were playing where a window had been broken and there was broken glass everywhere. It was like dancing on knives. My spine shivers with it still. And there sat Aileen—so lost in a dream that I had to put my hand on her shoulder to rouse here. 'Oh,' said she, when I showed her the glass, 'I thought it was ice!' She cried when I told her what a terribly dangerous thing she had done. Her tears come easily enough. A pretty little thing, but *so* stupid. I must do better for Martha."

"I thought," said Mrs. Blake hesitatingly, "that she didn't seem very warmly dressed the other day."

"I don't know why she shouldn't be. I gave her a very good coat. Come to think of it, she hasn't worn it. I wonder why?"

"My Delia told me she had a sister. Perhaps———"

"Sponging on her. Poor child! I like her—but, Martha dancing on broken glass. . . . There, that's done. Now, Martha can read it a hundred times more—'Goldilocks was naughty.'

"Now I must go—and dress. Symbol of degeneracy, as women; but of all that raises us above the Delias, if we *are* above them."

The road was icy and ill kept. Some half-dozen cottages with boarded windows showed silent and black against the red band of sunset and the gray, waving line of moors. The pound of winter surf was like distant hoof-beats over the frozen land. The only cottages that were open had children in them. Air is what we give them now. Air and careful food for the rearing of the best of the next generation. And for that purpose the half-dozen cottages on that island kept their warmth and life all winter, just for the sake of properly reddening the cheeks of a dozen little children for whom city streets and parks are not supposed to furnish enough of air.

"Lovely—lovely," thought Mrs. Waring as she walked crisply toward her own fair window. "The moors and the winter storms shall make up to them for having a middle-aged mother. They shall have all the youth and vigor that I had not—that I had not."

Suddenly she faced about. It was not a footfall or a sigh or a spoken word, though it gave the impression of all three. Something behind her had betrayed its presence. . . .

No. There was nothing.

"The wind in the grass," she thought, but was not satisfied. A caretaker had been murdered on the other side of the island the winter before. Being the mother of a Martha makes one a coward. If there were no Martha one would go striding anywhere disregarding fantastic dangers, but *when* there is a Martha, who waits at home for a mother to read the story of Goldilocks one hundred times more, why, a mother must not let the least shadow of danger come near her. Because there are so many ways besides reading Goldilocks in which a mother may be useful.

Therefore she thought sharply about the dead care-taker and vowed that on her next constitutional she would carry a pistol in her pocket—for Martha's sake. The black hedges with their white spots of snow gave no sign; the road behind and in front showed empty but for the gleam of frozen puddles. The wind rattled lightly in the frozen grass. . . .

"I hope ye'll excuse me, mum—" The voice was deprecatory and, thank Heaven, a woman's; though where she had come from out of all that emptiness——

"Ah!" gasped Martha's mother.

"I didn't want to scare ye, mum."

"I can't stop," said Mrs. Waring. "If you want to talk to me come to the house. I must get home to—to——"

"Yes, mum; I know, mum, to your little girl. But I can keep pace with you, by your leave, mum, for I was wishin' to speak to you about Aileen——"

"My nurse maid?"

"The same. I was hearin' she was not givin' ye satisfaction, mum, and would like to speak a word for her—widout offence."

"I have not complained of Aileen. It is true she is sometimes thoughtless. May I ask——"

The woman's figure was so shrouded and huddled that Mrs. Waring, looking all she could, might not distinguish the features. She fancied a resemblance to Mrs. Magillicuddy who came every week to help with the washing. No doubt it was Mrs. Magillicuddy. That would account for her knowledge of Aileen.

Mrs. Waring felt a twinge of annoyance at the thought of Aileen's complaining to Mrs. Magillicuddy. She walked on rapidly, but the other kept as close as her shadow.

"You mean, I suppose, about the broken glass."

"It was very bad, mum; so bad that . . . yet there's worse than broken glass in the world. There's other things that seems no more than the glitter of harmless ice and is really daggers for your heart's blood . . . an' so I was wishin' to speak to ye a word about Aileen. As to the glass, mum, there was no real harm done, an' could ye have seen the lass cryin' her eyes out in her little room that night. . . . Not because ye'd scolded her, but because she'd been that careless. And she could not sleep the night, that tender heart, for seein' the baby welterin' in gore that never was shed at all. Och—those eyes wid tears in them! Surely, mum—surely, ye must have noticed the eyes of her when she looks up at ye wid the hope in them that maybe she has pleased ye? Remember this is her first place and that she was reared gently among the sisters, orphanage as it was, and knows as little of the world as a fine lady-girl when she comes out from *her* convent school. She is not yet used to the rough ways of servants. . . .

"But she will be soon. Ah, wirra, wirra, she will be soon. . . .

"I would like her to stay wid ye. . . . I little thought, ten years ago, that she would be eatin' the bitter bread of service, for bitter it must be, however soft the life; bitter and dangerous for a young girl that is all alone and knows nothin' at all of the world's wickedness. . . . Do ye blame her for not seein' the broken glass? Can ye not guess that the eyes of her were blind with tears for a harsh word ye had given her about mixin' up the big baby's stockings with the little ones? Do ye mind that each of your children has two dozen little rolled up balls of stockings to be looked after and that they are very near of a size—very near? My Aileen—she never had but two pairs at a time and she washes out the wan pair at night so she can change to the other. And do ye mind that hers are thin cotton—twelve cints the pair they are—and her feet are cold to break yer heart as she sits in the cold wind watchin' your little girl at play, so warm in her English woollen stockings and leggins. And have ye ever been into Aileen's room? Do ye know that the fine gilt radiator in it is never warm and that she has but one thin blanket and a comforter so ragged your dog would scorn it? And when she had a bit of a cough ye were afraid it might be consumption, ye said, and if so ye couldn't have her with the children——"

"You seem to know my house and my servants remarkably well, Mrs. Magillicuddy. I will see to Aileen's room at once. I have been very busy, but—really——"

"Ah, save yer anger, mum, for one that deserves it. He's not far away. I am not angry with you, mum, though well I might be. I know with what love ye love yer own. But the world is so large and in such need of the kind and wise that, when one is truly kind and wise like you, mum, it is accounted a sin to let your kindness and wisdom go no further than the soft small heads that are your own. . . . There are so many children without any mothers at all . . . as yours might be had I been what you feared but now. . . .

"Broken glass! Is it not worse than broken glass for a young thing like that, as white-souled as that bit of snow on the hedge—have ye ever heard the talk of house servants? And the only place she can go to get away from it when ye do not want her for your children is her own little room that is so cold.

"She does not understand as yet, the whiteness in her is so white and the servants' hall is warm and pleasant and full of the laughter that ye sometimes hear and frown about. She knows no more than you do of the black heart beneath the white coat of the rascal that is so soft stepping and pleasant and keeps your silver so clean and bright an' says 'Very good, sir,' to everything the boss says to him——"

"Impossible!"

"Does it not happen every day? Do men and women leave off bein' men and women because they do your housework for you? Hearts as well as platters can break in the kitchen, and what do ye care what goes on among the help so long as your house is clean and quiet?"

"Broken glass. . . ." Her voice rose with the rising wind, thinly. . . . "Wirra, wirra—an' a colleen as innocent of the danger of it as your baby that danced upon it unharmed—praise the saints!—unharmed. . . ."

Between anger and fright, Mrs. Waring leaned forward to pluck at the shawl which the other held about her head. At the moment a shaft of light, probably the searchlight from some vessel close inshore—or was it something else?—fell upon the woman's face. It was gone so quickly that Mrs. Waring could not afterward swear to what she had seen. No. Not Mrs. Magillicuddy's face, but similar. Lined and worn, singularly noble.

"*Who are you?*"

"Do ye ask me *that?*" said the Voice.

The flash of light having passed, it seemed so dark that now Mrs. Waring could not even distinguish the film of shadow that had showed where the woman stood.

"Do ye ask me that, mother that loves her children? What would *ye* do, then, if ye were dead, and your children's tears fell upon ye in purgatory? What would ye do if the feet of yer own colleen were standing among broken glass that is broken glass indeed?"

"Who are you?" whimpered Mrs. Waring. But the little moon had risen now and showed the moor empty except for the silent lights of the cottages where little children were.

As she stumbled at her own doorstep her butler opened the door with obsequious concern, and obvious amazement when she cried out—"Aileen—where is she?"

"In her room, I think, m'm; the children being asleep. Shall I call her, m'm?"

"*No!*"

She hurried to the attic room and knocked. The door was locked. Something stirred softly and opened. Aileen's frightened eyes sought her mistress's face. Mrs. Waring read dread of something having been stolen, of some terrible oversight in the nursery, of instant dismissal.

The girl coughed and shivered. She was wearing her coat but her little cap and apron were ready for instant duty. Mrs. Waring remembered with a shock of contrition that Martha had cried because Aileen's hands were cold as she dressed her.

"Aileen—" sobbed Mrs. Waring. . . . "Oh, you poor *little* thing—Come down, child, where it is warm!"

CORNELIA A. P. COMER

(ca. 1869–1929)

Cornelia Atwood Pratt Comer combined successful careers as journalist and author. She was born in Seattle, Washington, and educated at Vassar, from which she graduated in 1889. She began writing for magazines and news-papers, and at one point was on the staff of the *New York Critic*. She later wrote editorials for the *St. Paul Globe* and the *Seattle Post-Intelligencer*. In 1905 she married William D. Pratt. Comer wrote several novels and collections of short fiction. "The Little Gray Ghost" appeared in the *Atlantic* in 1912.

The Little Gray Ghost

A MATTER-OF-FACT MAN'S STORY

I'M DENNYSON—DR. DENNYSON—AND THIS IS MY ONLY ghost-story. As a scientific man, I suppose I have no right even to a very little ghost, but this one came to me in the way of business.

Personally, I didn't want a ghost. I don't go in for anything of the kind, not even to the extent of reading the occult articles in the maga-zines. I see the thing this way. We're here to hold down the job—the long, long job of living—and it's enough to keep us busy. 'Functioning on this plane' is sufficiently stiff work for me. I've no time to waste thinking about other planes, and I don't believe anybody else has.

Besides, there is one thing I know—for I've seen it. The people who are really next to this 'functioning on the next plane' business aren't the ones who make a fuss about it. Spiritualism repels them. They don't go to sé-ances. They don't conduct investigations. They don't even join the Psychical Researchers, but, by the Lord Harry, *they know*. And they don't care very much, either. They take it for granted. They've always known. But they don't want people to think them queer; they don't want to get into the newspapers. Usually it's only when they think you're another that they will discuss it at all. They aren't what you'd pick out for the spooky kind. Plump and sensible and easy-going, mostly. You'd never in the world spot one by the way he looked or talked.

There was Carruthers. He talked to me more freely than any of the others. A little Canadian traveling-man from Vancouver. Scotch blood. Sandy, stocky, sane. A good jollier, and sold big bills of goods. It wouldn't have added to his popularity at the head-office, though, if they'd known he had the Eyes that See. So, naturally, he didn't tell them. He wouldn't have told me, only, that night I came across him at Calgary, he was threatened with pneumonia and pretty ill. And he was worried just then by the Little Gray One, and didn't know what to do about her. So he asked my professional advice, put himself in my hands, if you please, and I got interested and told him what I'd do in his place.

No, it wasn't delirium, and Carruthers wasn't any ordinary crank. Understand, I don't pronounce at all upon the value of his experiences as a basis for theorizing about the Beyond. I don't say they weren't hallucinations. I don't say they were. I suspend my judgment. So, by the way, did he. He didn't philosophize about them, himself. That attracted me.

We were snow-bound together at that hotel for three days. The first night he came in from a train that had been caught in the drifts for eighteen hours, and he slept in damp sheets on top of that. I wonder he escaped severe illness, but he knew enough to ask for a doctor, and my room happened to be next door to his, so I watched him pretty closely that night and it turned out all right. He escaped pneumonia—and I met my ghost.

Odd thought, isn't it, that perhaps—just perhaps, you know—the outer darkness a bit beyond our radiant, comfortable world of sense-perception, is full of pitiful, groping, bodiless folks? We take it from the scientists that there are colors we can't see and sounds we can't hear, but we're shy of believing there are people we can't touch. I like flesh and blood best, myself, but when I think about those possible Others, I feel sorry, the way one does about sick children or hurt animals. There is something in me that understands what being a maimed or naked soul might feel like.

Well, Carruthers and I talked for hours, and I think the man emptied his soul before me. What it all simmers down to, is this: those who have the Eyes claim that they begin to see queer things in childhood and get used to it. They learn early not to talk about it, too, for of course people call them little liars. It doesn't seem, essentially, to be a very thrilling experience or a very interesting one. Carruthers knew no more about the ways of God to man than you or I. And he didn't pretend to, either. He said seeing spirits wasn't a bit more interesting than seeing anything else, when you were used to it. The faculty shed no particular light on his own path and, apparently, wasn't designed to give him personally any form of help: Rather, it was the other way about. The benefactions were on his side.

I asked Carruthers a lot of questions. Didn't it worry him terribly, I wanted to know, this moving in the middle of a cloud of unseen witnesses? He said not at all, not any more than the hundreds of faces we pass on a crowded city street worry the rest of us; really, it was an effect almost identical with that. Occasionally one face would show with increased distinctness against the crowded background and he would see it oftener. If it finally became as definite to him as flesh and blood, he would accost it. I didn't get a very clear idea of their methods of communication. Carruthers used human speech to them, but usually 'heard in his consciousness' what they had to say. You may make what you please of that.

Considered as spirits, I should regard Carruthers's friends as an amœba-like bunch. There seemed to be hordes of them unable to move on. 'Earthbound' is the spiritualistic slang for the condition, I believe, but Carruthers didn't use any cant terms—that was another thing I liked about him. He simply said most of them are just dazed, dumb, helpless—amorphous Things that have slipped out of this world and haven't yet grasped the conditions of living elsewhere. They are like jellyfish rocking in a tide-deserted pool. They have to be helped to deeper water. His idea of his own relation to them, so far as he could be said to have an idea, was that he was a missionary of a sort, a kind of Little Brother to the Lost. Curious contravention of our accepted notions, isn't it? Yet it isn't hard to understand when you look about and see how many people there are right around us who couldn't draw living breath in anything like a spiritual atmosphere.

There are a few, however, who are different. If you love enough or hate enough it will keep you alive anywhere,—even in a world of shades.

I demanded some of his characteristic experiences. He told me lots of incidents, but he was curiously indifferent about them. After all, they were just what you might call the ghost-story of commerce, and rather a bore, you know. For instance, a man he had known came to him so vivid of aspect that he thought the creature still in the flesh, he was so actual. And, indeed, his death had only occurred a month before. But it was the flame of hate that gave him that glow. He was, as you might say, incandescent with the desire for revenge. He told Carruthers that his wife and the doctor conspired to poison him when he was ill, and that they were to be married. He wanted Carruthers to take it up—to frighten them; at least, to make their union impossible. But the traveling man refused to investigate. He said, sensibly enough, that it wasn't up to him; that if he had a part to play toward these people, it wasn't to execute their vengeances. He was willing to help them, but not to be played upon by them, nor taken possession of by their desires. So the man did not come to him any more.

He was shy of explaining what he said to his People. He called it giving them good advice. After he had once talked to one in this way, he seldom saw that one again. If they accepted his advice, they would mostly pass on out of his vision into farther and, he hoped, more blessed fields.

That's the gist of the situation as I got it from Carruthers. He didn't know the answers to most of the questions I asked, and, as I said, he didn't find any of these experiences very absorbing—until the one I am telling you about.

Mind you, now, I'm not pretending to give you a good ghost-story. This isn't that, at all. Carruthers was a matter-of-fact soul, and I'm another. This is just a plain account of what he told me, and what I experienced myself.

It began down in California in the early spring. He went down from Vancouver to San Francisco on some business for the firm, and a man he knew asked him out to one of the big ranches over Sunday. It was an old-fashioned estate—they are mostly cut up now—big enough for a principality. On it grew everything a son of Adam the Gardener could desire. In particular, there was a whole square mile of blossoming cherry-trees, their shining masses of white interspersed here and there with dashes of pink almond-boughs.

I could live without California myself, and so, he said, could he. There's something about it too positive, too magnetic, fertile, golden. It overwhelms you and wearies you with its gigantic beauty. But the pink-and-white glory of a square mile of cherry- and almond-boughs blooming in the spring sunshine—well, it's worth seeing once in a lifetime, just to know that it can be true. It overwhelmed Carruthers, Scotchman from the North though he was. They're used to big things in British Columbia, too, but there was something about the lavish beauty of that orchard that upset him. He wanted to walk there alone, and accordingly went out to do so.

What he thought, what he felt, was after this fashion: here, at last, was something that satisfied,—something as big and beautiful as we dream the mercy of the Merciful may be. In this bounteous, fertile spot, men had not beaten their brothers down, or fought like beasts for pitiful advantage. It was an untainted place where restless spirits would not come, a place where he might breathe deep and throw off the oppression which he sometimes felt his peculiar vision to be. In such an orchard one might be as free as the first man in Eden.

As he was thinking this, he turned his head suddenly and saw moving beside him, timidly, but with determination, a small, gray, insubstantial figure, woe-begone and desolate, yet full, in some curious way, of vital fire.

He described her to me over and over. Out of the things he said, a picture of her built itself up in my mind at last. I think of her as having been a girl with deep-set gray eyes, a small, square face, clean-cut chin, and a slight figure so charged with what we call temperament and personality, that even death spared something of its mutinous charm. You know the type. Carruthers said her very wraith had a glowing, passionate quality, like the leaping of the flame in the chimney-throat, but, even so, was unobtrusive. She was not alive as flesh is alive, heavily, almost rebelliously, but rather as fire is—*all* living, do you see? Her garments were gray, the color of a mist that the sun is about to pierce, wavering, luminous. Faint rose-color seemed to tremble on her cheeks, but it might have been reflected from the almond-blossoms. When she faced him with a bird's quick movement her gaze was wide but steady, like the stare of a child at bay.

'What are you doing here?' he demanded abruptly, almost harshly. Her coming disturbed his joy in the Sunday peace of the orchard. He resented her presence, for he had felt himself free from all obsession.

She shook her head, but made no answer. He looked at her again, more closely.

'What are you doing here?' he repeated, more gently. 'You are not one of the stupid, helpless ones. You don't need me. You ought to be away—far away, in some better place than this.'

She evaded his question, then, by asking another.

'How is it,' she demanded, 'that you see me and speak to me? The people I have known all my life pass me by and look as though I were not there and had said nothing—and yet I have cried and cried to them.'

'I'm just made that way,' said Carruthers vaguely. 'Most other people aren't. That's all. Tell me, what are you doing here?'

Already she began to look less indistinct, less woe-begone. The flush deepened on her cheek; there seemed to come a light in her eyes. It was as if she glowed all over with joy at being understood. It brought her into closer touch with earth.

'I have tried so hard to make them hear!' she cried, 'so hard and so long! But now I have found you it will be easy. You will help me! You will put it right for me! You will go fetch Teresita and take care of her. Then I can go—everywhere!'

Of all the apparitions he had ever encountered, Carruthers affirmed, she was the only one who had pronounced personality and the gift of beguilement. He felt like telling her at once that he would help her in whatever way she desired; then he remembered that this was not only unwise, but contrary to his fixed principles in such matters. He was vexed at himself for his instinct toward compliance, and so pressed his own side of the matter.

'Why,' he asked, 'have you not gone already?'

She looked at him in open wonder. 'You must know—if you know anything,' she said. 'I cannot go on while I hate. I must do my uttermost, my very uttermost, to set it right, and I must forgive.'

'Why have you not forgiven?'

The answer he received flashed into his consciousness as lightning flashes across the eyeball, as vivid, as intense as that.

'I cannot forgive Josefa—nor will I try—until Teresita is safe—with people who are good. Josefa took Teresita from me, and *that* is sin. There are things one must hate, and sins like that are of them. Sometimes to hate is almost sweet!'

Her eyes were on his face, but there was in them nothing evil, nothing malign. They were so limpid, childlike, and pure as she announced this transgression of the law of love, that Carruthers was puzzled and taken aback. So far as he knew, there is no exception to the rule that hate is Hell.

As he looked at her something recurred to him. Josefa—Teresita—where had he heard those names associated before? Suddenly he remembered. The remembrance was a horror. 'Are you Kitty Dundas?' he asked sharply. As he asked, he felt the stubbly hair rise slowly at the back of his neck; the scalp tightened upon his head, while his spine turned cold.

The Little Gray One nodded almost gayly, and with one small finger made an airy gesture toward a faint red line he now perceived about her neck.

'Good Lord!' Sandy Carruthers said. He was a gritty Scotchman, but he shivered, and fell back to think it over.

The name won't convey anything to most Easterners, but it did to me, for I was on the Pacific Coast when the region rang, briefly, with the case of Kitty Dundas. It was one of those things you can't get away from. Even in that land of outrageous crimes, there haven't been many stories so pitiful and terrible.

The facts were these: Kitty Dundas was the young daughter of a Scotch rancher in California. She had fallen in love with one of her father's workmen, a Spaniard named Pedro Rivara. Forbidden to have anything to do with him, she ran away and married him. Her father cast her off with curses for contaminating his blood. The girl and her husband struggled along until the birth of her child. She was ailing a long time, and absorbed in the baby, Teresita. Pedro neglected them both and became entangled with a Mexican woman, Josefa Josatti. When he disappeared with her, he most unnecessarily stole the child and took it along. The young mother worked with her hands until she had saved enough to follow them to San Francisco, where she believed they had gone. She had not been there long before, one day, in the street, she came upon Josefa carrying the baby, which was thin and ill. Kitty leaped for the child, but the other woman fought her off, and in the struggle, the Scotch girl stabbed her rival with the latter's own knife and killed her.

She was tried for murder and acquitted on the ground of self-defense,— that was a foregone conclusion,—but that was not the end of it. In some fierce revulsion of her hereditary conscience, the child proceeded to hang herself, leaving a note which said, baldly, that Josefa's blood was on her hands, and she found proper repentance impossible; so she refused to live.

She executed judgment on herself. Her father had come forward and stood by her during the trial, and she left the child to him. She said it would be better off without her. But that was a mistake. What really happened was that Rivara disappeared, old Dundas died of apoplexy on hearing of his daughter's suicide, leaving a will made after Kitty's marriage which consigned his property to charities, and the child was taken to an orphan asylum.

Think of living and dying in such a tangle of fierce passions and brutal deeds, such stark, gross tragedy as that! Carruthers said it took away his breath even to imagine it, and he watched the Little Gray One with fascinated eyes. She had come through so much, that scrap of a pale thing flitting just ahead of him. Save for that faint red line about her throat—where were her scars?

Twenty years old when she died, just a child herself, yet she had experienced everything. She knew lawless passion, mother-love, the agony of separation from her own, jealousy, hatred, the red rage that murders. Last of all, she knew the terrible self-revulsion of a being endowed with conscience and with character—revulsion against herself as all this heaped-up tragedy had made her. Evidently it had made her something alien to her inmost fibre. She had spirit; she would pay an eye for an eye, a tooth for a tooth, even though that meant surrendering her life for the base life she had taken.

Kitty Dundas had known and suffered all these things in her childish flesh. Yet, here, her spirit moved serenely in the Sabbath sunshine, under white cherry-boughs, with lifted head. She looked angelic, almost holy. Sandy Carruthers said it was beyond him.

I suppose he ought to have known the explanation. It was very simple. Everything in her earthly life had fallen away from Kitty Dundas, save one.

Carruthers had lagged behind her in his shocked bewilderment. She turned and waited for him to join her. If her last statement had been to him like a flash of lightning, what followed was a whole electrical storm. Literally, he staggered at the invasion of his consciousness by great waves of passionate pleading, of insistence, of assertion. He must get the child, she said, and take care of it, bring it up in the way it should go—the Scotch way. Teresita was Scotch, not Spanish, in her nature, her mother insisted; little, and plastic, and Scotch! And Teresita must be taken from the orphanage and reared in a home, as a girl should be, by people who were good. Carruthers was good, and he understood her. Simply, he must take the child. Not until this was done could she forgive Josefa and float free of earth. The thing *must* be.

She spoke as if it were all the simplest matter in the world, and as clear and desirable to him as to her. She was as direct, he said, as the Gospels, and as disconcerting.

The idea she proposed startled and repelled the man. As it happened, he was a married man, and childless. Thus, the thing she desired was possible to do, perhaps even natural. But he had never told his wife of his visions, and did not wish to tell her. Also, he resented deeply any suggestions as to his conduct in the world of sense from this other world with which he had been born entangled. It was his pride that his normal, natural life had never been affected by his second-sight. Furthermore, he had no desire to take a Pedro Rivara's child into his house or his heart.

'I'll not do it, indeed,' said Carruthers doggedly, squaring his shoulders and setting his lips.

He stalked along stiffly. The glorious morning was spoiled for him, and those wonderful aisles of bloom. He was as resentful and vexed as we all are when the call of practical philanthropy catches us in that mood of vague uplift. The Little Gray One drooped beside him, woe-begone again and fading, as though she had taken a mortal hurt. He felt himself brutal, and could not bear to look at her. It was a peculiarly unpleasant thought that he was adding the last touch to the cruelties that had been heaped upon her, and she such a slip of a thing! But he felt no further impulse to do her bidding.

'I wish you would go away,' he said shortly. 'You worry me.'

It seemed as if she were going to obey. She hesitated, wavered. Her garments grew fainter, her face indistinct. He found himself drawing a deep inhalation of triumph and relief. And then, sharply, distinctly, like the clashing of drawn swords, he felt the crossing of her will with his. The sense of opposition was so strong and sudden that he fairly gasped as he realized that of the two her weapon was not the weaker.

Looking at her, he saw that her radiant aspect had returned, stronger than before. She was more glowing, more vital. Her mutinous charm was more apparent. He dropped his lids uneasily, fairly dazzled by the sight of her. She said with her whole being,—

'No! No! I *cannot* go. Don't you see? There is no one but you whom I can make understand—and I must stay until you do my will!'

This was her explanation and her ultimatum. When he lifted his eyes she had disappeared, indeed, for the hour, but she had left with him an oppression of spirit that he was not to shake off. His heart felt as if some one had taken it and squeezed it in two hands. He was wretchedly unsure of himself. He could not dismiss the incident from his mind as he had learned, in the course of years, to dismiss other happenings of a super-normal nature.

To cut the story short, from that time forward Sandy Carruthers was hagridden, if you can apply such a term to such a visitation. The Little Gray Ghost haunted him, definitely, deliberately, persistently. She drifted beside him when he walked the streets; she took the vacant seat next him in the cars; she was visible against the plush cushions of his Pullman section; he saw her in restaurants, houses, theatres, even in church, where she seemed quite as much at home as himself. She followed him into offices and places of business. She came between him and his sales.

He ceased to see other apparitions. She had driven them away, perhaps. Instead, he was aware of a vast vacancy around him compared to which his previous world had been a cheerful, homelike place. He saw only her, and saw her constantly. Always he felt his spirit besieged; sometimes it was assaulted and shaken by the storms of pleading I have tried to describe. But Sandy Carruthers continued to go up and down the Canadian country and to and fro in it, selling goods for the firm at Vancouver, and smoking his old pipe between set lips. His grit was good.

He was an obstinate man and a hard-headed one, but grit is not everything. In time this pursuit got on his nerves. He had always taken his relations with the occult cheerfully and sensibly before this. He was 'born so,' that was all, and it was as much a matter of course as bread and butter, and as little to be dreaded. He found it impossible to take this in that way. He had controlled all other wraiths within his vision. He could neither control nor influence her. He argued, begged, commanded, but she came and went as if she did not hear.

For the first time in his life he was afraid. Yield he would not, and yet, if he persisted, what might not happen to him in this strange contest of wills? Who knew what yet unused weapon she might not have that she could turn against him? That she seemed gentle was no argument. She had seemed so when living, until the hour came for her to use the knife. Living, she had feared nothing for herself or others. Was she to be less daring, dead?

Carruthers mulled over these things until he felt his nerve begin to break. He found himself dreaming strange dreams which made his bed hideous. In them he roamed a universe of undreamed-of and terrible colors; he listened to unimagined and awful sounds. He seemed to be viewing the wrong side of creation; to be hearing the discords of a groaning and laboring universe; to be seeing the frightful shadows cast by life.

Words failed him when he tried to tell me how these things moved him, but it was easy to understand. He asked me flatly if there was imminent danger to his mind in his condition. I was forced to admit that, even if I respected his account of himself and did not classify him with other victims of hallucination, he was, nevertheless, in a desperate way. I thought very badly, not so much of the fact of his obsession, since that was really a condition normal to his organization, as of the fact that he was bearing that obsession ill. I considered that he might see as many ghosts as he pleased, if only he were not afraid of those that he saw! Fear plays the mischief with us all. After this admission from me, he put himself in my hands.

We discussed these matters the second night I was with him at Calgary. The first night he was too sick a man to speak of anything. The next morning he was better, and we talked most of that day and evening over the fire in his bedroom. There was a blizzard on, I remember, and I did not go out all day long. The howling wind, the driving crystals of the snow, the whiteness and impenetrability of the world outside the windows seemed, somehow, to isolate me from everyday life and shut me into Carruthers's world alone with him. Thus, I listened more patiently and sympathetically than I could have done in my office, or anywhere else. I put aside my natural impulse to say, 'Nonsense!' I tried to understand and accept. I ended by talking to him as if he were sane and sincere,—quite a feat for a man of my training!—but I told him frankly he was in as bad a way as a man can be, and he grimly acquiesced.

Turning his case over in my mind that night, I reached a definite, if unusual, conclusion at last. Accepting the data he had given me simply, just as he did himself, there was an obvious method of getting rid of his present trouble, and I resolved to try the experiment of advocating it as a therapeutic measure. It was worth trying, though I smiled to myself as I reflected what some of my colleagues would say to me if they knew it. Fortunately, we don't have to publish all our experiments! Anybody but a stubborn Scotchman would have thought of this one for himself.

The next morning dawned sharply cold, clear, radiant, a day to put fresh life into the dying. It was thirty degrees below, the sun was bright, the world was white and glittering. When I came up from my breakfast, I found Carruthers sitting over a bright fire, comfortably drinking his coffee. He was quite himself in every way, said that he had slept well and was waiting to hear my advice.

I sat down across the fireplace.

'Well, Carruthers,' I said, 'I'm ready to prescribe for you, but I'm afraid you won't like the prescription.'

'I'm going to take it just the same,' he answered.

'To me,' I said, 'it looks this way. I might recommend a rest-cure, feeding, massage, electricity, and all that, for you, and try to work on your mind by healthful suggestion. That would be the right procedure with a person who saw apparitions because his nerves were out of order. But if I am to act as if I believed you—and somehow I am tempted to do it—I must prescribe as if your nerves are out of order because you have been seeing apparitions— which would appear to be a different matter and call for different treatment. This apparition makes one request of you, and states that her disappearance is contingent upon its being granted. It is a simple request. Why don't you just grant it and see what happens? Go find her child. See what it is like and take it to your wife.'

In spite of the agonies he had been through, the man stared at me with absolute incredulity.

'And do you mean to say you would *give in* to the creature?' he demanded, with a whole-souled scorn of me and my faint-heartedness.

This was putting it rather crudely, and I hesitated. I was about to tell him that it was merely a matter of therapeutics, and I wished him to make the experiment—but when I spoke it was to utter words that shaped themselves, without my volition, on my lips.

'Give in to the logic of the situation!' I found myself urging. 'Give in to the impulse of humanity! Why, Carruthers, you yourself have made me see the pity of the thing! Here are we, in the bright, actual, comfortable world; yonder is that bit of a Thing you have described to me, roaming the outer darkness in unrest because her child is here, neglected and unhelped. And the blame for it is her very own, her fault, her grievous fault. She took herself away and left the child to others. Remember that—for *that* is her deadly sin!

'Take it home to yourself, man! If you were in the place of Kitty Dundas and by some miracle you found at last a human being you could appeal to, pray to, argue with, somebody in the same world with that child and able to help it, wouldn't you be fairly wild with joy at getting into touch with him? You or I would do just what you say that little Thing is doing. It seems to me it is inhuman not to help her out. You couldn't treat a living woman so. And the little Ghost is more helpless and more pitiful than any mother of flesh and blood. You are her only hope. Don't turn her down!

'Don't you see how it is? She was thinking about herself, her own soul, when she deserted the child. She was proud-spirited, going to pay with her life for her crime. But her right to do it was gone. Her life was mortgaged to the child. This business of being a parent is something you don't forget nor get away from—not in Heaven or in Hell! It is the tie that holds forever. It is the thing that binds His duties on the shoulders of God Himself!'

Carruthers looked at me blankly. The thing had not presented itself to him in that aspect. He communed with his Caledonian conscience, and his face softened.

'Man, there may be something in what you say,' he admitted. 'I promise you I'll see about it.'

I was silent. To tell you the truth, I was utterly staggered, both at what I had said and at its effect on myself. Those words seemed put into my mouth from without. I believed what I said while I was saying it. I was convinced as by another mind. As I realized this, I, too, felt the grip of fear. For the instant the wraith of Kitty Dundas was as real a thing to me as it was to him—and I felt myself merely her mouthpiece!

'*I promise you,*' I heard him repeating, but in an altered voice, '*that I will see about the child.*'

He was not looking at me or speaking to me. His eyes were fixed on the open door between our rooms. His seamed, red face was awed and pitiful, as if he looked upon and sorrowed for a passion of pleading that was beyond all speech. His sturdy features were twisted and his very mouth writhed with his pity.

I can't tell you how acutely this affected me. The air of that room was charged with something I had never felt before. My blood raced in my veins.

I heard the drumming of my heart. A door opened before me, and I, too, looked beyond the actual. It was as though the wind that blows between the worlds had caught me and lifted me up—up—. It was the strangest sensation—the most wonderful.

My gaze followed his. Did I see an outline of palpitant gray like a mist that the sun is about to pierce, wavering, luminous? Did I catch a glimpse of a face with deep-set eyes, more agonized and pitiful than any human face I ever saw?

'I promise you!' Carruthers cried again hoarsely.

Did I hear a sound like a sob of joy? A wonderful cry that was half farewell to the burdens of this world of sense, half welcome to the new emprises of the world of spirit? I would have sworn it then, by all the gods! Now, after years and in cold blood, I do not know. But I know this—that I fell on my knees in that place, shaken to the very soul, for the room seemed full of light, of cries, and I had a sudden consciousness of prayer and praise ineffable.

Sometimes I hear in my dreams a cry like that of hers. Always when I dream that death has set me free at last, I wake with that sound ringing in my ears as if it came from my own lips and were the breath of utter joy.

Well, that is all—quite all—except that Carruthers recovered quickly, and his wife doted upon the child. With his recovery vanished his dubious gift of second-sight.

As I told you, it is my only ghost-story. And even of it, you see, I am not sure. A man like me never is, and most men are like me. 'Neither will they be persuaded though one come from the dead.' For me, the Little Gray One walked in vain.

Thinking it over in my quiet hours, I say to myself that the Christ always knew whereof He spoke. There are no ghost-stories that are believed. There never will be, to the end of Time. I take it that there are not meant to be. For is it not the long anguish of walking by faith, and not by sight, that makes and keeps us men?

KATHARINE HOLLAND BROWN
(1876–1931)

Katharine Holland Brown was the author of nine books and a series of tales called *Stories from the Bible*. Born in Illinois, she was educated in Washington and at the University of Michigan, from which she graduated in 1924. She made her home eventually in Orlando, Florida. In 1927 she was the winner of the $25,000 John Day Prize for Fiction, an award affiliated with the *Woman's Home Companion*. "Hunger" was featured in *Scribner's Magazine* in March 1907.

Hunger

"IT'S A QUEER THING, ANYWAY," SAID ELEANOR, WITH SO-
ber eyes. She dropped down on the club-house steps, and pulled
absently at the scarlet leaves in her belt. The pale October sunlight struck gold sparkles from her ruffled curly head; her sun-
browned childish face was grave with thought. "Do you ever do that, Ned?"

"Do what, old lady?"

"Dream the same thing, over and over. I've dreamed this one three times now in the last four months, just since we were married, and dozens and dozens of times before. I can remember it as far back as the winter Grand-aunt Isabel took me to Italy with her. I was only five then. And it was always coming when I was with the sisters. I used to wake up and think it was one of them bending over me—the gray dress and all, you know. But one day I asked Sister Hyacinthe, who had charge of us minims, and she said that I always slept like a dormouse——"

"I'll wager."

"And that she hadn't gone to my alcove a single time in all the four years I'd stayed there. So it must have been just that same dream."

"Very likely." Her husband considered the wide, undulating green with placid gaze. "Watch Jimmy Curtis wallop that ball. He plays golf like a pleased Comanche."

"I can't help wondering why it keeps coming back," Eleanor went on, half to herself. "It makes me feel so dissatisfied, somehow; for I know that she's longing to ask me some question; and I can't answer."

"Why don't you wake up and talk back?"

"I do, goosey! That's what makes it so exasperating. My eyes are just popping out, wide awake, every time; but my tongue won't budge. I can't talk a bit, not a solitary word."

"Be sure it's a dream." Ned's wide blue cherub eyes lifted pensively to the tinted hills; his left shoulder lifted, too, in swift prescience of the wrath to come. But for once his ear escaped unchastened. Eleanor went on, unconscious of his gibe.

"She's always so eager! She stoops over me as I lie there, and peers down into my face as if she wanted to look clear through me, body and soul. I never see her so very clearly; she has long brown curls, and they blow across her face. But I don't need to see her, to know how curious she is. Her body leans over, as if it tried to see, too. Her hands are eager; they're warm and soft, and all sweet with some queer old-fashioned perfume, and they sort of flutter, she's in such a hurry, and I can always feel her eyes just begging me to tell her, quick, before she must go away. She's always hurrying—and yet she wants so to stay."

"He won't get out of that ditch if he digs till Christmas," murmured Ned. "Yes, it is queer, how dreams tag after you. I used to have 'em myself, when I was playing on the team. Used to wake up in a cold sweat, always in the last half, with the score a tie—and me fumbling the ball! Ugh, I wouldn't get over it all day! If it worries you, don't think about it, nor talk about it. Then it'll go away."

He scrambled up and drew her to her feet. Shoulder to shoulder, boy-husband and girl-wife might have posed as noble fragments from some antique shrine, miraculously copied in warm young flesh and radiant bloom. The girl, for all her dryad fairness of white-rose coloring and rounded lines, was moulded to a strength as poised and exquisite as that of the splendid body beside her. The boy's eyes met hers tranquilly. Their level gaze mirrored the lucent innocence of her own.

"I wish I knew what she wants," she pondered, as they sauntered down the wide, empty piazza, brown fingers interlaced and swinging. "If only——"

"Oh, dreams are all tommy-rot, anyway. Don't be so quiddly, Nell. You'll be shaking me awake to meet your gray lady every night in the week."

"My gray lady isn't half as quiddly as your falling down on a football play."
Eleanor rammed her arms belligerently into her white coat. "And I'll wager
I can beat you down to the gate. Let's start on this crack. Pig, don't you *dare*
put your foot past it! One—two—three—a-ah!"

With a breathless spurt, she gained the high arch, half a yard ahead.

"I just let you beat to please you," puffed Ned, with large masculine
indulgence. "Say, sis, I can stop that dream for you." He looked down at her,
his eyes rippling. A charming, shamefaced pink flared in his tanned cheek.
"Look sharp, now, I'm giving orders. You're not to dream about anybody or
anything on the face of the earth hereafter, world without end, except—Me.
Promise, now."

Eleanor considered.

"Turn about's fair play. How's that?"

"Sure thing."

They halted in the shadow of the gateway to crook ceremonious fingers
upon their compact, their faces set in solemn grins. Then, instinctively, they
leaned to each other. Shielded in vine-bound shadow, they kissed like royal
children, serenely blind to the unfathomable riches of their heritage, unknowing and content.

For all her promises, her questing dream followed Eleanor and clung in
her thought until it came to be a part of life, an ever-recurring figure in the
fabric of her days. In time, she came to take a fanciful delight in it; for it
drifted, a haze of mystery, across the happy, monotonous surface of her
world; and with it fleeted, like melting iridescence upon a bubble blown,
vague, gleaming recollections of other scenes where it had shadowed forth
to her. The wide, cool, frescoed room, all faded Loves and tarnished Graces,
its carven windows each a setting for a far blue jewel of Italian sea; the
narrow, cloistered niche, one maiden candle burning white before the little
shrine; the dim, home chamber where she had slept, the night of her betrothal, in Grand-aunt Isabel's tender arms; all these dear images blurred
and blent until they flowed, a luminous aura, about the clearer image of her
dream.

It was never a weird vision; it brought no thought of pain. Always it wore
but the one gentle semblance. She would fancy herself in her own bed, lying
broad awake in the gray day. Every sense would be aroused and eager; the
assurance of reality would be so strong that, days after, she could recall the
broadening path of light through the narrowed shutter, the faint cold morn-

ing smell of the rain-wet garden beyond. Yet her eyes never paused to prove their vision; for always beside her leaned the Vision itself; and every power strained with aching effort to meet its plea.

The figure was that of a young girl, younger than herself, beautiful with a beauty that glowed like a pale star through the twilight mist of dreams. Brown, heavy hair lay in great soft curls on her fair shoulders, and blew in airy rings around her face. A long majestic gown of velvet, ashen gray in shadow, paling to silver, dragged on her slender body and sheathed her little arms. Her hands were strung with jewels and smothered in falling lace; broad dulled chains of cameos shone on her neck and bound her tender wrists. In all her wide-flowing magnificence, she looked like a child playing at queen. For the first moment, Eleanor would feel herself patronizingly old and wise before her. Yet the eyes were never the eyes of a child. Nor was the answer that she had come to win a childish thing.

She hung over Eleanor, strung taut in every delicate muscle, her round throat tense, her young breast quivering. Her little hands hovered and groped, entreating; her body leaned and besought. Her brown eyes seized upon Eleanor's, clung to them, searched them with a gaze so urging and so passionate that Eleanor, bound and helpless in her net of silence, would fight for speech until her very soul rose up, in frantic, impotent aid. There was no anger in those dark, peering eyes; their look held neither wonderment nor fear. But all her beautiful, mysterious being throbbed with that one mighty impulse—that utter eagerness, that desperate curiosity which fuses body and soul into one flaming effort, leaping unavailingly upon the miracle which it will understand.

Shaken to consciousness by her longing to help, Eleanor would find herself awake in truth; and as her eyelids lifted to real day, the little pleading shape would glimmer from her sight. Yet the illusion was so strong, so clear, that she could feel that slender, hovering palm against her hair, the sweep of hurrying, scented robes against her knee. And always there lingered, like an echo of far bells, the ghost of a dim, sweet perfume, laden with mystic remembrance; the very perfume of dreams.

At length the vision came less frequently: and presently even the memory of it faded from her thought. For now her life had flushed awake, in sudden morning radiance, and her new day, so crowded and so joyous, held no more room for dreams. Yet she herself was not awakened. For all her days were dream days now, glorified, expectant, enthralling. The hours slipped through her waiting hands like beads upon her girlhood rosary. And all her dawns were rose-blown; and all her dews were pearl.

Once only, during her short, happy convalescence, the vision came to her again. As ever before, she roused to feel the fall of the light hand against her cheek, cool as wind-tossed apple-blossom, to see the frail, gray shape hovering near. But now those eager, questioning eyes were not for Eleanor alone. For as Eleanor awoke, she turned from her side and caught the baby up from his pillows, then drew back, glowing and triumphant, the tiny, yielding body cradled high in both slim arms. And from the beautiful searching face that bent above the child, there streamed an ecstasy that lay as white as joy upon the little face.

"Isn't he splendid!" Eleanor's heart of pride beat out the rapturous up-blown words. But even as she spoke, she knew again her dream. For the night-nurse dozed by the shaded lamp and the baby lay as he had lain, in her own breast.

The boy grew and flourished. He was a square, adorable princeling, brown-eyed, golden-headed, with a cheek like a pussy-willow bud, and the disposition of a well-bred puppy. His father, overgrown boy himself, alternately worshipped him and tinkered with him as if he had been a fascinating wound-up toy. Eleanor, for all her strange new mother-wisdom, hardly believed in him; he was entirely too good to be true. The months of his life lengthened past a year, and she still walked softly before the glory of her child.

It was easier for Ned to grow used to him than for her, she thought sometimes, a little wistfully. He had his father and mother and a phalanx of adoring sisters to share his transports; he could strut and boast to his heart's content, sure of an audience even more shamelessly exultant in its pride than he. Eleanor, on her side, stood alone. Her girl-mother had died in her babyhood; her father's name brought no recollection. Out of all her house, not one of her own blood remained to rejoice with her but the Grand-aunt Isabel, whose patient love had always been her refuge. So to Aunt Isabel she went, secure in an understanding that could never fail her. But the elder woman's largess of sympathy was tempered with gentle amused indulgence for her vain delight; and she owned herself still unsatisfied.

"If I just had somebody my own age, to show him to!" she longed. "Someone who didn't care which side he took after, nor whether he was going to have Grandfather Coleman's gout or Grandfather Underwood's nose, or would grow up High-church Presbyterian or Low-church Unitarian, but could just look at him and rave over him, and see how absurd and cunning and gorgeous he really is! If only——"

Her wistful eyes brightened with sudden tender laughter. "I just wish I could show him off to that dear little dream I used to have! *She'd* know how splendid he is! She thought he was the whole thing, that one time she did look at him. I almost——"

"Where did the kid go, Nell?" Her husband, lounging on the warm turf beside her hammock, cocked a drowsy eye.

"He posted off down the porch a while ago. Where are you, Neddy, son?"

The baby trotted ponderously around a corner of the piazza. His dumpling cheeks puffed with beatific smiles; his tight-curled head shone like a dandelion against the vivid grass.

"Where have you been, young man? Who have you been larking with, to make you look so cheerful?"

"Lady," said Neddy affably. Lady was his gallant term for everything in petticoats, from his stately grandmother to the giddy young thing in tissue frills who hung from his father's shaving-stand.

"What lady, my lamb?"

Neddy puckered crescent brows.

"Gone-away lady," he formulated presently, podgy hands outstretched to speak illimitable distance. "Way-way by. All gone!"

"The gone-away lady, is it? He's forever chortling about her," yawned Ned. "When I went up to the nursery last night he was standing at the window in those bear-cub pajamas of his, throwing juicy kisses to his gone-away lady. Somebody who stops outside to make love to him over the hedge, I suppose. It's disgusting, how daffy this entire neighborhood gets about him; and he nothing but an every-day common or garden child, you might say. Don't squeeze him so tight, Nell. You're scrouging his nose all to one side. Oh, I don't know that he's so dead common, after all. He does pretty well, for the likes of us. What is it, sis?"

Eleanor set the child on her knee. Slow wonder deepened in her eyes.

"Nothing. I was just thinking——"

Her voice trailed away in bewildered silence. She gathered her baby tightly into her arms, and laid her face against his dimpled shoulder. The lace and lawn against her cheek were faintly redolent of soft, mysterious perfume, unknown, yet keenly, poignantly familiar. She groped for recollection; but this fleeting phantom token, too evanescent to be called a fragrance, held for her no conscious memory. Only she glimpsed the shimmer of wan dawnlight upon a misty, gray-robed form. For an instant, she felt the hurrying touch of slender fingers upon her own.

"Come to your stern parent," commanded Ned, stretching out mighty arms. "Upon my honor, Nell, he's grown three inches since yesterday, lengthwise and crosswise and straight through. He must measure just about a yard each way. Twenty-seven cubic feet of angel infancy! Sounds like a baby hippopotamus. Here, you cannibal, are you eating grasshoppers again? Shame! Nice manners to gobble your little playmates like that!"

It was perhaps a fortnight later when Eleanor went again to spend a dutiful hour with Grand-aunt Isabel. Her afternoons there were always a happy interlude. The old house was her comrade; every turn in the deep, ancient staircase welcomed her; every tarnished mirror and wide-swinging door gave her familiar greeting. Aunt Isabel herself, imperious, merry, keen of sight, and keener still of tongue, was the ethereal spice that gave the final delicate zest to her atmosphere, and made its aroma of gracious age and high tradition a savor, not a cloying sweet.

As Eleanor entered, she turned from her heaped sewing-table with a brisk nod of her silvery capped head.

"You're just in time, child. March over here and sort those silk pieces for me. I'm planning an hereditary slumber-robe for that incomparable infant of yours, and it's to have bits of every wedding-gown and brocaded vest and damask petticoat that's peacocked through the family in four generations. You needn't smile, Miss Impudence. True, I'm piecing scraps, instead of cutting my days out of a full pattern, like you. But never mind. You'll be rising eighty in a year or so yourself, and you may well be proud if you turn out as neat a stent as mine.

"Put the stamped velvets all to themselves, dear. They're sniffy bachelor aristocrats, anyway; they won't like to rub elbows with the limp lady-silks, nor even the dowager damasks. Yes, they're magnificent fabrics, and just as masculine as if they wore side-whiskers and fat gold chains. That black piece with the little red lozenges standing up on their toes was the vest Uncle Dudley Coleman wore the day they tried to hiss him down in the Senate for his speech against the Dred Scott decision. I'll wager Uncle Dudley was standing on his toes just about then, too. The Colemans had faults enough and some to lend to the neighbors, but cowardice wasn't in the family motto. That pale-blue piece with the brocaded pink curlycues was Cousin Amariah Bradbury's. Do you remember when Amariah proposed to me? N-no, I suppose not. It was the spring of '42, I think. Amariah wore that very vest, and I recall how the blue matched his eyes, and the pink was just the shade of his little sprouting curly mustache——"

"Aunt Isabel, aren't you ashamed!"

"Indeed, I'm not, Sissy Pert. I'm proud of my memory. When I consider how many there were of them, that spring alone, I wonder that I can recall their names, even. That brown piece with the autumn leaves in raised work was Gran'ther Davenport's fourth-wedding vest. I always felt that Gran'ther showed a rare poetic spirit in choosing that pattern. The puce satin was father's. I've gone to sleep in church with my heard on the watch-pocket many's the time. The silvery stripe with the embossed cherries—that was your Uncle Richard's. No, dear, I don't remember whether he wore it the night he proposed to me or not. I wasn't interested in velvet waistcoats just then. I was so afraid one minute that he *would* ask me, in spite of all I could do, and so terrified the next for fear that he *wouldn't!*"

Her transparent face sparkled with April laughter.

"Ah, well, he sputtered it out at last, though I had to prod him on shamefully. But I've been thankful for sixty years that I did. Those plain velvets should go in a separate pile. The lilac one I wore when I danced with old Admiral Von Deyn at the Embassy, and he trod on the edge of my hoop and nearly tilted me over. The cinnamon was Augusta Chandler's; it was hideously unbecoming, and not at all what she wanted, but it was a great bargain, and Augusta never could resist a bargain. I sometimes think that was why she married Philemon. The peach-blow your Uncle Richard brought me from Paris. I had blond undersleeves, and a large Honiton bertha, and your Uncle Richard used to say——"

The sweet old voice rambled on contentedly. Eleanor did not hear. In the midst of the pile before her lay an odd exquisite bit—a velvet, ashen gray, gleaming silver as she turned it to the light. She picked it up eagerly. The downy fibres seemed to catch and cling upon her fingers. She laid her cheek against the luminous folds. Again that vague wonder encompassed her; for, as if woven into the glinting wrap, there breathed forth a far, dim perfume— the wan, elusive perfume of her dreams. It swayed her like a wind of magic; it swung her past her broad, familiar world, into another world, star-distant.

"What have you found, Eleanor? Oh!"

She put down her work and looked at the girl for a moment, without further speech. Then she took the velvet tenderly from Eleanor's hands. A shadowy pink warmed her soft withered cheek.

"That was one of Evelyn's dresses, child. I don't believe you ever saw it before. It was part of her trousseau—the most ridiculously unsuitable thing for a girl of nineteen. But she always loved such sumptuous, solemn clothes, the little dear! And your father loved to see her trail around in them; he'd have dressed her in cloth of gold, if he could. She loved her jewelry, too; I never saw her dressed for a party that her little neck and arms weren't decked with the cameo chains your grandfather bought for her. Perhaps it was childish of her to care so much for things to wear. But then she was only a little girl, younger by four years than you are now.

"Sometimes I can't help wondering what the Lord was thinking about to let her die. You two would have had such good times! I don't believe she ever would have grown up; and as for mothering you—you'd have been the mother, not she. But she was so cunning and winsome and whimsical and sweet! She had the oddest impatient curiosity about things, just like the child she was. She couldn't bear to read a story through; she must know how it ended before she was half-way down the first page. She hated a concert or a play—'Because you can't skip.' She was forever hurrying. Happy? Yes, dear. The happiest little creature that ever drew breath. But sometimes when I remember how eager she was, how she used to snatch at life, I wonder if— perhaps—she knew.

"She was curious about you, too, in that same whimsey way. She used to pick you up and kiss you and beg you to make haste and grow up, 'Oh, hurry, *hurry*, mother's love!' she'd say, over and over, 'so I can see what you're going to be like.' She used to beg you to be sure and have your father's eyes, 'But you can have my mouth, if you want it,' she'd assure you politely. And she was forever fretting about such nonsensical things, whether there might be some awful chance that you'd grow up to have shiny black hair, like Cousin Augusta's, or what if you should like cup-custards. 'Think of it, Aunt Isabel!' she'd wail, and she'd laugh, but with those curly lashes of hers all blazing with tears, 'Think of a child of mine liking them, actually *liking* them!' Oh, she was the dearest little foolish lovely thing!"

She laid the velvet on Eleanor's knee, and turned to her stitchery once more with a slow, tremulous sigh.

Eleanor worked on steadfastly, her heavy lashes drooping. The many-colored tangle yielded to flawless order beneath her flying hands. The long, fair afternoon waned; the two still sat together, speaking now and then a peaceful surface word, but for the most part in the tranquil silence of content.

"I'll have to run home to the boy, now," said Eleanor at length. She folded the last roll and bent her tall head for good-by. "Mind you don't sew too hard on this quilt, even if it is for the Incomparable. And," her strong young voice wavered with a sudden wistful thrill, "I wish you'd put all the pieces in."

"I will, child." The elder woman kissed her abruptly. Her keen eyes never lifted from her work; her tone fluted with swift understanding. "Be sure I'll put all the pieces in."

The new moon traced its gleaming paraph above the darkling elms as she went up the path to her own door. A belated robin piped importune confidences to the daffodils; the garden breathed deep in balmy April dusk. Eleanor pushed by its loveliness unheeding. Her eyes were dark with shadowing thought. For the first hour in all her brooded, shielded life, she found herself bewildered and alone. Through even the white glory of her happiness it clouded upon her; the pitiful, unknowing loneliness of the motherless child.

She climbed the stairs to Neddy's room. The nurse brushed past her in the dark hall. She turned with a quick word of surprise.

"Why, Mrs. Underwood! Why, I didn't know that you had gone out again! Did your friend want to stay with Neddy?"

"My friend? I've been gone all afternoon, Miss Trescott; and I brought no one home with me. Who do you mean?"

The nurse looked back at her helplessly.

"Why, the lady who is in the nursery with him now. I started to go in a while ago, but they were having such a lovely romp, I hated to spoil it. No, I only caught a glimpse—a slender little thing."

Eleanor thrust past her to the door. Her body throbbed with frantic haste. Intolerable hope surged through her veins. Her soul leaped within her in a terror of anticipation. She urged toward the door as one long blind might urge toward the promise of sight.

Neddy lay curled in his crib, rosy as anemones, his fists shut tight, the lashes golden on his milky cheek. She bent and snatched him up with trembling arms. The nursery lay hushed in fire-lit peace; she stood alone with her child.

Yet, for a breath, as she entered the room it had flickered upon her sight. The sweep of long gray gown, the bronzed hair, the clasping, hovering hands.

Neddy opened a brown, sleepy eye.

"Gone-away lady," he murmured, with a chuckle of content. His fat hands lifted and clung around his mother's neck. "Way-way by. All gone."

Then, with the weight of the warm little body against her arm, the joy of the silken head against her breast, great understanding came upon her. And she cried out, with an exceeding piteous and tender cry:

"Oh, you poor little love! You poor little hungry, eager thing! He's yours, too, dear. Yours and mine. I know all about it now. You'd waited till you were just starved, you wanted to have him so. And you couldn't stand it any longer. You just *had* to see him, and love him—and know."

"Lady," sighed Neddy. His petal cheek tucked down warm against her neck; and in a breath he slipped away, far on a sea of dreams.

———•◆•———

CHARLOTTE PERKINS GILMAN
(1860–1935)

An author and lecturer, Charlotte Perkins Gilman was the leading American feminist intellectual at the turn of the century. She authored nine novels, nearly two hundred short stories, and six books of essays, the most noteworthy of which is *Women and Economics* (1898). Born in Connecticut and raised by her mother after her father had deserted the family, Gilman's only formal education was a brief stint at the Rhode Island School of Design. In 1884 she married Walter Stetson, an artist. After the 1885 birth of their daughter, she fell into a depression and consulted a neurologist, Dr. S. Weir Mitchell. Her famous tale, "The Yellow Wallpaper," is a fictionalized account of her experience with his rest cure. Gilman's marriage failed and she moved to California, where she embarked on a career as a writer and lecturer on trade unions, socialism, and women's suffrage. Few people realize that "The Yellow Wallpaper" was not Gilman's sole foray into supernatural fiction. Like that tale and like Spofford's "Her Story," "The Giant Wistaria" combines the supernatural with real or perceived aberrant psychology, framed by sexual politics. In 1900 Gilman married George Houghton Gilman, and theirs was a successful relationship until his death in 1934. In 1935, after battling inoperable breast cancer for three years, Gilman put her affairs in order, bid family and friends farewell, and committed suicide. This deliberate, rational decision to end her life may serve to shed some light on the story that follows. "The Giant Wistaria" appeared in *New England Magazine* in June 1891 with the byline "Charlotte P. Stetson."

The Giant Wistaria

EDDLE NOT WITH MY NEW VINE, CHILD! SEE! THOU HAST already broken the tender shoot! Never needle or distaff for thee, and yet thou wilt not be quiet!"

The nervous fingers wavered, clutched at a small carnelian cross that hung from her neck, then fell despairingly.

"Give me my child, mother, and then I will be quiet!"

"Hush! hush! thou fool—some one might be near! See—there is thy father coming, even now! Get in quickly!"

She raised her eyes to her mother's face, weary eyes that yet had a flickering, uncertain blaze in their shaded depths.

"Art thou a mother and hast no pity on me, a mother? Give me my child!"

Her voice rose in a strange, low cry, broken by her father's hand upon her mouth.

"Shameless!" said he, with set teeth. "Get to thy chamber, and be not seen again to-night, or I will have thee bound!"

She went at that, and a hard-faced serving woman followed, and presently returned, bringing a key to her mistress.

"Is all well with her,—and the child also?"

"She is quiet, Mistress Dwining, well for the night, be sure. The child fretteth endlessly, but save for that it thriveth with me."

The parents were left alone together on the high square porch with its great pillars, and the rising moon began to make faint shadows of the young vine leaves that shot up luxuriantly around them: moving shadows, like little stretching fingers, on the broad and heavy planks of the oaken floor.

"It groweth well, this vine thou broughtest me in the ship, my husband."

"Aye," he broke in bitterly, "and so doth the shame I brought thee! Had I known of it I would sooner have had the ship founder beneath us, and have seen our child cleanly drowned, than live to this end!"

"Thou art very hard, Samuel, art thou not afeard for her life? She grieveth sore for the child, aye, and for the green fields to walk in!"

"Nay," said he grimly, "I fear not. She hath lost already what is more than life; and she shall have air enough soon. To-morrow the ship is ready, and we return to England. None knoweth of our stain here, not one, and if the town hath a child unaccounted for to rear in decent ways—why, it is not the first, even here. It will be well enough cared for! And truly we have matter for thankfulness, that her cousin is yet willing to marry her."

"Hast thou told him?"

"Aye! Thinkest thou I would cast shame into another man's house, unknowing it? He hath always desired her, but she would none of him, the stubborn! She hath small choice now!"

"Will he be kind, Samuel? can he—"

"Kind? What call'st thou it to take such as she to wife? Kind! How many men would take her, an' she had double the fortune? and being of the family already, he is glad to hide the blot forever."

"An' if she would not? He is but a coarse fellow, and she ever shunned him."

"Art thou mad, woman? She weddeth him ere we sail to-morrow, or she stayeth ever in that chamber. The girl is not so sheer a fool! He maketh an honest woman of her, and saveth our house from open shame. What other hope for her than a new life to cover the old? Let her have an honest child, an' she so longeth for one!"

He strode heavily across the porch, till the loose planks creaked again, strode back and forth, with his arms folded and his brows fiercely knit above his iron mouth.

Overhead the shadows flickered mockingly across a white face among the leaves, with eyes of wasted fire.

"O, George, what a house! what a lovely house! I am sure it's haunted! Let us get that house to live in this summer! We will have Kate and Jack and Susy and Jim of course, and a splendid time of it!"

Young husbands are indulgent, but still they have to recognize facts.

"My dear, the house may not be to rent; and it may also not be habitable."

"There is surely somebody in it. I am going to inquire!"

The great central gate was rusted off its hinges, and the long drive had trees in it, but a little footpath showed signs of steady usage, and up that Mrs. Jenny went, followed by her obedient George. The front windows of the old mansion were blank, but in a wing at the back they found white curtains and open doors. Outside, in the clear May sunshine, a woman was washing. She was polite and friendly, and evidently glad of visitors in that lonely place. She "guessed it could be rented—didn't know." The heirs were in Europe, but "there was a lawyer in New York had the lettin' of it." There had been folks there years ago, but not in her time. She and her husband had the rent of their part "for taking care of the place." "Not that they took much care on't either, but keepin' robbers out." It was furnished throughout, old-fashioned enough, but good; and "if they took it she could do the work for 'em herself, she guessed—if he was willin'!"

Never was a crazy scheme more easily arranged. George knew that lawyer in New York; the rent was not alarming; and the nearness to a rising sea-shore resort made it a still pleasanter place to spend the summer.

Kate and Jack and Susy and Jim cheerfully accepted, and the June moon found them all sitting on the high front porch.

They had explored the house from top to bottom, from the great room in the garret, with nothing in it but a rickety cradle, to the well in the cellar without a curb and with a rusty chain going down to unknown blackness below. They had explored the grounds, once beautiful with rare trees and shrubs, but now a gloomy wilderness of tangled shade.

The old lilacs and laburnums, the spirea and syringa, nodded against the second-story windows. What garden plants survived were great ragged bushes or great shapeless beds. A huge wistaria vine covered the whole front of the house. The trunk, it was too large to call a stem, rose at the corner of the porch by the high steps, and had once climbed its pillars; but now the pillars were wrenched from their places and held rigid and helpless by the tightly wound and knotted arms.

It fenced in all the upper story of the porch with a knitted wall of stem and leaf; it ran along the eaves, holding up the gutter that had once supported it; it shaded every window with heavy green; and the drooping, fragrant blossoms made a waving sheet of purple from roof to ground.

"Did you ever see such a wistaria!" cried ecstatic Mrs. Jenny. "It is worth the rent just to sit under such a vine,—a fig tree beside it would be sheer superfluity and wicked extravagance!"

"Jenny makes much of her wistaria," said George, "because she's so disappointed about the ghosts. She made up her mind at first sight to have ghosts in the house, and she can't find even one ghost story!"

"No," Jenny assented mournfully; "I pumped poor Mrs. Pepperill for three days, but could get nothing out of her. But I'm convinced there is a story, if we could only find it. You need not tell me that a house like this, with a garden like this, and a cellar like this, isn't haunted!"

"I agree with you," said Jack. Jack was a reporter on a New York daily, and engaged to Mrs. Jenny's pretty sister. "And if we don't find a real ghost, you may be very sure I shall make one. It's too good an opportunity to lose!"

The pretty sister, who sat next him, resented. "You shan't do anything of the sort, Jack! This is a *real* ghostly place, and I won't have you make fun of it! Look at that group of trees out there in the long grass—it looks for all the world like a crouching, hunted figure!"

"It looks to me like a woman picking huckleberries," said Jim, who was married to George's pretty sister.

"Be still, Jim!" said that fair young woman. "I believe in Jenny's ghost, as much as she does. Such a place! Just look at this great wistaria trunk crawling up by the steps here! It looks for all the world like a writhing body—cringing—beseeching!"

"Yes," answered the subdued Jim, "it does, Susy. See its waist,—about two yards of it, and twisted at that! A waste of good material!"

"Don't be so horrid, boys! Go off and smoke somewhere if you can't be congenial!"

"We can! We will! We'll be as ghostly as you please." And forthwith they began to see bloodstains and crouching figures so plentifully that the most delightful shivers multiplied, and the fair enthusiasts started for bed, declaring they should never sleep a wink.

"We shall all surely dream," cried Mrs. Jenny, "and we must all tell our dreams in the morning!"

"There's another thing certain," said George, catching Susy as she tripped over a loose plank; "and that is that you frisky creatures must use the side door till I get this Eiffel tower of a portico fixed, or we shall have some fresh ghosts on our hands! We found a plank here that yawns like a trap-door—big enough to swallow you,—and I believe the bottom of the thing is in China!"

The next morning found them all alive, and eating a substantial New England breakfast, to the accompaniment of saws and hammers on the porch, where carpenters of quite miraculous promptness were tearing things to pieces generally.

"It's got to come down mostly," they had said. "These timbers are clean rotted through, what ain't pulled out o' line by this great creeper. That's about all that holds the thing up."

There was clear reason in what they said, and with a caution from anxious Mrs. Jenny not to hurt the wistaria, they were left to demolish and repair at leisure.

"How about ghosts?" asked Jack after a fourth griddle cake. "I had one, and it's taken away my appetite!"

Mrs. Jenny gave a little shriek and dropped her knife and fork.

"Oh, so had I! I had the most awful—well, not dream exactly, but feeling. I had forgotten all about it!"

"Must have been awful," said Jack, taking another cake. "Do tell us about the feeling. My ghost will wait."

"It makes me creep to think of it even now," she said. "I woke up, all at once, with that dreadful feeling as if something were going to happen, you know! I was wide awake, and hearing every little sound for miles around, it seemed to me. There are so many strange little noises in the country for all it is so still. Millions of crickets and things outside, and all kinds of rustles in the trees! There wasn't much wind, and the moonlight came through in my three great windows in three white squares on the black old floor, and those fingery wistaria leaves we were talking of last night just seemed to crawl all over them. And—O, girls, you know that dreadful well in the cellar?"

A most gratifying impression was made by this, and Jenny proceeded cheerfully:

"Well, while it was so horridly still, and I lay there trying not to wake George, I heard as plainly as if it were right in the room, that old chain down there rattle and creak over the stones!"

"Bravo!" cried Jack. "That's fine! I'll put it in the Sunday edition!"

"Be still!" said Kate. "What was it, Jenny? Did you really see anything?"

"No, I didn't, I'm sorry to say. But just then I didn't want to. I woke George, and made such a fuss that he gave me bromide, and said he'd go and look, and that's the last I thought of it till Jack reminded me,—the bromide worked so well."

"Now, Jack, give us yours," said Jim. "Maybe, it will dovetail in somehow. Thirsty ghost, I imagine; maybe they had prohibition here even then!"

Jack folded his napkin, and leaned back in his most impressive manner.

"It was striking twelve by the great hall clock—" he began.

"There isn't any hall clock!"

"O hush, Jim, you spoil the current! It was just one o'clock then, by my old-fashioned repeater."

"Waterbury! Never mind what time it was!"

"Well, honestly, I woke up sharp, like our beloved hostess, and tried to go to sleep again, but couldn't. I experienced all those moonlight and grasshopper sensations, just like Jenny, and was wondering what could have been the matter with the supper, when in came my ghost, and I knew it was all a dream! It was a female ghost, and I imagine she was young and handsome, but all those crouching, hunted figures of last evening ran riot in my brain, and this poor creature looked just like them. She was all wrapped up in a shawl, and had a big bundle under her arm,—dear me, I am spoiling the story! With the air and gait of one in frantic haste and terror, the muffled figure glided to a dark old bureau, and seemed taking things from the drawers. As she turned, the moon-light shone full on a little red cross that hung from her neck by a thin gold chain—I saw it glitter as she crept noiselessly from the room! That's all."

"O Jack, don't be so horrid! Did you really? Is that all! What do you think it was?"

"I am not horrid by nature, only professionally. I really did. That was all. And I am fully convinced it was the genuine, legitimate ghost of an eloping chambermaid with kleptomania!"

"You are too bad, Jack!" cried Jenny. "You take all the horror out of it. There isn't a 'creep' left among us."

"It's no time for creeps at nine-thirty A. M., with sunlight and carpenters outside! However, if you can't wait till twilight for your creeps, I think I can furnish one or two," said George. "I went down cellar after Jenny's ghost!"

There was a delighted chorus of female voices, and Jenny cast upon her lord a glance of genuine gratitude.

"It's all very well to lie in bed and see ghosts, or hear them," he went on. "But the young householder suspecteth burglars, even though as a medical man he knoweth nerves, and after Jenny dropped off I started on a voyage of discovery. I never will again, I promise you!"

"Why, what *was* it?"

"Oh, George!"

"I got a candle——"

"Good mark for the burglars," murmured Jack.

"And went all over the house, gradually working down to the cellar and the well."

"Well?" said Jack.

"Now you can laugh; but that cellar is no joke by daylight, and a candle there at night is about as inspiring as a lightning-bug in the Mammoth Cave. I went along with the light, trying not to fall into the well prematurely; got to it all at once; held the light down and *then* I saw, right under my feet—(I nearly fell over her, or walked through her, perhaps),—a woman, hunched up under a shawl! She had hold of the chain, and the candle shone on her hands—white, thin hands,—on a little red cross that hung from her neck—*vide* Jack! I'm no believer in ghosts, and I firmly object to unknown parties in the house at night; so I spoke to her rather fiercely. She didn't seem to notice that, and I reached down to take hold of her,—then I came upstairs!"

"What for?"

"What happened?"

"What was the matter?"

"Well, nothing happened. Only she wasn't there! May have been indigestion, of course, but as a physician, I don't advise any one to court indigestion alone at midnight in a cellar!"

"This is the most interesting and peripatetic and evasive ghost I ever heard of!" said Jack. "It's my belief she has no end of silver tankards, and jewels galore, at the bottom of that well, and I move we go and see!"

"To the bottom of the well, Jack?"

"To the bottom of the mystery. Come on!"

There was unanimous assent, and the fresh cambrics and pretty boots were gallantly escorted below by gentlemen whose jokes were so frequent that many of them were a little forced.

The deep old cellar was so dark that they had to bring lights, and the well so gloomy in its blackness that the ladies recoiled.

"That well is enough to scare even a ghost. It's my opinion you'd better let well enough alone?" quoth Jim.

"Truth lies hid in a well, and we must get her out," said George. "Bear a hand with the chain?"

Jim pulled away on the chain, George turned the creaking windlass, and Jack was chorus.

"A wet sheet for this ghost, if not a flowing sea," said he. "Seems to be hard work raising spirits! I suppose he kicked the bucket when he went down!"

As the chain lightened and shortened, there grew a strained silence among them; and when at length the bucket appeared, rising slowly through the dark water, there was an eager, half reluctant peering, and a natural drawing back. They poked the gloomy contents. "Only water."

"Nothing but mud."

"Something—"

They emptied the bucket up on the dark earth, and then the girls all went out into the air, into the bright warm sunshine in front of the house, where was the sound of saw and hammer, and the smell of new wood. There was nothing said until the men joined them, and then Jenny timidly asked:

"How old should you think it was, George?"

"All of a century," he answered. "That water is a preservative,—lime in it. Oh!—you mean?—Not more than a month; a very little baby!"

There was another silence at this, broken by a cry from the workmen. They had removed the floor and the side walls of the old porch, so that the sunshine poured down to the dark stones of the cellar bottom. And there, in the strangling grasp of the roots of the great wistaria, lay the bones of a woman, from whose neck still hung a tiny scarlet cross on a thin chain of gold.

⚜ III ⚜

The "Other" Woman:
Sexuality

"Mr. Vanderbridge came in and sat down. . . ."

Illustration by Lejaren A. Hiller for Ellen Glasgow, "The Past," Good Housekeeping Magazine (October 1920). Photo courtesy Metropolitan Toronto Reference Library.

M. E. M. DAVIS
(1852–1909)

Mary Evelyn Moore Davis was a poet, novelist, and short-story writer. Born in Alabama, raised there and in Texas, she was the only daughter in a family with nine children. In 1874 she married Thomas Edward Davis. Although she had been publishing poetry since a young age, it wasn't until the 1880s that Davis began writing the short stories that gained her popularity in national literary magazines. Setting her fiction in Texas or Louisiana, Davis was skilled at portraying the different socioeconomic levels of Southern society. Her strength also lay in providing accurate historical detail—from clothing to mores. She wrote few actual ghost stories, but many more address the supernatural in the world of plantation voodoo. "At La Glorieuse" was first published in *Harper's* in 1898.

At La Glorieuse

ADAME RAYMONDE-ARNAULT LEANED HER HEAD against the back of her garden chair, and watched the young people furtively from beneath her half-closed eyelids. "He is about to speak," she murmured under her breath; "she, at least, will be happy!" and her heart fluttered violently, as if it had been her own thin bloodless hand which Richard Keith was holding in his; her dark sunken eyes, instead of Félice's brown ones, which drooped beneath his tender gaze.

Marcelite, the old *bonne*, who stood erect and stately behind her mistress, permitted herself also to regard them for a moment with something like a smile relaxing her sombre yellow face; then she too turned her turbaned head discreetly in another direction.

The plantation house at La Glorieuse is built in a shining loop of Bayou L'Eperon. A level grassy lawn, shaded by enormous live-oaks, stretches across from the broad stone steps to the sodded levee, where a flotilla of small boats, drawn up among the flags and lily-pads, rise and fall with the lapping waves. On the left of the house the white cabins of the quarter show their low roofs above the shrubbery; to the right the plantations of cane, following the inward curve of the bayou, sweep southward field after field, their billowy blue-green reaches blending far in the rear with the indistinct purple haze of the swamp. The great square house, raised high on massive stone pillars, dates back to the first quarter of the century; its sloping roof is set with rows of dormer-windows, the big red double chimneys rising oddly from their midst; wide galleries with fluted columns enclose it on three sides; from the fourth is projected a long narrow wing, two stories in height, which stands somewhat apart from the main building, but is connected with it by a roofed and latticed passageway. The lower rooms of this wing open upon small porticos, with balustrades of wrought ironwork rarely fanciful and delicate. From these you may step into the rose garden—a tangled pleasaunce which rambles away through alleys of wild-peach and magnolia to an orange grove, whose trees are gnarled and knotted with the growth of half a century.

The early shadows were cool and dewy there that morning; the breath of damask-roses was sweet on the air; brown, gold-dusted butterflies were hovering over the sweet-pease abloom in sunny corners; birds shot up now and then from the leafy aisles, singing, into the clear blue sky above; the chorus of the negroes at work among the young cane floated in, mellow and resonant, from the fields. The old mistress of La Glorieuse saw it all behind her drooped eyelids. Was it not April too, that long-gone unforgotten morning? And were not the bees busy in the hearts of the roses, and the birds singing, when Richard Keith, the first of the name who came to La Glorieuse, held her hand in his, and whispered his love-story yonder, by the ragged thicket of crêpe-myrtle? Ah, Félice, my child, thou art young, but I too have had my sixteen years; and yellow as are the curls on the head bent over thine, those of the first Richard were more golden still. And the second Richard, he who—

Marcelite's hand fell heavily on her mistress's shoulder. Madame Arnault opened her eyes and sat up, grasping the arms of her chair. A harsh grating sound had fallen suddenly into the stillness, and the shutters of one of the upper windows of the wing which overlooked the garden were swinging slowly outward. A ripple of laughter, musical and mocking, rang clearly on the air; at the same moment a woman appeared, framed like a portrait in the narrow casement. She crossed her arms on the iron window-bar, and gazed silently down on the startled group below. She was strangely beautiful and young, though an air of soft and subtle maturity pervaded her graceful figure. A glory of yellow hair encircled her pale oval face, and waved away in fluffy masses to her waist; her full lips were scarlet; her eyes, beneath their straight dark brows, were gray, with emerald shadows in their luminous depths. Her low-cut gown, of some thin, yellowish-white material, exposed her exquisitely rounded throat and perfect neck; long, flowing sleeves of spidery lace fell away from her shapely arms, leaving them bare to the shoulder; loose strings of pearls were wound around her small wrists, and about her throat was clasped a strand of blood-red coral, from which hung to the hollow of her bosom a single translucent drop of amber. A smile at once daring and derisive parted her lips; an elusive light came and went in her eyes.

Keith had started impatiently from his seat at the unwelcome interruption. He stood regarding the intruder with mute, half-frowning inquiry.

Félice turned a bewildered face to her grandmother. "Who is it, mère?" she whispered. "Did—did you give her leave?"

Madame Arnault had sunk back in her chair. Her hands trembled convulsively still, and the lace on her bosom rose and fell with the hurried beating of her heart. But she spoke in her ordinary measured, almost formal tones, as she put out a hand and drew the girl to her side. "I do not know, my child. Perhaps Suzette Beauvais has come over with her guests from Grandchamp. I thought I heard but now the sound of boats on the bayou. Suzette is ever ready with her pranks. Or perhaps—"

She stopped abruptly. The stranger was drawing the batten blinds together. Her ivory-white arms gleamed in the sun. For a moment they could see her face shining like a star against the dusky glooms within; then the bolt was shot sharply to its place.

Old Marcelite drew a long breath of relief as she disappeared. A smothered ejaculation had escaped her lips, under the girl's intent gaze; an ashen gray had overspread her dark face. "Mam'selle Suzette, she been an' dress up one o' her young ladies jes fer er trick," she said, slowly, wiping the great drops of perspiration from her wrinkled forehead.

"Suzette?" echoed Félice, incredulously. "She would never dare! Who *can* it be?"

"It is easy enough to find out," laughed Keith. "Let us go and see for ourselves who is masquerading in my quarters."

He drew her with him as he spoke along the winding violet-bordered walks which led to the house. She looked anxiously back over her shoulder at her grandmother. Madame Arnault half arose, and made an imperious gesture of dissent; but Marcelite forced her gently into her seat, and leaning forward, whispered a few words rapidly in her ear.

"Thou art right, Marcelite," she acquiesced, with a heavy sigh. "'Tis better so."

They spoke in *nègre*, that mysterious patois which is so uncouth in itself, so soft and caressing on the lips of women. Madame Arnault signed to the girl to go on. She shivered a little, watching their retreating figures. The old *bonne* threw a light shawl about her shoulders, and crouched affectionately at her feet. The murmur of their voices as they talked long and earnestly together hardly reached beyond the shadows of the wild-peachtree beneath which they sat.

"How beautiful she was!" Félice said, musingly, as they approached the latticed passageway.

"Well, yes," her companion returned, carelessly. "I confess I do not greatly fancy that style of beauty myself." And he glanced significantly down at her own flower-like face.

She flushed, and her brown eyes drooped, but a bright little smile played about her sensitive mouth. "I cannot see," she declared, "how Suzette could have dared to take her friends into the ballroom!"

"Why?" he asked, smiling at her vehemence.

She stopped short in her surprise. "Do you not know, then?" She sank her voice to a whisper. "The ballroom has never been opened since the night my mother died. I was but a baby then, though sometimes I imagine that I remember it all. There was a grand ball there that night. La Glorieuse was full of guests, and everybody from all the plantations around was here. Mère has never told me how it was, nor Marcelite; but the other servants used to talk to me about my beautiful young mother, and tell me how she died suddenly in her ball dress, while the ball was going on. My father had the whole wing closed at once, and no one was ever allowed to enter it. I used to be afraid to play in its shadow, and if I did stray anywhere near it, my father would always call me away. Her death must have broken his heart. He rarely spoke; I never saw him smile; and his eyes were so sad that I could weep now at remembering them. Then he too died while I was still a little girl, and now I have no one in the world but dear old mère." Her voice trembled a little, but she flushed, and smiled again beneath his meaning look. "It was many years before even the lower floor was reopened, and I am almost sure that yours is the only room there which has ever been used."

They stepped, as she concluded, into the hall.

"I have never been in here before," she said, looking about her with shy curiosity. A flood of sunlight poured through the wide arched window at the foot of the stair. The door of the room nearest the entrance stood open; the others, ranging along the narrow hall, were all closed.

"This is my room," he said, nodding towards the open door.

She turned her head quickly away, with an impulse of girlish modesty, and ran lightly up the stair. He glanced downward as he followed, and paused, surprised to see the flutter of white garments in a shaded corner of his room. Looking more closely, he saw that it was a glimmer of light from an open window on the dark polished floor.

The upper hall was filled with sombre shadows; the motionless air was heavy with a musty, choking odor. In the dimness a few tattered hangings were visible on the walls; a rope, with bits of crumbling evergreen clinging to it, trailed from above one of the low windows. The panelled double door of the ballroom was shut; no sound came from behind it.

"The girls have seen us coming," said Félice, picking her way daintily across the dust-covered floor, "and they have hidden themselves inside."

Keith pushed open the heavy valves, which creaked noisily on their rusty hinges. The gloom within was murkier still; the chill dampness, with its smell of mildew and mould, was like that of a funeral vault.

The large, low-ceilinged room ran the entire length of the house. A raised dais, whose faded carpet had half rotted away, occupied an alcove at one end; upon it four or five wooden stools were placed; one of these was overturned; on another a violin in its baggy green baize cover was lying. Straight high-backed chairs were pushed against the walls on either side; in front of an open fireplace was a low wooden mantel two small cushioned divans were drawn up, with a claw-footed table between them. A silver salver filled with tall glasses was set carelessly on one edge of the table; a half-open fan of sandal-wood lay beside it; a man's glove had fallen on the hearth just within the tarnished brass fender. Cobwebs depended from the ceiling, and hung in loose threads from the mantel; dust was upon everything, thick and motionless; a single ghostly ray of light that filtered in through a crevice in one of the shutters was weighted with gray lustreless motes. The room was empty and silent. The visitors, who had come so stealthily, had as stealthily departed, leaving no trace behind them.

"They have played us a pretty trick," said Keith, gayly. "They must have fled as soon as they saw us start towards the house." He went over to the window from which the girl had looked down into the rose garden, and gave it a shake. The dust flew up in a suffocating cloud, and the spoked nails which secured the upper sash rattled in their places.

"That is like Suzette Beauvais," Félice replied, absently. She was not thinking of Suzette. She had forgotten even the stranger, whose disdainful eyes, fixed upon herself, had moved her sweet nature to something like a rebellious anger. Her thoughts were on the beautiful young mother of alien race, whose name, for some reason, she was forbidden to speak. She saw her glide, gracious and smiling, along the smooth floor; she heard her voice above the call and response of the violins; she breathed the perfume of her laces, backward-blown by the swift motion of the dance!

She strayed dreamily about, touching with an almost reverent finger first one worm-eaten object and then another, as if by so doing she could make the imagined scene more real. Her eyes were downcast; the blood beneath her rich dark skin came and went in brilliant flushes on her cheeks; the bronze hair, piled in heavy coils on her small, well-poised head, fell in loose rings on her low forehead and against her white neck; her soft gray gown, following the harmonious lines of her slender figure, seemed to envelop her like a twilight cloud.

"She is adorable," said Richard Keith to himself.

It was the first time that he had been really alone with her, though this was the third week of his stay in the hospitable old mansion where his father and his grandfather before him had been welcome guests. Now that he came to think of it, in that bundle of yellow, time-worn letters from Félix Arnault to Richard Keith, which he had found among his father's papers, was one which described at length a ball in this very ballroom. Was it in celebration of his marriage, or of his home-coming after a tour abroad? Richard could not remember. But he idly recalled portions of other letters, as he stood with his elbow on the mantel watching Félix Arnault's daughter.

"*Your son and my daughter,*" the phrase which had made him smile when he read it yonder in his Maryland home, brought now a warm glow to his heart. The half-spoken avowal, the question that had trembled on his lips a few moments ago in the rose garden, stirred impetuously within him.

Félice stepped down from the dais where she had been standing, and came swiftly across the room, as if his unspoken thought had called her to him. A tender rapture possessed him to see her thus drawing towards him; he longed to stretch out his arms and fold her to his breast. He moved, and his hand came in contact with a small object on the mantel. He picked it up. It was a ring, a band of dull worn gold, with a confused tracery graven upon it. He merely glanced at it, slipping it mechanically on his finger. His eyes were full upon hers, which were suffused and shining.

"Did you speak?" she asked, timidly. She had stopped abruptly, and was looking at him with a hesitating, half-bewildered expression.

"No," he replied. His mood had changed. He walked again to the window and examined the clumsy bolt. "Strange!" he muttered. "I have never seen a face like hers," he sighed, dreamily.

"She was very beautiful," Félice returned, quietly. "I think we must be going," she added. "Mère will be growing impatient." The flush had died out of her cheek, her arms hung listlessly at her side. She shuddered as she gave a last look around the desolate room. "They were dancing here when my mother died," she said to herself.

He preceded her slowly down the stair. The remembrance of the woman began vaguely to stir his senses. He had hardly remarked her then, absorbed as he had been in another idea. Now she seemed to swim voluptuously before his vision; her tantalizing laugh rang in his ears; her pale perfumed hair was blown across his face; he felt its filmy strands upon his lips and eyelids. "Do you think," he asked, turning eagerly on the bottom step, "that they could have gone into any of these rooms?"

She shrank unaccountably from him. "Oh no," she cried. "They are in the rose garden with mère, or they have gone around to the lawn. Come"; and she hurried out before him.

Madame Arnault looked at them sharply as they came up to where she was sitting. "No one!" she echoed, in response to Keith's report. "Then they really have gone back?"

"Madame knows dat we is hear de boats pass up de bayou whilse m'sieu an' mam'selle was inside," interposed Marcelite, stooping to pick up her mistress's cane.

"I would not have thought Suzette so—so indiscreet," said Félice. There was a note of weariness in her voice.

Madame Arnault looked anxiously at her and then at Keith. The young man was staring abstractedly at the window, striving to recall the vision that had appeared there, and he felt, rather than saw, his hostess start and change color when her eyes fell upon the ring he was wearing. He lifted his hand covertly, and turned the trinket around in the light, but he tried in vain to decipher the irregular characters traced upon it.

"Let us go in," said the old madame. "Félice, my child, thou art fatigued."

Now when in all her life before was Félice ever fatigued? Félice, whose strong young arms could send a pirogue flying up the bayou for miles; Félice, who was ever ready for a tramp along the rose-hedged lanes to the swamp lakes when the water-lilies were in bloom; to the sugar-house in grinding-time, down the levee road to St. Joseph's, the little brown ivy-grown church, whose solitary spire arose slim and straight above the encircling trees.

Marcelite gave an arm to her mistress, though, in truth, she seemed to walk a little unsteadily herself. Félice followed with Keith, who was silent and self-absorbed.

The day passed slowly, a constraint had somehow fallen upon the little household. Madame Arnault's fine high-bred old face wore its customary look of calm repose, but her eyes now and then sought her guest with an expression which he could not have fathomed if he had observed it. But he saw nothing. A mocking red mouth; a throat made for the kisses of love; white arms strung with pearls—these were ever before him, shutting away even the pure sweet face of Félice Arnault.

"Why did I not look at her more closely when I had the opportunity, fool that I was?" he asked himself, savagely, again and again, revolving in his mind a dozen pretexts for going at once to the Beauvais plantation, a mile or so up the bayou. But he felt an inexplicable shyness at the thought of putting any of these plans into action, and so allowed the day to drift by. He arose gladly when the hour for retiring came—that hour which he had hitherto postponed by every means in his power. He kissed, as usual, the hand of his hostess, and held that of Félice in his for a moment; but he did not feel its trembling, or see the timid trouble in her soft eyes.

His room in the silent and deserted wing was full of fantastic shadows. He threw himself on a chair beside a window without lighting his lamp. The rose garden outside was steeped in moonlight; the magnolia bells gleamed waxen-white against their glossy green leaves; the vines on the tall trellises threw a soft network of dancing shadows on the white-shelled walks below; the night air stealing about was loaded with the perfume of roses and sweet-olive; a mocking-bird sang in an orange-tree, his mate responding sleepily from her nest in the old summer-house.

"To-morrow," he murmured, half aloud, "I will go to Grandchamp and give her the ring she left in the old ballroom."

He looked at it glowing dully in the moonlight; suddenly he lifted his head, listening. Did a door grind somewhere near on its hinges? He got up cautiously and looked out. It was not fancy. She was standing full in view on the small balcony of the room next his own. Her white robes waved to and fro in the breeze; the pearls on her arms glistened. Her face, framed in the pale gold of her hair, was turned towards him; a smile curved her lips; her mysterious eyes seemed to be searching his through the shadow. He drew back, confused and trembling, and when, a second later, he looked again, she was gone.

He sat far into the night, his brain whirling, his blood on fire. Who was she, and what was the mystery hidden in this isolated old plantation house?

His thoughts reverted to the scene in the rose garden, and he went over and over all its details. He remembered Madame Arnault's agitation when the window opened and the girl appeared; her evident discomfiture—of which at the time he had taken no heed, but which came back to him vividly enough now—at his proposal to visit the ballroom; her startled recognition of the ring on his finger; her slurring suggestion of visitors from Grandchamp; the look of terror on Marcelite's face. What did it all mean? Félice, he was sure, knew nothing. But here, in an unused portion of the house, which even the members of the family had never visited, a young and beautiful girl was shut up a prisoner, condemned perhaps to a life-long captivity.

"Good God!" He leaped to his feet at the thought. He would go and thunder at Madame Arnault's door, and demand an explanation. But no; not yet. He calmed himself with an effort. By too great haste he might injure her. "Insane?" He laughed aloud at the idea of madness in connection with that exquisite creature.

It dawned upon him, as he paced restlessly back and forth, that although his father had been here more than once in his youth and manhood, he had never heard him speak of La Glorieuse nor of Félix Arnault, whose letters he had read after his father's death a few months ago—those old letters whose affectionate warmth indeed had determined him, in the first desolation of his loss, to seek the family which seemed to have been so bound to his own. Morose and taciturn as his father had been, surely he would sometimes have spoken of his old friend if— Worn out at last with conjecture; beaten back, bruised and breathless, from an enigma which he could not solve; exhausted by listening with strained attention for some movement in the next room, he threw himself on his bed, dressed as he was, and fell into a heavy sleep, which lasted far into the forenoon of the next day.

When he came out (walking like one in a dream), he found a gay party assembled on the lawn in front of the house. Suzette Beauvais and her guests, a bevy of girls, had come from Grandchamp. They had been joined, as they rowed down the bayou, by the young people from the plantation houses on the way. Half a dozen boats, their long paddles laid across the seats, were added to the home fleet at the landing. Their stalwart black rowers were basking in the sun on the levee, or lounging about the quarter. At the moment of his appearance, Suzette herself was indignantly disclaiming any complicity in the jest of the day before.

"Myself, I was making o'ange-flower conserve," she declared; "an' anyhow I wouldn't go in that ballroom unless madame sent me."

"But who was it, then?" insisted Félice.

Mademoiselle Beauvais spread out her fat little hands and lifted her shoulders. "*Mo pas connais,*" she laughed, dropping into patois.

Madame Arnault here interposed. It was but the foolish conceit of some teasing neighbor, she said, and not worth further discussion. Keith's blood boiled in his veins at this calm dismissal of the subject, but he gave no sign. He saw her glance warily at himself from time to time.

"I will sift the matter to the bottom," he thought, "and I will force her to confess the truth, whatever it may be, before the world."

The noisy chatter and meaningless laughter around him jarred upon his nerves; he longed to be alone with his thoughts; and presently, pleading a headache—indeed his temples throbbed almost to bursting, and his eyes were hot and dry—he quitted the lawn, seeing but not noting until long afterwards, when they smote his memory like a two-edged knife, the pain in Félice's uplifted eyes, and the little sorrowful quiver of her mouth. He strolled around the corner of the house to his apartment. The blinds of the arched window were drawn, and a hazy twilight was diffused about the hall, though it was mid-afternoon outside. As he entered, closing the door behind him, the woman at that moment uppermost in his thoughts came down the dusky silence from the further end of the hall. She turned her inscrutable eyes upon him in passing, and flitted noiselessly and with languid grace up the stairway, the faint swish of her gown vanishing with her. He hesitated a moment, overpowered by conflicting emotion; then he sprang recklessly after her.

He pushed open the ballroom door, reaching his arms out blindly before him. Once more the great dust-covered room was empty. He strained his eyes helplessly into the obscurity. A chill reaction passed over him; he felt himself on the verge of a swoon. He did not this time even try to discover the secret door or exit by which she had disappeared; he looked, with a hopeless sense of discouragement, at the barred windows, and turned to leave the room. As he did so, he saw a handkerchief lying on the threshold of the door. He picked it up eagerly, and pressed it to his lips. A peculiar delicate perfume which thrilled his senses lurked in its gossamer folds. As he was about thrusting it into his breastpocket, he noticed in one corner a small blood-stain fresh and wet. He had then bitten his lip in his excitement.

"I need no further proof," he said aloud, and his own voice startled him, echoing down the long hall. "She is beyond all question a prisoner in this detached building, which has mysterious exits and entrances. She has been forced to promise that she will not go outside of its walls, or she is afraid to do so. I will bring home this monstrous crime. I will release this lovely young woman who dares not speak, yet so plainly appeals to me." Already he saw in fancy her starlike eyes raised to his in mute gratitude, her white hand laid confidingly on his arm.

The party of visitors remained at La Glorieuse overnight. The negro fiddlers came in, and there was dancing in the old-fashioned double parlors and on the moonlit galleries. Félice was unnaturally gay. Keith looked on gloomily, taking no part in the amusement.

"*Il est bien bête,* your yellow-haired Marylander," whispered Suzette Beauvais to her friend.

He went early to his room, but he watched in vain for some sign from his beautiful neighbor. He grew sick with apprehension. Had Madame Arnault—But no; she would not dare. "I will wait one more day," he finally decided; "and then—"

The next morning, after a late breakfast, some one proposed impromptu charades and tableaux. Madame Arnault good-naturedly sent for the keys to the tall presses built into the walls, which contained the accumulated trash and treasure of several generations. Mounted on a stepladder, Robert Beauvais explored the recesses, and threw down to the laughing crowd embroidered shawls and scarfs yellow with age, soft muslins of antique pattern, stiff big-flowered brocades, scraps of gauze ribbon, gossamer laces. On one topmost shelf he came upon a small wooden box inlaid with mother-of-pearl. Félice reached up for it, and, moved by some undefined impulse, Richard came and stood by her side while she opened it. A perfume which he recognized arose from it as she lifted a fold of tissue-paper. Some strings of Oriental pearls of extraordinary size, and perfect in shape and color, were coiled underneath, with a coral necklace, whose pendant of amber had broken off and rolled into a corner. With them—he hardly restrained an exclamation, and his hand involuntarily sought his breast-pocket at sight of the handkerchief with a drop of fresh blood in one corner! Félice trembled without knowing why. Madame Arnault, who had just entered the room, took the box from her quietly, and closed the lid with a snap. The girl, accustomed to implicit obedience, asked no questions; the others, engaged in turning over the old-time finery, had paid no attention.

"Does she think to disarm me by such puerile tricks?" he thought, turning a look of angry warning on the old madame; and in the steady gaze which she fixed on him he read a haughty defiance.

He forced himself to enter into the sports of the day, and he walked down to the boat-landing a little before sunset to see the guests depart. As the line of boats swept away, the black rowers dipping their oars lightly in the placid waves, he turned with a sense of release, leaving Madame Arnault and Félice still at the landing, and went down the levee road towards St. Joseph's. The field gang, whose red, blue, and brown blouses splotched the squares of cane with color, was preparing to quit work; loud laughter and noisy jests rang out on the air; high-wheeled plantation wagons creaked along the lanes; negro children, with dip-nets and fishing-poles over their shoulders, ran homeward along the levee, the dogs at their heels barking joyously; a schooner, with white sail outspread, was stealing like a fairy bark around a distant bend of the bayou; the silvery waters were turning to gold under a sunset sky.

It was twilight when he struck across the plantation, and came around by the edge of the swamp to the clump of trees in a corner of the home field which he had often remarked from his window. As he approached, he saw a woman come out of the dense shadow, as if intending to meet him, and then draw back again. His heart throbbed painfully, but he walked steadily forward. It was only Félice. *Only Félice!* She was sitting on a flat tombstone. The little spot was the Raymonde-Arnault family burying-ground. There were many marble head-stones and shafts, and two broad low tombs side by side and a little apart from the others. A tangle of rose-briers covered the sunken graves, a rank growth of grass choked the narrow paths, the little gate interlaced and overhung with honeysuckle sagged away from its posts, the fence itself had lost a picket here and there, and weeds flaunted boldly in the gaps. The girl looked wan and ghostly in the lonely dusk.

"This is my father's grave, and my mother is here," she said, abruptly, as he came up and stood beside her. Her head was drooped upon her breast, and he saw that she had been weeping. "See," she went on, drawing her finger along the mildewed lettering: " 'Félix Marie-Joseph Arnault . . . âgé de trente-quatre ans' . . . 'Hélène Pallacier, épouse de Félix Arnault . . . décédée à l'âge de dix-neuf ans.' Nineteen years old," she repeated, slowly. "My mother was one year younger than I am when she died—my beautiful mother!"

Her voice sounded like a far-away murmur in his ears. He looked at her, vaguely conscious that she was suffering. But he did not speak, and after a little she got up and went away. Her dress, which brushed him in passing, was wet with dew. He watched her slight figure, moving like a spirit along the lane, until a turn in the hedge hid her from sight. Then he turned again towards the swamp, and resumed his restless walk.

Some hours later he crossed the rose garden. The moon was under a cloud; the trunks of the crêpe-myrtles were like pale spectres in the uncertain light. The night wind blew in chill and moist from the swamp. The house was dark and quiet, but he heard the blind of an upper window turned stealthily as he stepped into the latticed arcade.

"The old madame is watching me—and her," he said to himself.

His agitation had now become supreme. The faint familiar perfume that stole about his room filled him with a kind of frenzy. Was this the chivalric devotion of which he had so boasted? this the desire to protect a young and defenceless woman? He no longer dared question himself. He seemed to feel her warm breath against his cheeks. He threw up his arms with a gesture of despair. A sigh stirred the deathlike stillness. At last! She was there, just within his doorway; the pale glimmer of the veiled moon fell upon her. Her trailing laces wrapped her about like a silver mist; her arms were folded across her bosom; her eyes—he dared not interpret the meaning which he read in those wonderful eyes. She turned slowly and went down the hall. He followed her, reeling like a drunkard. His feet seemed clogged, the blood ran thick in his veins, a strange roaring was in his ears. His hot eyes strained after her as she vanished, just beyond his touch, into the room next his own. He threw himself against the closed door in a transport of rage. It yielded suddenly, as if opened from within. A full blaze of light struck his eyes, blinding him for an instant; then he saw her. A huge four-posted bed with silken hangings occupied a recess in the room. Across its foot a low couch was drawn. She had thrown herself there. Her head was pillowed on crimson gold-embroidered cushions; her diaphanous draperies, billowing foam-like over her, half concealed, half revealed her lovely form; her hair waved away from her brows, and spread like a shower of gold over the cushions. One bare arm hung to the floor; something jewel-like gleamed in the half-closed hand; the other lay across her forehead, and from beneath it her eyes were fixed upon him. He sprang forward with a cry. . . .

At first he could remember nothing. The windows were open; the heavy curtains which shaded them moved lazily in the breeze; a shaft of sunlight that came in between them fell upon the polished surface of the marble mantel. He examined with languid curiosity some trifles that stood there—a pair of Dresden figures, a blue Sèvres vase of graceful shape, a bronze clock with gilded rose-wreathed Cupids; and then raised his eyes to the two portraits which hung above. One of these was familiar enough—the dark melancholy face of Félix Arnault, whose portrait by different hands and at different periods of his life hung in nearly every room of La Glorieuse. The blood surged into his face and receded again at sight of the other. Oh, so strangely like! The yellow hair, the slumberous eyes, the full throat clasped about with a single strand of coral. Yes, it was she! He lifted himself on his elbow. He was in bed. Surely this was the room into which she had drawn him with her eyes. Did he sink on the threshold, all his senses swooning into delicious faith? Or had he, indeed, in that last moment thrown himself on his knees by her couch? He could not remember, and he sank back with a sigh.

Instantly Madame Arnault was bending over him. Her cool hands were on his forehead. "*Dieu merci!*" she exclaimed, "thou art thyself once more, *mon fils.*"

He seized her hand imperiously. "Tell me, madame," he demanded—"tell me, for the love of God! What is she? Who is she? Why have you shut her away in this deserted place? Why—"

She was looking down at him with an expression half of pity, half of pain.

"Forgive me," he faltered, involuntarily, all his darker suspicions somehow vanishing; "but—oh, tell me!"

"Calm thyself, Richard," she said, soothingly, seating herself on the side of the bed, and stroking his hand gently. Too agitated to speak, he continued to gaze at her with imploring eyes. "Yes, yes, I will relate the whole story," she added, hastily, for he was panting and struggling for speech. "I heard you fall last night," she continued, relapsing for greater ease into French; "for I was full of anxiety about you, and I lingered long at my window watching for you. I came at once with Marcelite, and found you lying insensible across the threshold of this room. We lifted you to the bed, and bled you after the old fashion, and then I gave you a tisane of my own making, which threw you into a quiet sleep. I have watched beside you until your waking. Now you are but a little weak from fasting and excitement, and when you have rested and eaten—"

"No," he pleaded; "now, at once!"

"Very well," she said, simply. She was silent a moment, as if arranging her thoughts. "Your grandfather, a Richard Keith like yourself," she began, "was a collegiate-mate and friend of my brother, Henri Raymonde, and accompanied him to La Glorieuse during one of their vacations. I was already betrothed to Monsieur Arnault, but I— No matter! I never saw Richard Keith afterwards. But years later he sent your father, who also bore his name, to visit me here. My son, Félix, was but a year or so younger than his boy, and the two lads became at once warm friends. They went abroad, and pursued their studies side by side, like brothers. They came home together, and when Richard's father died, Félix spent nearly a year with him on his Maryland plantation. They exchanged, when apart, almost daily letters. Richard's marriage, which occurred soon after they left college, strengthened rather than weakened this extraordinary bond between them. Then came on the war. They were in the same command, and hardly lost sight of each other during their four years of service.

"When the war was ended, your father went back to his estates. Félix turned his face homeward, but drifted by some strange chance down to Florida, where he met *her*"—she glanced at the portrait over the mantel. "Hélène Pallacier was Greek by descent, her family having been among those brought over some time during the last century as colonists to Florida from the Greek islands. He married her, barely delaying his marriage long enough to write me that he was bringing home a bride. She was young, hardly more than a child, indeed, and marvellously beautiful"— Keith moved impatiently; he found these family details tedious and uninteresting—"a radiant soulless creature, whose only law was her own selfish enjoyment, and whose coming brought pain and bitterness to La Glorieuse. These were her rooms. She chose them because of the rose garden, for she had a sensuous and passionate love of nature. She used to lie for hours on the grass there, with her arms flung over her head, gazing dreamily on the fluttering leaves above her. The pearls—which she always wore—some coral ornaments, and a handful of amber beads were her only dower, but her caprices were the insolent and extravagant caprices of a queen. Félix, who adored her, gratified them at whatever expense; and I think at first she had a careless sort of regard for him. But she hated the little Félice, whose coming gave her the first pang of physical pain she had ever known. She never offered the child a caress. She sometimes looked at her with a suppressed rage which filled me with terror and anxiety.

When Félice was a little more than a year old, your father came to La Glorieuse to pay us a long-promised visit. His wife had died some months before, and you, a child of six or seven years, were left in charge of relatives in Maryland. Richard was in the full vigor of manhood, broad-shouldered, tall, blue-eyed, and blond-haired, like his father and like you. From the moment of their first meeting Hélène exerted all the power of her fascination to draw him to her. Never had she been so whimsical, so imperious, so bewitching! Loyal to his friend, faithful to his own high sense of honor, he struggled against a growing weakness, and finally fled. I will never forget the night he went away. A ball had been planned by Félix in honor of his friend. The ballroom was decorated under his own supervision. The house was filled with guests from adjoining parishes; everybody, young and old, came from the plantations around. Hélène was dazzling that night. The light of triumph in her cheeks; her eyes shone with a softness which I had never seen in them before. I watched her walking up and down the room with Richard, or floating with him in the dance. They were like a pair of radiant godlike visitants from another world. My heart ached for them in spite of my indignation and apprehension; for light whispers were beginning to circulate, and I saw more than one meaning smile directed at them. Félix, who was truth itself, was gayly unconscious.

"Towards midnight I heard far up the bayou the shrill whistle of the little packet which passed up and down then, as now, twice a week; and presently she swung up to our landing. Richard was standing with Hélène by the fireplace. They had been talking for some time in low earnest tones. A sudden look of determination came into his eyes. I saw him draw from his finger a ring which she had one day playfully bade him wear, and offer it to her. His face was white and strained; hers wore a look which I could not fathom. He quitted her side abruptly, and walked rapidly across the room, threading his way among the dancers, and disappeared in the press about the door. A few moments later a note was handed me. I heard the boat steam away from the landing as I read it. It was a hurried line from Richard. He said that he had been called away on urgent business, and he begged me to make his adieux to Madame Arnault and Félix. Félix was worried and perplexed by the sudden departure of his guest. Hélène said not a word, but very soon I saw her slipping down the stair, and I knew that she had gone to her room. Her absence was not remarked, for the ball was at its height. It was almost daylight when the last dance was concluded, and the guests who were staying in the house had retired to their rooms.

"Félix, having seen to the comfort of all, went at last to join his wife. He burst into my room a second later almost crazed with horror and grief. I followed him to this room. She was lying on a couch at the foot of the bed. One arm was thrown across her forehead, the other hung to the floor, and in her hand she held a tiny silver bottle with a jewelled stopper. A handkerchief, with a single drop of blood upon it, was lying on her bosom. A faint curious odor exhaled from her lips and hung about the room, but the poison had left no other trace.

"No one save ourselves and Marcelite ever knew the truth. She had danced too much at the ball that night, and she had died suddenly of heart-disease. We buried her out yonder in the old Raymonde-Arnault burying-ground. I do not know what the letter contained which Félix wrote to Richard. He never uttered his name afterwards. The ballroom, the whole wing, in truth, was at once closed. Everything was left exactly as it was on that fatal night. A few years ago, the house being unexpectedly full, I opened the room in which you have been staying, and it has been used from time to time as a guest-room since. My son lived some years, prematurely old, heart-broken, and desolate. He died with her name on his lips."

Madame Arnault stopped.

A suffocating sensation was creeping over her listener. Only in the past few moments had the signification of the story begun to dawn upon him. "Do you mean," he gasped, "that the girl whom I—that she is—was—"

"Hélène, the dead wife of Félix Arnault," she replied, gravely. "Her restless spirit has walked here before. I have sometimes heard her tantalizing laugh echo through the house, but no one had ever seen her until you came—so like the Richard Keith she loved!"

"When I read your letter," she went on, after a short silence, "which told me that you wished to come to those friends to whom your father had been so dear, all the past arose before me, and I felt that I ought to forbid your coming. But I remembered how Félix and Richard had loved each other before she came between them. I thought of the other Richard Keith whom I—I loved once; and I dreamed of a union at last between the families. I hoped, Richard, that you and Félice—"

But Richard was no longer listening. He wished to believe the whole fantastic story an invention of the keen-eyed old madame herself. Yet something within him confessed to its truth. A tumultuous storm of baffled desire, of impotent anger, swept over him. The ring he wore burned into his flesh. But he had no thought of removing it—the ring which had once belonged to the beautiful golden-haired woman who had come back from the grave to woo him to her!

He turned his face away and groaned.

Her eyes hardened. She rose stiffly. "I will send a servant with your breakfast," she said, with her hand on the door. "The down boat will pass La Glorieuse this afternoon. You will perhaps wish to take advantage of it."

He started. He had not thought of going—of leaving her—*her!* He looked at the portrait on the wall and laughed bitterly.

Madame Arnault accompanied him with ceremonious politeness to the front steps that afternoon.

"Mademoiselle Félice?" he murmured, inquiringly, glancing back at the windows of the sitting-room.

"Mademoiselle Arnault is occupied," she coldly returned. "I will convey to her your farewell."

He looked back as the boat chugged away. Peaceful shadows enwrapped the house and overspread the lawn. A single window in the wing gleamed like a bale-fire in the rays of the setting sun.

The years that followed were years of restless wandering for Richard Keith. He visited his estate but rarely. He went abroad and returned, hardly having set foot to land; he buried himself in the fastnesses of the Rockies; he made a long, aimless sea-voyage. Her image accompanied him everywhere. Between him and all he saw hovered her faultless face; her red mouth smiled at him; her white arms enticed him. His own face became worn and his step listless. He grew silent and gloomy. "He is madder than the old colonel, his father, was" his friends said, shrugging their shoulders.

One day, more than three years after his visit to La Glorieuse, he found himself on a deserted part of the Florida sea-coast. It was late in November, but the sky was soft and the air warm and balmy. He bared his head as he paced moodily to and fro on the silent beach. The waves rolled languidly to his feet and receded, leaving scattered half-wreaths of opalescent foam on the snowy sands. The wind that fanned his face was filled with the spicy odors of the sea. Seized by a capricious impulse, he threw off his clothes and dashed into the surf. The undulating billows closed around him; a singular lassitude passed into his limbs as he swam; he felt himself slowly sinking, as if drawn downward by an invisible hand. He opened his eyes. The waves lapped musically above his head; a tawny glory was all about him, a luminous expanse in which he saw strangely formed creatures moving, darting, rising, falling, coiling, uncoiling.

"You was jes on de eedge er drowndin', Mars Dick," said Wiley, his black body-servant, spreading his own clothes on the porch of the little fishing-hut to dry. "In de name o' Gawd whar mek you wanter go in swimmin' dis time o' de yea', anyhow? Ef I hadn' er splunge in an' fotch you out, dey'd er been mo'nin' yander at de plantation, sho!"

His master laughed lazily. "You are right, Wiley," he said; "and you are going to smoke the best tobacco in Maryland as long as you live." He felt buoyant. Youth and elasticity seemed to have come back to him at a bound. He stretched himself on the rough bench, and watched the blue rings of smoke curl lightly away from his cigar. Gradually he was aware of a pair of wistful eyes shining down on him. His heart leaped. They were the eyes of Félice Arnault! "My God, have I been mad!" he muttered. His eyes sought his hand. The ring, from which he had never been parted, was gone. It had been torn from his finger in his wrestle with the sea. "Get my traps together at once, Wiley," he said. "We are going to La Glorieuse."

"Now you *talkin',* Mars Dick," assented Wiley, cheerfully.

It was night when he reached the city. First of all, he made inquiries concerning the little packet. He was right; the *Assumption* would leave the next afternoon at five o'clock for Bayou L'Eperon. He went to the same hotel at which he had stopped before when on his way to La Glorieuse. The next morning, too joyous to sleep, he rose early, and went out into the street. A gray uncertain dawn was just struggling into the sky. A few people on their way to market or to early mass were passing along the narrow banquettes; sleepy-eyed women were unbarring the shutters of their tiny shops; high-wheeled milk-carts were rattling over the granite pavements; in the vine-hung court-yards, visible here and there through iron *grilles,* parrots were scolding on their perches; children pattered up and down the long, arched corridors; the prolonged cry of an early clothes-pole man echoed, like the note of a winding horn, through the close alleys. Keith sauntered carelessly along.

"In so many hours," he kept repeating to himself, "I shall be on my way to La Glorieuse. The boat will swing into the home landing; the negroes will swarm across the gang-plank, laughing and shouting; Madame Arnault and Félice will come out on the gallery and look, shading their eyes with their hands. Oh, I know quite well that the old madame will greet me coldly at first. Her eyes are like steel when she is angry. But when she knows that I am once more a sane man—And Félice, what if she— But no! Félice is not the kind of woman who loves more than once; and she did love me, God bless her! unworthy as I was."

A carriage, driven rapidly, passed him; his eyes followed it idly, until it turned far away into a side street. He strayed on to the market, where he seated himself on a high stool in *L'Appel du Matin* coffee stall. But a vague, teasing remembrance was beginning to stir in his brain. The turbaned woman on the front seat of the carriage that had rolled past him yonder, where had he seen that dark, grave, wrinkled face, with the great hoops of gold against either cheek? *Marcelite!* He left the stall and retraced his steps, quickening his pace almost to a run as he went. Félice herself, then, might be in the city. He hurried to the street into which the carriage had turned, and glanced down between the rows of white-eaved cottages with green doors and batten shutters. It had stopped several squares away; there seemed to be a number of people gathered about it. "I will at least satisfy myself," he thought.

As he came up, a bell in a little cross-crowned tower began to ring slowly. The carriage stood in front of a low red brick house, set directly on the street; a silent crowd pressed about the entrance. There was a hush within. He pushed his way along the banquette to the steps. A young nun, in a brown serge robe, kept guard at the door. She wore a wreath of white artificial roses above her long coarse veil. Something in his face appealed to her, and she found a place for him in the little convent chapel.

Madame Arnault, supported by Marcelite, was kneeling in front of the altar, which blazed with candles. She had grown frightfully old and frail. Her face was set, and her eyes were fixed with a rigid stare on the priest who was saying mass. Marcelite's dark cheeks were streaming with tears. The chapel, which wore a gala air with its lights and flowers, was filled with people. On the left of the altar, a bishop, in gorgeous robes, was sitting, attended by priests and acolytes; on the right, the wooden panel behind an iron grating had been removed, and beyond, in the nun's choir, the black-robed sisters of the order were gathered. Heavy veils shrouded their faces and fell to their feet. They held in their hands tall wax-candles, whose yellow flames burned steadily in the semi-darkness. Five or six young girls knelt, motionless as statues, in their midst. They also carried tapers, and their rapt faces were turned towards the unseen altar within, of which the outer one is but the visible token. Their eyelids were downcast. Their white veils were thrown back from their calm foreheads, and floated like wings from their shoulders.

He felt no surprise when he saw Félice among them. He seemed to have foreknown always that he should find her thus on the edge of another and mysterious world into which he could not follow her.

Her skin had lost a little of its warm rich tint; the soft rings of hair were drawn away under her veil; her hands were thin, and as waxen as the taper she held. An unearthly beauty glorified her pale face.

"Is it forever too late?" he asked himself in agony, covering his face with his hands. When he looked again the white veil on her head had been replaced by the sombre one of the order. "If I could but speak to her!" he thought; "if she would but once lift her eyes to mine, she would come to me even now!"

Félice! Did the name break from his lips in a hoarse cry that echoed through the hushed chapel, and silenced the voice of the priest? He never knew. But a faint color swept into her cheeks. Her eyelids trembled. In a flash the rose-garden at La Glorieuse was before him; he saw the turquoise sky, and heard the mellow chorus of the field gang; the smell of damask-roses was in the air; her little hand was in his . . . he saw her coming swiftly towards him across the dusk of the old ballroom; her limpid innocent eyes were smiling into his own . . . she was standing on the grassy lawn; the shadows of the leaves flickered over her white gown. . . .

At last the quivering eyelids were lifted. She turned her head slowly, and looked steadily at him. He held his breath. A cart rumbled along the cobblestones outside; the puny wail of a child sounded across the stillness; a handful of rose leaves from a vase at the foot of the altar dropped on the hem of Madame Arnault's dress. It might have been the gaze of an angel in a world where there is no marrying nor giving in marriage, so pure was it, so passionless, so free of anything like earthly desire.

As she turned her face again towards the altar the bell in the tower above ceased tolling; a triumphant chorus leaped into the air, borne aloft by joyous organ tones. The first rays of the morning sun streamed in through the small windows. Then light penetrated into the nuns' choir, and enveloped like a mantle of gold Sister Mary of the Cross, who in the world had been Félicité Arnault.

Ellen Glasgow

(1873–1945)

Ellen Glasgow was one of the American South's most prolific writers, and her fiction dominated bestseller lists for nearly four decades from the time she started publishing in the late 1890s. Glasgow was interested in portraying Virginia society after the Civil War, and her depiction was not sentimental. Her fiction often focuses on the lives of different classes of white women. Born in Richmond, Virginia, to a well-to-do family, she was educated largely at home. Glasgow experienced significant critical and financial success during her lifetime, earning literary awards and honorary degrees. She travelled extensively and knew many of the prominent literary figures of her time. Although she was once engaged, she never married. In addition to novels, Glasgow wrote essays and short fiction, among which is a body of superb ghost stories. "The Past" was published in the October 1920 issue of *Good Housekeeping Magazine*.

The Past

I HAD NO SOONER ENTERED THE HOUSE THAN I KNEW SOMEthing was wrong. Though I had never been in so splendid a place before—it was one of those big houses just off Fifth Avenue—I had a suspicion from the first that the magnificence covered a secret disturbance. I was always quick to receive impressions, and when the black iron doors swung together behind me, I felt as if I were shut inside a prison.

When I gave my name and explained that I was the new secretary, I was delivered into the charge of an elderly lady's-maid, who looked as if she had been crying. Without speaking a word, though she nodded kindly enough, she led me down the hall, and then up a flight of stairs at the back of the house to a pleasant bedroom in the third storey. There was a great deal of sunshine, and the walls, which were painted a soft yellow, made the room very cheerful. It would be a comfortable place to sit in when I was not working, I thought, while the sad-faced maid stood watching me remove my wraps and hat.

"If you are not tired, Mrs. Vanderbridge would like to dictate a few letters," she said presently, and they were the first words she had spoken.

"I am not a bit tired. Will you take me to her?" One of the reasons, I knew, which had decided Mrs. Vanderbridge to engage me was the remarkable similarity of our handwriting. We were both Southerners, and though she was now famous on two continents for her beauty, I couldn't forget that she had got her early education at the little academy for young ladies in Fredericksburg. This was a bond of sympathy in my thoughts at least, and, heaven knows, I needed to remember it while I followed the maid down the narrow stairs and along the wide hall to the front of the house.

In looking back after a year, I can recall every detail of that first meeting. Though it was barely four o'clock, the electric lamps were turned on in the hall, and I can still see the mellow light that shone over the staircase and lay in pools on the old pink rugs, which were so soft and fine that I felt as if I were walking on flowers. I remember the sound of music from a room somewhere on the first floor, and the scent of lilies and hyacinths that drifted from the conservatory. I remember it all, every note of music, every whiff of fragrance; but most vividly I remember Mrs. Vanderbridge as she looked round, when the door opened, from the wood fire into which she had been gazing. Her eyes caught me first. They were so wonderful that for a moment I couldn't see anything else; then I took in slowly the dark red of her hair, the clear pallor of her skin, and the long, flowing lines of her figure in a tea-gown of blue silk. There was a white bearskin rug under her feet, and while she stood there before the wood fire, she looked as if she had absorbed the beauty and colour of the house as a crystal vase absorbs the light. Only when she spoke to me, and I went nearer, did I detect the heaviness beneath her eyes and the nervous quiver of her mouth, which drooped a little at the corners. Tired and worn as she was, I never saw her afterwards—not even when she was dressed for the opera—look quite so lovely, so much like an exquisite flower, as she did on that first afternoon. When I knew her better, I discovered that she was a changeable beauty; there were days when all the colour seemed to go out of her, and she looked dull and haggard; but at her best no one I've ever seen could compare with her.

She asked me a few questions, and though she was pleasant and kind, I knew that she scarcely listened to my responses. While I sat down at the desk and dipped my pen into the ink, she flung herself on the couch before the fire with a movement which struck me as hopeless. I saw her feet tap the white fur rug, while she plucked nervously at the lace on the end of one of the gold-coloured sofa pillows. For an instant the thought flashed through my mind that she had been taking something—a drug of some sort—and that she was suffering now from the effects of it. Then she looked at me steadily, almost as if she were reading my thoughts, and I knew that I was wrong. Her large radiant eyes were as innocent as a child's.

She dictated a few notes—all declining invitations—and then, while I still waited pen in hand, she sat up on the couch with one of her quick movements, and said in a low voice, "I am not dining out to-night, Miss Wrenn. I am not well enough."

"I am sorry for that." It was all I could think of to say, for I did not understand why she should have told me.

"If you don't mind, I should like you to come down to dinner. There will be only Mr. Vanderbridge and myself."

"Of course I will come if you wish it." I couldn't very well refuse to do what she asked me, yet I told myself, while I answered, that if I had known she expected me to make one of the family, I should never, not even at twice the salary, have taken the place. It didn't take me a minute to go over my slender wardrobe in my mind and realize that I had nothing to wear that would look well enough.

"I can see you don't like it," she added after a moment, almost wistfully, "but it won't be often. It is only when we are dining alone."

This, I thought, was even queerer than the request—or command—for I knew from her tone, just as plainly as if she had told me in words, that she did not wish to dine alone with her husband.

"I am ready to help you in any way—in any way that I can," I replied, and I was so deeply moved by her appeal that my voice broke in spite of my effort to control it. After my lonely life I dare say I should have loved any one who really needed me, and from the first moment that I read the appeal in Mrs. Vanderbridge's face I felt that I was willing to work my fingers to the bone for her. Nothing that she asked of me was too much when she asked it in that voice, with that look.

"I am glad you are nice," she said, and for the first time she smiled—a charming, girlish smile with a hint of archness. "We shall get on beautifully, I know, because I can talk to you. My last secretary was English, and I frightened her almost to death whenever I tried to talk to her." Then her tone grew serious. "You won't mind dining with us. Roger—Mr. Vanderbridge—is the most charming man in the world."

"Is that his picture?"

"Yes, the one in the Florentine frame. The other is my brother. Do you think we are alike?"

"Since you've told me, I notice a likeness." Already I had picked up the Florentine frame from the desk, and was eagerly searching the features of Mr. Vanderbridge. It was an arresting face, dark, thoughtful, strangely appealing, and picturesque—though this may have been due, of course, to the photographer. The more I looked at it, the more there grew upon me an uncanny feeling of familiarity; but not until the next day, while I was still trying to account for the impression that I had seen the picture before, did there flash into my mind the memory of an old portrait of a Florentine nobleman in a loan collection last winter. I can't remember the name of the painter—I am not sure that it was known—but this photograph might have been taken from the painting. There was the same imaginative sadness in both faces, the same haunting beauty of feature, and one surmised that there must be the same rich darkness of colouring. The only striking difference was that the man in the photograph looked much older than the original of the portrait, and I remembered that the lady who had engaged me was the second wife of Mr. Vanderbridge and some ten or fifteen years younger, I had heard, than her husband.

"Have you ever seen a more wonderful face?" asked Mrs. Vanderbridge. "Doesn't he look as if he might have been painted by Titian?"

"Is he really so handsome as that?"

"He is a little older and sadder, that is all. When we were married it was exactly like him." For an instant she hesitated and then broke out almost bitterly, "Isn't that a face any woman might fall in love with, a face any woman—living or dead—would not be willing to give up?"

Poor child, I could see that she was overwrought and needed someone to talk to, but it seemed queer to me that she should speak so frankly to a stranger. I wondered why any one so rich and so beautiful should ever be unhappy—for I had been schooled by poverty to believe that money is the first essential of happiness—and yet her unhappiness was as evident as her beauty, or the luxury that enveloped her. At that instant I felt that I hated Mr. Vanderbridge, for whatever the secret tragedy of their marriage might be, I instinctively knew that the fault was not on the side of the wife. She was as sweet and winning as if she were still the reigning beauty in the academy for young ladies. I knew with a knowledge deeper than any conviction that she was not to blame, and if she wasn't to blame, then who under heaven could be at fault except her husband?

In a few minutes a friend came in to tea, and I went upstairs to my room, and unpacked the blue taffeta dress I had bought for my sister's wedding. I was still doubtfully regarding it when there was a knock at my door, and the maid with the sad face came in to bring me a pot of tea. After she had placed the tray on the table, she stood nervously twisting a napkin in her hands while she waited for me to leave my unpacking and sit down in the easy chair she had drawn up under the lamp.

"How do you think Mrs. Vanderbridge is looking?" she asked abruptly in a voice that held a breathless note of suspense. Her nervousness and the queer look in her face made me stare at her sharply. This was a house, I was beginning to feel, where everybody, from the mistress down, wanted to question me. Even the silent maid had found voice for interrogation.

"I think her the loveliest person I've ever seen," I answered after a moment's hesitation. There couldn't be any harm in telling her how much I admired her mistress.

"Yes, she is lovely—everyone thinks so—and her nature is as sweet as her face." She was becoming loquacious. "I have never had a lady who was so sweet and kind. She hasn't always been rich, and that may be the reason she never seems to grow hard and selfish, the reason she spends so much of her life thinking of other people. It's been six years now, ever since her marriage, that I've lived with her, and in all that time I've never had a cross word from her."

"One can see that. With everything she has she ought to be as happy as the day is long."

"She ought to be." Her voice dropped, and I saw her glance suspiciously at the door, which she had closed when she entered. "She ought to be, but she isn't. I have never seen any one so unhappy as she has been of late—ever since last summer. I suppose I oughtn't to talk about it, but I've kept it to myself so long that I feel as if it was killing me. If she was my own sister, I couldn't be any fonder of her, and yet I have to see her suffer day after day, and not say a word—not even to her. She isn't the sort of lady you could speak to about a thing like that."

She broke down, and dropping on the rug at my feet, hid her face in her hands. It was plain that she was suffering acutely, and while I patted her shoulder, I thought what a wonderful mistress Mrs. Vanderbridge must be to have attached a servant to her so strongly.

"You must remember that I am a stranger in the house, that I scarcely know her, that I've never so much as laid eyes on her husband," I said warningly, for I've always avoided, as far as possible, the confidences of servants.

"But you look as if you could be trusted." The maid's nerves, as well as the mistress's, were on edge, I could see. "And she needs somebody who can help her. She needs a real friend—somebody who will stand by her no matter what happens."

Again, as in the room downstairs, there flashed through my mind the suspicion that I had got into a place where people took drugs or drink—or were all out of their minds. I had heard of such houses.

"How can I help her? She won't confide in me, and even if she did, what could I do for her?"

"You can stand by and watch. You can come between her and harm—if you see it." She had risen from the floor and stood wiping her reddened eyes on the napkin. "I don't know what it is, but I know it is there. I feel it even when I can't see it."

Yes, they were all out of their minds; there couldn't be any other explanation. The whole episode was incredible. It was the kind of thing, I kept telling myself, that did not happen. Even in a book nobody could believe it.

"But her husband? He is the one who must protect her."

She gave me a blighting look. "He would if he could. He isn't to blame— you mustn't think that. He is one of the best men in the world, but he can't help her. He can't help her because he doesn't know. He doesn't see it."

A bell rang somewhere, and catching up the tea-tray, she paused just long enough to throw me a pleading word, "Stand between her and harm, if you see it."

When she had gone I locked the door after her, and turned on all the lights in the room. Was there really a tragic mystery in the house, or were they all mad, as I had first imagined? The feeling of apprehension, of vague uneasiness, which had come to me when I entered the iron doors, swept over me in a wave while I sat there in the soft glow of the shaded electric light. Something was wrong. Somebody was making that lovely woman unhappy, and who, in the name of reason, could this somebody be except her husband? Yet the maid had spoken of him as "one of the best men in the world," and it was impossible to doubt the tearful sincerity of her voice. Well, the riddle was too much for me. I gave it up at last with a sigh—dreading the hour that would call me downstairs to meet Mr. Vanderbridge. I felt in every nerve and fibre of my body that I should hate him the moment I looked at him.

But at eight o'clock, when I went reluctantly downstairs, I had a surprise. Nothing could have been kinder than the way Mr. Vanderbridge greeted me, and I could tell as soon as I met his eyes that there wasn't anything vicious or violent in his nature. He reminded me more than ever of the portrait in the loan collection, and though he was so much older than the Florentine nobleman, he had the same thoughtful look. Of course I am not an artist, but I have always tried, in my way, to be a reader of personality; and it didn't take a particularly keen observer to discern the character and intellect in Mr. Vanderbridge's face. Even now I remember it as the noblest face I have ever seen; and unless I had possessed at least a shade of penetration, I doubt if I should have detected the melancholy. For it was only when he was thinking deeply that this sadness seemed to spread like a veil over his features. At other times he was cheerful and even gay in his manner; and his rich dark eyes would light up now and then with irrepressible humour. From the way he looked at his wife I could tell that there was no lack of love or tenderness on his side any more than there was on hers. It was obvious that he was still as much in love with her as he had been before his marriage, and my immediate perception of this only deepened the mystery that enveloped them. If the fault wasn't his and wasn't hers, then who was responsible for the shadow that hung over the house?

For the shadow was there. I could feel it, vague and dark, while we talked about the war and the remote possibilities of peace in the spring. Mrs. Vanderbridge looked young and lovely in her gown of white satin with pearls on her bosom, but her violet eyes were almost black in the candlelight, and I had a curious feeling that this blackness was the colour of thought. Something troubled her to despair, yet I was as positive as I could be of anything I had ever been told that she had breathed no word of this anxiety or distress to her husband. Devoted as they were, a nameless dread, fear, or apprehension divided them. It was the thing I had felt from the moment I entered the house; the thing I had heard in the tearful voice of the maid. One could scarcely call it horror, because it was too vague, too impalpable, for so vivid a name; yet, after all these quiet months, horror is the only word I can think of that in any way expresses the emotion which pervaded the house.

I had never seen so beautiful a dinner table, and I was gazing with pleasure at the damask and glass and silver—there was a silver basket of chrysanthemums, I remember, in the centre of the table—when I noticed a nervous movement of Mrs. Vanderbridge's head, and saw her glance hastily towards the door and the staircase beyond. We had been talking animatedly, and as·

Mrs. Vanderbridge turned away, I had just made a remark to her husband, who appeared to have fallen into a sudden fit of abstraction, and was gazing thoughtfully over his soup-plate at the white and yellow chrysanthemums. It occurred to me, while I watched him, that he was probably absorbed in some financial problem, and I regretted that I had been so careless as to speak to him. To my surprise, however, he replied immediately in a natural tone, and I saw, or imagined that I saw, Mrs. Vanderbridge throw me a glance of gratitude and relief. I can't remember what we were talking about, but I recall perfectly that the conversation kept up pleasantly, without a break, until dinner was almost half over. The roast had been served, and I was in the act of helping myself to potatoes, when I became aware that Mr. Vanderbridge had again fallen into his reverie. This time he scarcely seemed to hear his wife's voice when she spoke to him, and I watched the sadness cloud his face while he continued to stare straight ahead of him with a look that was almost yearning in its intensity.

Again I saw Mrs. Vanderbridge, with her nervous gesture, glance in the direction of the hall, and to my amazement, as she did so, a woman's figure glided noiselessly over the old Persian rug at the door, and entered the dining-room. I was wondering why no one spoke to her, why she spoke to no one, when I saw her sink into a chair on the other side of Mr. Vanderbridge and unfold her napkin. She was quite young, younger even than Mrs. Vanderbridge, and though she was not really beautiful, she was the most graceful creature I had ever imagined. Her dress was of grey stuff, softer and more clinging than silk, and of a peculiar misty texture and colour, and her parted hair lay like twilight on either side of her forehead. She was not like any one I had ever seen before—she appeared so much frailer, so much more elusive, as if she would vanish if you touched her. I can't describe, even months afterwards, the singular way in which she attracted and repelled me.

At first I glanced inquiringly at Mrs. Vanderbridge, hoping that she would introduce me, but she went on talking rapidly in an intense, quivering voice, without noticing the presence of her guest by so much as the lifting of her eyelashes. Mr. Vanderbridge still sat there, silent and detached, and all the time the eyes of the stranger—starry eyes with a mist over them—looked straight through me at the tapestried wall at my back. I knew she didn't see me and that it wouldn't have made the slightest difference to her if she had seen me. In spite of her grace and her girlishness I did not like her, and I felt that this aversion was not on my side alone. I do not know how I received the impression that she hated Mrs. Vanderbridge—never once had she glanced in her direction—yet I was aware, from the moment of her entrance, that she was bristling with animosity, though animosity is too strong a word for the resentful spite, like the jealous rage of a spoiled child, which gleamed now and then in her eyes. I couldn't think of her as wicked any more than I could think of a bad child as wicked. She was merely wilful and undisciplined and—I hardly know how to convey what I mean—elfish.

After her entrance the dinner dragged on heavily. Mrs. Vanderbridge still kept up her nervous chatter, but nobody listened, for I was too embarrassed to pay any attention to what she said, and Mr. Vanderbridge had never recovered from his abstraction. He was like a man in a dream, not observing a thing that happened before him, while the strange woman sat there in the candlelight with her curious look of vagueness and unreality. To my astonishment not even the servants appeared to notice her, and though she had unfolded her napkin when she sat down, she wasn't served with either the roast or the salad. Once or twice, particularly when a new course was served, I glanced at Mrs. Vanderbridge to see if she would rectify the mistake, but she kept her gaze fixed on her plate. It was just as if there were a conspiracy to ignore the presence of the stranger, though she had been, from the moment of her entrance, the dominant figure at the table. You tried to pretend she wasn't there, and yet you knew—you knew vividly that she was gazing insolently straight through you.

The dinner lasted, it seemed, for hours, and you may imagine my relief when at last Mrs. Vanderbridge rose and led the way back into the drawing-room. At first I thought the stranger would follow us, but when I glanced round from the hall she was still sitting there beside Mr. Vanderbridge, who was smoking a cigar with his coffee.

"Usually he takes his coffee with me," said Mrs. Vanderbridge, "but tonight he has things to think over."

"I thought he seemed absent-minded."

"You noticed it, then?" She turned to me with her straightforward glance. "I always wonder how much strangers notice. He hasn't been well of late, and he has these spells of depression. Nerves are dreadful things, aren't they?"

I laughed. "So I've heard, but I've never been able to afford them."

"Well, they do cost a great deal, don't they?" She had a trick of ending her sentences with a question. "I hope your room is comfortable, and that you don't feel timid about being alone on that floor. If you haven't nerves, you can't get nervous, can you?"

"No, I can't get nervous." Yet while I spoke, I was conscious of a shiver deep down in me, as if my senses reacted again to the dread that permeated the atmosphere.

As soon as I could, I escaped to my room, and I was sitting there over a book, when the maid—her name was Hopkins, I had discovered—came in on the pretext of inquiring if I had everything I needed. One of the innumerable servants had already turned down my bed, so when Hopkins appeared at the door, I suspected at once that there was a hidden motive underlying her ostensible purpose.

"Mrs. Vanderbridge told me to look after you," she began. "She is afraid you will be lonely until you learn the way of things."

"No, I'm not lonely," I answered. "I've never had time to be lonely."

"I used to be like that; but time hangs heavy on my hands now. That's why I've taken to knitting." She held out a grey yarn muffler. "I had an operation a year ago, and since then Mrs. Vanderbridge has had another maid—a French one—to sit up for her at night and undress her. She is always so fearful of overtaxing us, though there isn't really enough work for two lady's-maids, because she is so thoughtful that she never gives any trouble if she can help it."

"It must be nice to be rich," I said idly, as I turned a page of my book. Then I added almost before I realized what I was saying, "The other lady doesn't look as if she had so much money."

Her face turned paler if that were possible, and for a minute I thought she was going to faint. "The other lady?"

"I mean the one who came down late to dinner—the one in the grey dress. She wore no jewels, and her dress wasn't low in the neck."

"Then you saw her?" There was a curious flicker in her face as if her pallor came and went.

"We were at the table when she came in. Has Mr. Vanderbridge a secretary who lives in the house?"

"No, he hasn't a secretary except at his office. When he wants one at the house, he telephones to his office."

"I wondered why she came, for she didn't eat any dinner, and nobody spoke to her—not even Mr. Vanderbridge."

"Oh, he never speaks to her. Thank God, it hasn't come to that yet."

"Then why does she come? It must be dreadful to be treated like that, and before the servants, too. Does she come often?"

"There are months and months when she doesn't. I can always tell by the way Mrs. Vanderbridge picks up. You wouldn't know her, she is so full of life—the very picture of happiness. Then one evening she—the Other One,

I mean—comes back again, just as she did to-night, just as she did last summer, and it all begins over from the beginning."

"But can't they keep her out—the Other One? Why do they let her in?"

"Mrs. Vanderbridge tries hard. She tries all she can every minute. You saw her to-night?"

"And Mr. Vanderbridge? Can't he help her?"

She shook her head with an ominous gesture. "He doesn't know."

"He doesn't know she is there? Why, she was close by him. She never took her eyes off him except when she was staring through me at the wall."

"Oh, he knows she is there, but not in that way. He doesn't know that any one else knows."

I gave it up, and after a minute she said in a suppressed voice, "It seems strange that you should have seen her. I never have."

"But you know all about her."

"I know and I don't know. Mrs. Vanderbridge lets things drop some-times—she gets ill and feverish very easily—but she never tells me anything outright. She isn't that sort."

"Haven't the servants told you about her—the Other One?"

At this, I thought, she seemed startled. "Oh, they don't know anything to tell. They feel that something is wrong; that is why they never stay longer than a week or two—we've had eight butlers since autumn—but they never see what it is."

She stooped to pick up the ball of yarn which had rolled under my chair. "If the time ever comes when you can stand between them, you will do it?" she asked.

"Between Mrs. Vanderbridge and the Other One?"

Her look answered me.

"You think, then, that she means harm to her?"

"I don't know. Nobody knows—but she is killing her."

The clock struck ten, and I returned to my book with a yawn, while Hopkins gathered up her work and went out, after wishing me a formal goodnight. The odd part about our secret conferences was that as soon as they were over, we began to pretend so elaborately to each other that they had never been.

"I'll tell Mrs. Vanderbridge that you are very comfortable," was the last remark Hopkins made before she sidled out of the door and left me alone with the mystery. It was one of those situations—I am obliged to repeat this over and over—that was too preposterous for me to believe in even while I was surrounded and overwhelmed by its reality. I didn't dare face what I thought, I didn't dare face even what I felt; but I went to bed shivering in a warm room, while I resolved passionately that if the chance ever came to me I would stand between Mrs. Vanderbridge and this unknown evil that threatened her.

In the morning Mrs. Vanderbridge went out shopping, and I did not see her until the evening, when she passed me on the staircase as she was going out to dinner and the opera. She was radiant in blue velvet, with diamonds in her hair and at her throat, and I wondered again how any one so lovely could ever be troubled.

"I hope you had a pleasant day, Miss Wrenn," she said kindly. "I have been too busy to get off any letters, but to-morrow we shall begin early." Then, as if from an afterthought, she looked back and added, "There are some new novels in my sitting-room. You might care to look over them."

When she had gone, I went upstairs to the sitting-room and turned over the books, but I couldn't, to save my life, force an interest in printed romances after meeting Mrs. Vanderbridge and remembering the mystery that surrounded her. I wondered if "the Other One," as Hopkins called her, lived in the house, and I was still wondering this when the maid came in and began putting the table to rights.

"Do they dine out often?" I asked.

"They used to, but since Mr. Vanderbridge hasn't been so well, Mrs. Vanderbridge doesn't like to go without him. She only went to-night because he begged her to."

She had barely finished speaking when the door opened, and Mr. Vanderbridge came in and sat down in one of the big velvet chairs before the wood fire. He had not noticed us, for one of his moods was upon him, and I was about to slip out as noiselessly as I could when I saw that the Other One was standing in the patch of firelight on the hearthrug. I had not seen her come in, and Hopkins evidently was still unaware of her presence, for while I was watching, I saw the maid turn towards her with a fresh log for the fire. At the moment it occurred to me that Hopkins must be either blind or drunk, for without hesitating in her advance, she moved on the stranger, holding the huge hickory log out in front of her. Then, before I could utter a sound or stretch out a hand to stop her, I saw her walk straight through the grey figure and carefully place the log on the andirons.

So she isn't real, after all, she is merely a phantom, I found myself thinking, as I fled from the room, and hurried along the hall to the staircase. She is only a ghost, and nobody believes in ghosts any longer. She is something that I know doesn't exist, yet even, though she can't possibly be, I can swear that I have seen her. My nerves were so shaken by the discovery that as soon as I reached my room I sank in a heap on the rug, and it was here that Hopkins found me a little later when she came to bring me an extra blanket.

"You looked so upset I thought you might have seen something," she said. "Did anything happen while you were in the room?"

"She was there all the time—every blessed minute. You walked right through her when you put the log on the fire. Is it possible that you didn't see her?"

"No, I didn't see anything out of the way." She was plainly frightened. "Where was she standing?"

"On the hearthrug in front of Mr. Vanderbridge. To reach the fire you had to walk straight through her, for she didn't move. She didn't give way an inch."

"Oh, she never gives way. She never gives way living or dead."

This was more than human nature could stand.

"In heaven's name," I cried irritably, "who is she?"

"Don't you know?" She appeared genuinely surprised. "Why, she is the other Mrs. Vanderbridge. She died fifteen years ago, just a year after they were married, and people say a scandal was hushed up about her, which he never knew. She isn't a good sort, that's what I think of her, though they say he almost worshipped her."

"And she still has this hold on him?"

"He can't shake it off, that's what's the matter with him, and if it goes on, he will end his days in an asylum. You see, she was very young, scarcely more than a girl, and he got the idea in his head that it was marrying him that killed her. If you want to know what I think, I believe she puts it there for a purpose."

"You mean—?" I was so completely at sea that I couldn't frame a rational question.

"I mean she haunts him purposely in order to drive him out of his mind. She was always that sort, jealous and exacting, the kind that clutches and strangles a man, and I've often thought, though I've no head for speculation, that we carry into the next world the traits and feelings that have got the better of us in this one. It seems to me only common sense to believe that we're obliged to work them off somewhere until we are free of them. That is the way my first lady used to talk, anyhow, and I've never found anybody that could give me a more sensible idea."

"And isn't there any way to stop it? What has Mrs. Vanderbridge done?"

"Oh, she can't do anything now. It has got beyond her, though she has had doctor after doctor, and tried everything she could think of. But, you see, she is handicapped because she can't mention it to her husband. He doesn't know that she knows."

"And she won't tell him?"

"She is the sort that would die first—just the opposite from the Other One—for she leaves him free, she never clutches and strangles. It isn't her way." For a moment she hesitated, and then added grimly—"I've wondered if you could do anything?"

"If I could? Why, I am a perfect stranger to them all."

"That's why I've been thinking it. Now, if you could corner her some day—the Other One—and tell her up and down to her face what you think of her."

The idea was so ludicrous that it made me laugh in spite of my shaken nerves. "They would fancy me out of my wits! Imagine stopping an apparition and telling it what you think of it!"

"Then you might try talking it over with Mrs. Vanderbridge. It would help her to know that you see her also."

But the next morning, when I went down to Mrs. Vanderbridge's room, I found that she was too ill to see me. At noon a trained nurse came on the case, and for a week we took our meals together in the morning-room upstairs. She appeared competent enough, but I am sure that she didn't so much as suspect that there was anything wrong in the house except the influenza which had attacked Mrs. Vanderbridge the night of the opera. Never once during that week did I catch a glimpse of the Other One, though I felt her presence whenever I left my room and passed through the hall below. I knew all the time as well as if I had seen her that she was hidden there, watching, watching—

At the end of the week Mrs. Vanderbridge sent for me to write some letters, and when I went into her room, I found her lying on the couch with a tea-table in front of her. She asked me to make the tea because she was still so weak, and I saw that she looked flushed and feverish, and that her eyes were unnaturally large and bright. I hoped she wouldn't talk to me, because people in that state are apt to talk too much and then to blame the listener; but I had hardly taken my seat at the tea-table before she said in a hoarse voice—the cold had settled on her chest:

"Miss Wrenn, I have wanted to ask you ever since the other evening—did you—did you see anything unusual at dinner? From your face when you came out I thought—I thought—"

I met this squarely. "That I might have? Yes, I did see something."

"You saw her?"

"I saw a woman come in and sit down at the table, and I wondered why no one served her. I saw her quite distinctly."

"A small woman, thin and pale, in a grey dress?"

"She was so vague and—and misty, you know what I mean, that it is hard to describe her; but I should know her again anywhere. She wore her hair parted and drawn down over her ears. It was very dark and fine—as fine as spun silk."

We were speaking in low voices, and unconsciously we had moved closer together while my idle hands left the tea things.

"Then you know," she said earnestly, "that she really comes—that I am not out of my mind—that it is not an hallucination?"

"I know that I saw her. I would swear to it. But doesn't Mr. Vanderbridge see her also?"

"Not as we see her. He thinks that she is in his mind only." Then, after an uncomfortable silence, she added suddenly, "She is really a thought, you know. She is his thought of her—but he doesn't know that she is visible to the rest of us."

"And he brings her back by thinking of her?"

She leaned nearer while a quiver passed over her features and the flush deepened in her cheeks. "That is the only way she comes back—the only way she has the power to come back—as a thought. There are months and months when she leaves us in peace because he is thinking of other things, but of late, since his illness, she has been with him almost constantly." A sob broke from her, and she buried her face in her hands. "I suppose she is always trying to come—only she is too vague—and hasn't any form that we can see except when he thinks of her as she used to look when she was alive. His thought of her is like that, hurt and tragic and revengeful. You see, he feels that he ruined her life because she died when the child was coming—a month before it would have been born."

"And if he were to see her differently, would she change? Would she cease to be revengeful if he stopped thinking her so?"

"God only knows. I've wondered and wondered how I might move her to pity."

"Then you feel that she is really there? That she exists outside of his mind?"

"How can I tell? What do any of us know of the world beyond? She exists as much as I exist to you or you to me. Isn't thought all that there is—all that we know?"

This was deeper than I could follow; but in order not to appear stupid, I murmured sympathetically,

"And does she make him unhappy when she comes?"

"She is killing him—and me. I believe that is why she does it."

"Are you sure that she could stay away? When he thinks of her isn't she obliged to come back?"

"Oh, I've asked that question over and over! In spite of his calling her so unconsciously, I believe she comes of her own will. I have always the feeling—it has never left me for an instant—that she could appear differently if she would. I have studied her for years until I know her like a book, and though she is only an apparition, I am perfectly positive that she wills evil to us both. Don't you think he would change that if he could? Don't you think he would make her kind instead of vindictive if he had the power?"

"But if he could remember her as loving and tender?"

"I don't know. I give it up—but it is killing me."

It *was* killing her. As the days passed I began to realize that she had spoken the truth. I watched her bloom fade slowly and her lovely features grow pinched and thin like the features of a starved person. The harder she fought the apparition, the more I saw that the battle was a losing one, and that she was only wasting her strength. So impalpable yet so pervasive was the enemy that it was like fighting a poisonous odour. There was nothing to wrestle with, and yet there was everything. The struggle was wearing her out—was, as she had said, actually "killing her"; but the physician who dosed her daily with drugs—there was need now of a physician—had not the faintest idea of the malady he was treating. In those dreadful days I think that even Mr. Vanderbridge hadn't a suspicion of the truth. The past was with him so constantly—he was so steeped in the memories of it—that the present was scarcely more than a dream to him. It was, you see, a reversal of the natural order of things; the thought had become more vivid to his perceptions than any object. The phantom had been victorious so far, and he was like a man recovering from the effects of a narcotic. He was only half awake, only half alive to the events through which he lived and the people who surrounded him. Oh, I realize that I am telling my story badly!—that I am slurring over the significant interludes! My mind has dealt so long with external details that I have almost forgotten the words that express invisible things. Though the phantom in the house was more real to me than the bread I ate or the floor on which I trod, I can give you no impression of the atmosphere in which we lived day after day—of the suspense, of the dread of something we could not define, of the brooding horror that seemed to lurk in the shadows of the firelight, of the feeling always, day and night, that some unseen person was watching us. How Mrs. Vanderbridge stood it without losing her mind, I have never known; and even now I am not sure that she could have kept her reason if the end had not come when it did. That I accidentally brought it about is one of the things in my life I am most thankful to remember.

It was an afternoon in late winter, and I had just come up from luncheon, when Mrs. Vanderbridge asked me to empty an old desk in one of the upstairs rooms. "I am sending all the furniture in that room away," she said; "it was bought in a bad period, and I want to clear it out and make room for the lovely things we picked up in Italy. There is nothing in the desk worth saving except some old letters from Mr. Vanderbridge's mother before her marriage."

I was glad that she could think of anything so practical as furniture, and it was with relief that I followed her into the dim, rather musty room over the library, where the windows were all tightly closed. Years ago, Hopkins had once told me, the first Mrs. Vanderbridge had used this room for a while, and after her death her husband had been in the habit of shutting himself up alone here in the evenings. This, I inferred, was the secret reason why my employer was sending the furniture away. She had resolved to clear the house of every association with the past.

For a few minutes we sorted the letters in the drawers of the desk, and then, as I expected, Mrs. Vanderbridge became suddenly bored by the task she had undertaken. She was subject to these nervous reactions, and I was prepared for them even when they seized her so spasmodically. I remember that she was in the very act of glancing over an old letter when she rose impatiently, tossed it into the fire unread, and picked up a magazine she had thrown down on a chair.

"Go over them by yourself, Miss Wrenn," she said, and it was characteristic of her nature that she should assume my trustworthiness. "If anything seems worth saving you can file it—but I'd rather die than have to wade through all this."

They were mostly personal letters, and while I went on, carefully filing them, I thought how absurd it was of people to preserve so many papers that were entirely without value. Mr. Vanderbridge I had imagined to be a methodical man, and yet the disorder of the desk produced a painful effect on my systematic temperament. The drawers were filled with letters evidently unsorted, for now and then I came upon a mass of business receipts and acknowledgments crammed in among wedding invitations or letters from some elderly lady, who wrote interminable pale epistles in the finest and most feminine of Italian hands. That a man of Mr. Vanderbridge's wealth and position should have been so careless about his correspondence amazed me until I recalled the dark hints Hopkins had dropped in some of her midnight conversations. Was it possible that he had actually lost his reason for months after the death of his first wife, during that year when he had shut himself alone with her memory? The question was still in my mind when my eyes fell on the envelope in my hand, and I saw that it was addressed to Mrs. Roger Vanderbridge. So this explained, in a measure at least, the carelessness and the disorder! The desk was not his, but hers, and after her death he had used it only during those desperate months when he barely opened a letter. What he had done in those long evenings when he sat alone here it was beyond me to imagine. Was it any wonder that the brooding should have permanently unbalanced his mind?

At the end of an hour I had sorted and filed the papers, with the intention of asking Mrs. Vanderbridge if she wished me to destroy the ones that seemed to be unimportant. The letters she had instructed me to keep had not come to my hand, and I was about to give up the search for them, when, in shaking the lock of one of the drawers, the door of a secret compartment fell open, and I discovered a dark object, which crumbled and dropped apart when I touched it. Bending nearer, I saw that the crumbled mass had once been a bunch of flowers, and that a streamer of purple ribbon still held together the frail structure of wire and stems. In this drawer someone had hidden a sacred treasure, and moved by a sense of romance and adventure, I gathered the dust tenderly in tissue paper, and prepare to take it downstairs to Mrs. Vanderbridge. It was not until then that some letters tied loosely together with a silver cord caught my eye, and while I picked them up, I remember thinking that they must be the ones for which I had been looking so long. Then, as the cord broke in my grasp and I gathered the letters from the lid of the desk, a word or two flashed back at me through the torn edges of the envelopes, and I realized that they were love letters written, I surmised, some fifteen years ago, by Mr. Vanderbridge to his first wife.

"It may hurt her to see them," I thought, "but I don't dare destroy them. There is nothing I can do except give them to her."

As I left the room, carrying the letters and the ashes of the flowers, the idea of taking them to the husband instead of to the wife flashed through my mind. Then—I think it was some jealous feeling about the phantom that decided me—I quickened my steps to a run down the staircase.

"They would bring her back. He would think of her more than ever," I told myself, "so he shall never see them. He shall never see them if I can prevent it." I believe it occurred to me that Mrs. Vanderbridge would be generous enough to give them to him—she was capable of rising above her jealousy, I knew—but I determined that she shouldn't do it until I had reasoned it out with her. "If anything on earth would bring back the Other One for good, it would be his seeing these old letters," I repeated as I hastened down the hall.

Mrs. Vanderbridge was lying on the couch before the fire, and I noticed at once that she had been crying. The drawn look in her sweet face went to my heart, and I felt that I would do anything in the world to comfort her. Though she had a book in her hand, I could see that she had not been reading. The electric lamp on the table by her side was already lighted, leaving the rest of the room in shadow, for it was a grey day with a biting edge of snow in the air. It was all very charming in the soft light; but as soon as I entered I had a feeling of oppression that made me want to run out into the wind. If you have ever lived in a haunted house—a house pervaded by an unforgettable past—you will understand the sensation of melancholy that crept over me the minute the shadows began to fall. It was not in myself—of this I am sure, for I have naturally a cheerful temperament—it was in the space that surrounded us and the air we breathed.

I explained to her about the letters, and then, kneeling on the rug in front of her, I emptied the dust of the flowers into the fire. There was, though I hate to confess it, a vindictive pleasure in watching it melt into the flames; and at the moment I believe I could have burned the apparition as thankfully. The more I saw of the Other One, the more I found myself accepting Hopkins's judgment of her. Yes, her behaviour, living and dead, proved that she was not "a good sort."

My eyes were still on the flames when a sound from Mrs. Vanderbridge— half a sigh, half a sob—made me turn quickly and look up at her.

"But this isn't his handwriting," she said in a puzzled tone. "They are love letters, and they are to her—but they are not from him." For a moment or two she was silent, and I heard the pages rustle in her hands as she turned them impatiently. "They are not from him," she repeated presently, with an exultant ring in her voice. "They are written after her marriage, but they are from another man." She was as sternly tragic as an avenging fate. "She wasn't faithful to him while she lived. She wasn't faithful to him even while he was hers—"

With a spring I had risen from my knees and was bending over her.

"Then you can save him from her. You can win him back! You have only to show him the letters, and he will believe."

"Yes, I have only to show him the letters." She was looking beyond me into the dusky shadows of the firelight, as if she saw the Other One standing there before her. "I have only to show him the letters," I knew now that she was not speaking to me, "and he will believe."

"Her power over him will be broken," I cried out. "He will think of her differently. Oh, don't you see? Can't you see? It is the only way to make him think of her differently. It is the only way to break for ever the thought that draws her back to him."

"Yes, I see, it is the only way," she said slowly; and the words were still on her lips when the door opened and Mr. Vanderbridge entered.

"I came for a cup of tea," he began, and added with playful tenderness, "What is the only way?"

It was the crucial moment, I realized—it was the hour of destiny for these two—and while he sank wearily into a chair, I looked imploringly at his wife and then at the letters lying scattered loosely about her. If I had had my will I should have flung them at him with a violence which would have startled him out of his lethargy. Violence, I felt, was what he needed—violence, a storm, tears, reproaches—all the things he would never get from his wife.

For a minute or two she sat there, with the letters before her, and watched him with her thoughtful and tender gaze. I knew from her face, so lovely and yet so sad, that she was looking again at invisible things—at the soul of the man she loved, not at the body. She saw him, detached and spiritualized, and she saw also the Other One—for while we waited I became slowly aware of the apparition in the firelight—of the white face and the cloudy hair and the look of animosity and bitterness in the eyes. Never before had I been so profoundly convinced of the malignant will veiled by that thin figure. It was as if the visible form were only a spiral of grey smoke covering a sinister purpose.

"The only way," said Mrs. Vanderbridge, "is to fight fairly even when one fights evil." Her voice was like a bell, and as she spoke, she rose from the couch and stood there in her glowing beauty confronting the pale ghost of the past. There was a light about her that was almost unearthly—the light of triumph. The radiance of it blinded me for an instant. It was like a flame, clearing the atmosphere of all that was evil, of all that was poisonous and deadly. She was looking directly at the phantom, and there was no hate in her voice—there was only a great pity, a great sorrow and sweetness.

"I can't fight you that way," she said, and I knew that for the first time she had swept aside subterfuge and evasion, and was speaking straight to the presence before her. "After all, you are dead and I am living, and I cannot fight you that way. I give up everything. I give him back to you. Nothing is mine that I cannot win and keep fairly. Nothing is mine that belongs really to you."

Then, while Mr. Vanderbridge rose, with a start of fear, and came towards her, she bent quickly, and flung the letters into the fire. When he would have stooped to gather the unburned pages, her lovely flowing body curved between his hands and the flames; and so transparent, so ethereal she looked, that I saw—or imagined that I saw—the firelight shine through her. "The only way, my dear, is the right way," she said softly.

The next instant—I don't know to this day how or when it began—I was aware that the apparition had drawn nearer, and that the dread and fear, the evil purpose, were no longer a part of her. I saw her clearly for a moment—saw her as I had never seen her before—young and gentle and—yes, this is the only word for it—loving. It was just as if a curse had turned into a blessing, for, while she stood there, I had a curious sensation of being enfolded in a kind of spiritual glow and comfort—only words are useless to describe the feeling because it wasn't in the least like anything else I had ever known in my life. It was light without heat, glow without light—and yet it was none of these things. The nearest I can come to it is to call it a sense of blessedness—of blessedness that made you at peace with everything you had once hated.

Not until afterwards did I realize that it was the victory of good over evil. Not until afterwards did I discover that Mrs. Vanderbridge had triumphed over the past in the only way that she could triumph. She had won, not by resisting, but by accepting; not by violence, but by gentleness; not by grasping, but by renouncing. Oh, long, long afterwards, I knew that she had robbed the phantom of power over her by robbing it of hatred. She had changed the thought of the past, in that lay her victory.

At the moment I did not understand this. I did not understand it even when I looked again for the apparition in the firelight, and saw that it had vanished. There was nothing there—nothing except the pleasant flicker of light and shadow on the old Persian rug.

<hr />

MRS. WILSON WOODROW
(ca. 1870–1935)

Nancy Mann Waddel Woodrow was born in Ohio around 1870. She received a private education and in 1896 commenced a newspaper career as assistant editor of Ohio's *Chillicothe Daily News*. In 1897 she married Dr. James Wilson Woodrow, and it is his name that she used afterward as her pen name. Although Woodrow published short fiction in the leading magazines, she was known primarily as a novelist. Unfortunately, little information is available about her today. She was certainly well read in the gothic, as "Secret Chambers" reveals. The scene in which the servant Judy shows Sylvia the chambers of her beloved first mistress is reminiscent of an incident in Ann Radcliffe's *The Mysteries of Udolpho*. In turn, Daphne DuMaurier's *Rebecca* contains a startlingly similar scene in which the housekeeper, Mrs. Danvers, shows the nameless second wife the room and wardrobe of the compelling first Mrs. de Winter. "Secret Chambers" was published in *Harper's* in June 1909.

Secret Chambers

NATURALLY, THEY WERE DISCUSSING THE COMMISSION AS they sat drinking their coffee in the drawing-room after dinner—Arnold Hartzfield, the artist who had received it, his mother, and Sylvia, his wife; and although it had been the one topic mentioned among them for the last few days, it still remained the immediate and exclusive interest in the lives of these three people. Why not? It was a matter of vast importance in Arnold's career. One of the larger American towns had recently builded a magnificent public library, and Hartzfield had been asked to paint ten pictures to fill the ten large panels.

"Isn't it odd, mother," Arnold's hazel eyes were brilliant with twinkling reflections, and there was a sparkle, even a momentary content, on his keen, eager face, "and isn't it fortunate that I should actually have a studio to my hand so near L——? A railway runs through the village now, and it's only an hour's ride to town. A beautifully restful old spot! I'm speaking of Altamont, Sylvia, the place mother owned and gave to me, and where I built an outdoor studio. Whew! The dreams I used to dream there!" He passed his hand across his brow in brief reverie, his face again assuming its customary expression in repose, a sort of baffled, disappointed eagerness, repression, even a faint cynical bitterness; but these in turn faded in the glow of purpose, the new determination of achievement which the bestowal of the Commission had aroused in him.

"Of course," he went on, "it is absolutely necessary that I should be near the library for a time and give a thorough study to the lighting and proportions. So," in quite matter-of-fact tones, "we will go back there instead of my trying to do the work here."

Sylvia looked up bewildered, and gazed about the harmonious room, admittedly one of the most artistic in Paris, with its pieces of silver and pewter shining against the subdued peacock hues of walls and hangings, blues and greens and bronzes suavely blended. What had he been saying? Impossibilities.

But although her first quick glance about had been one of dismay, she said nothing. That was like Sylvia. She was not in the least impulsive, and this quality of inner balance and harmony, the antithesis of his own mercurial temperament, was what had at first attracted Hartzfield to her.

His mother was the first to break the silence. "Do you remember the picture of Love that you painted at Altamont, Arnold? I wish—" she paused suddenly, with a hasty, almost furtive glance at Sylvia.

Hartzfield threw back his head with a flash of storm in his eyes. "I beg you will never mention that subject to me again," he cried, with harsh irritability. He pushed back his chair gratingly and left the room; a few moments later the two women heard him open the piano and begin to play, crashing volcanic chords.

"Mother," said Sylvia presently, her clear, gray eyes fixed steadily on those of the older woman, "what did you mean and why was Arnold annoyed when that picture, of Love, was mentioned?"

"Nothing, really," she said, hesitating, and frankly appearing to ponder. "I assure you of that, Sylvia. A buried incident in his career. Since he has not spoken of it to you, and since you are a wise woman, I advise you to let it sink into oblivion, but—" she spoke with an earnestness and depth of feeling unusual with her. "Take my advice. Amuse yourself by having the whole house done over as soon as you get to Altamont."

"But why?" asked Sylvia, in surprise. "Arnold said that it was charming."
"He forgets," said Mrs. Hartzfield, shortly. "All men forget. He has never
been near the place since Adele died, and at that time, in the first—" she
hesitated—"sentimentality," Sylvia noticed that she did not say grief—"he
gave orders that nothing be changed; but I stayed there a month, two years
ago, and let me tell you, my dear, that I have never had anything get so on
my nerves. I am not impressionable nor superstitious, but—" she shivered
and lifted her eyebrows expressively.

"Why?" asked Sylvia.

Mrs. Hartzfield threw out her hands with an expansive gesture. "The
whole place is full of her," she said—"full of her. She was a feminine Narcissus, and every person she met must be a pool and reflect her. She would
tolerate no backgrounds, nor vistas, nor any relieving scenery; she wanted to
fill the whole picture from frame to frame, and she could not even have
conceived the idea of being one of a group. When she entered a room, she
filled it. She filled a house. She took complete possession of your imagination, your will, or she knew the reason why, and she crowded everything else
out of Arnold. In the few years they were married, the promise of his youth,
his high dreams, his consecration of purpose, all went down in ashes. You
did not know him in those first years after her death. When you met him,
his interest in his work was gradually reviving, his individuality was beginning to assert itself, to flutter vaguely its maimed wings; and you, Sylvia,"
the bitterness of her tones lost in unwonted tenderness, "you have helped to
heal and restore and obliterate."

Sylvia laid her cheek against the older woman's in one of her rare caresses;
but she did not speak. Her eyes had a peculiar inward glow. She had never
thought much about Adele before, but Mrs. Hartzfield's words had aroused
a curiosity, acute, sudden, almost stinging. Arnold rarely spoke of his first
wife, and then almost casually, and Mrs. Hartzfield had never mentioned
her to Sylvia before. And now, all at once, Sylvia felt that she longed,
thirsted to know more of this love of Arnold's youth.

"Were you not fond of her? Was she not attractive?" she asked.

"Oh, adorable, in a way," returned Mrs. Hartzfield, carelessly, "but the
most pervasive—yes, altogether the most pervasive—personality I have ever
encountered."

"Was she very delicate? An invalid?"

"Adele?" in evident surprise. "Oh, not at all. Full of life."

"Of what did she die?"

Mrs. Hartzfield was intently examining a photograph on the table. "Oh, her death was very sudden." Her tone was infused with a cold, even curt, finality. "But why," impatiently, "are we on such depressing themes?"

That was the last as well as the first time that the subject either of Adele or of the picture was ever mentioned between them. In the late summer Arnold and Sylvia sailed, and whatever apprehensions her homesick heart may have nursed on the voyage, Sylvia felt them all vanish on the day they arrived at Altamont. She always retained a delightful memory of the drive first through the village and then through a long stretch of woodland. She affirmed that it was a revelation of color to her; a sky as blue and as brilliant as a sapphire, and against it bold columns of maple-flame, the yellow, fluttering gold of elms and beeches, and the gorgeous sombre bronze of oaks; a splendid trumpet-call of color lifting the heart as on waves of music.

The house stood on a little knoll, hardly a hill, but rising ground. Houses which have harbored many generations have a very distinct character of their own, and this mansion was no exception to the rule. The impression it created on the mind was of a sort of stately serenity. It was built in the Colonial style, with a row of Corinthian pillars across the front, and a flight of stone steps leading up to a flagged porch. Of a soft cream-color, it was flanked on either side by some fine old oaks and beeches, not too near to impede the view of far-stretching woods and noble hills.

"By Jove!" said Hartzfield, his head out of the carriage window, "the old place isn't so bad, after all, is it? That is my studio yonder, Sylvia," pointing out a small building at some distance from the house. "And here is good old Judy to meet us," as a tall, dark, angular Irish-woman came across the porch and to the top of the steps to welcome them.

Judy herself showed the new mistress through the hall and up the wide, shallow stairs to a suite of three rooms.

"These are the guest chambers, Mrs. Hartzfield,"—her words allayed a latent and shrinking fear of Sylvia's that through some stupidity she might have been given the apartments of Adele. "The bedroom, bath, and sitting-room. They are all done in blue, you see. I hope you like blue?"

As Judy asked this commonplace question, Sylvia was struck by something in her manner; she seemed to wait with anxiety the answer.

"Indeed, I am very fond of blue," replied Sylvia. "It is my favorite color. I will slip into another gown and then come down. I am hungry. Will dinner be ready soon?"

"It shall be served whenever you wish, Mrs. Hartzfield." Judy was already unpacking the trunks with the skill and touch of much experience.

Half an hour later, Sylvia was smiling at Arnold across the dinner table.

"Judy is wonderful, an artist!" she exclaimed. "Look at the arrangement of those flowers! It is worthy of Japan. But, Arnold," as a beautiful dish of grapes and peaches was offered her, "is this an American custom, having fruit served first at dinner?"

"An American custom!" he repeated. "Oh dear, no. It is a stupid custom of this house." His mouth twisted wryly. "Abolish it. Abolish it by all means."

"Why? It is rather odd and pleasing." Then, a few moments later: "Arnold! What dreams of candle-shades! Ah," examining them more closely, "they have been painted by no tyro. Have you looked at them?"

Arnold barely glanced at the pink candle-shades, painted with tiny crimson roses wreathing the miniatures of lovely women.

"Yes," went on Sylvia, "done by a master. Sorchon? Would he condescend—"

There was a sardonic smile on Hartzfield's face. His eyes were hard. Sylvia did not know before that hazel eyes could look like steel.

"No," he said, grimly. "Emphatically Sorchon would not condescend. It was I—I."

"You!" she cried, incredulously. "You who must always have a canvas as wide as a church door!"

He was looking at her with a peculiar intensity, and yet she felt as if he did not see her at all. His mouth was twisted in a smile of cynical mirth, the steel of his eyes flashed. "My hair was clipped to the roots, and my eyes were blinded, and I was put in the treadmill." He passed his hand over the thick, short growth. "I resisted. Believe me, I resisted; but Delilah is sure to win."

He twirled one of the candle-shades nearest him for a few minutes, his face still contracted in that distorted smile; and then slightly shrugging his shoulders after his mother's fashion, devoted himself to his dinner.

He scarcely spoke again, and at the conclusion of the meal wandered into the hall, and opening the piano, began to play; and Sylvia, after listening a bit, got up from her chair and strolled restlessly about. Most of the rooms on the first floor opened into the hall, and they were all brilliantly lighted, apparently inviting inspection. Her first impression of the house, gained from its exterior, was but enhanced and confirmed by her view of the interior. It was remarkably light and spacious, one might say even gay in effect.

"I wonder if I am out of the picture completely," smiled Sylvia to herself. "This seems the chosen nest, the loved retreat of an enchantingly pretty and coquettish woman. If my grave and sedate self is to be part of the composition, I should be in the sombre and flowing robes of a French abbess."

She had moved slowly through the library and a charming sitting-room, and had now reached the drawing-room. It was by far the most brilliant apartment of the series, lacking entirely the rather severe formality characteristic of drawing-rooms in general. All in pink and silver, it gave out a sheen and shimmer that Sylvia found almost dazzling.

Overcrowded, overdecorated as it was, its ornaments, many of them, beautiful and unique, yet Sylvia's eye was almost immediately caught and held by a picture on the opposite wall, the portrait of a beautiful woman. Her exquisitely rounded shoulders rose from billows of tulle which fell low over the arms; the head, literally sunning over with curls, was bent, and the eyes glanced upward through long lashes with an arch and petulant coquetry.

"Pretty creature!" exclaimed Sylvia. Then, which a shock, followed by a vivid increase of interest, she realized that this must be Adele.

She had been standing with one hand on the back of a straight little chair, and now she drew it toward her and sat down, the involuntary smile with which we greet an image of beauty fading from her face. What radiance! Here in this room, so decorated that it gave out sparkles like a jewel, where there were any number of objects, each beautiful in itself, to attract the attention, the picture dominated and eclipsed them all. Sylvia felt as if she had never seen feminine loveliness before, nor realized its possibilities for expressing the joy of life. But as she continued to study the portrait she saw there was that in the face which all the glow and radiance of a most seductive beauty but thinly masked. It had been in the flesh a mutable face, and as Sylvia continued to gaze steadily at it she seemed to see it change before her eyes. There was something in those pictured eyes that mocked and refuted the appealing sweetness of that rose-leaf smile. He who ran might read that it was an emotional face passionate to weakness; but few would discern beneath that soft, peach-bloom flesh the iron of a powerful will and of a tenacious and unscrupulous purpose.

Sylvia did not see all this clarity, but something of it she divined dimly and in part. "What a power!" she muttered, rising—"what a power!" and then stopped suddenly; the portrait appeared to surround her, for the several large mirrors which the room contained seemed to give back a thousand reflections of it. Her own image, too, was presented from half a dozen angles. Slender, erect, her long, dull blue gown falling about her, her pale, upheld, cameo face, the dark, cloudy hair—yet she, the living, breathing woman, was as the shadow, while the portrait, a thing of paint, conveyed infinitely more effectively the illusion of life, the pride of the flesh.

She strolled out into the hall again. A wood fire was burning on the broad hearth, there were no other lights, and Arnold still sat at the piano; but the music his fingers evoked was evidently the mere accompaniment of his thoughts. His head was thrown back, his eyes gazed unseeingly before him, narrowed, concentrated, introspective. He did not even see Sylvia as she stood for a moment beside him. He had entirely abandoned himself to the absorbed contemplation of the vision. The creative mood was upon him. These were the signs by which she had grown to recognize it. Noiselessly she moved away from him and sank softly into a chair by the fire. Even before their marriage she had become accustomed to these moods and knew when to efface herself. Their love, she rejoiced to think, had been an unhindered progression. Begun in genuine comradeship, it seemed to her that they were always graduating through various phases of friendship into an ever rarer and more understanding love and sympathy.

For perhaps an hour they sat there, she gazing into the flames, and he drifting from one bit of melody into another, until at last he closed with a crash of chords and jumped to his feet.

"Sylvia!" he cried, his eyes shining, his face palely irradiated, "I've got it, the whole conception! It has been more or less hazy, lacking coherence and definiteness. Oh, you can't dream how disturbing that is! But now it is perfectly clear. I shall begin work tomorrow."

"Oh, what is it?" she cried, all eager sympathy.

"No. I shall keep it for a surprise. Oh, truly," at her obvious disappointment, "I am not saying that to tease you; but because I value your criticism above that of any one I know, and I am determined in this important instance to have the benefit of your first, fresh impression of the completed work."

"Very well," she smiled, although a bit ruefully. "I see what you mean, and if I can help you best that way, well and good; but I cannot pretend that I am not disappointed, because I am dreadfully. I thought the Commission would be our principal interest and topic of conversation here; but I shall manage to put in my time very well without you, since I have to. It is a charming, restful spot, and I shall devote my time to my music and those other studies that I have been meaning to take up for a long time."

For the next two or three weeks the weather continued fine, October at its mellowest and best, and Sylvia spent the greater part of each day out-of-doors. She never grew tired of wandering through the woods, watching the leaves flutter down through the dreamy sunlight, and the hazes on the hills melt through all the shades of sun-dusted violet and amethyst. But in spite of her books and her music, the studies that she had contemplated with so much enthusiasm, she suffered a growing dread of her evenings—in fact, of any of the time that she must remain indoors; for, take herself to task as she would for such irrational vagaries, she felt more and more during the hours she spent within the house as if she were not the rather solitary mistress of Arnold's home, but a guest thrown into a constant enforced intimacy with her hostess.

One day Judy suggested to Sylvia that she make a tour of the house. It seemed only fitting that as mistress of the mansion she should do so, and Sylvia assented. Over the whole place, from attic to cellar, they went, Sylvia bestowing encomiums on the perfect order in which everything was kept. But when Judy unlocked the door leading to Adele's apartments, Sylvia was aware of a mental reluctance, a dread of entering, and yet a tingling curiosity which would not be assuaged save by a sight of these rooms which had always been kept just as Adele left them.

As Judy stood aside for her to enter, Sylvia thought of all the tales she had read in which the apartments of the departed are kept intact, and almost she expected to be met by a waft of musty air, laden with dead and sorrowful memories; but the sunlight streamed through the open windows, and the breath of the autumn morning was sweet and fresh. In the draught created by the opening and closing of doors there was the stir and movement of draperies, the sudden sweep inward of a long silken curtain, creating the momentary illusion of the advance of a rose-gowned, buoyant figure, an illusion enhanced by the wafting fragrance of roses and jasmine with which the very hangings on the walls were impregnated; and the shimmer and play of moted sunbeams over white rugs and polished floor was like dancing feet running to greet a guest.

The rooms were crowded, full of all the thousand and one absurd costly trinkets that Adele had loved, and portraits, photographs, taken at every angle and in every possible type of costume, filled every available space.

"Would you like to see her dresses?" asked Judy. "There are presses full of them."

"Oh, no, no, no!" cried Sylvia, sharply. "I couldn't pry like that."

Judy glanced at her with an odd, grim little smile. "She'd have rummaged through everything before now," she said.

Sylvia had picked up a photograph in an ornate gold and silver frame. "How lovely she must have been!"

"There's no photograph or even paintings that can give an idea of her,"

Judy said. "The photographs can't give her color and the paintings can't give her life, not even an idea of it. That's what she was, all life and color. She could wheedle a stick or a stone, and she did it, too. She couldn't let anything pass her without paying toll. She'd lay herself out to please; but she got more than she gave, Miss Sylvia, she got more than she gave." Judy's always grim tones had grown grimmer, almost reminiscently tragic, while her eyes bent on Sylvia held a strange Celtic insight. "You were telling me a few days ago that there wasn't anything I couldn't do. Well, I was trained in a hard school, the school of Miss Adele. She had no mercy on any one. She took a fancy to me, and I had to do everything—be housekeeper, lady's-maid, sempstress, everything. Why, I'm only thirty-five, Mrs. Hartzfield, and I look fifty. Miss Adele wore me out. You see, everything had to be just right, or she'd know why, and times when I thought I'd drop, it would be, 'Brush my hair, Judy; I'm tired,' or ringing me up in the dead of night to read to her because she couldn't sleep. Oh, she was cruel hard, Miss Sylvia; and yet, since she's gone, her and her tempers and her tears and her smiles and her coaxings, someway the color and laughter and excitement's gone out of life. It's like a dish without salt."

"But how did a person like that endure the country here?" Sylvia could not forbear the question.

"She was in love with her husband." Judy lifted her eyes. "Lord! How she loved him!"

"Was she long ill, Judy?" Sylvia's voice was low.

"Ill! Her? Oh, you mean at the last. No, Mrs. Hartzfield." The tone was curt with a repressed emotion Sylvia could not translate, and from maid to mistress authoritatively final. "It is getting late. It must be luncheon-time." Judy fingered her keys and moved toward the door.

Daily, Sylvia found her interest focussed more steadily upon one subject— Adele. There was always something, some trifle either by way of incident or discovery, to incite her in following mentally the mazes of this fascinating personality; but not without protest. Ah no. There was the continual struggle, the wearing mental argument, when all the sane and healthy and normal forces of her nature rebelled against this obsession.

As a last stand she suggested to Arnold one morning at the breakfast table that they have some people to stop with them; but he immediately negatived this idea, looking at her meanwhile with a surprised and almost unbelieving irritation.

"Sylvia! Of what are you thinking? You know that at this stage of my work

I cannot have a lot of people to bother me. If you are lonely or bored here, and"—in quick afterthought—"no doubt you are, my dear, why do you not run off somewhere and amuse yourself?"

"You forget," she said, coldly and gently, "that it is many years since I have lived in America, and that I have very few affiliations here."

He threw out his hands with a quick gesture as if disclaiming all responsibility and resenting having it thrust upon him. "I'm sorry, my dear, but really you'll have to arrange those things to suit yourself." Then in contrition he jumped from his chair, and running around the table, threw an arm about her shoulders. "You know, Sylvia, how outside things torture me when I've got the mood, and, by Jove! I've got it, or it's got me." There was a strong, almost wondering exultation in his voice.

"I know," she smiled up at him, herself again. "Go right on with your work and never give me a thought. You know that I always do very well. And you understand that 'the mood' is not to be disturbed for a moment by any little vagaries of mine."

"Dear Sylvia," he touched her hair lightly with his lips, "you have made me understand that in the past, to my eternal gratitude."

For two or three days thereafter she succeeded in banishing her disquieting fancies, but gradually they asserted themselves more positively than before, and her resistance to this influence which permeated the atmosphere in which she moved gave way. The delicacy which had withheld her from probing into the psychological relations of Arnold and Adele began to appear to her as a wire-drawn and imaginary scruple. In this new point of view Arnold already seemed a different person to her, and her analysis of him, her supposition of the traits of character and phases of emotion he would exhibit under different conditions occupied her mind. She strove to reason clearly and logically from the known to the unknown of him, without particular success, but the deepening suspicion of injustice, neglect, misunderstanding to the point of cruelty to this long-dead Adele was unchecked; and as she opened her thought to it the stream of conjecture widened and increased in volume. Adele had so far revealed herself as to show that she was broken-hearted. Had she died of a broken heart? Absurd! Impossible! That superabundant vitality had never so succumbed.

But what was the malady which had cut her off in the splendid tide of her health? Why had she, Sylvia, never heard? When she had asked Mrs. Hartzfield and again when she had asked Judy, they had both looked at her so strangely, with the same quick, furtive glance, and had answered with the same curt inflection, "Yes, she died very suddenly." Surely it was odd!

Then through the unbroken silence of the room there seemed to peal the question, infinitely more startling and compelling than if audible, "How did Adele die?" The very walls echoed it. Sylvia suddenly sat upright, her hand on her wildly beating heart, while the question thundered its reiterations in her brain.

She started up. She would go now at once and ask Judy. No; she knew instinctively that Judy would evade her, perhaps lie to her. Judy was out of the question. She would demand of Arnold that he tell her. She was half-way across the porch going toward the studio, when she gave the matter consideration, her finger on her lip. Perhaps in this new Arnold, this stranger with whom she dwelt, she would also encounter evasions and subterfuges. Why turn to either Judy or himself, when she had a far surer method of discovery? She had so far resented the encroachments and invasions of Adele, but now the foundations of her resistance, long undermined, gave way, her bulwarks fell, her barriers crumbled. She was defenceless.

Her poise, her calm strength, had entirely deserted her. Through the very violence of her emotions, shades and subtleties of feeling of which she had hitherto been ignorant were revealed to her, and in the silence of this snow-bound, ice-locked winter, in this strange, featureless, incalculable world of visions wherein she groped, she was conscious of a more thrilling and intense life than she had ever dreamed of. It seemed to her that she was a harp, ever being tuned higher and higher for some mighty theme.

One evening as Arnold sat dreaming over the piano, striking vague chords and drifting into broken harmonies, an almost irresistible impulse seized her to go to him, to cry to him: "Shake off this obsession to work, Arnold. Stop grasping after the ideal. Come back to earth, sweetheart, to love, and to me."

She crushed back this inclination, but she could not repress her desire to woo him, to win him to remember her.

Slipping gently behind him, she threw her arms about his neck and pressed her cheek against his. "Dearest," she murmured—"dearest." He suffered her caress, even leaned his cheek upon hers, but did not speak. His eyes were still fixed upon some point beyond the mortal vision, and he still weaved his broken, improvised harmonies.

She could not bear it. A wave of anguish engulfed her. "Arnold!" she cried, her voice broken, "it is weeks since you have kissed me. It is months since you have treated me with the old intimacy and tenderness. Do you no longer love me?"

The lines so perceptible now in his sensitive face deepened; chords crashed and broke under his fingers. "Don't!" he cried, sharply. "My work gives me all the emotion that I can bear. Ah-h-h!" He shivered and leaned more heavily against her. "The tortures of the last few days! How I have groped for the proper treatment, how it has haunted and eluded me! This is not like you, Sylvia." He turned to her with a deep reproach in his eyes, and then seemed to see her for the first time. "Adele!" he gasped, hoarsely, almost inaudibly. "Ah," recovering himself, although the beads of sweat stood out on his pale forehead. "I thought for a moment—Why are you wearing rose-color?"

"There is no reason why I should not," she answered, coldly. "I had on this gown at dinner, but you did not notice it." She turned and left him, going into the drawing-room, and there again walked the floor, her hands pressed to her temples, her whole figure shaken by tearless gusts of passion. She looked up at the portrait of Adele, the exquisite shoulders rising from the billows of tulle, the eyes looking upward through the long lashes with the most alluring coquetry.

"What would you do?" Sylvia whispered. "What would you do? Oh, you poor thing, what *did* you do?"

The sound of Arnold's music came softly to her ears. It was no longer broken, but continuous and flowing. He was lost in his visions again; visions over which he so dreamed and gloated that he could not even see her in her gown like crushed rose-leaves. She determined now that she, too, would see them and in tangible form; so, snatching up a cloak, she stole silently from the house.

It was a moonless night, but a pallid light was reflected from the snow which stretched far and white. The black trees were like a mighty guard of sentinel shadows, and Sylvia sped among them, flying over the snow in her light slippers, indifferent to cold or wet. Swept along as a leaf without volition of her own, a wild exultation shook her. Now, now she meant to search the springs of Arnold's passion, all those secret chambers of his soul so securely locked from her.

A dim light shone from the studio. She tried the outer door. It was unlocked, and with a sigh of relief she passed through it. The inner door, too, yielded to her touch, and softly she pushed it open and crept in. The lofty sky-lighted room was warm and very quiet, with shaded lights dimly burning, and the atmosphere was soothingly calm and peaceful; but although it arrested her for a moment, it could not long assuage the storm of her spirit. Hastily she turned high the lights and glanced eagerly, hungrily, about her. The room was full of tall canvases leaning against easels. One or two of the panels were almost finished; the rest were in various stages of completion.

Above the central canvas were great golden letters:

"YE SHALL KNOW THE TRUTH,
AND THE TRUTH SHALL MAKE YOU FREE"

and on this panel Arnold had depicted Jesus of Nazareth as He toiled a prisoner up the slope of Calvary, bearing upon His back the cross of this world's hatred.

Sylvia stood before it a long moment, breathless, motionless, awed, and then, still profoundly self-forgetful and absorbed, began to study it in its effect and details, bending forward and then moving back, stepping to this side and then to that. For the time that her entire attention was focussed upon the picture she was the old Sylvia again, Sylvia of the tranquil eyes and the gentle, deliberate movements.

She recognized at once that this was the highest expression of Arnold's career; that it represented an almost incredible growth in his art. Not in any previous work had he shown such concentrated power, such exaltation and high nobility of feeling, and such mastery and such subordination of treatment; and Sylvia's appreciation, for she had ever been an enthusiastic lover of the best that man has wrought, rose like a lark from the depths of her imprisoned spirit and lifted its wings and sang an answer to this clarion-call of genius.

In an intense but still tranquil absorption she moved from one canvas to another, inspecting each minutely, comparing one with another, then studying them as a whole.

The great golden letters set forth plainly Arnold's theme: "Ye shall know the truth, and the truth shall make you free," and on each panel was portrayed the supreme moment in the life of the world's greatest dreamers—discerners and proclaimers of the Truth, that Truth which makes all things new and sends out unsuspected, undivined thought-worlds like golden balls spinning through the ether from the dim looms of Chaos.

Arnold had chosen that hour in the life of each of his conquerors when Man—the fearer and hater of dreams—rises in all the might of temporal power to crush Man the reflector of the Idea, and he had invested the bleak hill of Calvary, the gaunt and ghastly scaffold, the foul and narrow dungeon, with a splendor of light which made them antechambers to the Kingdom of God; while the purple and scarlet and gold of pomp and power, the machinery of repression, appeared as pitiful deceptions; and the ermined kings and prelates, the armored soldiery gathered to set the machinery in motion, as mad maskers and mummers cowering purblind before the light.

From each dreamer, manacled, crowned with thorns, twisted with torture, or hung with chains, there emanated the majesty and might of the soul's eternal freedom, the white, ineffable irradiation of light, so that they, dying, seemed the manifestation of life at its fullest, most rapturous, and immortal moment; and the mob, which shrieked triumphant, the spawn of death spewed from some bitter maelstrom of ignorance and horror.

And Sylvia, trembling, admiring, adoring, still passed from one to the other, still leaned and looked, and looked again, until at last she drew a chair to her where her eyes might cling to the canvases, and leaning her chin upon her hand, gradually sank into reverie.

So this was what the veiled, mysterious, beckoning figure had given to Arnold! No visions of sensuous beauty; but austere and lofty images of the soul's struggles and triumphs. Ah, well, what matter? She sighed heavily; what matter whether it were the flower-crowned, dancing daughters of the Venusberg, or some wan and tortured victor over illusion, with eyes unsealed and lips touched with the flame of his message? What mattered the character of the visions? Had they not taken him from her?

For a long time she sat thus, her head averted from the pictures, her eyes cast on the floor, her depression deepening, until at last her tranquillity fell from her, and she rose and began again her hurried, uneven pacing of the floor. Some dreadful tide with a sinister, hissing lap seemed creeping nearer and nearer her, until at last the black waters of hate rushed and roared and seethed about her, and she felt the awful, inexorable drag of the undertow. She was lost in whirlpools of tortured thought, and then the undertow dragged her down.

On one of the tables near her she saw the sharp, thin, gleaming edge of steel, and she caught it up and made a rush, straight as an arrow from the bow, toward the central panel.

"Sylvia!" Hartzfield standing in the doorway had almost whispered the words, and yet she heard him, although the roar of many waters was in her ears. "Sylvia, what are you doing here?"

Instinctively she folded the knife in her cloak. "I—I came to see them." She fought for controlled utterance. Her lips were dry. She could barely form the words. "I had to come." The anguished heart of her burst through her lips. "I would not have chosen to come, but I had to. I could bear no more. I had to see what it was that had stolen your heart from me, what had pushed me out of my place in your life, what it was that had changed your whole nature. I had to see in tangible form the work to which I had been sacrificed. Oh, Arnold, have I not a right to some of you, to some of your thought and consideration? Has love no rights?"

He did not answer her. He could not, but leaned the more heavily against the door, as though chained in some horrible nightmare, unable to move. His breath came in audible, painful gasps.

"You have thrust me out into some cold isolation as desolate and ice-bound as this awful winter"—she made no effort to wipe away the tears rolling down her emotion-tortured face—"and I am young and alive. I am a woman, and I want to be loved."

His eyes never left hers, but, wide and staring, clung to her as if fascinated by some image of unbelievable horror.

"And I am your wife," her voice growing higher and shriller, "and yet I am completely shut out from all your interests. Do you call that being one? Do you call that union? And look!" her wild, gasping laughter rose and fell and echoed through the room. From the folds of her heavy cloak she drew the knife. "If you had not come just when you did, just when you did, I should have slashed the canvases to bits, slashed them to bits and trampled on them."

He was across the room in a bound, his hand like a steel vise on her wrist. "Adele!" the name seemed forced from him, his white lips twisted over it.

"Adele!" she repeated, and grew suddenly calm, not even striving to free herself from the grip of his tense fingers pressing cruelly into her flesh. "Why do you say her name? Twice this evening you have called me Adele."

His face was more ghastly than ever. "It was so she looked; so she spoke the night she stole here."

"The night she stole here?" Sylvia repeated, still calmly. "What night?" The knife fell from her fingers and clattered on the floor; he thrust it far with his foot.

"The night she cut my picture to ribbons; my just finished picture of *Love;* and then drove the knife into her own heart, here, where you stand. And you, Sylvia, have spoken her very words, duplicated her very actions. Oh, in what horrible dreams are we groping?" His voice broke poignantly. He looked wildly about him as if to assure himself of some fantastic dream-surroundings from which they would presently emerge; and then upon his face dawned a great light as of horror and awakening commingled. "I see it. I see it now." He cast his arms about her, clasping her close as if to shield her from some dreaded menace. "Oh, my God, is it possible? May a passionate and powerful consciousness so stamp its personality upon the environment in which it lived that it persists and continues to exert its subtle and poisonous influence upon sensitive natures?"

"An influence?" she repeated, dazedly, winding her arms more tightly about his neck, and shrinking, shuddering against him—"an influence—Oh, you do not know—!"

"Ah, Sylvia, poor Sylvia, do I not know? Have I not struggled in those coils? But during her life. I have never felt it since."

"But how did you save yourself? How did you save yourself?" She slipped through his arms and fell on her knees before him, clutching him with gripping fingers.

"My work saved me." He drew his hand across his brow. "Yes, my work saved me. Living or dead, she could not touch the best in me, the longing to create images of truth and beauty."

"But I have no art to save me, no highest in me." She swayed brokenly from her knees to the floor and lay there, her proud and delicate head on her out-thrown arms.

"Oh, Sylvia!" he knelt beside her, covering her cloudy hair with kisses, "the highest in you is so high that I have never dreamed of reaching it; but it has lifted me; oh, it has. This work, the best of my life, would have been an impossibility without you. Idea after idea, conception after conception, has been rejected, because I saw you always, your head uplifted in a purer ether, the stars a scarf about your shoulders, beckoning me higher. The crystal stream of your affection has soothed and restored my fevered spirit. It is in your love, Sylvia, your understanding and sympathy, which never bound nor fettered me, that I have found the freedom of the spirit which has enabled me to work out my dreams."

"Ah, tell me again! Make me believe it!" Her voice was as the voice of a sobbing child.

Again and again he told her with words and caresses, and Sylvia, listening, lifted her fallen head, rose to her knees and then to her feet. She breathed a rarer ether again; the light of the morning was in her eyes. "Then I, too, am free," she cried. "If the best of me has helped you to create these pictures, then the best of me is too high to be reached by any lower influences. Look, Arnold, look! It is dawn. Come, we must go home."

He shrank, his face darkening. "Not there. You cannot go back there. Not into that rose-colored hell."

She raised her eyes to his, clear and tranquil to their depths. "There is nothing there that can touch me now. To-day I shall begin to change every-thing. Come."

They left the studio; the glory of another day was flashing across the sky and over the hilltops, and in one brief moment of clear vision Arnold and Sylvia saw a new heaven and a new earth, for the former things were passed away. Then, hand in hand, through the black, sentinel trees stretching away to the sunrise and across the dawn-flushed snow, they walked together in love's great and happy silence.

———————◆•◆•◆———————

KATE CHOPIN
(1850–1904)

Kate Chopin's brief but illustrious literary career spanned from 1890 to 1899. During that time she published more than one hundred short stories and three novels, the last of which was *The Awakening*. Now considered her masterpiece, its bold exploration of Edna Pontellier's rebellion against the restrictive roles of wife and mother and growing awareness of her sexuality brought critical condemnation and a virtual end to Chopin's career. Born Katherine O'Flaherty in Missouri, Chopin lost her Irish father at the age of five and was raised by her mother, grandmother, and great-grandmother—three generations of French-speaking widows. Receiving a Catholic education, she married a successful Louisiana cotton broker, Oscar Chopin, at age twenty. After living for ten years in New Orleans, the Chopins moved to Cloutierville, a tiny town in Natchitoches Parish that provides the rural background to Chopin's many brilliant stories of Creoles and Acadians. Chopin was widowed in 1882, the mother of five young children. She eventually returned to St. Louis and commenced writing professionally. Chopin was primarily a realist; "Her Letters" is her only supernatural tale. Featured in *Vogue* in April 1895, it is particularly interesting when considered as a precursor to *The Awakening*.

Her Letters

I

SHE HAD GIVEN ORDERS THAT SHE WISHED TO REMAIN UN-disturbed and moreover had locked the doors of her rooms.

The house was very still. The rain was falling steadily from a leaden sky in which there was no gleam, no rift, no promise. A generous wood fire had been lighted in the ample fireplace and it brightened and illumined the luxurious apartment to its furthermost corner.

HER LETTERS

From some remote nook of her writing desk the woman took a thick bundle of letters, bound tightly together with strong, coarse twine, and placed it upon the table in the centre of the room.

For weeks she had been schooling herself for what she was about to do. There was a strong deliberation in the lines of her long, thin, sensitive face; her hands, too, were long and delicate and blue-veined.

With a pair of scissors she snapped the cord binding the letters together. Thus released the ones which were top-most slid down to the table and she, with a quick movement thrust her fingers among them, scattering and turning them over till they quite covered the broad surface of the table.

Before her were envelopes of various sizes and shapes, all of them addressed in the handwriting of one man and one woman. He had sent her letters all back to her one day when, sick with dread of possibilities, she had asked to have them returned. She had meant, then, to destroy them all, his and her own. That was four years ago, and she had been feeding upon them ever since; they had sustained her, she believed, and kept her spirit from perishing utterly.

But now the days had come when the premonition of danger could no longer remain unheeded. She knew that before many months were past she would have to part from her treasure, leaving it unguarded. She shrank from inflicting the pain, the anguish which the discovery of those letters would bring to others; to one, above all, who was near to her, and whose tenderness and years of devotion had made him, in a manner, dear to her.

She calmly selected a letter at random from the pile and cast it into the roaring fire. A second one followed almost as calmly, with the third her hand began to tremble; when, in a sudden paroxysm she cast a fourth, a fifth, and a sixth into the flames in breathless succession.

Then she stopped and began to pant—for she was far from strong, and she stayed staring into the fire with pained and savage eyes. Oh, what had she done! What had she not done! With feverish apprehension she began to search among the letters before her. Which of them had she so ruthlessly, so cruelly put out of her existence? Heaven grant, not the first, that very first one, written before they had learned, or dared to say to each other "I love you." No, no; there it was, safe enough. She laughed with pleasure, and held it to her lips. But what if that other most precious and most imprudent one were missing! in which every word of untempered passion had long ago eaten its way into her brain; and which stirred her still to-day, as it had done a hundred times before when she thought of it. She crushed it between her palms when she found it. She kissed it again and again. With her sharp white teeth she tore the far corner from the letter, where the name was written; she bit the torn scrap and tasted it between her lips and upon her tongue like some god-given morsel.

What unbounded thankfulness she felt at not having destroyed them all! How desolate and empty would have been her remaining days without them; with only her thoughts, illusive thoughts that she could not hold in her hands and press, as she did these, to her cheeks and her heart.

This man had changed the water in her veins to wine, whose taste had brought delirium to both of them. It was all one and past now, save for these letters that she held encircled in her arms. She stayed breathing softly and contentedly, with the hectic cheek resting upon them.

She was thinking; thinking of a way to keep them without possible ultimate injury to that other one whom they would stab more cruelly than keen knife blades.

At last she found the way. It was a way that frightened and bewildered her to think of at first, but she had reached it by deduction too sure to admit of doubt. She meant, of course, to destroy them herself before the end came. But how does the end come and when? Who may tell? She would guard against the possibility of accident by leaving them in charge of the very one who, above all, should be spared a knowledge of their contents.

She roused herself from the stupor of thought and gathered the scattered letters once more together, binding them again with the rough twine. She wrapped the compact bundle in a thick sheet of white polished paper. Then she wrote in ink upon the back of it, in large, firm characters:

"I leave this package to the care of my husband. With perfect faith in his loyalty and his love, I ask him to destroy it unopened."

It was not sealed; only a bit of string held the wrapper, which she could remove and replace at will whenever the humor came to her to pass an hour in some intoxicating dream of the days when she felt she had lived.

II

If he had come upon that bundle of letters in the first flush of his poignant sorrow there would not have been an instant's hesitancy. To destroy it promptly and without question would have seemed a welcome expression of devotion—a way of reaching her, of crying out his love to her while the world was still filled with the illusion of her presence. But months had passed since that spring day when they had found her stretched upon the floor, clutching the key of her writing desk, which she appeared to have been attempting to reach when death overtook her.

The day was much like that day a year ago when the leaves were falling and the rain pouring steadily from a leaden sky which held no gleam, no promise. He had happened accidentally upon the package in that remote nook of her desk. And just as she herself had done a year ago, he carried it to the table and laid it down there, standing, staring with puzzled eyes at the message which confronted him:

"I leave this package to the care of my husband. With perfect faith in his loyalty and his love, I ask him to destroy it unopened."

She had made no mistake; every line of his face—no longer young—spoke loyalty and honesty, and his eyes were as faithful as a dog's and as loving. He was a tall, powerful man, standing there in the firelight, with shoulders that stooped a little, and hair that was growing somewhat thin and gray, and a face that was distinguished, and must have been handsome when he smiled. But he was slow. "Destroy it unopened," he re-read, half aloud, "but why unopened?"

He took the package again in his hands, and turning it about and feeling it, discovered that it was composed of many letters tightly packed together.

So here were letters which she was asking him to destroy unopened. She had never seemed in her lifetime to have had a secret from him. He knew her to have been cold and passionless, but true, and watchful of his comfort and his happiness. Might he not be holding in his hands the secret of some other one, which had been confided to her and which she had promised to guard? But, no, she would have indicated the fact by some additional word or line. The secret was her own, something contained in these letters, and she wanted it to die with her.

If he could have thought of her as on some distant shadowy shore waiting for him throughout the years with outstretched hands to come and join her again, he would not have hesitated. With hopeful confidence he would have thought "in that blessed meeting-time, soul to soul, she will tell me all; till then I can wait and trust." But he could not think of her in any far-off paradise awaiting him. He felt that there was no smallest part of her anywhere in the universe, more than there had been before she was born into the world. But she had embodied herself with terrible significance in an intangible wish, uttered when life still coursed through her veins; knowing that it would reach him when the annihilation of death was between them, but uttered with all confidence in its power and potency. He was moved by the splendid daring, the magnificence of the act, which at the same time exalted him and lifted him above the head of common mortals.

What secret save one could a woman choose to have die with her? As quickly as the suggestion came to his mind, so swiftly did the man-instinct of possession creep into his blood. His fingers cramped about the package in his hands, and he sank into a chair beside the table. The agonizing suspicion that perhaps another hand shared with him her thoughts, her affections, her life, deprived him for a swift instant of honor and reason. He thrust the end of his strong thumb beneath the string which, with a single turn would have yielded—"with perfect faith in your loyalty and your love." It was not the written characters addressing themselves to the eye; it was like a voice speaking to his soul. With a tremor of anguish he bowed his head down upon the letters.

He had once seen a clairvoyant hold a letter to his forehead and purport in so doing to discover its contents. He wondered for a wild moment if such a gift, for force of wishing it, might not come to him. But he was only conscious of the smooth surface of the paper, cold against his brow, like the touch of a dead woman's hand.

A half-hour passed before he lifted his head. An unspeakable conflict had raged within him, but his loyalty and his love had conquered. His face was pale and deep-lined with suffering, but there was no more hesitancy to be seen there.

He did not for a moment think of casting the thick package into the flames to be licked by the fiery tongues, and charred and half-revealed to his eyes. That was not what she meant. He arose, and taking a heavy bronze paper-weight from the table, bound it securely to the package. He walked to the window and looked out into the street below. Darkness had come, and it was still raining. He could hear the rain dashing against the window-panes, and could see it falling through the dull yellow rim of light cast by the lighted street lamp.

He prepared himself to go out, and when quite ready to leave the house thrust the weighted package into the deep pocket of his top-coat.

He did not hurry along the street as most people were doing at that hour, but walked with a long, slow, deliberate step, not seeming to mind the penetrating chill and rain driving into his face despite the shelter of his umbrella.

His dwelling was not far removed from the business section of the city; and it was not a great while before he found himself at the entrance of the bridge that spanned the river—the deep, broad, swift, black river dividing two States. He walked on and out to the very centre of the structure. The wind was blowing fiercely and keenly. The darkness where he stood was impenetrable. The thousands of lights in the city he had left seemed like all the stars of heaven massed together, sinking into some distant mysterious horizon, leaving him alone in a black, boundless universe.

He drew the package from his pocket and leaning as far as he could over the broad stone rail of the bridge, cast it from him into the river. It fell straight and swiftly from his hand. He could not follow its descent through the darkness, nor hear its dip into the water far below. It vanished silently; seemingly into some inky unfathomable space. He felt as if he were flinging it back to her in that unknown world whither she had gone.

III

An hour or two later he sat at his table in the company of several men whom he had invited that day to dine with him. A weight had settled upon his spirit, a conviction, a certitude that there could be but one secret which a woman would choose to have die with her. This one thought was possessing him. It occupied his brain, keeping it nimble and alert with suspicion. It clutched his heart, making every breath of existence a fresh moment of pain.

The men about him were no longer the friends of yesterday; in each one he discerned a possible enemy. He attended absently to their talk. He was remembering how she had conducted herself toward this one and that one; striving to recall conversations, subtleties of facial expression that might have meant what he did not suspect at the moment, shades of meaning in words that had seemed the ordinary interchange of social amenities.

He led the conversation to the subject of women, probing these men for their opinions and experiences. There was not one but claimed some infallible power to command the affections of any woman whom his fancy might select. He had heard the empty boast before from the same group and had always met it with good-humored contempt. But to-night every flagrant, inane utterance was charged with a new meaning, revealing possibilities that he had hitherto never taken into account.

He was glad when they were gone. He was eager to be alone, not from any desire or intention to sleep. He was impatient to regain her room, that room in which she had lived a large portion of her life, and where he had found those letters. There must surely be more of them somewhere, he thought; some forgotten scrap, some written thought or expression lying unguarded by an inviolable command.

At the hour when he usually retired for the night he sat himself down before her writing desk and began the search of drawers, slides, pigeon-holes, nooks and corners. He did not leave a scrap of anything unread. Many of the letters which he found were old; some he had read before; others were new to him. But in none did her find a faintest evidence that his wife had not been the true and loyal woman he had always believed her to be. The night was nearly spent before the fruitless search ended. The brief, troubled sleep which he snatched before his hour for rising was freighted with feverish, grotesque dreams, through all of which he could hear and could see dimly the dark river rushing by, carrying away his heart, his ambitions, his life.

But it was not alone in letters that women betrayed their emotions, he thought. Often he had known them, especially when in love, to mark fugitive, sentimental passages in books of verse or prose, thus expressing and revealing their own hidden thought. Might she not have done the same?

Then began a second and far more exhausting and arduous quest than the first, turning, page by page, the volumes that crowded her room—books of fiction, poetry, philosophy. She had read them all; but nowhere, by the shadow of a sign, could he find that the author had echoed the secret of her existence—the secret which he had held in his hands and had cast into the river.

He began cautiously and gradually to question this one and that one, striving to learn by indirect ways what each had thought of her. Foremost he learned she had been unsympathetic because of her coldness of manner. One had admired her intellect; another her accomplishments; a third had thought her beautiful before disease claimed her, regretting, however, that her beauty had lacked warmth of color and expression. She was praised by some for gentleness and kindness, and by others for cleverness and tact. Oh, it was useless to try to discover anything from men! he might have known. It was women who would talk of what they knew.

They did talk, unreservedly. Most of them had loved her; those who had not had held her in respect and esteem.

IV

And yet, and yet, "there is but one secret which a woman would choose to have die with her," was the thought which continued to haunt him and deprive him of rest. Days and nights of uncertainty began slowly to unnerve him and to torture him. An assurance of the worst that he dreaded would have offered him peace most welcome, even at the price of happiness.

It seemed no longer of any moment to him that men should come and go; and fall or rise in the world; and wed and die. It did not signify if money came to him by a turn of chance or eluded him. Empty and meaningless seemed to him all devices which the world offers for man's entertainment. The food and the drink set before him had lost their flavor. He did not longer know or care if the sun shone or the clouds lowered about him. A cruel hazard had struck him there where he was weakest, shattering his whole being, leaving him with but one wish in his soul, one gnawing desire, to know the mystery which he had held in his hands and had cast into the river.

One night when there were no stars shining he wandered, restless, upon the streets. He no longer sought to know from men and women what they dared not or could not tell him. Only the river knew. He went and stood again upon the bridge where he had stood many an hour since that night when the darkness then had closed around him and engulfed his manhood.

Only the river knew. It babbled, and he listened to it, and it told him nothing, but it promised all. He could hear it promising him with caressing voice, peace and sweet repose. He could hear the sweep, the song of the water inviting him.

A moment more and he had gone to seek her, and to join her and her secret thought in the immeasurable rest.

⊰ IV ⊱

Madwomen or Mad Women?
The Medicalization of the Female

"What were you doing in the window?"

Illustration by C. E. Hart for Mary Heaton Vorse, "The Second Wife," Harper's Magazine 124 (February 1912). Photo courtesy Metropolitan Toronto Reference Library.

MARY HEATON VORSE
(1874–1966)

Mary Heaton Vorse led a most active and interesting life. She married three times, in 1898, 1912, and 1920, and bore three children. With her first husband, she founded the A Club, an experimental, cooperative living arrangement in Greenwich Village. After his death she supported herself by writing, becoming a popular journalist, novelist, and short-story writer. During World War I, Vorse was a war correspondent. For more than thirty years she worked as a journalist, reporting on current events in labor and on battlefronts in Europe, the Soviet Union, and the United States. Interested in education, she organized a Montessori school and was among the founding members of the Provincetown Players. The fact that Vorse published "The Second Wife" in 1912, the same year that she married for the second time, lends itself to some interesting speculation. The tale appeared in the February 1912 issue of *Harper's*.

<hr>

The Second Wife

ORE POIGNANT THAN THE FACTS OF LIFE, WITH AS MUCH power as the elemental needs of the body, The Unseen still shapes the lives of vast peoples. In some black corners of the earth strange demons still call out for human sacrifice. Mysterious and powerful are these voiceless companions of men.

We alone, of all ages and peoples, have denied them; we have cut away our shadows from our spirits, and perhaps that is why the spirits of modern men seem unsubstantial, as a body would which could cast no dark silhouette behind it.

Around the paths of men The Unseen exists always, and it may come to any one and at any moment as it did to Beata and to Graham.

The mellow afternoon light shone through the quiet spaces of the room, which, simple as it was—bare almost, some would have said—had the supreme beauty of proportion. It had an air about it, a gracious gravity, which proclaimed it of the honorable lineage of lovingly built houses. It gave the effect of space, even of elegance, if for no other reason than that its three dimensions were in harmony.

For the first time its charm failed with Beata. Its beneficent dignity mocked at her, affecting her with the same anger that the unthinking beauty of a glorious day does to one in deep trouble. This room, her room, her creature—how dared it breathe peace while she suffered with unrest?

If there had been any reason for it she could have borne it. She had stood up with gallantry to all the blows that fate had handed out to her. No matter what had happened, her inner self had been serene and unshaken. And now, for no reason, with all the surfaces of life fair and smiling before her, a horror unspeakable, reasonless, invaded the secret places of her being.

She sat there saying to herself:

"I will not! I will not! I will not! They can't make me! They can't make me! They can't make me!"

And with the words once spoken it was as though her spirit cried out against something unknown, as though she fought for her own self and something very dear to her, and yet she didn't know what she was fighting.

The outward symbol of this struggle was so trivial, so meaningless, that she shivered at herself as though her reason was failing her. There was a bowl of yellow jonquils gleaming out of a dark corner of the room, reflecting themselves on the dark floor in a splash of color. Beata had been moved with an impulse to take these flowers and place them between the windows where the light would shine through them on a small, round table on which was inlaid a landscape in mother-of-pearl—a table that might have been hideous, but had turned out to be only a charming indiscretion of some cabinet-maker.

This whim, so harmless in its outer meaning, had come over her like an overpowering wave; yet it had come not as her own wish. It was as though it arose from the passionate desire of some will outside her own. To steady herself Beata sat down in the rosewood chair and said to herself: "I will not! I will not!" as though fighting for her own individuality.

This impulse, with its meaningless madness, had come as suddenly, as shatteringly, as some explosion. Dread shook her through and through—a dread that left her tense and expectant. Why, she hadn't felt that way for three years, not since she had waited for one of Alène's terrible, meaningless, heart-rending scenes—scenes that Graham and she knew were caused by Alène's illness, and yet scenes that gave the effect of wantonness, as if Alène wanted to make them suffer, too. Since her nerves were diseased, since her soul was poisoned in God knows what mysterious fashion, she couldn't let them off—the two creatures dearest to her—but must encompass them also in the hell where she lived.

In spite of Beata's care and Graham's devotion, Alène had got worse and worse, until it seemed to them that madness stared from her eyes. She had died from an overdose of her sleeping-potion—an accidental death, the doctor had insisted.

This had been three years ago. After Alène's death, Graham had gone abroad, and for a year Beata hadn't seen him. Just when, after his return, she had begun to care for him, she couldn't now tell. They had drifted into it—gone in step by step. She couldn't even remember when he had asked her to marry him, so well had they understood.

She had been married six months now, and until this moment she had been happier than she had ever been in her life—happier than she had known it was possible to be. The eighteen months that she had spent nursing Alène, and the final catastrophe, had left her stunned, asking of life only quiet. She had had peace and rest and then happiness, and now it was broken—for no reason; broken—for so absurd a thing.

It was especially hard for Beata to bear; she didn't know how to meet moods—she had never had any. It was almost her first experience with any unhappiness from within, her first experience of that overwhelming misery that comes unreasoning from the inner recesses of the spirit, something more full of anguish than pain, something that makes grief seem God's compassion, and sorrow as sweet as a gray day in midsummer.

She sought for some cause of such disturbance, her trained mind running rapidly through the events of the last few days as an expert might riffle a deck of cards. There was no explanatory spot or fleck on the fair surface of the kindly and familiar events.

"I must be sick," she thought, and again sought for some symptom that might satisfy her. There was nothing. It was as ghostly to have her spirit so disturbed as for doors to slam and windows rattle when the trees remain quiet without. And while her heart beat and while the tortured nerves of her cried out the more torturingly that she did not know the source of her pain, her tranquil head thought, "I must treat this mood as I used to Alène's."

At this thought her heart stood still—then leaped like a frightened animal in fear for its very life, and as though in actual physical terror of some unseen menace she fled toward the sunshine of the garden, glancing apprehensively behind her, not for fear of what she might see, but from a feeling as inexplicable as all the rest, that she wished no one to see her go. Not the servants, not Graham—especially not Graham. She heard his voice call to her:

"Beata–dear Beata!" So happy it was, so reassuring, that suddenly her fear vanished as though it had wakened her from torturing nightmare. She felt her actual body coming back to life as one breathes easily for the first time again after one has been overwhelmed by a crashing wave. Her heart beat freely again; the intolerable racking of her spirit passed by; color returned to her cheeks. Only as she saw Graham coming toward her through the open door she repressed an impulse to throw herself about his neck as though he had really delivered her from herself.

That evening the idea of telling Graham flitted through her mind, coming and going like a shadow cast by a flickering flame. In the end she decided not to, and, as she did, a sadness fell over her spirit, while her mind argued:

Poor Graham—why should I tell him anything so vague, and at the same time so fantastic? Hasn't he had enough of the inexplicable in his life?

Then, at this thought of Alène, it seemed as if Alène was there. Beata had all the sensation of seeing her without the actual visualization—Alène, sitting, her dark-rimmed eyes on Graham. She watched them fill slowly with tears; watched Alène's face quiver like that of a hurt child that asks, "Oh, why do you so wound me?" Beata had sat there often enough through what seemed a long lifetime of vicarious pain, pretending not to notice Graham's irrepressible discomfort; pretending not to notice Alène's gathering nerve-storm which sometimes threatened and threatened, poisoning their lives, poisoning the very air; sometimes passing over, leaving sunlight behind.

Recalling these things, Beata let her eyes rest on vacancy. What prevented one, she wondered, from seeing with one's actual eyes any one whom one could see with what is called "the mind's eye"? There have always been people, sick and well, who could project their inner visions into space and thus behold their own imaginings and realities. Beata dwelt in this way on the image of Alène, absorbed as a devotee is absorbed in the contemplation of the attributes of Deity. After a time it was as though her visualization of Alène had been projected into space, and that this thought of her was there clothed in form and invisible, but existing somehow in another medium. She wondered if it were true that the things seen by dreamers have their real existence in some fluid which we may not perceive.

Here Graham's voice broke in upon her, asking:

"What are you thinking of, Beata, so intensely?"

She had been plunged so profoundly in her train of thought, the crystal mirror of her reflection had been shattered so unexpectedly, that she jumped nervously. It seemed as if her spirit had come swimming up from some far depth in which it had plunged itself. She realized, too, that she had been looking directly at Graham, but through him and beyond him, as if she had penetrated far enough into this land which she had so fantastically imagined, so that the things of this world had become for the moment nonexistent, as are usually the things we cannot see. For a moment her mind and eyes and all of her had dwelt in some almost luminous vacancy which had been cleared of so-called actuality for a new creation of her own. Her return to the physical world, to Graham, and to familiar things in the room was a shock as of physical pain.

She had been awakened too abruptly. She looked at him, dazed, frowning, at the same time registering the troubled and anxious look on his face— a look of doubt, a look of wonder, a look of some deeper trouble also. In answer to his question came unbidden the words:

"Why do you look at me like that, Graham?"

He arose and put his arms around her, but before he spoke he swallowed, as though speech came to him with an effort. With his arms around her, his face close to her, something snapped in Beata's mind, like a joint coming back into place. She had yet the impression of having been away a very great distance.

"What were you thinking of just now?" he repeated.

She answered with absolute truthfulness:

"I don't know—I almost seemed to be hypnotized." The shock of his voice had for the second obliterated the object of her deep absorption.

Graham shook her roughly.

"Well, don't do it again, please," he said. "I don't like your looks."

"What do I look like?" She was perfectly natural now; the whole phantasmagoria had vanished out of her spirit as though it had not been.

"I don't like your looks," he repeated—"that's all." He had the evasive and uneasy air of a man who doesn't like to tell what is in his mind.

The following day Beata succeeded in overcoming the feeling of distrust with the whole universe which the inexplicable breeds in a direct and common-sense temperament. She overcame herself, yet she didn't go into the drawing-room, and the drawing-room was as much lived in by her as was Graham's library by him; for the effect of that terrible and spectral battle remained with her as though some shadow had been cast across her spirit. Pushed into the farthest recesses of her mind was the question, "Why? Why? Why?" Nor could she rid herself of the idea that there was more to come, nor of a nameless and reasonless fear that in some strange way she had given up some of her personality.

With the passing of the days the shadow dwindled, until one day Beata went again into her room. Yellow flowers picked freshly stood in a bowl upon her secretary. At the sight of them there, hot anger surged up within her, making her tingle from head to foot. Swiftly and yet with a certain furtiveness, as though she were being watched, she picked them up and carried them back to their place in the window and placed them on the little inlaid table between the windows where the light would shine through them. As she did so there came over her a very agony of desire to see Graham; she wanted him to come home; she wondered where he was and with whom. An impatience to go out and find him wherever he was plucked at her feet. She looked at her watch; it was almost time for his return to luncheon, and she posted herself at the window before which the flowers stood and which commanded a view of the elm-shaded street to wait for him. As she stood there in a fever of impatience and longing and affection, she felt as though her whole personality had been invaded by an emotion foreign to her own temperament. Her love had been from the first deep and profound, the surface of it radiant, but without anguish of spirit. They knew each other too well for uncertainties or surprises—they had been friends so long before they had become lovers.

The knowledge that he would soon come, that he would come when he said he would, had been enough for her; why this impatience, she wondered—where did it come from, this passionate agony of longing for the sight of his face? She stood there peering out from the window. She was so sure he must come down that road, her gaze so lost in the distance for the first glimpse of him, that she did not hear his step behind her. His words, in a tone through which a sharp anxiety pierced, "Beata, what are you doing there?" made her turn upon him, her nervous hand clutching the heavy, old-gold drapery of the curtain.

For a moment they stood gazing at each other, startled. Then she laughed with attempted lightness:

"What's the matter, Graham? You look frightened!"

"What were you doing in the window?" he insisted.

"Why—just waiting for you."

"Come—let's get out of here. If you wait staring like that— Waiting for me! Good God! One would have thought that you expected me to be brought home on a stretcher! You'll be getting yourself hypnotized again, Beata, before you know it." He put his arm around her and drew her out on the piazza. "I've just got a letter from mother," he told her. "She's coming back."

"Oh, I *am* glad," Beata cried.

For some time during her son's first marriage Mrs. Yates had made her home with the young people, and then, under the pressure of Alène's nervous disorder and her final illness, she had left their home to live with her sister. The pressure was too much for her gentle spirit; she couldn't weather the storms which swept and devastated the household; she suffered, too, with a keen inner shame that she hadn't strength enough to help this tormented daughter of hers, whose peculiar loveliness and charm she had so cared for before illness blighted it. After Graham's second marriage she had again made his house her headquarters, finding in Beata's tranquillity something more akin to her own nature, something nearer to what her own daughter might have been than Alène's more fascinating personality had ever been able to give her.

To Beata's heartfelt "Oh, I'm glad!" Graham echoed:

"You can believe I am."

There was an unmistakable passion of relief in his tone, as if Beata's cry had voiced the hope of deliverance—as if the presence of this beloved older woman would dispel the shadow that was drifting in upon them, shutting out the sun from their lives. It was their first recognition of the nameless fear that had come over them.

Now Beata was sure that never for a moment had Graham failed to recognize this awful something which was crawling upon them like some dark spiritual tide. If only he would help her—if he would ask her what was the matter! She felt his anxious look resting on her; then he made some excuse and left her. It was as though he had deserted her in a moment of great peril. Scorn for his cowardice and for his stupidity flashed over her; then darkness settled over her spirit. Perhaps she was going mad; perhaps her nerves were only shaken—this was what her intelligence kept telling her with irritating, ineffectual persistency, while her heart cried out that the very springs of life in her had been poisoned, the very depths of her personality shaken.

At any rate, she was adrift in a strange and unfamiliar world, and there was no one anywhere to help her. A great pity for the stricken soul of Alène poured over her. Alène had put out her hands and had pleaded to be saved from herself—and no one had helped her. Now, at the first touch of her own distress, Graham turned from her—Graham wasn't going to help her. This thought walked through her mind: "Both of us together, we could have fought it! Alone—I cannot!"

She heard the gate click and saw Graham walking down the street. No doubt he was going to meet his mother—going without her.

"He's running away from me," she thought.

They had always gone to meet Mrs. Yates together. How many times they had walked down this street side by side, long before Alène died, whenever Graham's mother came! They would go down and tell her the news and how Alène was at that moment. Now *she* was left behind while Graham walked down alone to the station to see his mother first; to warn her, no doubt, that Beata was "not quite well."

She went into the house and began shoving around the ornaments, rearranging them with a sort of bitter satisfaction, an inward glow quite out of keeping with her trivial occupation. The noise of carriage wheels checked her suddenly. She stopped, a little dazed, like a person who has forgotten what he came into a room for—as an actor searches for a cue.

Now she remembered—Graham's mother was coming, and she must run out to meet her.

For the next few days the house was as though bathed in sunshine; calm returned to it. Beata was continually with the older woman, sheltering herself in her loving presence. It was as though all around was some fog which concealed menacing and terrible shapes—some terror that walked in the darkness, but for the moment Beata could escape from it, though she felt as insecure as if she were living in a soap-bubble; in a moment the force of the invading shadows—or whatever they were—might come upon her, and the agony of her rent personality would begin again.

They were all touchingly happy—Beata as from a relief from pain, Graham in his recovered peace—until one day when the two women sat sewing in the drawing-room. Graham was lounging near them, reading. Then Mrs. Yates raised her head toward the window and said:

"There's something different about this room since I've been away. You haven't moved things, have you?"

Beata didn't answer; her spirit, it seemed, ceased to breathe. The same shock that she had felt communicated itself to Graham, and he arose and walked around restlessly.

"I don't quite make out what's changed," she pursued, with serenity. "I see you keep yellow flowers in the window the way poor Alène did— Why, Beata, what ails you, child?"

For Beata had let her sewing fall and was gazing at Graham's mother in fascinated horror. Never once to herself had she clothed her thoughts in any words. At her fixed look and hopeless gesture Mrs. Yates stared, and for a moment the two women looked one at the other, horror in the eyes of each. Mrs. Yates broke the silence with:

"Are you ill, Beata—what is it?"

"I'm faint—a sudden pain—" The words came without her volition; her hand sought her heart.

There was a second of taut silence, when the very air of the room seemed to share the suspense, while mother and son looked at each other. Then Beata arose.

"I'm better now—I'm going to lie down."

For several days she remained on a couch in Graham's library on a pretext of illness, hiding from life by her inactivity; trying by her very quietness to put off the next move in the drama, which came like an unexpected verdict of a physician, when Mrs. Yates announced, after the mail had come one day:

"Ella wants me to visit her; I think I shall go."

"When does she want you?" Beata inquired.

With that command of herself which guileless older women know so well how to use, Mrs. Yates answered in an irreproachably natural tone:

"Why, right away. I shall go tomorrow, my dear—if you are feeling better, Beata."

"Oh yes," she replied. "I'm perfectly well now, I think. I've just been a little run down for some reason."

"It's very natural with his heat," Mrs. Yates replied, tranquilly. There was not a break in her surface anywhere.

After her departure—they both took her to the train—Beata and Graham turned into the garden. Suddenly she stopped.

"Why did mother go?" she asked him.

"Why, to see Ella, of course," Graham replied.

"You know what I mean—what was her real reason?"

Oh, how she waited for his answer—how she prayed for it in his one little second of indecision!

"You've had a lot of odd little streaks lately, Beata," he said.

Beata wanted to cry aloud to him: "You know she won't come back—you know I've driven her away!" But she couldn't speak. She waited for him to help her; she was sure that if she could drag the obscure events out into the light of day and clothe them with commonplace speech it would kill their horror. But what to say—where to begin? Her heart cried out, "Now—now!" Her whole being urged her into her vague confession, while her obstinate common sense leagued itself with the shadowy impulse from without which placed itself in the way of her desire.

Again Beata fought the unknown force as of an awful voiceless conflict of wills; common sense, by paradox, fighting on the side of The Unseen. Only now Beata knew she was fighting for her very existence. She no longer struggled with something that was no more than some strange and shattering nervous attack. Herself—her own personality—was her battle. Some mysterious door had been opened that allowed to flow through it emotions and acts not her own. She guessed that the very gestures of her hands, the look of her eyes, had been used. She had seen it mirrored on Graham's face; she had seen it in the momentary leaping horror of his glance.

But while their troubled eyes looked into each other's with comprehension, their obstinate tongues refused to voice their fear of this lurking peril. Peril was what it was, and Beata knew it—peril of their happiness—peril of her own sanity.

She looked at him, tears swimming in her eyes; longing to throw herself on his beloved heart and to lie there as in a safe haven and to beg him to save her, or at least to give her relief from pain. But he was gazing at her speculatively; to her racked mind it seemed that his gaze was hostile. She turned and fled to her room to give herself up for the first time in her life to the sort of weeping that made her feel that she had wept forth all the strength of her body; that with her weeping some virtue had gone out of her. She said out loud:

"There is no use fighting any more." A melancholy sense of rest enveloped her. No one would help her, and she wouldn't fight any more. She relaxed the muscles of her spirit. Now let the flood overwhelm her if it would; let it drown her utterly—she didn't care.

As the last shred of her resistance died, the enveloping shadow receded. She had expected some sort of a cataclysm. She had been fighting The Unseen, whatever it was—madness, visions—with all her strength; opposing her puny might to its force. At times, it seemed to her, coming near victory—with Graham's help, almost sure victory. But now it stood aloof.

Days passed and nothing happened. The outer surfaces of life were serene, and yet—all of life was altered, and Beata must go through her miserable treadmill of thought. She would sit long hours staring into vacancy, thinking over the minutest details of the events of the day. She dwelt on each small, meaningless act, half of whose torment lay in its very insignificance; the fact that there was nothing to tell, that you couldn't touch or taste or explain, not to anybody, not even to yourself, without seeming to talk in terms of madness. Such things, she would say to herself, didn't happen. And yet, while nothing happened, from one day to another there was a steady onflow of small details—whatever it was, this nameless and faceless thing was crawling upon her, Beata realized, like some dark tide, unceasing, unresting; while she slept, while she walked; without let-up, without rest.

Oh, that something would happen to hasten it! Oh, that some tangible event would happen so that she could cry out: "I've seen! I know!"

The only thing to be seen with the eyes was that the house, her creature, was changing in aspect under her hand. Her own hand eagerly obliterated the changes she had made when she had become Graham's wife. Yet the changes came with terrible and relentless slowness. One day a shade pulled down, a window shut, a picture of her choosing suppressed, the order of some books changed—nothing more, but each change accomplished by her hand and with a sense of fierce, inner joy.

She would walk up and down, up and down, absorbed in her own emotions, unconscious of the flight of time, and obscurely conscious that time dragged, that time stood still, that the hours whirled around her unnoticed, and that she and her sick fear alone stood still in the swirling, shifting universe.

Sometimes she would fill hours with balancing up which she would prefer—this nameless horror, this thing that couldn't be, that was poisoning her, perhaps killing her—or madness. She would laugh long, silent laughter on the irony of fate that put such a choice before her, of all people—she, who had been praised always for her sanity; she, to whom Alène had turned in her first illness of the spirit as a friend.

Meantime her life with Graham went on with unbroken surface—so unbroken that she could have screamed at him. Yet she knew with a sickening certainty that he watched her covertly, from around some doors, as it were; that he was always pretending to be doing something else, and yet was watching her. He, too, with smiling face and frozen heart was living in an obscure hell, spying upon her, watching for a look of the eye, for a gesture of the hand, while he had let the whole change in the house pass by unnoticed.

Anyway, if he watched her, then she watched him, for ever growing in her was a curious distrust of him—distrust of what she couldn't tell; she didn't trust him, that was all. Her logical mind that rejected the whole situation had to go through its torment and had to ask questions of her tormented heart. Did she distrust his love? There was no reason for it, and yet he never left the house but suspicion, nameless and groundless, filled her whole being with an ever-increasing anguish.

She suffered when he was with her; suffered from the suspicion of his suspicion—that he must read into her heart and hate and despise her for her ever-growing distrust—a distrust that didn't even seek to pin itself to anything. If she could only have accused him of something; if only for one little moment there was some real complaint against him. She herself would cry, even if she watched, even if she peered from behind a closed blind at him:

"Oh, my dear, I know you are good and true! It isn't *I* watching you—it isn't *I* accusing you—and yet I must suffer as though I knew you were waiting, a knife in your hand, to stab me when my back is turned!"

Beata waited as loving women wait who knew that their hour is come when the beloved is gone from them, and, worse than that—that he lies. They must wait with loving and beating hearts for the death of their spirits to be dealt out to them, shamefully and coward-wise. And since they cannot believe their lovers cowards as well as traitors, they still believe in the face of unbelief.

This was Beata's torment: believing him upright, believing him true, she must suffer for an unbelief; knowing that he loved her alone, she must watch each mood as it passed by for corroboration of what she knew was not. She must watch all his comings and goings; she must read dislike and suspicion in his gaze—the dislike that a man has for a woman whose claims sever him from the beloved. Then, as to thousands of women before her, came the need of knowing. Certainty! Certainty was what she wanted; for good or bad, to know the torment in which she lived.

"Oh," she would think to herself, "if I could only know!" But her mind would answer, "Know what?"

She lived continually as though on the eve of some discovery. A little further, and she would know what the monstrous certainty was of which she wished to be sure. If she looked into the black pool of her uncertainty long enough, she felt the answer would come; there must be an answer to all this that she suffered, and somehow she felt it lay in Graham—somehow in Graham she must find it. His very dumbness was to her the corroboration of his blameless guilt. She hated his smiling face; she hated his pretense; she wanted with all her strength to cry out:

"Say what you think! Say what you suspect!"

Then one night, as she sat in his room, and while their lips talked the pleasant commonplaces of happily married people, she realized that the answer to the riddle lay in his desk.

She knew it was there. There, in tangible form was the answer of all her torment and all her suspicion, if she could only look. She waited frozen in her own impatience for the slow moments to drag past on their leaden feet; she sat waiting until Graham should go upstairs and go to sleep beside her, so she could come down and find out what lay there.

There was no fight now. She, Beata—Beata with honor like a man's honor—waited with beating heart, her breath coming short, for the evening to pass and for Graham to sleep, that she might commit the one unforgivable crime.

He slept at last. Beata got out of bed, put on her dressing-gown and slippers, and went noiselessly down the stairs. She made no sound; not a stair creaked. It was as though she went through each one of the little acts like some highly trained mechanism, as though all her life had been one rehearsal for this moment. It was as though she had been rehearsing all her life for this—that without noise she might get up, dress herself, go downstairs without noise and light her candle in the library, then walk swiftly and with the directness of a homing pigeon to Graham's desk—to Graham's desk, where the answer of everything lay.

In the strange and painful universe in which Beata had been living the only certainty that she had was that there was the answer, the explanation of the riddle, and that she was about to find it. That she must find it even at the price of her own honor, at the breaking-down of the things most essential in her nature, meant nothing.

She went unfalteringly to where the desk stood, with the candle in her hand; unfalteringly she pulled out a little drawer and took from it a bundle of letters. They were tied neatly—Graham was exact and methodical in all his ways. As she opened them a little picture fluttered down—a snapshot of herself sent to Graham long ago, and then she recognized in the letters her own handwriting—nothing else. Her letters were what she had come to find—her letters written to Graham long ago! Written during his brief absences from Alène, telling of Alène's change from day to day; written to him when she was away. Letters for all the world to read; letters without one word of affection beyond that of a kindly friendship.

Her own letters—that was the answer! Her friendship and Graham's—that was the key-note of this mystery! For a second she stood there, not willing to understand. Then came crowding on her memories of Alène's looks and her sudden appearances in the room where she and Graham sat talking innocently—so innocently that no thought of what Alène meant had crossed their minds. So Beata stood motionless, her own letters in her hand, a terrible figure, as though she held there a proof of her own blood-guilt. And the question now arose to her mind:

"When did we first begin to care for each other? And was I here for Alène, or was I here for Graham's sake?"

She had come for Alène, but she had stayed for Graham, and before Alène's tragic death she had been the only comfort that he had had.

Then she heard his step behind her, and then his voice, and instead of her own name—"Alène!" he called. And then with a face of horror and her hands outstretched in a gesture terrible and tragic, a gesture they knew well and that was not her own, she cried:

"Yes—Alène, if you like! Why did you keep these letters—you, who never keep any letters?"

He tried to recover himself.

"Are you mad, Beata?" he said, but the sternness of his voice faltered.

"Oh," she took up, "I wish I were—you could shut me up then! Madness would be easy! We killed her—you and I between us killed her! She trusted us and we killed her—she trusted us and we tortured her!"

"Hush!" said Graham. "You don't know what you're saying, Beata. You're not well—you've not been well for a long time."

"No," she agreed. "I've not been well—but you've said nothing about it, Graham. It's a very strange illness I've had—what's been its name, Graham? What doctors cure it? You've tried not to believe—what couldn't be believed. Such things *can't* happen—that's what you've said to yourself when my face has frightened you—when you came into the room and thought Alène was standing here. But how should I have come where I am now, to find my own letters—my letters that you kept—my letters that I've been waiting so long to find?"

"Listen, Beata—we'll go away. You're ill. We'll go away!"

She saw that he couldn't admit what he had seen. In his man's world such things couldn't be. But it made no difference to her now. She held her proof in her hand.

"We'll go away and forget these weeks," he repeated.

"We'll do what you like—it won't alter anything. *We know now,*" Beata answered, dully; for she knew, as Graham did, that there was no flight possible for them, no refuge that they could take anywhere in the world, apart or together. They had heard the voice from the other side of silence; there was no country where they could take refuge, no place to go that would blot out from Graham's memory the picture of Beata leaning over his desk, her letters in her hand.

———•◆•———

HARRIETT PRESCOTT SPOFFORD
(1835–1921)

Poet, essayist, short-story writer, and novelist, Harriet Prescott Spofford was one of America's most widely published authors. Born in Maine, she attended the Putnam Free School and Pinkerton Academy. In the 1850s she began publishing anonymously, as did many women. In 1859, however, publication of the brilliant story "In a Cellar" in the *Atlantic Monthly* launched her on a lengthy and lucrative writing career. In 1865 she married Richard S. Spofford, Jr., a Newburyport lawyer, and all accounts of her life describe theirs as a long, successful marriage. Spofford's family had deep roots in New England, the locale and inspiration for much of her fiction. She wrote a number of haunting works, characterized by the lush romanticism of the earlier nineteenth century. The prose of "Her Story" has an almost biblical cadence and grandeur. It first appeared in *Lippincott's Magazine* in 1872.

* * *

Her Story

WELLNIGH THE WORST OF IT ALL IS THE MYSTERY.
If it were true, that accounts for my being here. If it were not true, then the best thing they could do with me was to bring me here. Then, too, if it were true, they would save themselves by hurrying me away; and if it were not true— You see, just as all roads lead to Rome, all roads led me to this Retreat. If it were true, it was enough to craze me; and if it were not true, I was already crazed. And there it is! I can't make out, sometimes, whether I am really beside myself or not; for it seems that whether I was crazed or sane, if it were true, they would naturally put me out of sight and hearing—bury me alive, as they have done, in this Retreat. They? Well, no—he. She stayed at home, I hear. If she had come with us, doubtless I should have found reason enough to say to the physician at once that she was the mad woman, not I—she, who, for the sake of her own brief pleasure, could make a whole after-life of misery for three of us. She— Oh

no, don't rise, don't go. I am quite myself, I am perfectly calm. Mad! There was never a drop of crazy blood in the Ridgleys or the Bruces, or any of the generations behind them, and why should it suddenly break out like a smothered fire in me? That is one of the things that puzzle me—why should it come to light all at once in me if it were not true?

Now, I am not going to be incoherent. It was too kind in you to be at such trouble to come and see me in this prison, this grave. I will not cry out once: I will just tell you the story of it all exactly as it was, and you shall judge. If I can, that is—oh, if I can! For sometimes, when I think of it, it seems as if Heaven itself would fail to take my part if I did not lift my own voice. And I cry, and I tear my hair and my flesh, till I know my anguish weighs down their joy, and the little scale that holds that joy flies up under the scorching of the sun, and God sees the festering thing for what it is! Ah, it is not injured reason that cries out in that way: it is a breaking heart!

How cool your hand is, how pleasant your face is, how good it is to see you! Don't be afraid of me: I am as much myself, I tell you, as you are. What an absurdity! Certainly any one who heard me make such a speech would think I was insane and without benefit of clergy. To ask you not to be afraid of me because I am myself. Isn't it what they call a vicious circle? And then to cap the climax by adding that I am as much myself as you are myself! But no matter—you know better. Did you say it was ten years? Yes, I knew it was as much as that—oh, it seems a hundred years! But we hardly show it: your hair is still the same as when we were at school; and mine— Look at this lock— I cannot understand why it is only sprinkled here and there: it ought to be white as the driven snow. My babies are almost grown women, Elizabeth. How could he do without me all this time? Hush now! I am not going to be disturbed at all; only that color of your hair puts me so in mind of his: perhaps there was just one trifle more of gold in his. Do you remember that lock that used to fall over his forehead and which he always tossed back so impatiently. I used to think that the golden Apollo of Rhodes had just such massive, splendid locks of hair as that; but I never told him; I never had the face to praise him; she had. She could exclaim how like ivory the forehead was—that great wide forehead—how that keen aquiline was to be found in the portrait of the Spencer of two hundred years ago. She could tell of the proud lip, of the fire burning in the hazel eye. She knew how, by a silent flattery, as she shrank away and looked up at him, to admire his haughty stature, and make him feel the strength and glory of his manhood and the delicacy of her womanhood.

She was a little thing—a little thing, but wondrous fair. Fair, did I say?

No: she was dark as an Egyptian, but such perfect features, such rich and splendid color, such great soft eyes—so soft, so black—so superb a smile; and then such hair! When she let it down, the backward curling ends lay on the ground and she stood on them, or the children lifted them and carried them behind her as pages carry a queen's train. If I had my two hands twisted in that hair! Oh, how I hate that hair! It would make as good a bowstring as ever any Carthaginian woman's made.

Ah, that is atrocious! I am sure you think so. But living all these lonesome years as I have done seems to double back one's sinfulness upon one's self. Because one is sane it does not follow that one is a saint. And when I think of my innocent babies playing with the hair that once I saw him lift and pass across his lips! But I will not think of it!

Well, well! I was a pleasant thing to look at myself once on a time, you know, Elizabeth. He used to tell me so: those were his very words. I was tall and slender, and if my skin was pale it was clear with a pearly clearness, and the lashes of my gray eyes were black as shadows; but now those eyes are only the color of tears.

I never told a syllable about it—I never could. It was so deep down in my heart, that love I had for him: it slept there so dark and still and full, for he was all I had in the world. I was alone, an orphan—if not friendless, yet quite dependent. I see you remember it all. I did not even sit in the pew with my cousin's family,—there were so many to fill it,—but down in one beneath the gallery, you know. And altogether life was a thing to me that hardly seemed worth the living. I went to church one Sunday, I recollect, idly and dreamingly as usual. I did not look off my book till a voice filled my ear—a strange new voice, a deep sweet voice, that invited you and yet commanded you—a voice whose sound divided the core of my heart, and sent thrills that were half joy, half pain, coursing through me. And then I looked up and saw him at the desk. He was reading the first lesson: "Fear not, for I have redeemed thee, I have called thee by thy name: thou art mine." And I saw the bright hair, the bright upturned face, the white surplice, and I said to myself, It is a vision, it is an angel; and I cast down my eyes. But the voice went on, and when I looked again he was still there. Then I bethought me that it must be the one who was coming to take the place of our superannuated rector—the last of a fine line, they had been saying the day before, who, instead of finding his pleasure otherwise, had taken all his wealth and prestige into the Church.

Why will a trifle melt you so—a strain of music, a color in the sky, a perfume? Have you never leaned from the window at evening, and had the scent of a flower float by and fill you with as keen a sorrow as if it had been disaster touching you? Long ago, I mean—we never lean from any windows here. I don't know how, but it was in that same invisible way that this voice melted me; and when I heard it saying, "Behold, I will do a new thing; now it shall spring forth; shall ye not know it? I will even make a way in the wilderness, and rivers in the desert," I was fairly crying. Oh, nervous tears, I dare say. The doctor here would tell you so, at any rate. And that is what I complain of here: they give a physiological reason for every emotion—they could give you a chemical formula for your very soul, I have no doubt. Well, perhaps they were nervous tears, for certainly there was nothing to cry for, and the mood went as suddenly as it came—changed to a sort of exaltation, I suppose—and when they sang the psalm, and he had swept in, in his black gown, and had mounted the pulpit stairs, and was resting that fair head on the big Bible in his silent prayer, I too was singing—singing like one possessed:

> "Then, to thy courts when I repair,
>   My soul shall rise on joyful wing,
>   The wonders of thy love declare,
>   And join the strain which angels sing."

And as he rose I saw him searching for the voice unconsciously, and our eyes met. Oh, it was a fresh young voice, let it be mine or whose. I can hear it now as if it were someone else singing. Ah, ah, it has been silent so many years! Does it make you smile to hear me pity myself? It is not myself I am pitying: it is that fresh young girl that loved so. But it used to rejoice me to think that I loved him before I laid eyes on him.

He came to my cousin's in the week—not to see Sylvia or to see Laura: he talked of church-music with my cousin, and then crossed the room and sat down by me. I remember how I grew cold and trembled—how glad, how shy I was; and then he had me sing; and at first Sylvia sang with us, but by and by we sang alone—I sang alone. He brought me yellow old church music, written in quaint characters: he said those characters, those old square breves, were a text guarding secrets of enchantment as much as the text of Merlin's book did; and so we used to find it. Once he brought a copy of an old Roman hymn, written only in the Roman letters: he said it was a hymn which the ancients sang to Maia, the mother-earth, and which the Church fathers adopted, singing it stealthily in the hidden places of the Catacombs; and together we translated it into tones. A rude but majestic thing it was.

And once— The sunshine was falling all about us in the bright lonely room, and the shadows of the rose leaves at the window were dancing over us. I had been singing a Gloria while he walked up and down the room, and he came up behind me: he stooped and kissed me on the mouth. And after that there was no more singing, for, lovely as the singing was, the love was lovelier yet. Why do I complain of such a hell as this is now? I had my heaven one—oh, I had my heaven once! And as for the other, perhaps I deserve it all, for I saw God only through him: it was he that waked me to worship. I had no faith but Spencer's faith; if he had been a heathen, I should have been the same, and creeds and systems might have perished for me had he only been spared from the wreck. And he had loved me from the first moment that his eyes met mine. "When I looked at you," he said, "singing that simple hymn that first day, I felt as I do when I look at the evening star leaning out of the clear sunset lustre: there is something in your face as pure, as remote, as shining. It will always be there," he said, "though you should live a hundred years." He little knew, he little knew!

But he loved me then—oh yes, I never doubted that. There were no happier lovers trod the earth. We took our pleasure as lovers do: we walked in the fields; we sat on the river's side; together we visited the poor and sick; he read me the passages he liked best in his writing from week to week; he brought me the verse from which he meant to preach, and up in the organ-loft I improvised to him the thoughts that it inspired in me. I did that timidly indeed: I could not think my thoughts were worth his hearing till I forgot myself, and only thought of him and the glory I would have revealed to him, and then the great clustering chords and the full music of the diapason swept out beneath my hands—swept along the aisles and swelled up the raftered roof as if they would find the stars, and sunset and twilight stole around us there as we sat still in the succeeding silence. I was happy: I was humble too. I wondered why I had been chosen for such a blest and sacred lot. It was so blessed to be allowed to minister one delight to him. I had a little print of the angel of the Lord appearing to Mary with the lily of annunciation in his hand, and I thought— I dare not tell you what I thought. I made an idol of my piece of clay.

When the leaves had turned we were married, and he took me home. Ah, what a happy home it was! Luxury and beauty filled it. When I first went into it and left the chill October night without, fires blazed upon the hearths; flowers bloomed in every room; a marble Eros held a light up, searching for his Psyche. "*Our* love has found its soul," said he. He led me to the music-room—a temple in itself, for its rounded ceiling towered to the height of the house. There were golden organ-pipes and banks of keys fit for St. Cecilia's use; there were all the delightful outlines of violin and piccolo and harp and horn for any who would use them; there was a pianoforte near the door for me—one such as I had never touched before; and there were cases on all sides filled with the rarest musical works. The floor was bare and inlaid; the windows were latticed in stained glass, so that no common light of day ever filtered through, but light bluer than the sky, gold as the dawn, purple as the night; and then there were vast embowering chairs, in any of which he could hide himself away while I made my incantation, as he sometimes called it, of the great spirits of song. As I tried the piano that night he tuned the old Amati which he himself now and then played upon, and together we improvised our own epithalamium. It was the violin that took the strong assuring part with strains of piercing sweetness, and the music of the piano flowed along in a soft cantabile of undersong. It seemed to me as if his part was like the flight of some white and strong-winged bird above a sunny brook.

But he had hardly created this place for the love of me alone. He adored music as a regenerator; he meant to use it so among his people: here were to be pursued those labors which should work miracles when produced in the open church. For he was building a church with the half of his fortune—a church full of restoration of the old and creation of the new: the walls within were to be a frosty tracery of vines running to break into the gigantic passion-flower that formed the rose-window; the lectern a golden globe upon a tripod, clasped by a silver dove holding on outstretched wings the book.

I have feared, since I have been here, that Spencer's piety was less piety than partisanship: I have doubted if faith were so much alive in him as the love of a great perfect system, and the pride in it I know he always felt. But I never thought about it then: I believed in him as I would have believed in an apostle. So stone by stone the church went up, and stone by stone our lives followed it—lives of such peace, such bliss! Then fresh hopes came into it—sweet trembling hopes; and by and by our first child was born. And if I had been happy before, what was I then? There are some compensations in this world: such happiness could not come twice, such happiness as there was in that moment when I lay, painless and at peace, with the little cheek nestled beside my own, while he bent above us both, proud and glad and tender. It was a dear little baby—so fair, so bright! and when she could walk she could sing. Her sister sang earlier yet; and what music their two shrill sweet voices made as they sat in their little chairs together at twilight before the fire, their curls glistening and their red shoes glistening, while they sang the evening hymn, Spencer on one side of the hearth and I upon the other! Sometimes we let the dear things sit up for a later hour in the music-room—for many a canticle we tried and practised there that hushed hearts and awed them when the choir gave them on succeeding Sundays—and always afterward I heard them singing in their sleep, just as a bird stirs in his nest and sings his stave in the night. Oh, we were happy then; and it was then she came.

She was the step-child of his uncle, and had a small fortune of her own, and Spencer had been left her guardian; and so she was to live with us—at any rate, for a while. I dreaded her coming. I did not want the intrusion; I did not like the things I heard about her; I knew she would be a discord in our harmony. But Spencer, who had only seen her once in her childhood, had been told by some one who travelled in Europe with her that she was delightful and had a rare intelligence. She was one of those women often delightful to men indeed, but whom other women—by virtue of their own kindred instincts, it may be, perhaps by virtue of temptations overcome—see through and know for what they are. But she had her own way of charming: she was the being of infinite variety—to-day glad, to-morrow sad, freakish, and always exciting you by curiosity as to her next caprice, and so moody that after a season of the lowering weather of one of her dull humors you were ready to sacrifice something for the sake of the sunshine that she knew how to make so vivid and so sweet. Then, too, she brought forward her forces by detachment. At first she was the soul of domestic life, sitting at night beneath the light and embossing on weblike muslin designs of flower and leaf which she had learned in her convent, listening to Spencer as he read, and taking from the little wallet of her work-basket apropos scraps which she had preserved from the sermon of some Italian father of the Church or of some French divine. As for me, the only thing I knew was my poor music; and I used to burn with indignation when she interposed that unknown tongue between my husband and myself. Presently her horses came, and then, graceful in her dark riding-habit, she would spend a morn-ing fearlessly subduing one of the fiery fellows, and dash away at last with plume and veil streaming behind her. In the early evening she would dance with the children—witch-dances they were—with her round arms linked above her head, and her feet weaving the measure in and out as deftly as any flashing-footed Bayadere might do—only when Spencer was there to see: at other times I saw she pushed the little hindering things aside without a glance.

By and by she began to display a strange dramatic sort of power: she would rehearse to Spencer scenes that she had met with from day to day in the place, giving now the old churchwarden's voice and now the sexton's, their gestures and very faces; she could tell the ailments of half the old women in the parish who came to me with them, and in their own tone and manner to the life; she told us once of a street-scene, with the crier crying a lost child, the mother following with lamentations, the passing strangers questioning, the boys hooting, and the child's reappearance, followed by a tumult, with kisses and blows and cries, so that I thought I saw it all; and presently she had found the secret and vulnerable spot of every friend we had, and could personate them all as vividly as if she did it by necromancy.

One night she began to sketch our portraits in charcoal: the likenesses were not perfect; she exaggerated the careless elegance of Spencer's attitude; perhaps the primness of my own. But yet he saw there the ungraceful trait for the first time, I think. And so much led to more: she brought out her portfolios, and there were her pencil-sketches from the Rhine and from the Guadalquivir, rich water-colors of Venetian scenes; interiors of old churches, and sheet after sheet covered with details of church architecture. Spencer had been admiring all the others—in spite of something that I thought I saw in them, a something that was not true, a trait of her own identity, for I had come to criticise her sharply—but when his eye rested on those sheets I saw it sparkle, and he caught them up and pored over them one by one.

"I see you have mastered the whole thing," he said: "you must instruct me here." And so she did. And there were hours, while I was busied with servants and accounts or with the children, when she was closeted with Spencer in the study, criticising, comparing, making drawings, hunting up authorities; other hours when they walked away together to the site of the new church that was building, and here an arch was destroyed, and there an aisle was extended, and here a row of cloisters sketched into the plan, and there a row of windows, till the whole design was reversed and made over. And they had the thing between them, for, admire and sympathize as I might, I did not know. At first Spencer would repeat the day's achievement to me, but the contempt for my ignorance which she did not deign to hide soon put an end to it when she was present.

It was this interest that now unveiled a new phase of her character: she was devout. She had a little altar in her room; she knew all about albs and chasubles; she would have persuaded Spencer to burn candles in the chancel; she talked of a hundred mysteries and symbols; she wanted to embroider a stole to lay across his shoulders. She was full of small church sentimentalities, and as one after another she uttered them, it seemed to me that her belief was no sound fruit of any system—if it were belief, and not a mere bunch of fancies—but only, as you might say, a rotten windfall of the Romish Church: it had none of the round splendor of that Church's creed, none of the pure simplicity of ours: it would be no stay in trouble, no shield in temptation. I said as much to Spencer.

"You are prejudiced," said he: "her belief is the result of long observation abroad, I think. She has found the need of outward observances: they are, she has told me, a shrine to the body of her faith, like that commanded in the building of the tabernacle, where the ark of the covenant was enclosed in the holy of holies."

"And you didn't think it profane in her to speak so? But I don't believe it, Spencer," I said. "She has no faith: she has some sentimentalisms."

"You are prejudiced," he repeated. "She seems to me a wonderful and gifted being."

"Too gifted," I said. "Her very gifts are unnatural in their abundance. There must be scrofula there to keep such a fire in the blood and sting the brain to such action: she will die in a madhouse, depend upon it." Think of my saying such a thing as that!

"I have never heard you speak so before," he replied coldly. "I hope you do not envy her her powers."

"I envy her nothing," I cried. "For she is as false as she is beautiful!" But I did—oh I did!

"Beautiful?" said Spencer. "Is she beautiful? I never thought of that."

"You are very blind, then," I said with a glad smile.

Spencer smiled too. "It is not the kind of beauty I admire," said he.

"Then I must teach you, sir," said she. And we both started to see her in the doorway, and I, for one, did not know, till shortly before I found myself here, how much or how little she had learned of what we said.

"Then I must teach you, sir," said she again. And she came deliberately into the firelight and paused upon the rug, drew out the silver arrows and shook down all her hair about her, till the great snake-like coils unrolled upon the floor.

"Hyacinthine," said Spencer.

"Indeed it is," said she. "The very color of the jacinth, with that red tint in its darkness that they call black in the shade and gold in the sun. Now look at me."

"Shut your eyes, Spencer," I cried, and laughed.

But he did not shut his eyes. The firelight flashed over her: the color in her cheeks and on her lips sprang ripe and red in it as she held the hair away from them with her rosy finger-tips; her throat curved small and cream-white from the bosom that the lace of her dinner-dress scarcely hid; and the dark eyes glowed with a great light as they lay full on his.

"You mustn't call it vanity," said she. "It is only that it is impossible, looking at the picture in the glass, not to see it as I see any other picture. But for all that, I know it is not every fool's beauty: it is no daub for the vulgar gaze, but a masterpiece that it needs the educated eye to find. I could tell you how this nostril is like that in a famous marble, how the curve of this cheek is that of a certain Venus, the line of this forehead like the line in the dreamy Antinous' forehead. Are you taught? Is it—?"

Then she twisted her hair again and fastened the arrows, and laughed and turned away to look over the evening paper. But as for Spencer, as he lay back in his lordly way, surveying the vision from crown to toe, I saw him flush—I saw him flush and start and quiver, and then he closed his eyes and pressed his fingers on them, and lay back again and said not a word.

She began to read aloud something concerning services at the recent dedication of a church. I was called out as she read. When I came back, a half hour afterward, they were talking. I stopped at my work-table in the next room for a skein of floss that she had asked me for, and I heard her saying, "You cannot expect me to treat you with reverence. You are a married priest, and you know what opinion I necessarily must have of married priests." Then I came in and she was silent.

But I knew, I always knew, that if Spencer had not felt himself weak, had not found himself stirred, if he had not recognized that, when he flushed and quivered before her charm, it was the flesh and not the spirit that tempted him, he would not have listened to her subtle invitation to austerity. As it was, he did. He did—partly in shame, partly in punishment; but to my mind the listening was confession. She had set the wedge that was to sever our union—the little seed in a mere idle cleft that grows and grows and splits the rock asunder.

Well, I had my duties, you know. I never felt my husband's wealth a reason why I should neglect them any more than another wife should neglect her duties. I was wanted in the parish, sent for here and waited for there: the dying liked to see me comfort their living, the living liked to see me touch their dead; some wanted help, and others wanted consolation; and where I felt myself too young and unlearned to give advice, I could at least give sympathy. Perhaps I was the more called upon for such detail of duty because Spencer was busy with the greater things, the church-building and the sermons—sermons that once on a time lifted you and held you on their strong wings. But of late Spencer had been preaching old sermons. He had been moody and morose too: sometimes he seemed oppressed with melancholy. He had spoken to me strangely, had looked at me as if he pitied me, had kept away from me. But she had not regarded his moods: she had followed him in his solitary strolls, had sought him in his study; and she had ever a mystery or symbol to be interpreted, the picture of a private chapel that she had heard of when abroad, or the ground-plan of an ancient one, or some new temptation to his ambition, as I divine. And soon he was himself again.

I was wrong to leave him so to her, but what was there else for me to do? And as for those duties of mine, as I followed them I grew restive; I abridged them, I hastened home. I was impatient even with the detentions the children caused. I could not leave them to their nurses, for all that; but they kept me away from him, and he was alone with her.

One day at last he told me that his mind was troubled by the suspicion that his marriage was a mistake; that on his part at least it had been wrong; that he had been thinking a priest should have the Church only for his bride, and should wait at the altar mortified in every affection; that it was not for hands that were full of caresses and lips that were covered with kisses to touch the sacrament, to offer praise. But for answer I brought my children and put them in his arms. I was white and cold and shaking, but I asked him if they were not justification enough. And I told him that he did his duty better abroad for the heartening of a wife at home, and that he knew better how to interpret God's love to men through his own love for his children. And I laid my head on his breast beside them, and he clasped us all and we cried together, he and I.

But that was not enough, I found. And when our good bishop came, who had always been like a father to Spencer, I led the conversation to that point one evening, and he discovered Spencer's trouble, and took him away and reasoned with him. The bishop was a power with Spencer, and I think that was the end of it.

The end of that, but only the beginning of the rest. For she had accustomed him to the idea of separation from me—the idea of doing without me. He had put me away from himself once in his mind: we had been one soul, and now we were two.

One day, as I stood in my sleeping-room with the door ajar, she came in. She had never been there before, and I cannot tell you how insolently she looked about her. There was a bunch of flowers on a stand that Spencer himself placed there for me every morning. He had always done so, and there had been no reason for breaking off the habit; and I had always worn one of them at my throat. She advanced a hand to pull out a blossom. "Do not touch them," I cried: "my husband puts them there."

"Suppose he does," said she lightly. "For how long?" Then she overlooked me with a long sweeping glance of search and contempt, shrugged her shoulders, and with a French sentence that I did not understand turned back and coolly broke off the blossom she had marked and hung it in her hair. I could not take her by the shoulders and put her from the room. I could not touch the flowers that she had desecrated. I left the room myself, and left her in it, and went down to dinner for the first time without the flower at my throat. I saw Spencer's eye note the omission: perhaps he took it as a release from me, for he never put the flowers in my room again after that day.

Nor did he ask me any more into his study, as he had been used, or read his sermons to me. There was no need of his talking over the church-building with me—he had her to talk it over with. And as for our music, that had been a rare thing since she arrived, for her conversation had been such as to leave but little time for it, and somehow when she came into the music-room and began to dictate to me the time in which I should take an Inflammatus and the spirit in which I should sing a ballad, I could not bear it. Then, too, to tell you the truth, my voice was hoarse and choked with tears full half the time.

It was some weeks after the flowers ceased that our youngest child fell ill. She was very ill—I don't think Spencer knew how ill. I dared not to trust her with any one, and Spencer said no one could take such care of her as her mother could; so, although we had nurses in plenty, I hardly left the room by night or day. I heard their voices down below, I saw them go out for their walks. It was a hard fight, but I saved her.

But I was worn to a shadow when all was done—worn with anxiety for her, with alternate fevers of hope and fear, with the weight of my responsibility as to her life; and with anxiety for Spencer too, with a despairing sense that the end of peace had come, and with the total sleeplessness of many nights. Now, when the child was mending and gaining every day, I could not sleep if I would.

The doctor gave me anodynes, but to no purpose: they only nerved me wide awake. My eyes ached, and my brain ached, and my body ached, but it was of no use: I could not sleep. I counted the spots on the wall, the motes upon my eyes, the notes of all the sheets of music I could recall. I remembered the Eastern punishment of keeping the condemned awake till they die, and wondered what my crime was; I thought if I could but sleep I might forget my trouble, or take it up freshly and master it. But no, it was always there—a heavy cloud, a horror of foreboding. As I heard that woman's step go by the door I longed to rid the house of it, and I dinted my palms with my nails till she had passed.

I did not know what to do. It seemed to me that I was wicked in letting the thing go on, in suffering Spencer to be any longer exposed to her power; but then I feared to take a step lest I should thereby rivet the chains she was casting on him. And then I longed so for one hour of the old dear happiness—the days when I and the children had been all and enough. I did not know what to do; I had no one to counsel with; I was wild within myself, and all distraught. Once I thought if I could not rid the house of her I could rid it of myself; and as I went through a dark passage and chanced to look up where a bright-headed nail glittered, I questioned if it would bear my weight. For days the idea haunted me. I fancied that when I was gone perhaps he would love me again, and at any rate I might be asleep and at rest. But the thought of the children prevented me, and one other thought—I was not certain that even my sorrows would excuse me before God.

I went down to dinner again at last. How she glowed and abounded in her beauty as she sat there! And I—I must have been very thin and ghastly: perhaps I looked a little wild in all my bewilderment and hurt. His heart smote him, it may be, for he came round to where I sat by the fire afterward and smoothed my hair and kissed my forehead. He could not tell all I was suffering then—all I was struggling with; for I thought I had better put him out of the world than let him, who was once so pure and good, stay in it to sin. I could have done it, you know. For though I still lay with the little girl, I could have stolen back into our own room with the chloroform, and he would never have known. I turned the handle of the door one night, but the bolt was slipped. I never thought of killing her, you see: let her live and sin, if she would. She was the thing of slime and sin, a splendid tropical growth of the passionate heat and the slime: it was only her nature. But then we think it no harm to kill reptiles, however splendid.

But it was by that time that the voices had begun to talk with me—all night long, all day. It was they, I found, that had kept me so sleepless. Go where I might, they were ever before me. If I went to the woods, I heard them in the whisper of every pine tree. If I went down to the seashore, I heard them in the plash of every wave. I heard them in the wind, in the singing of my ears, in the children's breath as I hung above them,—for I had decided that if I went out of the world I would take the children with me. If

I sat down to play, the things would twist the chords into discords; if I sat down to read, they would come between me and the page.

Then I could see the creatures: they had wings like bats. I did not dare speak of them, although I fancied she suspected me, for once she said, as I was kissing my little girl, "When you are gone to a madhouse, don't think they'll have many such kisses." Did she say it? or did I think she said it? I did not answer her, I did not look up: I suppose I should have flown at her throat if I had.

I took the children out with me on my rambles: we went for miles; sometimes I carried one, sometimes the other. I took such long, long walks to escape those noisome things: they would never leave me till I was quite tired out. Now and then I was gone the whole day; and all the time that I was gone he was with her, I knew, and she was tricking out her beauty and practising her arts.

I went to a little festival with them, for Spencer insisted. And she made shadow-pictures on the wall, wonderful things with her perfect profile and her perfect arms and her subtle curves—she out of sight, the shadow only seen. Now it was Isis, I remember, and now it was the head and shoulders and trailing hair of a floating sea-nymph. And then there were charades in which she played; and I can't tell you the glorious thing she looked when she came on as Helen of Troy with all her "beauty shadowed in white veils," you know—that brown and red beauty with its smiles and radiance under the wavering of the flower-wrought veil. I sat by Spencer, and I felt him shiver. He was fighting and struggling too within himself, very likely; only he knew that he was going to yield after all—only he longed to yield while he feared. But as for me, I saw one of those bat-like things perched on her ear as she stood before us, and when she opened her mouth to speak I saw them flying in and out. And I said to Spencer, "She is tormenting me. I cannot stay and see her swallowing the souls of men in this way." And I would have gone, but he held me down fast in my seat. But if I was crazy then—as they say I was, I suppose—it was only with a metaphor, for she was sucking Spencer's soul out of his body.

But I was not crazy. I should admit I might have been if I alone had seen those evil spirits. But Spencer saw them too. He never told me so, but— there are subtle ways—I knew he did; for when I opened the church door late, as I often did at that time after my long walks, they would rush in past me with a whizz, and as I sat in the pew I would see him steadily avoid looking at me; and if he looked by any chance, he would turn so pale that I have thought he would drop where he stood; and he would redden afterward as though one had struck him. He knew then what I endured with them; but I was not the one to speak of it. Don't tell me that his color changed and he shuddered so because I sat there mumbling and nodding to myself. It was because he saw those things mopping and mowing beside me and whispering in my ear. Oh what loathsomeness the obscene creatures whispered! Foul quips and evil words I had never heard before, ribald songs and oaths; and I would clap my hands over my mouth to keep from crying out at them. Creatures of the imagination, you may say. It is possible. But they were so vivid that they seem real to me even now. I burn and tingle as I recall them. And how could I have imagined such sounds, such shapes, of things I had never heard or seen or dreamed?

And Spencer was very unhappy, I am sure. I was the mother of his children, and if he loved me no more, he had an old kindness for me still, and my distress distressed him. But for all that the glamour was on him, and he could not give up that woman and her beauty and her charm. Once or twice he may have thought about sending her away, but perhaps he could not bring himself to do it—perhaps he reflected it was too late, and now it was no matter. But every day she stayed he was the more like wax in her hands. Oh, he was weaker than water that is poured out. He was abandoning himself, and forgetting earth and heaven and hell itself, before a passion—a passion that soon would cloy, and then would sting.

It was the spring season: I had been out several hours. The sunset fell while I was in the wood, and the stars came out; and at one time I thought I would lie down there on last year's leaves and never get up again. But I remembered the children, and went home to them. They were in bed and asleep when I took off my shoes and opened the door of their room— breathing so sweetly and evenly, the little yellow heads close together on one pillow, their hands tossed about the coverlid, their parted lips, their rosy cheeks. I knelt to feel the warm breath on my own cold cheek, and then the voices began whispering again: "If only they never waked! they never waked!"

And all I could do was to spring to my feet and run from the room. I ran shoeless down the great staircase and through the long hall. I thought I would go to Spencer and tell him all—all my sorrows, all the suggestions of the voices, and maybe in the endeavor to save me he would save himself. And I ran down the long dimly-lighted drawing-room, led by the sound I heard, to the music-room, whose doors were open just beyond. It was lighted only by the pale glimmer from the other room and by the moonlight through the painted panes. And I paused to listen to what I had never listened to there—the sound of the harp and a voice with it. Of course they had not heard me coming, and I hesitated and looked, and then I glided within the door and stood just by the open piano there.

She sat at the harp singing—the huge gilded harp. I did not know she sang—she had kept that for her last reserve—but she struck the harp so that it sang itself, like some great prisoned soul, and her voice followed it—oh so rich a voice! My own was white and thin, I felt, beside it. But mine had soared, and hers still clung to earth—a contralto sweet with honeyed sweetness—the sweetness of unstrained honey that has the earth-taste and the heavy blossom-dust yet in it—sweet, though it grew hoarse and trembling with passion. He sat in one of the great arm-chairs just before her: he was white with feeling, with rapture, with forgetfulness; his eyes shone like stars. He moved restlessly, a strange smile kindled all his face: he bent toward her, and the music broke off in the middle as they threw their arms around each other, and hung there lip to lip and heart to heart. And suddenly I crashed down both my hands on the keyboard before me, and stood and glared upon them.

And I never knew anything more till I woke up here.

And that is the whole of it. That is the puzzle of it—was it a horrid nightmare, an insane vision, or was it true? Was it true that I saw Spencer, my white, clean lover, my husband, a man of God, the father of our spotless babies,—was it true that I saw him so, or was it only some wild, vile conjuration of disease? Oh, I would be willing to have been crazed a lifetime, a whole lifetime, only to wake one moment before I died and find that that had never been!

Well, well, well! When time passed and I became more quiet, I told the doctor here about the voices—I never told him of Spencer or of her—and he bade me dismiss care. He said I was ill—excitement and sleeplessness had surcharged my nerves with that strange magnetic fluid that has worked so much mischief in the world. There was no organic disease, you see; only when my nerves were rested and right, my brain would be right. And the doctor gave me medicines and books and work, and when I saw the bat-like things again I was to go instantly to him. And after a little while I was not sure that I did see them. And in a little while longer they had ceased to come altogether. And I have had no more of them. I was on my parole then in the parlor, at the table, in the grounds. I felt that I was cured of whatever had ailed me: I could escape at any moment that I wished.

And it came Christmas time. A terrible longing for home overcame me— for my children. I thought of them at this time when I had been used to take such pains for their pleasure. I thought of the little empty stockings, the sad faces; I fancied I could hear them crying for me. I forgot all about my word of honor. It seemed to me that I should die, that I might as well die, if I could not see my little darlings, and hold them on my knees, and sing to them while the chimes were ringing in the Christmas Eve. And winter was here and there was so much to do for them. And I walked down the garden, and looked out at the gate, and opened it and went through. And I slept that night in a barn—so free, so free and glad! And the next day an old farmer and his sons, who thought they did me a service, brought me back, and of course I shrieked and raved. And so would you.

But since then I have been in this ward and a prisoner. I have my work, my amusement. I send such little things as I can make to my girls. I read. Sometimes of late I sing in the Sunday service. The place is a sightly place; the grounds, when we are taken out, are fine; the halls are spacious and pleasant.

Pleasant—but ah, when you have trodden them ten years!

And so, you see, if I were a clod, if I had no memory, no desires, if I had never been happy before, I might be happy now. I am confident the doctor thinks me well. But he has no orders to let me go. Sometimes it is so wearisome. And it might be worse if lately I had not been allowed a new service. And that is to try to make a woman smile who came here a year ago. She is a little woman, swarthy as a Malay, but her hair, that grows as rapidly as a fungus grows in the night, is whiter than leprosy: her eyebrows are so long and white that they veil and blanch her dark dim eyes; and she has no front teeth. A stone from a falling spire struck her from her horse, they say. The blow battered her and beat out reason and beauty. Her mind is dead: she remembers nothing, knows nothing; but she follows me about like a dog: she seems to want to do something for me, to propitiate me. All she ever says is to beg me to do her no harm. She will not go to sleep without my hand in hers. Sometimes, after long effort, I think there is a gleam of intelligence, but the doctor says there was once too much intelligence, and her case is hopeless.

Hopeless, poor thing!—that is an awful word: I could not wish it said for my worst enemy.

In spite of these ten years I cannot feel that it has yet been said for me.

If I am strange just now, it is only the excitement of seeing you, only the habit of the strange sights and sounds here. I should be calm and well enough at home. I sit and picture to myself that some time Spencer will come for me—will take me to my girls, my fireside, my music. I shall hear his voice, I shall rest in his arms, I shall be blest again. For, oh, Elizabeth, I do forgive him all!

Or if he will not dare to trust himself at first, I picture to myself how he will send another—some old friend who knew me before my trouble—who will see me and judge, and carry back report that I am all I used to be—some friend who will open the gates of heaven to me, or close the gates of hell upon me—who will hold my life and my fate.

If—oh if it should be you, Elizabeth!

JOSEPHINE DASKAM BACON
(1876–1961)

Josephine Dodge Daskam Bacon enjoyed a literary career that spanned more than four decades. Born in Connecticut, she attended Smith College. After graduating in 1898, she launched her reputation with a volume of short stories about that institution. In 1903 she married Selden Bacon and continued to write, publishing thirty-six volumes of poetry and short stories in all. Bacon was also a pioneer in the Girl Scouts Movement and compiled the handbook used by that organization. One chatty biographical dictionary from 1914 listed her interests as "all country sports, farming, stock breeding, amateur dramatics and music." The two ghostly tales that appear in this volume were taken from *The Strange Cases of Dr. Stanchon* (1913), a collection of stories loosely connected by the figure of Dr. Stanchon, a turn-of-the-century alienist.

The Gospel

FOR THE FIRST FEW DAYS OF HER STAY THERE, SHE thought little enough of the strangeness of the situation. To think of it, to marvel at the neat stillness, the quiet precision of all the domestic arrangements, would have been to let her mind dwell on just what she had to avoid. She was sick to her very soul of all that the words "domestic arrangements" implied; sick with an actual spiritual nausea. It was honestly no exaggeration to say that she would gladly have died rather than take the trouble to arrange the details of living.

So every morning she woke when her dreams ended and lay staring idly, through the cross-bars of the primitive window-netting, at the swaying, sinking, tree-tops, and the floating white above them, so white between the blue and green; and then her breakfast came, fresh and chill and shining, with a flaming nasturtium on the snowy linen; and then a dreamy time, when thought ranged among stray lines of poetry and memories of childhood; and then some one rubbed and kneaded and ironed out her tired muscles and she slept again. Sometimes foaming milk came in a beaded brown pitcher that smelt of dairies; sometimes luscious, quartered fruits, smothered in clotting cream, tempted a palate nearly dulled beyond recall; sometimes rich, salted broth steamed in a dim, blue bowl till she regretted to see the bottom of it.

And just at that time she was lifted into a long, basket chair and, propped in lavendered pillows, looked dreamily into the hills and pastures rolling out in front of her. Cows wandered here and there, birds swooped lazily through the June blue, the faintest scent of grapevines hung on the wind. But no human figures blotted the landscape; only the faint, musical clash of distant scythes (a sound as natural as the cawing and loving and interminable twittering of the busy animal world all around) spoke of men.

Then one day (it might have been a week's time) she caught herself listening for sounds of household labour. Where was the breaking, the slamming, the whistling, the quarrelling, the brushing and the rattling that these thin partitions ought to filter through? Simply, it was not. A little faint, suspicious worry came to her: the house was a tomb, then? Did it have to be? Was she as bad as that?

And when her tray came next, some kind of savoury stew, by now, with fresh picked strawberries on a sea-green grape leaf, she looked directly at the woman who brought it to the bed.

"How still this house is!" she said, and flushed with weakness, for it was her first real sentence, and it occurred to her that only little sighs of fatigue or groans of relief and halting exclamations of, "That feels good," or "No more, thanks," had passed her lips.

The woman smiled. She wore a straight gown of some cool stripe of white and grey and her eyes were grey.

"We live in a quiet place," she said, and lifted the pillows higher.

But it seemed that after that—perhaps it was because she listened—she began to hear faint sounds. The clear falling of poured out water, and the tinkling of dish on dish, now and then, and later, the soft murmur of exchanging women's voices.

Another day she spoke of the freshness of her morning egg, and that afternoon she leaned nearer the casement to catch the cluck of a motherly hen with her brood, and smiled at the scurry of wing and feet as grain was scattered somewhere.

It must have been at that time that the doctor came up to see her, a big brown man, whose beard hid his smile when he chose, but nothing could cover the keen, reading beam of the eye.

"I see you are doing well," he said.

"It is wonderful," she answered him, "but I am sure it is not the world."

"The world is very large," he said, and went away.

"And I never asked about—about anybody," she murmured, her eyes filling, "but I am sure they are all right, or he would have said!"

She was ashamed, afterward, to remember for how long she had thought the woman who attended on her a servant. And yet she did think her so until the morning when it suddenly occurred to her that it was not possible any ordinary servant should be so deft and self-contained at once: servants were not so calm—that was it, so calm. Even the best of them were hurried and anxious, and if they were old and valued, they got on one's nerves the more: one had to consider them. Of course, this was a trained nurse. She had decided suddenly that she felt equal to rising for her bath, and congratulated herself on discerning the nurse in time, for now she could ask for help, if she needed it.

"If you will show me the bathroom," she said, "and will be there to help me over the edge of the tub, in case I feel weak——"

"I will be there," said the woman, "but I must get it ready: the tub is not high."

And when she stepped into the next room she realised, with a little smile, how far she was from white porcelain and tiled walls. On the scrubbed deal floor there stood a white deal tub, clean as new milk, round and copper bound. Towels and soaps and sponges were there in plenty, and great metal ewers full of hot and cold water, and nothing else but one chair in all the scrubbed cleanliness. The woman poured the water over her as she crouched in the fragrant wooden pool and dried her gently and quickly in towels pressed away in lavender, with the deft, sure movements of one well practised in her business; but when she lay, just happily tired from the new exertion, among the fragrant sheets, a tiny shadow seemed about to haunt her sleep. She placed the little discomfort with difficulty, but at length expressed it.

"That tub is very heavy, now," she said drowsily. "Is there a man to lift it?"

For the first time the woman smiled. Till then she had been hands and feet merely, tireless and tactful, but impersonal: now she smiled, and her face was very sweet.

"I shall empty it," she said. "I am quite strong. Go to sleep, now."

Very soon again the doctor came, and at her quiet request gave her news of husband, children and home; all well, it seemed, and smoothly ordered. Days of absolute stillness had broken the habit of insistent speech, and many things that once would have said themselves before she thought, now halted behind her lips and seemed not worth the muscular effort. But one thing she did mention.

"Ought not the nurses here to have more help?" she asked. "Mine lifts out my bath-water every day. Are there not servants enough? I could pay for it . . ."

"There are no servants here at all," he said, "and there is nobody you could pay more than you are already paying."

"Then they are all nurses?"

"There are no trained nurses here, if you mean that," he said.

"Then who—what is the woman who takes care of me?" she asked, vaguely displeased.

"She is one of the daughters of the house," he said. "She is no more a nurse than her mother is a cook or her sister a laundress. They do what is to be done, that is all. Each has done and can do the others' tasks."

She felt in some way corrected, yet it was hard to say in what she had offended. But Dr. Stanchon was an odd man in many ways. "All the same," she persisted, "I think I had better have a nurse, now. I shall feel more comfortable. Ask Miss Jessop if she could come out to me. I believe I could get along with her, now. I'm afraid I was childish, before."

But he only shook his head. "The time for Miss Jessop has passed, dear friend," he said quietly. "No nurse ever comes here."

"Then this is a private house," she began again, "their own home. And I do not even know their names!"

"It is private because it *is* their own home—just that," he said. "That is what a home is. It is a simple fact, but one that seems not to have been included in your education."

"Why, Dr. Stanchon, what can you mean?" she cried. "My mother's hospitality——"

"I mean that I do not consider an art museum a home, no matter how highly the chef is paid," he said shortly.

"But there is the place on the Hudson——"

"That is a country club, nothing more," he interrupted. "Your mother dismissed a butler once, because, though he offered eight liqueurs to a guest, the guest asked for a ninth and the butler had neglected to order it. I have attended her there for a really painful attack of sciatica when none of her visitors knew that anything ailed her, though she had been away from them for forty-eight hours."

"But that is mother's house, not mine," she protested, "and I do not pretend to keep up——"

"You do not pretend to, because you could not do it," he interrupted again. "Your father is a multimillionaire and your husband is not. But it is your constant ideal, nevertheless, and your failures to realise it, even in the degree to which you have tried, have sapped your vitality to a point which even you can understand now, I should suppose."

She looked doubtingly at him.

"Do you really mean, Dr. Stanchon," she began, "that this dreadful attack———"

"'Attack!'" he muttered brusquely, "'attack'! One would imagine I had pulled you through pneumonia or peritonitis! If, after constant sapping and mining and starving-out the garrison, it gives way and falls defeated, you choose to call the day of surrender a yielding to an attack, then you have had an attack."

And again he left her abruptly, a prey to creeping, ugly doubts. For she had been very sorry for herself and the fatality that had stranded her on the dreary coast where so many of her friends had met mysterious wreckage.

"Has the doctor sent patients here before?" she asked her attendant the next morning, when she sat, fresh and fragrant in her invalid ruffles, at the window, watching the poultry yard, which somehow she had not noticed before, and the cow browsing beside the brook where the white ducks paddled, gossiping.

"Oh, yes, often," said the busy sister (she was Hester; the other was Ann). "We are never without some one. So many people are ill in the city. Now I am going to clean your room, and perhaps you will feel like stepping out on the balcony?"

Surprised, for she had not seen any such addition to the simple frame house, she stepped through a window cut down somewhat clumsily, but efficiently enough, and hinged to swing outward, onto a shallow, roofed *loggia* with vines grown from boxes on the sides and two long, low chairs faced to the view of the hills. In one of these sat a woman, slender and motionless, whose glistening white wrapper seemed to melt in the strong sun into the white of the painted wooden balustrade that protected the balcony. Flushed with an invalid's quick irritation and resentful of any other occupant, for her raw nerves were not yet healed, she was about to turn back hastily into the room when a second glance assured her that it was only one of her own white wrappers draped along the chair. The face and hands that her vexed irritation must have supplied amazed her, in retrospect, with their distinctness of outline, and she trembled at her weak nerves.

From inside the room came the swishing of water and the sound of scrubbing; soon the strong clean flavour of soapy boards floated out, and the flick of the drops into the pail; from where she sat she could see out of the corner of her eye the fluff of snowy suds that foamed over the shining bucket as Hester rubbed the milky cake of soap with the bristles. Her strong strokes had a definite rhythm and set the time for the stern old hymn-tune she crooned. The listener on the balcony obeyed her growing interest and turned her chair to face into the room. The kilted Hester, on her knees, her brow bound with a glistening towel, threw her body forward with the regularity of a rower, her strong, muscled arms shot out in a measured curve; on her little island of dry boards she sang amid her clean, damp sea, high-priestess of a lustral service as old as the oldest temple of man, and the odour of her incense, the keen, sweet freshness of her cleansing soap, rose to the heaven of her hymn.

"You sing as if you liked it," said the watcher.

"And so I do," said Hester. "Things must be clean, and I like to make them so."

"Why, you are doing just what we did in the gymnasium the year I went there," cried the invalid, with the first real interest she had felt in anything outside herself. "We kneeled on the floor and swept our arms out just like that!"

"If there were many of you, it must soon have been clean," said Hester, moving the rug she knelt on deftly.

"Oh, we were not cleaning it," said the invalid smiling. "It was only the same motion."

"Indeed? Then why were you doing it?" Hester asked, turning her flushed face in surprise toward the ruffled whiteness in the window.

She stared at the worker, but even as she stared she frowned uncomfortably.

"Why, for—for exercise—for strength," she said slowly, and coloured under Hester's smile. . . .

Later in the day she moved out again upon the balcony, regretful for the first time that no one of her own world could be there to talk with her. Hester, wiping bed, chair and mirror with the white cloth that never seemed to soil, whipping the braided rag rugs below her on the green with strong, firm strokes that recalled the scheduled blows she had practised at a swinging leather ball, vexed her, somehow, and she was conscious of a whimsical wish that her delusion of the white wrapper stretched along the reclining chair had proved a reality. The soft grey shadows of early evening covered the little balcony, the chairs were plunged in it, and it was with a cry of apology that she stepped into a grey gown, so soft and thin that she had taken it for a deeper shadow, merely, and had actually started to seat herself in the long chair where the slender woman lay. Her own body appeared so robust beside this delicate creature's that pity smothered the surprise at her quiet presence there, and the swift feeling that she herself was by no means the frailest of the doctor's patients added to her composure as she begged pardon for her clumsiness.

"I thought I was the only patient here," she explained. "Miss Hester and Miss Ann have a wonderful way of getting quiet and privacy in their little house, haven't they?"

"Is it so little?" the stranger asked. She felt embarrassed, suddenly, and tactless, for she had taken it for granted that they were both of the class to which the modest cottage must seem small.

"I only meant," she added hastily, for it seemed that at any cost this gentle, pale creature must not be hurt, "I only meant that to take in strangers, in this way, and to keep the family life entirely separate requires, usually, much more space."

"But do they keep it separate—the family life!"

("Evidently," she thought, "they have not been able to give her a private room, like mine, or perhaps she eats with them.")

"I think that is how they do it," the stranger went on, "by not having any separate life, really. It is all one life, with them."

"All one life . . ." the other repeated, vaguely, recalling, for some reason, the doctor's words, "but, of course, in a larger establishment that would not be possible. With servants . . ."

"I suppose that is why they have no servants," said the stranger.

There was a soft assurance in the tone, soft, but undoubtedly there. And yet what assurance should a woman have who did not find this house small? She discovered that she was still a little irritable, for she spoke brusquely.

"People do not employ servants, I imagine, for the very simple reason that they cannot afford to."

"Not always," said the other quietly. "I have known Ann and Hester many years, and there has never been a time when they could not have afforded at the least one servant."

"Tastes differ, I suppose," she answered shortly, "I should have supposed that every woman would take the first opportunity of relieving herself from the strain of household drudgery, which any ignorant person can accomplish."

"Have you found so many of them to accomplish it for you?"

She flushed angrily.

"Dr. Stanchon has been talking about me!" she cried with hot memories of her interminable domestic woes.

"Indeed not," said the grey lady. "I knew nothing . . . I only asked if ignorant persons really accomplished their drudgery to any one's satisfaction nowadays? They used not to when—when I employed them. . . ."

So she had been wrecked beyond repair, this shadowy, large-eyed thing! She spoke as of a day long over. The other woman felt ashamed of her suspicion.

"No, indeed," she answered wearily, "that was an exaggeration, naturally. But they might, if they would take pains. They are paid enough for it, heaven knows."

"Ann and Hester are not paid," said the voice from the dim chair. "Perhaps that is why they take pains."

The woman nodded fretfully.

"That is all very well," she said, "and sounds very poetic, but it would be rather impractical for us all to do, on that account."

"Impractical? *Impractical?*"

A hint of gentle laughter from the long chair. "But it seems to me that Ann and Hester are the least impractical of people—are they not? They are surely less harassed than you were?"

("I must have been very sleepy: I don't remember telling her all about it," thought the woman, "but she seems to know.")

"Yes," she said aloud, "I was harassed. Nearly to death, it seems. I am hardly myself yet. I suppose you have been through it all?"

"I have been through a great deal, yes."

The shadows deepened and a thin, new moon sank lower and lower. The grey figure grew less and less distinct to her, and before she knew it, she slept. When she woke, she was alone on the balcony, and the sunlight lay in blue-white pools upon the floor. For the first time in her life she had slept alone under the stars, with no one to settle her into her dreams or to attend on her when she woke from them, and suspicion and displeasure darkened for a moment the freshest awakening she could remember. Had they really forgotten her? No one seemed to be coming, and after a quarter of an hour's impatient waiting she left the long, couch-like chair, opened the door of her room and went with quick determined steps down the narrow hall, down the stairs, straight to the sounds of women's voices in the distance. They led her through a shining kitchen, where a patient, old clock presided, through a cool, dim buttery into a primitive laundry, or washing shed, with deal tubs and big copper cauldrons and a swept stone floor. But no odour of the keen cleanliness she had learned to connect with Hester's soap ruled the wash-house this morning: a breeze from Araby the blest blew through the piles of dewy crimson strawberries that heaped themselves in yellow bowls, in silver-tinted pans, in leaf-lined wicker baskets, and brought all the gardens of June into the bare, stone room. Hester's quick fingers twisted the delicate hulls from the scarlet, scented globes, and near her, measuring mounds of glittering sugar, stood a broader, squarer woman with greying hair, who smiled gravely at her, facing her.

"Here she is, now," said this woman, whom she guessed to be Ann, and Hester, turning to her, added, as one who finishes a sentence, merely,

"And I was just getting ready a dish of strawberries for you. Mother has stepped out for your egg; the brown hen has just laid. The rolls are in the oven and mother has the chocolate ready. I thought you would be early this morning, you were sleeping so soundly."

"Early? early?" she repeated, taken aback by their easy greeting of her. "Why, what do you mean?" And just then the clock struck seven, deliberately.

"Why—why, I thought—then you did not forget—" she began, uncertainly.

"There is nothing like the open air for sleeping, when one is ready for it," said Hester. "Did you not notice the cover I threw over you? You must have gone off before it grew dark, quite."

"Oh, no, because I was with—" then she stopped abruptly. For it dawned on her that the other woman must have been a dream, since she perceived that she was unwilling to ask about her, so faintly did that conversation recall itself to her, so uncertain her memory proved as to how that other came and went, or when.

"It was a dream, of course," she thought, and said, a shade resentful still, "I never slept—that way—before."

"It seems to suit you," said Ann briskly, "for you have never left your room till now."

Then it dawned on her suddenly.

"Why, I am well!" she said.

"Very nearly, I think," Hester answered her. "Will you have your break-fast under the tree, while sister picks the berries?"

To this she agreed gladly and found herself, still wondering at the new strength that filled her, under a pear-tree, in a pleasant patch of shadow, eating with relish from Hester's morning tray. Ann knelt not far from her in the sun, not too hot at this hour for a hardy worker, and soon her low humming rose like a bee's note from under her broad hat.

"The wash is all ready for you, sister, on the landing," she called. "Tell mother her new towels bleached to a marvel: they are on the currant-bushes now. I'll wet them down and iron them off while the syrup is cooking, I think—I know she's anxious to handle them."

"Are you always busy, Miss Ann?" her guest inquired, for Ann's fingers never stopped even while she looked toward the house-door.

"Always in the morning, of course," she answered, directly. "Every one must be, if things are to get done."

"But in the afternoon you are ironing, and Miss Hester tells me you do a great deal in the garden. When do you rest?"

"In my bed," said Ann briefly.

She was less sweetly grave than her sister, and it was easy to see that her tongue was sharper. She would not have been so soothing to an invalid, but the woman under the pear-tree had her nerves better in hand by now, and felt, somehow, upon her mettle to prove to this broad, curt Ann that there were tasks in the world beyond her sturdy rule-of-thumb.

"But surely every one needs time to think—to consider," she began gently. "Don't you find it so?"

"To plan out the day, do you mean?" said Ann, moving to a new patch. "I generally do that at night before I go to sleep."

"No, no," she explained, "not the day's work—that must be done, of course—but the whole Scheme, life, and one's relation to it . . ."

"I don't feel any call to study that out," said Ann. "I haven't the headpiece for it."

"No, but some people have, and so——"

"Have you?" said Ann.

She bit her lip.

"It is surely every woman's duty to cultivate herself as far as she can," she began. "Nobody denies that nowadays."

Ann was silent.

"Don't you agree with me?" the woman persisted. "You surely know what I mean?"

"Oh, yes, I know what you mean, well enough," Ann said at last. "I know you have to cultivate strawberries, if you want to get more of 'em—and bigger. The question is, what do *you* get out of it?"

A flood of explanations pressed to her lips, but just as they brimmed over, some quick surmise of Ann's shrewd replies choked them back. After all, what *had* she got out of it? What that she could show? She rose slowly and walked back to her room, where the bath, fresh, uncreased clothes, and Hester's deft ministry waited ready for her. Later, she lay again in the balcony chair, not so soothed by her little pile of books as she had looked to be. Beautiful, pellucid thought, deep-flowing philosophies, knife-edged epigrams and measured verse lay to her hand, but they seemed unreal, somehow, and their music echoed like meaningless words shouted, for the echo merely, in empty halls. She drowsed discontentedly and woke from a dream of the grey lady to see her stretched in the companion chair, herself asleep, it seemed, for it was only after a long doubtful stare from the other that she opened her great dark eyes.

"And I almost thought I had dreamed of meeting you before! Wasn't it absurd? I am only now realising how ill I have been—things were all so confused . . . I find that I can't even reply to Miss Ann as I ought to be able to, when she scorns the effects of culture!"

"Does Ann scorn culture?" the grey lady asked in mild surprise. "I never knew that."

"She scorns the leisure that goes to produce it, anyway."

"Did you give her a concrete instance of any special culture?"

She moved uneasily in her chair.

"Oh—concrete, *concrete!*" she repeated deprecatingly. "Must I be as concrete with you as with her? Surely culture, and all that it implies, need not be forced to defend itself with concrete examples?"

"I'm afraid that I agree with Ann," said the soft voice in the shadow. "I'm afraid that so far as I am concerned, culture needs just that defence."

She tried to smile the superior smile she had mastered for Ann, kneeling in her checked sunbonnet, but this was difficult, with a woman so obviously of her own class and kind. Still the woman was clearly unreasonable, and she was able, at least, to speak forcibly as she replied,

"Aren't you rather severe on the enormous majority of us, in that case? We can't all be great philosophers or productive artists, you know, and yet between us and Ann's preserved strawberries and Hester's scrubbing there's a wide gulf—you must admit that!"

The stranger rose lightly from her chair and walked, with a swaying motion like a long-stemmed wild flower, toward the home-made window-door. At the sill she paused and fixed her great eyes on the stronger woman—stronger, plainly, for the frail white hand on the china knob supported her while she stood, and she seemed to cling to the woodwork and press against it as she sank into the shadow of the eaves.

"A wide gulf, indeed," she said slowly, in her soft, breathless voice, with an intonation almost like a foreigner's, her listener decided suddenly, "a gulf so wide that unless you can cross it with some bridge of honest accomplishment, it will swallow you all very soon—you women of culture!"

She slipped across the sill and presently Hester's clear, firm voice was heard in the narrow hall,

"Yes, yes, I'm coming!" and the balcony was drowned in the dusk, and the woman on it yielded consciously to the great desire for sleep that possessed her. But before she drifted off, not afraid, this time, of night under the sky, it occurred to her dimly that Hester's other patient must come through her own room whenever she used the little *loggia*.

"What is she—an anarchist? a socialist?" she thought. "I must surely ask Hester about her. 'You women of culture,' indeed! What does she call herself, I wonder?"

The next morning as she waited idly for bath and breakfast, the stranger possessed her thoughts more and more. Only in such an absolutely unconventional place, she told herself, could a completely unknown woman appear (in her own apartments, really) and discuss with her so nonchalantly such strange questions. In many ways this delicate creature's words seemed to echo Dr. Stanchon's, and this seemed all the more natural, now, since she was so obviously still his patient. Hester had said that he sent many there—this one was perhaps too frail ever to leave them, and felt so much at home that no one thought to speak of her.

A healthy hunger checked these musings, and more amused than irritated at such unusual desertion, she bathed and dressed unaided and went down to the kitchen.

"They will soon see by the way I keep my temper, now," she thought, "and my strength, that I am quite able to go back. I really must see how the children are getting on."

Following the ways of her last journey through the house she found the kitchen, where an oven-door ajar and a half-dozen small, fragrant loaves in the opening showed her that though empty, the room was deserted only for a housewife's rapid moment. She sat down therefore beneath the patient old clock, and waited. Soon she heard a quick, bustling step, unlike Hester's lithe quietness or the heavier stride of Ann, and knew that the little old lady who entered, fresh and tidy as a clean withered apple, was their mother. She had a pan of new-picked peas in one arm and a saucer of milk balanced in the other hand, plainly the breakfast for the sleek black cat that bounded in beside her. This she set carefully on a flagstone corner before she noticed her visitor, it seemed, and yet she did not appear startled at company, and showed all of the younger women's untroubled ease as she explained that a message from Dr. Stanchon had called them both away suddenly, very early.

"It was perhaps some other patient in the house?" the guest suggested curiously, with a vivid memory of the grey lady's frail white hand and breathless voice.

"Perhaps," said the old woman equably, and tied a checked apron over the white one, the better to attack the peas.

From the shining pan she tossed the fairy green globes into the rich yellow bowl of earthenware at her side, with the quick ease of those veined, old hands that outwork the young ones, and her guest watched her in silence for a few minutes, hypnotised, almost, by the steady pit-pat of the little green balls against the bowl.

"And when do you expect them back?" she asked finally.

"I don't know," said the old lady, "but they'll be back as soon as the work is over, you may depend—they don't lag, my girls, neither of 'em."

"I am sure of that," she assented quickly. "They are the hardest workers I ever saw: I wonder that they never rest, and tell them so."

"Time enough for resting when all's done," said the old lady briskly. "That was my mother's word before me and I've handed it down to Ann and Hester."

"But then, at that rate, none of us would ever rest, would we?" she protested humourously.

"This side o' green grave?" the old lady shot out. "Maybe so. But podding peas is a kind of rest—after picking 'em!"

"And have you really picked all these—and in the sun, too?" she said, surprised. "I trust not for me—I could get along perfectly . . ."

The old lady jumped briskly after her loaves, tapped the bottoms knowingly, then stood each one on its inverted pan in a fragrant row on the dresser.

"Peas or beans or corn—it makes no odds, my dear," she cried cheerfully. "It's all to be done, one way or another, you see."

An inspiration came to the idler by the window, and before she had quite caught at the humour of it, she spoke.

"Why should you get my breakfast—for I am sure you are going to?" she said. "Why shouldn't I—if you think I could—for I don't like to sit here and have you do it all!"

"Why not, indeed?" the old woman replied, with a shrewd smile at her. "Hester judged you might offer, and left the tray ready set."

"Hester judged?" she repeated wonderingly. "Why, how could she, possibly? How could she know I would come down, even?"

"She judged so," the mother nodded imperturbably. "The kettle's on the boil, now, and I've two of the rusks you relished yesterday on the pantry shelf. Just dip 'em in that bowl of milk in the window and slip 'em in the oven—it makes a tasty crust. She keeps some chocolate grated in a little blue dish in the corner and the butter's in a crock in the well. The brown hen will show you her own egg, I'll warrant that."

Amused, she followed all these directions, and poured herself a cup of steaming chocolate, the first meal of her own preparing since childish banquets filched from an indulgent cook. And then, the breakfast over, she would have left the kitchen, empty just then, for the mistress of it had pottered out on one of her endless little errands, had not a sudden thought sent a flush to her forehead, so that she turned abruptly at the threshold and walking swiftly to the water spigot, sent a stream into a tiny brass-bound tub she took from the deep window seats, frothed it with Hester's herb-scented soap, and rinsed and dipped and dried each dish and cup of her own using before the old woman returned.

"It is surprising how—how *satisfactory* it makes one feel, really," she began hastily at the housewife's friendly returning nod, "to deal with this sort of work. One seems to have accomplished something that—that had to be done . . . I don't know whether you see what I mean, exactly. . . ."

"Bless you, my dear, and why shouldn't I see?" cried the other, scrubbing the coats of a lapful of brown jacketed potatoes at the spigot. "Every woman knows that feeling, surely?"

"I never did," she said, simply. "I thought it was greasy, thankless work, and felt very sorry for those who did it."

"Did they look sad?" asked the old worker.

In a flash of memory they passed before her, those white-aproned, bare-elbowed girls she had watched idly in many countries and at many seasons; from the nurse that bathed and combed her own children, singing, to the laundry-maids whose laughter and ringing talk had waked her from more than one uneasy afternoon sleep.

"Why, no, I can't say that they did," she answered slowly, "but to do it steadily, I should think . . ."

"It's the steady work that puts the taste into the holiday, my mother used to say," said the old woman shortly.

"Where's the change, else?"

"But of course there are many different forms of work," she began, slowly, as though she were once for all making the matter clear to herself, and not at all explaining obvious distinctions to an uneducated old woman, "and brain workers need rest and change as much, yes, more, than mere labourers."

"So they tell me," said Hester's mother respectfully, "though of course I know next to nothing of it myself. Ann says it's that makes it so dangerous for women folks to worry at their brains too much, for she's taken notice, she says, that mostly they're sickly or cranky that works too much that way. Hard to get on with, she says they are, the best of 'em."

"Indeed!" she cried indignantly, "and I suppose to be 'easy to get on with' is the main business of women, then!"

"Why, Lord above us, child!" answered the old woman briskly, dropping her white potatoes into a brown dish of fresh-drawn water, "if the women are not to be easy got on with, who's to be looked to for it, then; the children—or the men?"

She gathered up the brown peelings and bagged them carefully with the pea pods.

"For the blacksmith's pig," she said. "We don't keep one and he gives us a ham every year. . . . Not that it's not a different matter with you, of course," she added politely. "There's some, of course, that's needed by the world, for books and music and the like o' that—I don't need Hester to tell me so. There's never an evening in winter, when all's swept and the lamp trimmed and a bowl of apples out, and Ann and I sit with our bit of sewing, that I don't thank God for the books Hester reads out to us. One was written by a woman writer that the doctor sent us here for a long, long time—poor dear, but she was feeble!

"She worked with the girls at everything they did, that she could, by doctor's orders, and it put a little peace into her, she told me. You've a look in the eyes like her—there were thousands read her books."

The guest rose abruptly.

"I never wrote a book—or did anything," she said briefly, and turned to the door.

"You don't tell me!" the old mother stammered. "Why, I made sure by your look—what made ye so mortal tired, then, deary?"

"I must find that out," she said, slowly, her hand on the knob. "I—must—find—that—out!"

And on the balcony she paced and thought for an hour, but there was no calmness in her forehead till the afternoon, when alone with Hester's mother, for the daughters did not return all that day, she worked with pressed lips at their tasks, picking Ann's evening salad, sprinkling cool drops over Hester's fresh-dried linen, brought in by armfuls from the currant-bushes, spreading the supper-table, pressing out the ivory-moulded cottage cheese and ringing its dish with grape-leaves gathered from the well-house.

So intent was she at these tasks, that she heard no footsteps along the grass, and only as she put the fifth chair at the white-spread table (for the old mother had been mysteriously firm in her certainty that they should need it) did she turn to look into the keen brown eyes of the wise physician who had left her weeks ago in the bed above them. He gave her a long, piercing look. then,

"I thought so," he said quietly. "We will go back to-morrow, you and I—I need your bedroom."

Through the open door she caught a quick glimpse of Ann and Hester half supporting, half carrying up the stairs a woman heavily veiled in black crêpe; Hester did not join them till late in the meal, and went through the room with a glass of milk afterward. No one spoke further of her presence among them; no one thanked her for her services; all was assumed and she blessed them for it.

The doctor passed the evening with his new patient, and when she mounted the stairs for her last night she found her simple luggage in the room next hers: there was no question of helping her to bed, and she undressed thoughtfully alone. The house was very still.

Her window was a deep dormer, and as she leaned out of it, for a breath of the stars, she saw Dr. Stanchon stretched in her chair on the balcony, his face white and tired in the moonlight. In the chair near her, so near that she could touch it, lay the frail creature in the grey dress, black now at night.

"It is his old patient!" she thought contentedly, remembering with vexation that she had absolutely forgotten to ask the house-mother about her and why she had not appeared; and she began to speak, when the other raised her hand warningly, and she saw that Dr. Stanchon slept.

Why she began to whisper she did not know, but she remembered afterward that their conversation, below breath as it was, was the longest they had yet had, though she could recall only the veriest scraps of it. For instance:

"But Mary and Martha?" she had urged, "surely there is a deep meaning in that, too? It was Martha who was reproved. . . ."

"One would imagine that every woman to-day judged herself a Mary—and that is a dangerous judgment to form, one's self," the other whispered.

"But to deliberately assume these tasks—simple because they clear my life and keep me balanced—when I have no need to do them, seems to me an affectation, absurd!"

"How can a thing be absurd if it brings you ease?"

"But I don't need to do them, really, for myself."

"For some one else, then?"

It was then that another veil dropped from before her.

"Then is that why, do you think, people devote themselves to those low, common things—great saints and those that give up their own lives?"

"I think so, yes."

"It is a real relief to them?"

"Why not? . . ."

She fell asleep on the broad window-seat, her head on her arms, and when she woke and groped for her bed in the dark, the balcony was empty.

There was no bustle of departure: a grave hand-shaking from the daughters, a kiss on the mother's withered, rosy cheek.

"Come back again, do," said the old woman and the doctor commented upon this as they sat in the train.

"That is a great compliment," he said. "I never knew her to say that except to a long-time patient of mine that stayed a long time (more's the pity!) with them. 'Come back,' said Mother to her. 'Come soon, deary, for the house will miss your grey dress so soft on the floor.' They would have cured her if anybody could."

"Then you don't consider her cured?" she said with a shock of disappointment. "I am so sorry. But it is surely a wonderful place—one can't talk about it, but I see you know."

"Oh, yes, I know," he said briefly. "I saw you would pull through in great shape there. This patient I spoke of used to tell me that the duty of her life, here and through Eternity, ought by rights to be the preaching of the gospel she learned there. Well—maybe it is, for all we know. If I could have cured her, she would have been a great—a really great novelist, I think."

"If you could have—" she gasped, seizing his arm, "you mean——"

"I mean that I couldn't," he answered simply. "She died there. I dreamed of her last night."

<hr />

HELEN R. HULL

(1888–1971)

Helen Rose Hull distinguished herself as both an author and an educator. Born in Michigan, she was educated in the Midwest, then embarked on a teaching career at Wellesley College, Barnard College, and finally at Columbia University, where she was a professor of creative writing for forty years. Concurrent with this, she published twenty novels, two collections of short stories, and two novelettes. Although early in life she had been active in radical politics, she later became somewhat politically reticent—a fact that has been attributed in part to her publisher's caution that her lesbianism would be detrimental to her career. Hull's fiction often explores women's options in marriage, career, and parenting. Indictment of the nuclear family on both personal and economic grounds, given such horrifying form in "Clay-Shuttered Doors," is a frequent theme in her powerful fiction. The May 1926 issue of *Harper's* is the original source of this tale.

Clay-Shuttered Doors

OR MONTHS I HAVE TRIED NOT TO THINK ABOUT THALIA Corson. Anything may invoke her, with her langorous fragility, thin wrists and throat, her elusive face with its long eyelids. I can't quite remember her mouth. When I try to visualize her sharply I get soft pale hair, the lovely curve from her temple to chin, and eyes blue and intense. Her boy, Fletcher, has eyes like hers.

To-day I came back to New York, and my taxi to an uptown hotel was held for a few minutes in Broadway traffic where the afternoon sunlight fused into a dazzle a great expanse of plateglass and elaborate show motor cars. The "Regal Eight"—Winchester Corson's establishment. I huddled as the taxi jerked ahead, in spite of knowledge that Winchester would scarcely peer out of that elegant setting into taxi cabs. I didn't wish to see him, nor would he care to see me. But the glimpse had started the whole affair churning again, and I went through it deliberately, hoping that it might have smoothed out into some rational explanation. Sometimes things do, if you leave them alone, like logs submerged in water that float up later, encrusted thickly. This affair won't add to itself. It stays unique and smooth, sliding through the rest of life without annexing a scrap of seaweed.

I suppose, for an outsider, it all begins with the moment on Brooklyn Bridge; behind that are the years of my friendship with Thalia. Our families had summer cottages on the Cape. She was just enough older, however, so that not until I had finished college did I catch up to any intimacy with her. She had married Winchester Corson, who at that time fitted snugly into the phrase "a rising young man." During those first years, while his yeast sent up preliminary bubbles, Thalia continued to spend her summers near Boston, with Winchester coming for occasional weekends. Fletcher was, unintentionally, born there; he began his difficult existence by arriving as a seven-months baby. Two years later Thalia had a second baby to bring down with her. Those were the summers which gave my friendship for Thalia its sturdy roots. They made me wonder, too, why she had chosen Winchester Corson. He was personable enough; tall, with prominent dark eyes and full mouth under a neat mustache, restless hands, and an uncertain disposition. He could be a charming companion, sailing the catboat with dash, managing lobster parties on the shore; or he would, unaccountably, settle into a foggy grouch, when everyone—children and females particularly—was supposed to approach only on tiptoe, bearing burnt offerings. The last time he spent a fortnight there, before he moved the family to the new Long Island estate, I had my own difficulties with him. There had always been an undertone of sex in his attitude toward me, but I had thought "that's just his male conceit." That summer he was a nuisance, coming upon me with his insistent, messy kisses, usually with Thalia in the next room. They were the insulting kind of kisses that aren't at all personal, and I could have ended them fast enough if there hadn't been the complication of Thalia and my love for her. If I made Winchester angry he'd put an end to Thalia's relationship to me. I didn't, anyway, want her to know what a fool he was. Of course she did know, but I thought then that I could protect her.

There are, I have decided, two ways with love. You can hold one love, knowing that, if it is a living thing, it must develop and change. That takes maturity, and care, and a consciousness of the other person. That was Thalia's way. Or you enjoy the beginning of love and, once you're past that, you have to hunt for a new love, because the excitement seems to be gone. Men like Winchester, who use all their brains on their jobs, never grow up;

they go on thinking that preliminary stir and snap is love itself. Cut flowers, that was Winchester's idea, while to Thalia love was a tree.

But I said Brooklyn Bridge was the point at which the affair had its start. It seems impossible to begin there, or anywhere, as I try to account for what happened. Ten years after the summer when Winchester made himself such a nuisance—that last summer the Corsons spent at the Cape—I went down at the end of the season for a week with Thalia and the children at the Long Island place. Winchester drove out for the weekend. The children were mournful because they didn't wish to leave the shore for school; a sharp September wind brought rain and fog down the Sound, and Winchester nourished all that Sunday a disagreeable grouch. I had seen nothing of them for most of the ten intervening years, as I had been first in France and then in China, after feature-article stuff. The week had been pleasant: good servants, comfortable house, a half-moon of white beach below the drop of lawn; Thalia a stimulating listener, with Fletcher, a thin, eager boy of twelve, like her in his intensity of interest. Dorothy, a plump, pink child of ten, had no use for stories of French villages or Chinese temples. Nug, the wire-haired terrier, and her dolls were more immediate and convincing. Thalia was thin and noncommittal, except for her interest in what I had seen and done. I couldn't, for all my affection, establish any real contact. She spoke casually of the town house, of dinners she gave for Winchester, of his absorption in business affairs. But she was sheathed in polished aloofness and told me nothing of herself. She did say, one evening, that she was glad I was to be in New York that winter. Winchester, like his daughter Dorothy, had no interest in foreign parts once he had ascertained that I hadn't even seen the Chinese quarters of the motor company in which he was concerned. He had an amusing attitude toward me: careful indifference, no doubt calculated to put me in my place as no longer alluring. Thalia tried to coax him into listening to some of my best stories. "Tell him about the bandits, Mary"—but his sulkiness brought, after dinner, a casual explanation from her, untinged with apology. "He's working on an enormous project, a merging of several companies, and he's so soaked in it he can't come up for a breath."

In the late afternoon the maid set out high tea for us, before our departure for New York. Thalia suggested that perhaps one highball was enough if Winchester intended to drive over the wet roads. Win immediately mixed a second, asking if she had ever seen him in the least affected. "Be better for you than tea before a long damp drive, too." He clinked the ice in his glass. "Jazz you up a bit." Nug was begging for food and Thalia, bending to give him a corner of her sandwich, apparently did not hear Winchester. He looked about the room, a smug, owning look. The fire and candlelight shone in the heavy waxed rafters, made silver beads of the rain on the French windows. I watched him—heavier, more dominant, his prominent dark eyes and his lips sullen, as if the whiskey banked up his temper rather than appeased it.

Then Jim, the gardener, brought the car to the door; the children scrambled in. Dorothy wanted to take Nug, but her father said not if she wanted to sit with him and drive.

"How about chains, sir?" Jim held the umbrella for Thalia.

"Too damned noisy. Don't need them." Winchester slammed the door and slid under the wheel. Thalia and I, with Fletcher between us, sat comfortably in the rear.

"I like it better when Walter drives, don't you, Mother?" said Fletcher as we slid down the drive out to the road.

"Sh—Father likes to drive. And Walter likes Sunday off, too." Thalia's voice was cautious.

"It's too dark to see anything."

"I can see lots," announced Dorothy, whereupon Fletcher promptly turned the handle that pushed up the glass between the chauffeur's seat and the rear.

The heavy car ran smoothly over the wet narrow road, with an occasional rumble and flare of headlights as some car swung past. Not till we reached the turnpike was there much traffic. There Winchester had to slacken his speed for other shiny beetles slipping along through the rain. Sometimes he cut past a car, weaving back into line in the glaring teeth of a car rushing down on him, and Fletcher would turn inquiringly toward his mother. The gleaming, wet darkness and the smooth motion made me drowsy, and I paid little heed until we slowed in a congestion of cars at the approach to the bridge. Far below on the black river, spaced red and white stars suggested slow-moving tugs, and beyond, faint lights splintered in the rain hinted at the city.

"Let's look for the cliff dwellers, Mother."

Thalia leaned forward, her fine, sharp profile dimly outlined against the shifting background of arches, and Fletcher slipped to his feet, his arm about her neck. "There!"

We were reaching the New York end of the bridge, and I had a swift glimpse of their cliff dwellers—lights in massed buildings, like ancient camp fires along a receding mountain side. Just then Winchester nosed out of the slow line, Dorothy screamed, the light from another car tunnelled through our windows, the car trembled under the sudden grip of brakes, and like a crazy top spun sickeningly about, with a final thud against the stone abutment. A shatter of glass, a confusion of motor horns about us, a moment while the tautness of shock held me rigid.

Around me that periphery of turmoil—the usual recriminations, "what the hell you think you're doing?"—the shriek of a siren on an approaching motor cycle. Within the circle I tried to move across the narrow space of the car. Fletcher was crying; vaguely I knew that the door had swung open, that Thalia was crouching on her knees, the rain and the lights pouring on her head and shoulders; her hat was gone, her wide fur collar looked like a drenched and lifeless animal. "Hush, Fletcher." I managed to force movement into my stiff body. "Are you hurt? Thalia—" Then outside Winchester, with the bristling fury of panic, was trying to lift her drooping head. "Thalia! My God, you aren't hurt!" Someone focussed a searchlight on the car as Winchester got his arms about her and lifted her out through the shattered door.

Over the springing line of the stone arch I saw the cliff dwellers' fires and I thought as I scrambled out to follow Winchester, "She was leaning forward, looking at those, and that terrific spin of the car must have knocked her head on the door as it lurched open."

"Lay her down, man!" An important little fellow had rushed up, a doctor evidently. "Lay her down, you fool!" Someone threw down a robe, and Winchester, as if Thalia were a drowned feather, knelt with her, laid her there on the pavement. I was down beside her and the fussy little man also. She did look drowned, drowned in that beating sea of tumult, that terrific honking of motors, unwilling to stop an instant even for—was it death? Under the white glare of headlights her lovely face had the empty shallowness, the husk-likeness of death. The little doctor had his pointed beard close to her breast; he lifted one of her long eyelids. "She's just fainted, eh, doctor?" Winchester's angry voice tore at him.

The little man rose slowly. "She your wife? I'm sorry. Death must have been instantaneous. A blow on the temple."

With a kind of roar Winchester was down there beside Thalia, lifting her, her head lolling against his shoulder, his face bent over her. "Thalia! Thalia! Do you hear? Wake up!" I think he even shook her in his baffled fright and rage. "Thalia, do you hear me? I want you to open your eyes. You weren't hurt. That was nothing." And then, "Dearest, you must!" and more words, frantic, wild words, mouthed close to her empty face. I touched his shoulder, sick with pity, but he staggered up to his feet, lifting her with him. Fletcher pressed shivering against me, and I turned for an instant to the child. Then I heard Thalia's voice, blurred and queer, "You called me, Win?" and Winchester's sudden, triumphant laugh. She was standing against his shoulder, still with that husklike face, but she spoke again, "You did call me?"

"Here, let's get out of this." Winchester was again the efficient, competent man of affairs. The traffic cops were shouting, the lines of cars began to move. Winchester couldn't start his motor. Something had smashed. His card and a few words left responsibility with an officer, and even as an ambulance shrilled up, he was helping Thalia into a taxi. "You take the children, will you?" to me, and "Get her another taxi, will you?" to the officer. He had closed the taxi door after himself, and was gone, leaving us to the waning curiosity of passing cars. As we rode off in a second taxi, I had a glimpse of the little doctor, his face incredulous, his beard wagging, as he spoke to the officer.

Dorothy was, characteristically, tearfully indignant that her father had left her to me. Fletcher was silent as we bumped along under the elevated tracks, but presently he tugged at my sleeve, and I heard his faint whisper. "What is it?" I asked.

"Is my mother really dead?" he repeated.

"Of course not, Fletcher. You saw her get into the cab with your father."

"Why didn't Daddy take us too?" wailed Dorothy, and I had to turn to her, although my nerves echoed her question.

The house door swung open even as the taxi bumped the curb, and the butler hurried out with umbrella which we were too draggled to need.

"Mr. Corson instructed me to pay the man, madam." He led us into the hall, where a waiting maid popped the children at once into the tiny elevator.

"Will you wait for the elevator, madam? The library is one flight." The butler led me up the stairs, and I dropped into a low chair near the fire, vaguely aware of the long, narrow room, with discreet gold of the walls giving back light from soft lamps. "I'll tell Mr. Corson you have come."

"Is Mrs. Corson—does she seem all right?" I asked.

"Quite, madam. It was a fortunate accident, with no one hurt."

Well, perhaps it had addled my brain! I waited in a kind of numbness for Winchester to come.

Presently he strode in, his feet silent on the thick rugs.

"Sorry," he began, abruptly. "I wanted to look the children over. Not a scratch on them. You're all right, of course?"

"Oh, yes. But Thalia—"

"She won't even have a doctor. I put her straight to bed—she's so damned nervous, you know. Hot-water bottles . . . she was cold. I think she's asleep now. Said she'd see you in the morning. You'll stay here, of course." He swallowed in a gulp the whiskey he had poured. "Have some, Mary? Or would you like something hot?"

"No, thanks. If you're sure she's all right I'll go to bed."

"Sure?" His laugh was defiant. "Did that damn fool on the bridge throw a scare into you? He gave me a bad minute, I'll say. If that car hadn't cut in on me— I told Walter last week the brakes needed looking at. They shouldn't grab like that. Might have been serious."

"Since it wasn't—" I rose, wearily, watching him pour amber liquid slowly into his glass—"if you'll have someone show me my room—"

"After Chinese bandits, a little skid ought not to matter to you." His prominent eyes gleamed hostilely at me; he wanted some assurance offered that the skidding wasn't his fault, that only his skill had saved all our lives.

"I can't see Thalia?" I said.

"She's asleep. Nobody can see her." His eyes moved coldly from my face, down to my muddy shoes. "Better give your clothes to the maid for a pressing. You're smeared quite a bit."

I woke early, with clear September sun at the windows of the room, with blue sky behind the sharp city contours beyond the windows. There was none too much time to make the morning train for Albany, where I had an engagement that day, an interview for an article. The maid who answered my ring insisted on serving breakfast to me in borrowed elegance of satin negligee. Mrs. Corson was resting, and would see me before I left. Something—the formality and luxury, the complicated household so unlike the old days at the Cape—accented the queer dread which had filtered all night through my dreams.

I saw Thalia for only a moment. The heavy silk curtains were drawn against the light and in the dimness her face seemed to gather shadows.

"Are you quite all right, Thalia?" I hesitated beside her bed, as if my voice might tear apart the veils of drowsiness in which she rested.

"Why, yes—" as if she wondered. Then she added, so low that I wasn't sure what I heard, "It is hard to get back in."

"What, Thalia?" I bent toward her.

"I'll be myself once I've slept enough." Her voice was clearer. "Come back soon, won't you, Mary?" Then her eyelids closed and her face merged into the shadows of the room. I tiptoed away, thinking she slept.

It was late November before I returned to New York. Free-lancing has a way of drawing herrings across your trail and, when I might have drifted back in early November, a younger sister wanted me to come home to Arlington for her marriage. I had written to Thalia, first a note of courtesy for my week with her, and then a letter begging for news. Like many people of charm, she wrote indifferent letters, stiff and childlike, lacking in her personal quality. Her brief reply was more unsatisfactory than usual. The children were away in school, lots of cold rainy weather, everything was going well. At the end, in writing unlike hers, as if she scribbled the line in haste, "I am lonely. When are you coming?" I answered that I'd show up as soon as the wedding was over.

The night I reached Arlington was rainy, too, and I insisted upon a taxi equipped with chains. My brother thought that amusing, and at dinner gave the family an exaggerated account of my caution. I tried to offer him some futile sisterly advice and, to point up my remarks, told about that drive in from Long Island with the Corsons. I had never spoken of it before; I found that an inexplicable inhibition kept me from making much of a story.

"Well, nothing happened, did it?" Richard was triumphant.

"A great deal might have," I insisted. "Thalia was stunned, and I was disagreeably startled."

"Thalia was stunned, was she?" An elderly cousin of ours from New Jersey picked out that item. I saw her fitting it into some pigeon hole, but she said nothing until late that evening when she stopped at the door of my room.

"Have you seen Thalia Corson lately?" she asked.

"I haven't been in New York since September."

She closed the door and lowered her voice, a kind of avid curiosity riding astride the decorous pity she expressed.

"I called there, one day last week. I didn't know what was the matter with her. I hadn't heard of that accident."

I waited, an old antagonism for my proper cousin blurring the fear that shot up through my thoughts.

"Thalia was always *individual*, of course." She used the word like a reproach. "But she had *savoir faire*. But now she's—well—*queer*. Do you suppose her head was affected?"

"How is she queer?"

"She looks miserable, too. Thin and white."

"But how—"

"I am telling you, Mary. She was quite rude. First she didn't come down for ever so long, although I sent up word that I'd come up to her room if she was resting. Then her whole manner—well, I was really offended. She scarcely heard a word I said to her, just sat with her back to a window, so I couldn't get a good look at her. When I said, 'You don't look like yourself,' she actually sneered. 'Myself?' she said. 'How do you know?' Imagine! I tried to chatter along as if I noticed nothing. I flatter myself I can manage awkward moments rather well. But Thalia sat there and I am sure she muttered under her breath. Finally I rose to go and I said, meaning well, 'You'd better take a good rest. You look half dead.' Mary, I wish you'd seen the look she gave me! Really I was frightened. Just then their dog came in, you know, Dorothy's little terrier. Thalia used to be silly about him. Well, she actually tried to hide in the folds of the curtain, and I don't wonder! The dog was terrified at her. He crawled on his belly out of the room. Now she must have been cruel to him if he acts like that. I think Winchester should have a specialist. I didn't know how to account for any of it; but of course a blow on the head can affect a person."

Fortunately my mother interrupted us just then, and I didn't, by my probable rudeness, give my cousin reason to suppose that the accident had affected me, too. I sifted through her remarks and decided they might mean only that Thalia found her more of a bore than usual. As for Nug, perhaps he retreated from the cousin! During the next few days the house had so much wedding turmoil that she found a chance only for a few more dribbles: one that Thalia had given up all her clubs—she had belonged to several—the other that she had sent the children to boarding schools instead of keeping them at home. "Just when her husband is doing so well, too!"

I was glad when the wedding party had departed, and I could plan to go back to New York. Personally I think a low-caste Chinese wedding is saner and more interesting than a modern American affair. My cousin "should think I could stay home with the family," and "couldn't we go to New York together, if I insisted upon gadding off?" We couldn't. I saw to that. She hoped that I'd look up Thalia. Maybe I could advise Winchester about a specialist.

I did telephone as soon as I got in. That sentence "I am lonely," in her brief note kept recurring. Her voice sounded thin and remote, a poor connection, I thought. She was sorry. She was giving a dinner for Winchester that evening. The next day?

I had piles of proof to wade through that next day, and it was late afternoon when I finally went to the Corson house. The butler looked doubtful
but I insisted, and he left me in the hall while he went off with my card. He
returned a little smug in his message: Mrs. Corson was resting and had left
word she must not be disturbed. Well, you can't protest to a perfect butler,
and I started down the steps, indignant, when a car stopped in front of the
house, a liveried chauffeur opened the door, and Winchester emerged. He
glanced at me in the twilight and extended an abrupt hand.

"Would Thalia see you?" he asked.

"No." For a moment I hoped he might convoy me past the butler. "Isn't
she well? She asked me to come to-day."

"I hoped she'd see you." Winchester's hand smoothed at his little mustache. "She's just tired from her dinner last night. She overexerted herself,
was quite the old Thalia." He looked at me slowly in the dusk, and I had a
brief feeling that he was really looking at me, no, *for* me, for the first time in
all our meetings, as if he considered me without relation to himself for once.
"Come in again, will you?" He thrust away whatever else he thought of
saying. "Thalia really would like to see you. Can I give you a lift?"

"No, thanks. I need a walk." As I started off I knew the moment had just
missed some real significance. If I had ventured a question . . . but, after all,
what could I ask him? He had said that Thalia was "just tired." That night I
sent a note to her, saying I had called and asking when I might see her.

She telephoned me the next day. Would I come in for Thanksgiving? The
children would be home, and she wanted an old-fashioned day, everything
but the sleigh ride New York couldn't furnish. Dinner would be at six, for
the children; perhaps I could come in early. I felt a small grievance at being
put off for almost a week, but I promised to come.

That was the week I heard gossip about Winchester, in the curious de-
vious way of gossip. Atlantic City, and a gaudy lady. Someone having an
inconspicuous fortnight of convalescence there had seen them. I wasn't
surprised, except perhaps that Winchester chose Atlantic City. Thalia was
too fine; he couldn't grow up to her. I wondered how much she knew. She
must, years ago, with her sensitiveness, have discovered that Winchester was
stationary so far as love went and, being stationary himself, was inclined to
move the object toward which he directed his passion.

On Thursday, as I walked across Central Park, gaunt and deserted in the
chilly afternoon light, I decided that Thalia probably knew more about
Winchester's affairs than gossip had given me. Perhaps that was why she
had sent the children away. He had always been conventionally discreet, but
discretion would be a tawdry coin among Thalia's shining values.

I was shown up to the nursery, with a message from Thalia that she would join me there soon. Fletcher seemed glad to see me, in a shy, excited way, and stood close to my chair while Dorothy wound up her phonograph for a dance record and pirouetted about us with her doll.

"Mother keeps her door tight locked all the time," whispered Fletcher doubtfully. "We can't go in. This morning I knocked and knocked but no one answered."

"Do you like your school?" I asked cheerfully.

"I like my home better." His eyes, so like Thalia's with their long, arched lids, had young bewilderment under their lashes.

"See me!" called Dorothy. "Watch me do this!"

While she twirled I felt Fletcher's thin body stiffen against my arm, as if a kind of panic froze him. Thalia stood in the doorway. Was the boy afraid of her? Dorothy wasn't. She cried, "See me, Mother! Look at me!" and in her lusty confusion, I had a moment to look at Thalia before she greeted me. She was thin, but she had always been that. She did not heed Dorothy's shrieks, but watched Fletcher, a kind of slanting dread on her white, proud face. I had thought, that week on Long Island, that she shut herself away from me, refusing to restore the intimacy of ten years earlier. But now a stiff loneliness hedged her as if she were rimmed in ice and snow. She smiled. "Dear Mary," she said. At the sound of her voice I lost my slightly cherished injury that she had refused earlier to see me. "Let's go down to the library," she went on. "It's almost time for the turkey." I felt Fletcher break his intent watchfulness with a long sigh, and as the children went ahead of us, I caught at Thalia's arm. "Thalia—" She drew away, and her arm, under the soft flowing sleeve of dull blue stuff, was so slight it seemed brittle. I thought suddenly that she must have chosen that gown because it concealed so much beneath its lovely embroidered folds. "You aren't well, Thalia. What *is* it?"

"Well enough! Don't fuss about me." And even as I stared reproachfully she seemed to gather vitality, so that the dry pallor of her face became smooth ivory and her eyes were no longer hollow and distressed. "Come."

The dinner was amazingly like one of our old holidays. Winchester wore his best mood, the children were delighted and happy. Thalia, under the gold flames of the tall black candles, was a gracious and lovely hostess. I almost forgot my troublesome anxiety, wondering whether my imagination hadn't been playing me tricks.

We had coffee by the library fire and some of Winchester's old Chartreuse. Then he insisted upon exhibiting his new radio. Thalia demurred, but the children begged for a concert. "This is their party, Tally!" Winches-

ter opened the doors of the old teakwood cabinet which housed the appara-
tus. Thalia sank back into the shadows of a wing chair, and I watched her
over my cigarette. Off guard, she had relaxed into strange apathy. Was it the
firelight or my unaccustomed Chartreuse? Her features seemed blurred as if
a clumsy hand trying to trace a drawing made uncertain outlines. Strange
groans and whirrs from the radio.

"Win, I can't stand it!" Her voice dragged from some great distance. "Not
to-night." She swayed to her feet, her hands restless under the loose sleeves.

"Static," growled Winchester. "Wait a minute."

"No!" Again it was as if vitality flowed into her. "Come, children. You
have had your party. Time to go upstairs. I'll go with you."

They were well trained, I thought. Kisses for their father, a curtsy from
Dorothy for me, and a grave little hand extended by Fletcher. Then Winchester came toward the fire as the three of them disappeared.

"You're good for Thalia," he said, in an undertone. "She's—well, what do
you make of her?"

"Why," I fenced, unwilling to indulge him in my vague anxieties.

"You saw how she acted about the radio. She has whims like that. Funny,
she was herself at dinner. Last week she gave a dinner for me, important
affair, pulled it off brilliantly. Then she shuts herself up and won't open her
door for days. I can't make it out. She's thin—"

"Have you had a doctor?" I asked, banally.

"That's another thing. She absolutely refuses. Made a fool of me when
I brought one here. Wouldn't unlock her door. Says she just wants to
rest. But—" he glanced toward the door—"do you know that fool on the
bridge . . . that little runt? The other night, I swear I saw him rushing down
the steps as I came home. Thalia just laughed when I asked about it."

Something clicked in my thoughts, a quick suspicion, drawing a parallel
between her conduct and that of people I had seen in the East. Was it some
drug? That lethargy, and the quick spring into vitality? Days behind a closed
door—

"I wish you'd persuade her to go off for a few weeks. I'm frightfully
pressed just now, in an important business matter, but if she'd go off—maybe
you'd go with her?"

"Where, Winchester?" We both started, with the guilt of conspirators.
Thalia came slowly into the room. "Where shall I go? Would you suggest—
Atlantic City?"

"Perhaps. Although some place farther south this time of year—" Winchester's imperturbability seemed to me far worse than some slight sign of

embarrassment; it marked him as so rooted in successful deceit whether Thalia's inquiry were innocent or not. "If Mary would go with you. I can't get away just now."

"I shall not go anywhere until your deal goes through. Then—" Thalia seated herself again in the wing chair. The hand she lifted to her cheek, fingers just touching her temple beneath the soft drift of hair, seemed transparent against the firelight. "Have you told Mary about your deal? Winchester plans to be the most important man on Automobile Row." Was there mockery in her tone? "I can't tell you the details, but he's buying out all the rest."

"Don't be absurd. Not all of them. It's a big merging of companies, that's all."

"We entertain the lords at dinner, and in some mysterious way that smooths the merging. It makes a wife almost necessary."

"Invite Mary to the next shebang, and let her see how well you do it." Winchester was irritated. "For all your scoffing, there's as much politics to being president of such a concern as of the United States."

"Yes, I'll invite Mary. Then she'll see that you don't really want to dispense with me—yet."

"Good God, I meant for a week or two."

As Winchester, lighting a cigarette, snapped the head from several matches in succession, I moved my chair a little backward, distressed. There was a thin wire of significance drawn so taut between the two that I felt at any moment it might splinter in my face.

"It's so lucky—" malice flickered on her thin face—"that you weren't hurt in that skid on the bridge, Mary. Winchester would just have tossed you in the river to conceal your body."

"If you're going over that again!" Winchester strode out of the room. As Thalia turned her head slightly to watch him, her face and throat had the taut rigidity of pain so great that it congeals the nerves.

I was silent. With Thalia I had never dared intrude except when she admitted me. In another moment she too had risen. "You'd better go home, Mary," she said, slowly. "I might tell you things you wouldn't care to live with."

I tried to touch her hand, but she retreated. If I had been wiser or more courageous, I might have helped her. I shall always have that regret, and that can't be much better to live with than whatever she might have told me. All I could say was stupidly, "Thalia, if there's anything I can do! You know I love you."

"Love? That's a strange word," she said, and her laugh in the quiet room was like the shrilling of a grasshopper on a hot afternoon. "One thing I will tell you." (She stood now on the stairway above me.) "Love has no power. It never shouts out across great space. Only fear and self-desire are strong."

Then she had gone, and the butler appeared silently, to lead me to the little dressing room.

"The car is waiting for you, madam," he assured me, opening the door. I didn't want it, but Winchester was waiting, too, hunched angrily in a corner.

"That's the way she acts," he began. "Now you've seen her I'll talk about it. Thalia never bore grudges, you know that."

"It seems deeper than a grudge," I said cautiously.

"That reference to the . . . the accident. That's a careless remark I made. I don't even remember just what I said. Something entirely inconsequential. Just that it was damned lucky no one was hurt when I was putting this merger across. You know if it'd got in the papers it would have queered me. Wrecking my own car . . . there's always a suspicion you've been drinking. She picked it up and won't drop it. It's like a fixed idea. If you can suggest something. I want her to see a nerve specialist. What does she do behind that locked door?"

"What about Atlantic City?" I asked, abruptly. I saw his dark eyes bulge, trying to ferret out my meaning, there in the dusky interior of the car.

"A week there with you might do her good." That was all he would say, and I hadn't courage enough to accuse him, even in Thalia's name.

"At least you'll try to see her again," he said, as the car stopped in front of my apartment house.

I couldn't sleep that night. I felt that just over the edge of my squirming thoughts there lay clear and whole the meaning of it all, but I couldn't reach past thought. And then, stupidly enough, I couldn't get up the next day. Just a feverish cold, but the doctor insisted on a week in bed and subdued me with warnings about influenza.

I had begun to feel steady enough on my feet to consider venturing outside my apartment when the invitation came, for a formal dinner at the Corson's. Scrawled under the engraving was a line, "Please come. T." I sent a note, explaining that I had been ill, and that I should come—the dinner was a fortnight away—unless I stayed too wobbly.

I meant that night to arrive properly with the other guests, but my watch, which had never before done anything except lose a few minutes a day, had gained an unsuspected hour. Perhaps the hands stuck—perhaps— Well, I was told I was early, Thalia was dressing, and only the children, home for the Christmas holidays, were available. So I went again to the nursery. Dorothy was as plump and unconcerned as ever, but Fletcher had a strained, listening effect and he looked too thin and white for a little boy. They were having their supper on a small table, and Fletcher kept going to the door, looking out into the hall. "Mother promised to come up," he said.

The maid cleared away their dishes, and Dorothy, who was in a beguiling mood, chose to sit on my lap and entertain me with stories. One was about Nug the terrier; he had been sent out to the country because Mother didn't like him any more.

"I think," interrupted Fletcher, "she likes him, but he has a queer notion about her."

"She doesn't like him," repeated Dorothy. Then she dismissed that subject, and Fletcher too, for curiosity about the old silver chain I wore. I didn't notice that the boy had slipped away, but he must have gone down stairs; for presently his fingers closed over my wrist, like a frightened bird's claw, and I turned to see him, trembling, his eyes dark with terror. He couldn't speak but he clawed at me, and I shook Dorothy from my knees and let him pull me out to the hall.

"What is it, Fletcher?" He only pointed down the stairway, toward his mother's door, and I fled down those stairs. *What* had the child seen?

"The door wasn't locked—" he gasped behind me—"I opened it very still and went in—"

I pushed it ajar. Thalia sat before her dressing table, with the threefold mirrors reiterating like a macabre symphony her rigid, contorted face. Her gown, burnished blue and green like peacock's feathers, sheathed her gaudily, and silver, blue, and green chiffon clouded her shoulders. Her hands clutched at the edge of the dressing table. For an instant I could not move, thrust through with a terror like the boy's. Then I stumbled across the room. Before I reached her, the mirrors echoed her long shudder, her eyelids dragged open, and I saw her stare at my reflection wavering toward her. Then her hands relaxed, moved quickly toward the crystal jars along the heavy glass of the table and, without a word, she leaned softly forward, to draw a scarlet line along her white lips.

"How cold it is in here," I said, stupidly, glancing toward the windows, where the heavy silk damask, drawn across, lay in motionless folds. "Fletcher said—" I was awkward, an intruder.

"He startled me." Her voice came huskily. She rouged her hollow cheeks. It was as if she drew another face for herself. "I didn't have time to lock the door." Then turning, she sought him out, huddled at the doorway, like a moth on a pin of fear. "It wasn't nice of you, Son. It's all right now. You see?" She rose, drawing her lovely scarf over her shoulders. "You should never open closed doors." She blew him a kiss from her finger tips. "Now run along and forget you were so careless."

The icy stir of air against my skin had ceased. I stared at her, my mind racing back over what I knew of various drugs and the stigmata of their victims. But her eyes were clear and undilated, a little piteous. "This," she said, "is the last time. I can't endure it." And then, with that amazing flood of vitality, as if a sudden connection had been made and current flowed again, "Come, Mary. It is time we were down stairs."

I thought Fletcher peered over the railing as we went down. But a swift upward glance failed to detect him.

The dinner itself I don't remember definitely except that it glittered and sparkled, moving with slightly alcoholic wit through elaborate courses, while I sat like an abashed poor relation at a feast, unable to stop watching Thalia, wondering whether my week of fever had given me a tendency to hallucinations. At the end a toast was proposed, to Winchester Corson and his extraordinary success. "It's done, then?" Thalia's gaiety had sudden malice—as she looked across at Winchester, seating himself after a slightly pompous speech. "Sealed and cemented forever?"

"Thanks to his charming wife, too," cried a plump, bald man, waving his glass. "A toast to Mrs. Corson!"

Thalia rose, her rouge like flecked scarlet on white paper. One hand drew her floating scarf about her throat, and her painted lips moved without a sound. There was an instant of agitated discomfort, as the guests felt their mood broken so abruptly, into which her voice pierced, thin, high. "I . . . deserve . . . such a toast—"

I pushed back my chair and reached her side.

"I'll take her—" I saw Winchester's face, wine-flushed, angry rather than concerned. "Come, Thalia."

"Don't bother. I'll be all right—now." But she moved ahead of me so swiftly that I couldn't touch her. I thought she tried to close her door against me, but I was too quick for that. The silver candelabra still burned above the mirrors. "Mary!" Her voice was low again as she spoke a telephone number. "Tell him *at once.*" She stood away from me, her face a white mask with spots of scarlet, her peacock dress ashimmer. I did as I was bid and when I had said, "Mrs. Corson wishes you at once," there was an emptiness where a man's voice had come which suggested a sudden leap out of a room somewhere.

"I can never get in again!" Her fingers curled under the chiffon scarf.

"Never! The black agony of fighting back— If he—" She bent her head, listening. "Go down to the door and let him in," she said.

I crept down the stairs. Voices from the drawing-room. Winchester was seeing the party through. Almost as I reached the door and opened it I found him there: the little doctor with the pointed beard. He brushed past me up the stairs. He knew the way, then! I was scarcely surprised to find Thalia's door fast shut when I reached it. Behind it came not a sound. Fletcher, like an unhappy sleepwalker, his eyes heavy, slipped down beside me, clinging to my hand. I heard farewells, churring of taxis and cars. Then Winchester came up the stairs.

"She's shut you out?" He raised his fist and pounded on the door. "I'm going to stop this nonsense!"

"I sent for a doctor," I said. "He's in there."

"Is it—" his face was puffy and gray—"that same fool?"

Then the door opened, and the man confronted us.

"It is over," he said.

"What have you done to her?" Winchester lunged toward the door, but the little man's lifted hand had dignity enough somehow to stop him.

"She won't come back again." He spoke slowly. "You may look if you care to."

"She's dead?"

"She died—months ago. There on the bridge. But you called to her, and she thought you wanted—*her.*"

Winchester thrust him aside and strode into the room. I dared one glance and saw only pale hair shining on the pillow. Then Fletcher flung himself against me, sobbing, and I knelt to hold him close against the fear we both felt.

What Winchester saw I never knew. He hurled himself past us, down the stairs. And Thalia was buried with the coffin lid fast closed under the flowers.

Shades of Discontent:
Widows and Spinsters

"All but Luella shone white in the moonlight."

Illustration by Peter Newell for Mary E. Wilkins Freeman, "Luella Miller," Everybody's
Magazine 7 (December 1902). Photo courtesy Metropolitan Toronto Reference Library.

ANNE PAGE

(DATES UNCERTAIN)

Anne Page's fiction often appeared in the leading American magazines. She also wrote poetry, some for children. No other information is available about her. Given the unsung heroism of Lois Benson in the story that follows, this lack of biographical information about Page holds a particular pathos.

Lois Benson's Love Story

"WHAT DO YE S'POSE HAS COME OVER YER GIRL LOIS, MISS Benson? I never see sech a change in any one in my life. If I didn't know better, I'd say she's in love. Haven't noticed it? Waal, 'pears to me parents is awful blind! Lois has allus been quiet like, but lately, since a month or so, she seems different—brighter seeming; ye'd almost say younger."

The speaker rested her water-pail on the steps of the low, rambling house, which wind and rain had painted a dull gray. She stood talking to a woman of her own age sitting inside at the open window. Her calico sun-bonnet concealed her face, but her rasping voice and strong, knotted hands betrayed a hard-working woman—one of the carriers of water.

The woman sitting at the window had been handsome, and her face, though youth had long since left it, was still fair and smooth. For all its fairness, however, it was not attractive; hard, fretful lines were about the mouth, and the eyelids were hooded, drooping low at the corners over rather dull gray eyes: an immense reserve of stubborn determination was written in every feature.

"No, I haven't noticed any change in Lois. She never was a hand to talk much. I do believe, now that ye speak of it, she *has* been a little different lately. I guess she ain't in love though: there ain't any one to be in love with; besides, Lois ain't so very young any longer, and she ain't the kind men like."

"No, she ain't young, to be sure," replied the neighbor; "but an old fool's the worst fool, some say, and 'love's blind,' ye know, and it don't make much difference who't is, the age don't make any difference, either. Waal, I 'low Lois's a good girl, and I've often thought she'd make some man a good wife; but what ye and Mr. Benson'd do without her, I don't see."

"Waal, don't trouble, Miss Hammett. Lois ain't a-goin' to leave us, I guess; leastways not jist yet."

Mrs. Hammett took up her pail and went on to the next house, where she lived with a widowed sister.

The "girl" in question was a woman past forty, whose whole life had been devoted to her father and mother; they—as it seemed to her—had always been old and needing her care. Many years before, when she was still a young girl in her teens, Mr. Benson had lived on a large farm, and Lois still recalled the beautiful country about their home; but when he grew too old to care for it alone—his sons had all left him—he sold it, and went to live in the village street, which since then had been the boundary of Lois's horizon.

She had once timidly hinted that she would like to go to the neighboring city to learn a trade and do something for herself.

This suggestion had been met with such a burst of indignation on her father's part, with such a look of speechless horror on her mother's face, that she had said no more. To her father's "I guess I can take care o' my daughter without her goin' into service or learnin' any trade" she had been silent. It was her one feeble effort; and seeing it so futile she had relapsed into the daily drudge, bearing her mother's fretful fault-finding and her father's rough, exacting authority.

Lois Benson herself was no saint, and she carried her cross at times with only a wayward spirit; the thorns were often almost too sharp to bear, and she would gladly have plucked them out. Her youth had slipped away in days of petty duties and wearying service in trying to smooth the path of her aged parents; elder brothers and sisters had married and left the home. She had not married, and to her remained the care which they forgot was partly their duty as well as hers. She did the work of a domestic without receiving a domestic's wages. A new gown was an event in her existence, and the old straw hat had for many seasons received a fresh coat of shoe-gloss that its rustiness might not too plainly betray its wearer's slender purse.

She seldom touched any money. Weren't her wants supplied by her father? She was fed and clothed, and she was under the shelter of her father's house. Of her *wants* there was no question.

Lois had none of her mother's beauty. Her hair was of a dull auburn; her skin was covered with freckles; her eyes, though full of a kindly expression, were devoid of all beauty of shape or color. Her pinched nose and thin, compressed lips completed the thought suggested by her figure, which bore the marks of a heavy burden imposed too early and carried without respite. Lois, like the house she lived in, was weather-beaten. She had not been sheltered from wind and rain; and yet her life had passed without events, the very absence of which perhaps—the dreary, unbroken monotony of a leaden sky that never cleared—had made the horizon narrower and the outlook more utterly barren.

Of love she had known nothing; the few young men she had seen had never whispered tender words in her ear. There had never been a springtime in her life. Lois Benson was a pleasant girl, they said, but not the kind to fall in love with; besides, they never could see much of her—she was always waiting on her father and mother. And in this way Lois's youth had faded, and with it all the freshness of her face and figure.

"Lois, Lois come and help me unhitch the mare!" called Mr. Benson as he drove into the barn back of the house. He had brought a horse and cow, pigs and chickens from the farm, and kept them on his little place.

He often drove to the neighboring city: it was only twelve miles, and the roads over the smooth, rolling prairie were always good; he got his newspaper there, sometimes a letter, and spent a few hours in gossip with men like himself. He seldom asked his wife or Lois to go with him. "What did women folks want with goin' to town?—it was allus to spend money." Mrs. Benson did not care, the drive wearied her; Lois often longed to ask her father to take her, but she dreaded a refusal.

"Lois, why don't ye come? Where are ye? Are ye dreamin' or star-gazin' somewhere? Women's allus dreamin' or star-gazin'," he added to himself, as he saw Lois hurrying from the house, where she had been making biscuits for supper.

She helped her father out of the high buggy, and then went to unharness the old brown mare, that turned to sniff affectionately at Lois. The animal knew the friend who had often brought her food and drink, and had many a time rubbed her and put on a warm blanket when she came in wet and worn from a hard drive with her master. Lois knew that her father was often merciless, especially if he had chanced to stay too long at the inn where he met his cronies. Bessie loved Lois. The dumb animals perhaps knew best what a great wealth of tender affection lay dormant in Lois Benson's nature.

"Lois, do you still feel the same? Are you still willing to marry me?"

The strong man bends towards her with a searching look into her face, while he takes her trembling hands in his. She lets them lie in his firm grasp;

she looks up at him—for he stands much above the small, shrunken figure—while she tells him that her feelings have not changed. How glad she is! What an ineffable happiness fills her!

This man whom she loves, loves her in return and wishes to keep and protect her always.

Her voice almost chokes, her whole frame quivers as she tells him that she is ready. He still holds her hand; together they step before the clergyman, who in a few minutes has spoken the sacred words to bind them together for all their lives.

What is this room where they are standing? It seems to Lois like her grandfather's house, which she faintly remembers as a vision of her childhood; things about her are strange, and yet familiar. Who is this man, whom she has promised to take for better or for worse? Does she know him? Has she ever seen him before? She feels that she has known him always; she loves him, and he loves her, and he will make her life sweet and happy. His strong arm will protect her, he will help to bear the burdens which have lately grown so heavy. Strange—his face she thinks she does not know, and yet every feature is vivid to her; she hears the tones of his voice as if they had always been dear to her; she feels the touch of his hand—a broad, working hand, whose touch, however, is very gentle; his face is not handsome,—there are many wrinkles, and the thick, brown hair shows streaks of gray,—but it smiles kindly, lovingly, upon her.

How strange she feels!—as if she were hardly herself. Can it be really she to whom this man has promised love and protection? She has never known either. He stoops to her, puts his arm about her, and presses his lips to hers. Why should he? Who is he? Why is she not frightened? He is her husband now, and she is joyful in the thought.

"What's the matter with ye, Lois?" said her mother two days later, as they sat at their comfortable supper which Lois had prepared and was serving. "Miss Hammett was here the other day, and she thinks ye're wonderful changed; says she'd almost b'lieve ye're in love. What's the matter with ye, anyhow?"

A vivid flush flew over the younger woman's face and neck. She felt as if some one had struck her. Had any one—no, that was impossible.

"I want ye to help me dig Mr. Luscombe's potatoes to-morrow, Lois; he says I can have a third of all I dig, and diggin' makes my back ache so." The flush left Lois's face; her father's words diverted the conversation, and she was not forced to answer her mother's question.

After the dishes were washed and put away she crept wearily to her room to be ready for the next day's work.

The room was spotlessly clean, though bare of ornament. A narrow cot filled one side, while the rest of the small space was taken up by a chest of drawers, a table, and two cane-seated chairs; muslin curtains hung at the two narrow windows, and a strip of rag carpet lay before the bed on the pine floor, the narrow boards of which were as white as snow. On the walls hung a few small prints; over the table there was a woodcut from an illustrated paper; and near it, in a wood frame, a small sea-weed cross, brought from the sea-coast. Lois had never seen the ocean, and the sea-weeds suggested a beautiful unknown world.

"This is your new home, Lois. Do you like it? You must tell me, dear, if there is anything you want changed. It won't be much trouble to make any little changes to please you, and I want my wife to like her home." How kind he is! He calls her "Lois" and bids her tell him all her wishes: it is strange and sweet to be so cherished.

"You are very kind to me," she answers, looking up gratefully into his plain, benevolent face. The house Lois sees is not large, but more comfortable and beautiful than anything she has ever known. She goes with the delight of a child from the large kitchen into a long, low room flooded with sunshine, showing a carpet of soft moss colors; a large, easy lounge; tables; chairs; and, best of all, a small bookcase, in which Lois discovers more books than she has ever seen together before.

"O Reuben! where did you get the books?" she cries eagerly.

"Are you glad, Lois? We will read them together. They were my mother's, and are all dear to me for her sake as well as their own. There is Scott's 'Lady of the Lake,' and there's 'Childe Harold,' telling of foreign places we can't hope to see ourselves, Lois, as I'm a workingman, you know, but we can read about them; and here's dear Robert Burns, a plowman like myself, and yet was there ever another poet like him? He understood the human heart, Lois. Ah, my dear little wife, I'm glad I've got you at last. I thought I should find you. I had to look and wait a long time, and sometimes I was very lonely; and you, Lois, were you—"

"Lois, Lois, are ye goin' to sleep all day? Have ye forgotten all about Mr. Luscombe's potatoes?"

Lois sprang from her cot. The voice was her father's, admonishing her that she was late. She had always dreaded, she dreaded still, no longer the physical punishments borne in childhood, but a mental lash whose sting was almost harder to bear.

She could hardly rouse herself. She must have slept very heavily, she thought. It was hard to have daylight return, and hard to take up her burden again.

The breakfast was eaten amid the fretting of her mother, who had not slept well, and the impatience of her father, with whom it had become chronic. All day, while filling the bushel basket and staggering under its weight, Lois thought of the long, low room, of the sunshine, of the quiet; she heard a voice saying, "We will read them together."

Where is he? Why—oh, why does he not come to help her now? The day dragged wearily on until the last of the potatoes were finally divided, and Mr. Benson's tottering steps were turned towards home. Lois watched him with a pang of remorse. "How can I be rebellious," she thought, "when I see the old, feeble form, and remember that his life has been hard?" She knew that it had not been sweetened by her mother, whose vanity and ambition had been disappointed, whose whole life had been embittered, because her father had turned out nothing but a poor farmer. She could but pity them both; to each she gave what help she could. It was the service of a faithful slave, and was accepted by both as such. To her mother Lois's lack of beauty was an unpardonable fault; her poor, shrunken form was good to bear its burden, but it was not to be admired or spared from hardship. If she had been handsome, like herself, the mother thought, she would have married, but an unmarried woman couldn't look for the consideration that was shown to her married sisters. She, of course, was useful, but not of much account in the world.

To her father she was a woman, and though he knew better than his wife how noble Lois had always been in her devotion to them, her particular thoughts and wishes were womanish and contemptible.

Lois could not remember ever going to either father or mother with a thought or feeling. She had passed through the glowing, happy years of girlhood and early womanhood in silence, repressing every feeling until she felt pinched and warped, as if every spring of emotion were dry. Her affections, except as they lived in her strong sense of filial duty and in her devotion to animals, were starved. She blushed at the mere thought of kissing her mother's cheek, for the ridicule she knew it would excite, as something foolish and sentimental.

Yet she was naturally of a loving, dependent disposition, tenderly, deeply affectionate. Why was she placed in the midst of such surroundings? She was only a simple woman whose mind was untrained, whose tastes were uncultivated, whose every faculty was shriveled, and yet she had a delicate nature which hungered ceaselessly for what she could never hope to attain.

To her father and mother this was unknown, while she herself did not understand: she had never analyzed her needs; she knew only that she had longed for a sympathy she had never received. Lately it had been different. Life had been just as hard, and yet she had been able to bear it more easily. She did not understand, but now she no longer lost heart as the dreary days went slowly by.

Lois was a woman of strong religious belief: her faith was simple; she knew nothing of theological controversies; she had never heard a religious discussion. She had listened every Sunday to the hard, dry teachings of a pastor whose dogmas she accepted, finding help and comfort in her own humble way. She never questioned or doubted. Although she sometimes chafed against her lot, she believed that it had been so ordered by her Creator. "Perhaps," she thought, in a vague way which she could not have expressed in words—"perhaps this is a boon to make the weary days easier; perhaps angels are whispering to me so that I may not lose courage; or is it— can it have a meaning I may hope, even in this world, to understand?"

From the long, low room full of the mellow autumn sunlight Lois looks out upon wide fields and orchards; it is a beautiful, warm day, and the trees are heavy with ripened fruit.

Near the house are gardens, and Lois smells sweet flowers growing under the windows. She sees sweet-peas and nasturtiums still brilliant with a few last blossoms. She sees vines climbing over the low stone wall that shuts out the high-road. Off beyond the road stretch acres of farm land, and still beyond, in the distance, are hills enveloped in a soft autumn haze.

The house Lois sees when she goes out into the garden is a one-story cottage built of stone, covered on one side by an ivy, hanging like a curtain over some of the small windows. Lois does not remember seeing this place before Reuben brought her here; and yet it is not new, and Reuben tells her it belonged to his father and to his grandfather before him—that the family has been one of only sons for four generations. The gardens, Reuben is telling her, were his mother's. "And now, dear, they belong to you."

She wanders on by her husband's side to the stables, where they stop to look at the horses and cattle, which come up to the fence to be petted. The soft-eyed Jerseys receive a bunch of clover from her hand as if they were glad to see her. "Ah, dear, they love you already," Reuben is saying, with evident pleasure. "Do you know, I believe that animals possess something keener, finer than intelligence, that tells them where to look for a friend. They say you can tell a man's real nature from the way he drives a horse; I think the way all his animals act when he's around shows what sort of man he is. You may be pretty sure when you see a horse or a dog shrink away as if he expected to be struck or kicked that sometime he has received such treatment. Animals don't know how to pretend; they either love you or they don't, and a man makes a mistake, if he's a-trying to seem kinder than he really is, when he goes near his animals; they will soon betray his secret."

Lois knows that the hand that drives a span of restive colts is gentle but firm; she knows that the temper of the man near her is always under restraint. In his presence she feels a new strength; the peaceful life by his side is resting her wearied body and overstrained nerves. His constant care, his loving tenderness, are to her what sunshine is to flowers; new color has come into her life, there are bits of scarlet and gold where before all was dull gray—as if a few brilliant leaves were still clinging to the otherwise bare trees in the autumn landscape. She is surprised at her own happiness, at the power of gladness, which she had thought dead; she believes that her face is losing a little of the pinched look, and that she is growing young again, and—what is Reuben telling her, that she is really pretty?

"Yes, Miss Benson, I'm jest cert'in yer girl's in love. I've been watchin' her since I spoke to you, and I know the signs; why, she's as different as different kin be."

Lois heard the words this time, as she stood over her ironing, while her mother and Mrs. Hammett were talking under the kitchen window. She looked up, and caught the reflection of her face in a little mirror hanging on the kitchen wall.

Could the speakers under the window have seen the hot flush that stained her cheeks Mrs. Hammett would have thought her suspicions well grounded. Had Mrs. Benson been observing she herself could have noticed a change: she could have seen that Lois looked less weary; that there was an unwonted brightness in her eyes; that her step was lighter; that she went about her duties, not more consciously, but with more spirit; that she had even of late been heard to sing at her work, and that one day it was an old and tender love-song.

But Mrs. Benson's thought was of herself and her unsatisfactory life, and Lois had gone about as usual, and her mother had not noticed what the kinder, more unselfish neighbor believed she had seen.

There was no visible change in her life; how could she be different? "That was another of the silly notions some people got into their heads; *she* had believed things only when she could see a reason for believin'."

"Lois, dear, will you go to the pine woods with me to-day, and then on to where we caught a glimpse of the ocean? You have told me that you have never seen it."

Reuben is hardly giving her time to put on her bonnet and the soft, warm cloak he has given her—Lois thinks it a very pretty cloak, with its fur trimming—before the "grays" are at the door. Is it the keen autumn air or something else that brings the color to Lois's faded cheek? Reuben has carefully tucked the blanket about her, "for the air will grow chilly," he is saying, "as we near the ocean."

Soon the road enters the forest, and Lois looks up, vainly trying to see the tops of the tall, spire-like trees, while on every side, on the road itself, lie the brown pine needles, and the delicious odor of the balsam fills the air.

Slowly they drive, that Lois may enjoy the stillness; that she may not lose the effect of the perfect forest calm.

To Reuben her quiet joy is a compensation for all his devotion; his large, generous nature has taken her into its keeping, and she yields to the loving care as a tired bird might lie at rest in the palm of a gentle hand.

Lois shrinks from telling him how dear he is to her, but the responsive glance, the fleeting blush, tell him better than words. Suddenly the forest opens, and in the distance Lois sees the ocean; she sees the waves breaking ceaselessly on the beach; she can faintly hear their roar. Were she nearer she could perhaps find the delicate weeds that are washed upon the sands—that's a pretty sea-weed cross upon her wall: oh, no, that was long ago, she hardly remembers when or where; this is the ocean itself she has dreamed of, and Reuben is by her side, and he loves her.

"If ye like, Lois, I'll take ye over to Burton this afternoon; ye was sayin' that ye wanted a pair o' shoes and a calico dress. I suppose girls has to have things in fashion whatever happens. Waal, ye can't say I've stinted ye for anythin'."

It was a year since Lois had driven into the main street of Burton, and she felt a flutter of nervous excitement at the many teams driving up and down the streets, and at the hurry of men and women on the pavement. The shop windows were gorgeous to her in their display of new autumn goods. What beautiful dress materials—soft cashmeres and even shining silks; but Lois would not stop to look at them, for her father was urging her into the shop.

Her small purchases were soon made—a calico-gown, a pair of shoes, and, what seemed to her father a frightful extravagance, which he would never have allowed if he had not been ashamed to exhibit his feelings before the clerk, a new felt bonnet for the coming winter.

She would have liked to linger in front of one window, where beautiful crayons, engravings, and water-colors were framed and hanging. She did not understand what many of them meant; she thought they were perhaps of people she didn't know; but there were some she could appreciate. A young girl, with a beautiful Jersey cow and calf walking beside her, seemed to Lois as lovely as anything she had ever seen. There were colored prints too; but Lois's taste, though uncultivated, was naturally good, and she looked longest at what was really best. How she longed for more! If she could but go inside, and be allowed to look as long as she wished; she wondered if she might.

"Come, Lois, don't be all day standin' starin' in that window. Folks'll think ye never was in town before; there ain't anythin' new in that window, anyhow; those picters has been there for three months. Come along."

Mr. Benson had forgotten that Lois had not been in the city for a year, and that everything was strange and beautiful to her. She had been upon the point of asking permission to go in to stay while her father finished the errands; but she dreaded his impatience, and she stifled her wish, and went on quietly by his side—a plain, unattractive little woman past forty.

She felt shy in the crowded, bustling streets; she shrank from the gaze of those she met; her self-consciousness was painful, though there was so much to look at, so much to make her forget herself.

"O father!" she exclaimed, grasping her father's arm (they were nearly ready to get their horse before starting for home)—"O father! Who's that man standing over there?—the tall man with broad shoulders, talking with those two men. Don't you see, father?"

Her voice, in spite of her effort at self-control, faltered; her hands quivered, their veins were swollen, their pulses throbbed.

"What's the matter with ye?" cried her father, irritably. "Where's the use in gettin' all excited up at jest seein' a strange man on a street corner?"

Lois did not heed her father's impatience. "Who is he, father. Do you know who he is?"

"What difference does it make *who* he is? I don't know him; never seen him before."

"But, father," she pleaded, "haven't you heard what his name is?"

"His name!" ejaculated Mr. Benson, with scorn. "I don't care a tinker's curse for a man's name. Ye allus want to know a person's name. What difference does it make, anyhow? A woman's curiosity beats anythin' I ever see; sech empty-headed things as women are, allus askin' questions and never waitin' for the answers. I'd jest like to know what ye want to know that man's name for; 'pears to me ye'r' unusual cur'us, even for a woman. Waal, I don't know his name, if that'll satisfy ye. But come along, let's be off. I don't know nothin' about the man, and, what's more, I don't care."

Lois was thankful that her father did not again look at her; thankful that she could sit by his side unnoticed, while her thoughts rushed through her brain until she feared the throbbing temples would burst.

Her fingers worked convulsively, and her heart fluttered. After a while she was a little calmer, and a dull ache about her heart followed the violent beating.

Who was this man? What could it, what could it mean? Her father said he did not know him, that he had never seen him before. Was it possible that he had come to live in Burton, and that she should really—how her heart beat! Could her father hear it, she wondered? No, he was nagging at old Bess.

She began to feel dizzy; was she really awake? Could she go on living, she wondered piteously, with this ache always at her heart? Could she go on just as she had before?

"Beloved, my beloved, I thought that I had lost you, that you had vanished from my sight. Tell me, tell me, Lois, that you will never leave me. Remember that my life has been very lonely, that I have waited so long; and remember that I love you. Tell me, Lois." It is Reuben's voice. She hears no more: a blank wall stretches endlessly before her; she cannot see it; darkness gathers about her; in the darkness and the deathlike stillness she seems to hear faintly, as she strains her ear to listen, "Lois, Lois, my wife!"

The autumn had passed, and what the village people prophesied would be a severe winter had set in. Mr. Benson, who had come from Burton cold and tired, was sitting with his wife beside the kitchen fire. Mrs. Benson was dozing in her chair, while Lois was sewing near a table on which stood a large lamp, throwing its bright light on her pale and weary face. The lines about her mouth were deeper, and the brightness had gone from her eyes; in its place was a puzzled wistfulness as of a little child who has been asked a question he cannot fully understand. She was as one who after long blindness has seen the light and the beauty of the world, only to find himself again shut in by an impenetrable darkness, which he vainly struggles to push aside.

Her life had never been easy, but she had accepted it without trying to explain things to herself. She had gone on quietly, *doing*, not *thinking*. But the rhythm, dull and monotonous though it had been, was disturbed, and she was bewildered. She wondered if every one was living in the same puzzled way?—if every one was going on day after day in a dim twilight, or even in perfect darkness? Was there always something that one could not understand?

Thus she groped helplessly, without thinking of asking any one what it might mean. She had grown used to the dull ache about her heart; she would grow accustomed to this bewildered feeling, to the sense of expecting something that never came.

"How strange," she mused, "for *me* to be looking for something or some one; for *me* to be *missing* some one."

She had not been to Burton again: her winter purchases were made; there was no further excuse for her going. And the autumn days had worn slowly and dully away,—as other days would in their turn,—and nothing had come.

"Ye recollec' that stranger, Lois," said her father, after his comfortable supper and the warm room had soothed his irritability. His voice awakened Mrs. Benson and startled Lois from her thoughts. "Ye recollec' him—the one ye 'peared to take sech an interest in, though, for the life o' me, I couldn't see why. I heerd some men talkin' on the sidewalk today, an' they was tellin' about a railway accident. A train run into an open switch and jammed right into a freight train standin' there. It was a fearful smash-up, and about a dozen was killed, and a good many more hurt bad. It was the very night we come from Burton, ye recollec'? And it 'pears this stranger was aboard. Some letters that was sent to him has come back, and then word come that he was killed. I didn't stop to ask any questions, as I wa'n't interested particular; but as I come along home I remembered that he was the man ye was so anxious to know about. I didn't hear his name, but somethin' they said made me know 't was him. Waal, he was killed—cur'us, ain't it?—that very same night."

"O father, don't!" faltered Lois, dropping her work.

"What ails ye?—what makes ye so pale? 'Pears to me ye'r' awful tender-hearted," said Mrs. Benson, sneeringly. "For a while ye was as chipper as a cricket, and Miss Hammett she said ye was in *love;* but now ye are as mopy as—it must be the cold weather. I do think some folks is the queerest; first they're one way and then another, without any livin' reason. I'd jest like to know what's the matter with ye, anyhow."

To Lois her mother's critical scrutiny was like a scorching breath upon her face. She rose, turning to take a candle from its shelf.

She felt as if a glare of light had suddenly flashed before her, in whose garish blaze she saw plainly a long, unbroken road upon which, wearily and alone, she must journey.

"Nothing, mother; nothing," she replied, huskily. "I'm only a little tired to-night. I think I'll go to my room."

She went out quietly, closing the door behind her.

Annie Trumbull Slosson

(1838–1926)

Annie Trumbull Slosson was a popular short-story writer of critical acclaim. Born and raised in Connecticut, she married Edward Slosson in 1867. Between 1878 and 1912 she published fifteen collections of short stories. Slosson was one of the first authors to be named a local color or regional realist. This type of fiction drew much of its appeal from the depiction of authentic regional detail—dialects, typical characters, real settings, the customs and dress of an area. Much local color fiction depicts a world inhabited by women and filled with their experiences, and Slosson's numerous ghost stories are written in this tradition. Another defining characteristic of this sort of fiction is its narration; the narrators are outsiders—defined to a certain extent as superior to the region and as able therefore to poke fun at it. The frame narrative of "A Dissatisfied Soul" corresponds to this pattern. The tale was published in the *Atlantic* in 1904.

A Dissatisfied Soul

IT WAS WHEN ELDER LINCOLN WAS SUPPLYING THE PULPIT of the old Union Meeting-House in Franconia. He was a Congregationalist, but was always styled Elder, as was also any clergyman of any denomination; it was, and is now, considered there the fit and proper title for a minister. There were three places of worship in the village representing as many denominations, called colloquially by the residents the Congo, the Freewill, and the Second-Ad, these names being "short" for the Congregationalist, Freewill Baptist, and Second-Adventist churches.

The Congregationalists and plain Baptists held their services in the same house of worship, each taking its turn, yearly I think, in providing a clergyman. Elder Lincoln was the choice of the Congos at that time, a dear, simple-hearted old man whom we loved well.

We were sitting together, the good Elder and I, on the piazza of the little inn—it was when uncle Eben kept it—and talking quietly of many things. I do not recall just how it came about, but I know that our conversation at last veered around to the subject of the soul's immortality, its condition immediately after it left the body, possible probation, and the intermediate state, technically so called. In the midst of this talk I saw an odd look upon the face of the Elder, a sort of whimsical smile, as if he were thinking of something not so grave as the topic of which we talked, and when he spoke, his words seemed strangely irrelevant. "Do you know," he asked, "who has taken the old mill-house on the Landaff road, the one, you know, where Captain Noyes lived?" I did not know; I had heard that somebody had lately moved into the old house, but had not heard the name of the new occupant.

"Well," said the Elder, still with that quaint smile upon his face, "before you form any definite opinions upon this subject of the intermediate state you should talk with the good woman who lives in that old house." He would not explain further, save to tell me that Mrs. Weaver of Bradford had taken the house, that she was an elderly woman, practically alone in the world, anxious to know her new neighbors and to make new friends.

It was largely owing to this hint that, soon after our Sunday evening talk, I came to know Mrs. Apollos Weaver, to gain her friendship and confidence, and to hear her strange story.

It was not told me all at one time, but intermittently as the summer days went by. Yet every word of the tale was spoken in the old mill-house, and I never pass that ancient brown dwelling, standing high above the road on its steep, grassy bank, with the two tall elms in front, the big lilac bush at the door, and the cinnamon rosebushes straggling down to the road, that I do not think of Mrs. Weaver and her story.

It was not in reply to any question of mine that she told it, for, notwithstanding Elder Lincoln's suggestion, I somehow shrank from asking her directly about her theological views and beliefs. I had received a telegram one day relating to a business matter, and as I sat with Mrs. Weaver at the open door of the mill-house, I spoke of it, and of the nervous dread the sight of one of those dull yellow envelopes always brought me.

"Yes," she said, "they're scary things, any way you take it; but sometimes the writing one is worse than getting one. I never shall forget, as long as I live, the time I tried and tried, till I thought I should go crazy trying, to put just the right words, and not more than ten of them, into a telegraph to John Nelson. Over and over I went with it, saying the words to myself, and trying to pick out something that would sort of break the news easy, and yet have him sense it without any mistake: 'Maria has come back, don't be scared, all well here.' No, the first part of that was too dreadful sudden. 'Don't be surprised to hear Maria is with us now!' Oh no, how could he help being surprised, and how could I help making him so?

"For you see, Maria was dead and buried, and had been for three whole weeks!

"John Nelson had stood by her dying bed at the very end; he'd been at the funeral, one of the mourners, being her own half-brother and her nighest relation. He was the last one of the family to view the remains, and had stayed behind with Mr. Weaver and one of the neighbors to see the grave filled up. So to hear she was staying with us now would be amazing enough to him, however I could break it or smooth it down. It was amazing to us, and is now to look back at, only we sort of got used to it after a spell, as you do to anything.

"Maria Bliven wasn't a near relation of ours, being only my first husband's sister,—I was Mrs. Bliven when I married Mr. Weaver, you know,—but she had lived with us off and on for years, and she'd been buried from our house. Mr. Weaver'd been real good about having her there, though lots of men wouldn't have been, she belonging, as you might say, to another dispensation, my first husband's relations. The fact was, she didn't stay to our house long enough at a time for anybody to get tired of her,—never stayed anywheres long enough for that. She was the fittiest, restlessest, changeablest person I ever saw or heard of; and never, never quite satisfied. A week in one place was enough, and more than enough, for Maria. She'd fidget and fuss and walk up and down, and twitch her feet and wiggle her fingers, and make you too nervous for anything, if she had to stay in one spot twenty-four hours, I was going to say. So always just as I was going to be afraid Mr. Weaver would get sick of seeing Maria around and having a distant relation like her at the table every meal, she'd come down some morning with carpet-bag in her hand, and say she guessed she'd go over to Haverhill and spend a few days with Mrs. Deacon Colby, or she'd take the cars for Newbury or Fairlee to visit with the Bishops or Captain Sanborn's folks, and sometimes as far as Littleton to Jane Spooner's. Then Mr. Weaver and me, we'd have a nice quiet spell all to ourselves, and just when we were ready for a change and a mite of company and talk, Maria would come traipsing back. Something didn't suit her, and she wasn't satisfied, but she'd always have lots of news to tell, and we were glad to see her.

"Off and on, off and on, that was Maria all over, and more off than on. Why, the time she got her last sickness—the last one, I mean, before the time I'm telling you about—it was her getting so restless after she'd been staying three or four days with aunt Ellen Bragg over to Piermont, and starting for home in a driving snowstorm. She got chilled through and through, took lung fever, and only lived about ten days.

"We did everything we could for her, had the best doctor in the neighborhood, and nursed her day and night. Mr. Weaver was real kind, she being only a distant relation, but nothing could raise her up, and she died. We had a real nice funeral, Elder Fuller attending it, and we buried her in our own lot next to Mr. Bliven. It seemed dreadful quiet, and so queer to think that this time she'd gone for good and all, and that she'd got to stay now where she was, and not keep coming back in her restless, changing kind of way whether she was satisfied or not. I really did miss her, and I believe Mr. Weaver did, too, though he wouldn't own it.

"And here she was, and here was I half crazy over making up a telegraph to tell John Nelson about it.

"She'd been gone just exactly three weeks to a day, she having died the 11th of March, and it being now the second day of April.

"I was sitting at the window about ten o'clock in the forenoon peeling potatoes for dinner. I'd brought them into the sitting-room because it had a better lookout and was lighter and pleasanter in the morning. It was an early spring that year, though it came out real wintry afterwards, and the grass was starting up, and the buds showing on the trees, and somehow I got thinking about Maria. She was always glad when it came round spring, and she could get about more and visit with folks, and I was thinking where she was, and how she could ever stand it with her changing ways, to stay put, as you might say. Just then I looked out from the window over towards the river and the bridge, and I saw a woman coming. The minute I saw her I says to myself, 'She walks something like Maria Biven.' She was coming along pretty quick, though not exactly hurrying, and she had somehow a real Bliven way about her. She came straight on in the direction of our house, and the closer she came, the more she walked like Maria. I didn't think it was her, of course, but it gave me a queer feeling to see anybody that favored her so much. The window was open, and I got nearer and nearer to it, and at last stretched my head out and stared down the street, a potato in one hand and the knife in the other. The sun was warm when you were out in it, exercising, and I saw the woman untying her bonnet-strings and throwing them back. Dear me! that was a real Bliven trick. I'd seen Maria do it herself fifty times. She was getting pretty nigh now, and the first thing I knew she looked up at the house and nodded her head just as Maria used to when she came home from visiting. Then in a minute I saw her plain as day. It was Maria Bliven, sure enough; there was no mistaking her.

"I see by your face what you are thinking about; it's what strikes every soul I ever tell this to. You're wondering why I take this so cool, as if it wasn't anything so much out of the common. Well, first place, it all happened a good many years ago, and I've gone through a heap of things since then, good and bad both, enough to wear off some of the remembering. And again, somehow, I took it kind of cool even then. It appeared to come about so natural, just in the course of things, as you might say, and only what you might have expected from Maria with her fitty, unsatisfied ways. And then— well, you'll see it yourself as I go on—there was something about Maria and the way she took it, and seemed to expect us to take it, that kept us from getting excited or scared or so dreadful amazed.

"Why, what do you think was the first and only single remark I made as she came in at the door just as she had come in fifty times before after visiting a spell? I says, 'Why, good-morning, Maria, you've come back.' And she says, 'Good-morning, Lyddy; yes, I have.'

"That was all, outside, I mean, for I won't deny there was a swimmy feeling in my head and a choky feeling down my throat, and a sort of trembly feeling all over as I see Maria drop into a chair and push her bonnet-strings a mite further back. She sat there a few minutes, I don't recollect just how long, and I don't seem to remember what either one of us said. Appears to me Maria made some remark about its being warm weather for the beginning of April, and that I said 't was so. Then sometimes I seem to remember that I asked her if she'd walked all the way or got a lift any part of it. But it don't hardly appear as if I could have said such a foolish thing as that, and anyways, I don't recollect what she answered. But I know she got up pretty soon and said she guessed she'd go up and take off her things, and she went.

"There was one potato dished up that day for dinner with the skin on, and it must have been the one I was holding when I first caught sight of Maria down the road. So that goes to show I was a good deal flustered and upset, after all. The first thing was to tell Mr. Weaver. He was in the barn, and out I went. I didn't stop to break the news then, but gave it to him whole, right out. 'Pollos,' I says, all out of breath, 'Maria Bliven's come back. She's in her bedroom this minute, taking off her things.' I never can bring back to my mind what he said first. He took it kind of calm and cool, as he always took everything that ever happened since I first knew him. And in a minute he told me to go and telegraph to John Nelson. You see, besides John's being

Maria's nearest relation, he had charge of the little property she'd left, and so 't was pretty important he should know right off that she hadn't left it for good.

"Now I've got back to where I begun about that telegraph. Well, I sent it, and John came over from Hanover next day. I can't go on in a very regular, straight-ahead way with this account now, but I'll tell what went on as things come into my head, or I'll answer any questions you want to ask, as you appear so interested. Everything went on natural and in the old way after the first. Of course, folks found out pretty quick. Bradford's a small place now, and 't was smaller then, and I don't suppose there was a man, woman, or child there that didn't know within twenty-four hours that Maria had come back. There was some talk naturally, but not as much as you'd think. Folks dropped in, and when they'd see her looking about as she did before she left, and we going on just the same, why, they got used to it themselves, and the talk most stopped.

"But though they thought she was the same as she used to be, I knew she wasn't. It's hard to put it into words to make you understand, but Maria hadn't been many hours in the house before I saw she was dreadful changed. First place, she didn't talk near so much. Before she left she was a great hand to tell about all her doings after she'd been on one of her visits. She'd go all over it to Mr. Weaver and me, and it was real interesting. But she never said one single word now about anything that had happened since we saw her last, where she'd been, what she'd done, or anything. She and me, we were together by ourselves a great deal, more than ever before, in fact, for somehow the neighbors didn't come in as much as they used to. Maria was always pleasant to them, but though they said she was just the same as ever, with nothing queer or alarming about her, I saw they didn't feel quite at home with her now, and didn't drop in so often. But sit together, she and me, hours at a time as we might, never one word of what I couldn't help hankering to know passed Maria's lips. Why didn't I ask her, you say? Well, I don't know. Seems to me now, as I think it all over, that I would do it if I could only have the chance again. You wouldn't hardly believe how I wish and wish now it's too late that I had asked her things I'm just longing to know about, now I'm growing old and need to look ahead a little, and particular now Mr. Weaver's gone, and I'm so hungry to know something about him, we having lived together most fifty years, you know. But there was something about Maria that kept me from asking. And sometimes I think there was something that kept her from telling. I feel sure she was on the point of making some statement sometimes, but she couldn't; the words wouldn't come; there didn't seem to be any way of putting the information into words she knew, or that was used in our part of the country, anyway. Dear me, what lots of times I've heard her begin something this way, 'When I first got there, I'—'Before I come back, I'—Oh, how I'd prick up my ears and most stop breathing to hear! But she'd just stop, seem to be a-thinking about something way, way off, and never, never finish her remarks. Yes, I know you wonder I didn't question her about things. As I said before, I can't hardly explain why I didn't. But there was something about her looks and her ways, something that, spite of her being the old Maria Bliven I had lived in and out with so many years, somehow made her most like a stranger that I couldn't take liberties with.

"Mr. Weaver and me, of course, we talked about it when we were all by ourselves, mostly at night, when it was still and dark. It did seem real strange and out of the common someways. Neither one of us had ever had anything like it happen before to anybody we knew or heard of. Folks who'd died, generally,—no, always, I guess, up to this time,—died for good, and stayed dead. We were brought up Methodists; we were both professors, and knew our Bibles and the doctrines of the church pretty well. We knew about two futures for the soul,—the joyful, happy one for the good and faithful, and the dreadful one for the wicked. And we'd always been learnt that to one of these localities the soul went the very minute, or second, it left the body. That there were folks that held different opinions, and thought there was a be-twixt and between district where you stayed on the road, where even the good and faithful might rest and take breath before going into the wonderful glory prepared for them, and where the poor, mistaken, or ignorant, or careless souls would be allowed one more chance of choosing the right, we didn't know that. I never 'd heard of that doctrine then, though a spell after that I hardly heard anything else.

"I don't know as I told you about Elder Janeway from down South some-where coming to board with us one summer. He was writing a book called *Probation*, and he had a way of reading out loud what he was writing in a preaching kind of way, so that you couldn't help hearing it all, even if you wanted to. And all day long, while I sat sewing or knitting, or went about my work, baking and ironing and all, I'd hear that solemn, rumbling voice of his going on about the 'place of departed spirits,' the Scripture proofs of there being such a place, what it was like, how long folks stayed there, and I don't know what all. That was just before I came down with the fever that I most died with, as I was telling you the other day, and they say this talk of the

Elder's appeared to run in my mind when I was light headed and wandering, and I'd get dreadful excited about it.

"But at the time I was telling about I hadn't heard this, so Mr. Weaver and I would talk it over, and wonder and guess and suppose. 'Oh, Pollos,' I whispered one night, 'you don't presume Maria is a—ghost?' 'No more than you be,' says Mr. Weaver, trying to whisper, but not doing it very well, his voice naturally being a bass one. 'Ghosts,' he says, 'are all in white, and go about in a creepy way, allowing there are any such things, which I don't.' 'But what else can she be, Pollos,' I says, 'she having died and been buried, and now back again? Where's she, or her soul or spirit, been these three weeks, since that?'

"'Well, come to that, I don't know,' Mr. Weaver would say. And he didn't. No more did I.

"Where had she come from that morning when she appeared so unexpected as I sat peeling the potatoes? Not a single soul had seen her, as far as we could find out, before the very minute I catched sight of her at the turn of the road. Folks had been at their windows or doors, or in their yards all along that very road for miles back, and on the two different roads that come into the main one there were plenty of houses full of people, but nobody, not one of them, saw her go by. There was Almy Woolett, whose whole business in life was to know who passed her house, and what they did it for. She was at her front window every minute that forenoon, and it looked right out on the road, not fifteen foot back of where I first saw Maria, and she never saw her.

"Then, as to what clothes she came in, folks have asked about that, and I can't give them a mite of satisfaction. For the life of me I can't remember what she had on before she went up to her room and took off her things. I'm certain sure she wasn't wearing what she went away in, for that was a shroud. In those days, you know, bodies was laid out in regular appropriate burying things, made for the occasion, instead of being dressed all up like living beings, as they do nowadays. And Maria didn't come back in that way, or I might have thought her a ghost sure enough. Sometimes I seem to recollect that she had on something sort of grayish, not black or white, but just about the color of those clouds out there, just over the mill, almost the color of nothing, you might say. But there, I ain't sure, it's so long ago. But I know she had on something I never 'd seen her wear before, and she never wore again, for when she came downstairs she was dressed in her old blue gingham, with a white tie apron. I own up I did look about everywheres I could think of for the things she came in, but I couldn't find them high nor low. Not a sign of them was there in her bed-room, in the closet or chest of drawers, or her little leather trunk, and I'm certain sure they wasn't anywheres in the house when I ransacked for them, and that wasn't two hours after Maria came back.

"It's only little specks of things I can tell you about that happened after this, anything, I mean, that had to do with her queer experience. I watched her close, and took notice of the least thing that seemed to bear on that. She complained a good deal of being lonesome, and when I recommended her going out more and visiting with the neighbors, she'd say so sorrowful and sad, 'There ain't anybody of my kind here, not a single one; I'm all alone in the world.' And, take it one way, she was.

"One day she and me were sitting together in the kitchen, and one of Billy Lane's boys came to the door to borrow some saleratus. After he'd gone, I says to Maria, 'I told you, didn't I, that Billy Lane died last month? He died of lock-jaw, and it came on so sudden and violent he wasn't able to tell how he hurt himself. They found a wound on his foot, but don't know how it came.' 'Oh,' say, Maria, as quiet and natural as you please, 'he told me he stepped on a rusty nail down by the new fence.' I was just going to speak up quick, and ask how in the world he could have told her that, when he didn't die till a week after she did, when she started, put on one of her queer looks, and says, 'There, I forgot to shut my blinds, and it's real sunny,' and went upstairs.

"The first death that we had in Bradford after her coming back was little Susan Garret. We'd heard she was sick, but didn't know she was dangerous, and were dreadful surprised when Mr. Weaver came in to supper and told us she was dead. I felt sorry for Mrs. Garret, a widow with only one other child, and that a sickly boy, but I must say I was surprised to see how Maria took it to heart. She turned real white, kept twisting her hands together, and sort of moaning out, 'Oh, I wish I'd knowed she was going, I wish I'd knowed. If she'd only wait just a minute for me,' and crazy, nervy things like that. I had to get her upstairs and give her some camphor and make her lay down, she was so excited like. She didn't calm down right away, and when I heard her say sort of to herself, 'Oh, if I could only a seen her!' I says, 'Why, Maria, you can see her. We'll run right over there now. I guess they've laid the poor child out by this time, and they'll let us see the body.' Such a look as Maria gave me, real scornful, as you might say, as she says, 'That! see that! What good would it do to see *that* I want to know.' Why, I tell you it made me feel for a minute as if a body was of no account at all, leastways in Maria's opinion. And yet she'd used hers to come back in anyways! 'T was quite a spell before she cooled down, and she never explained why it worked her up so, and I'm sure I don't know. Whether it was because she thought little Susan had gone to the place she herself had come away from, and wished she had known in time to go back along with her just for company, or again, whether she felt bad because she hadn't had a chance to give the child some advice or directions that would have helped her along the road that Maria knew and nobody else probably in all that county did know, why, I haven't an idea.

"I believe I told you a ways back that after she got home Maria all the time had a kind of look and way as if she'd done something she hadn't ought to done, or was somewhere she hadn't any business to be, somehow as if she belonged somewhere else.

"In the old days she wasn't ever satisfied long at a time in any place, but she was always pleased to get back, leastways for a spell. But from the minute she came this time she was troubled and worried. And that grew on her. She was always sort of listening and watching, as if she expected something to happen, starting at the least bit of noise, and jumping if anybody knocked or even came by the gate. She got dreadful white, and so poor she didn't weigh no more than a child, and such little trifling things worked her up. For instance, we had heard a spell before, Mr. Weaver and me, that Mr. Tewksbury over at South Newbury was dead, and we believed it, not knowing anything to the contrary. But one day Mr. Weaver came in and he says, Lyddy, you recollect we heard the other day that Silas Tewksbury was dead? Well, I met him just now coming over the bridge.' Maria was in the room, and first thing we knew she gave a kind of screech, and put her two hands together, and she says, 'Oh, no, no, no, not another of us! I thought 't was only me. Oh, deary, deary me, that's what they meant. They said it wouldn't end with me; they begged me not to try; and now I've started it, and it won't never stop. They'll all come back, all, every single one of 'em,' and she cried and moaned till we were at our wits' ends what to do. It wasn't till she found out that Mr. Tewksbury hadn't ever died at all, but 't was his brother at White River Junction that was taken off, that she got quiet.

"So it went on, Maria sort of wearing out with worrying and grieving about something she couldn't seem to tell us about except by little hintings and such, and Mr. Weaver and me, we wondering and surmising and talking all alone nights in whispers. We didn't understand it, of course, but we'd made up our minds on one or two points, and agreed on them. Maria had never been to heaven, we felt sure of that. There were lots of reasons for that belief, but one is enough. Nobody, even the most discontented and changeablest being ever made, would leave that place of perfect rest and peace for this lonesome, dying, changing world, now would they? And as for the other locality, why, I just know certain, certain sure she'd never been there. That would have showed in her face, and her talk, and her ways. If it is one little mite like what I've always been learnt it is, one minute, one second spent there would alter you so dreadfully you'd never be recognized again by your nighest and dearest. And Maria was a good woman, a Christian woman. Her biggest fault was only her fretting and finding fault, and wanting to change about and find something better. Oh no, no; wherever Maria Bliven had come from that morning in April it wasn't from that place of punishment, we felt sure of that, Mr. Weaver and me. As I said once before, we hadn't heard then that there was any other place for the dead to go to. But from things Maria let drop, and the way she behaved, and our own thinking and studying over it, we began to come to this, that maybe there was a stopping-place on the road before it forked,—to put it into this world's sort of talk,—where folks could rest and straighten out their beliefs and learn what to expect, how to look at things, and try and be tried. Last summer I heard a new word, and it struck me hard. Mrs. Deacon Spinner told me her son had gone off to learn new ways of farming and gardening and such. She said they had places nowadays where they learnt boys all that, and they called them 'Experiment Stations.' The minute I heard that I says to myself, 'That's the name! That's what the place where Maria came back from, and that Elder Janeway knew so much about, had ought to be called, an Experiment Station.' But at that time, in Maria's day, I'd never heard of this name no more than I had of Elder Janeway, and the place or state he was always writing and talking about. But, after all, I don't believe I care to go back on what ma and pa and all the good folks of old times held on those subjects. There wasn't any mincing matters those days; 't was the very best or the very worst for everybody as soon as they departed this life, and no complaints made. I'm certain sure any of those ancestors of mine, particular of the Wells side—that was pa's, you know—would have taken the worst, and been cheerful about it, too, rather than have had the whole plan upset and a half-and-half place interduced. But then, if there ain't such a locality, where in the world did Maria come from that time? I tell you, it beats me.

"Now this very minute something comes into my head that I haven't told you about, that I don't believe I ever told anybody about; I don't know as I can tell it now. It is like a sound that comes to you from way, way off, that you think you catch, and then it's gone. It was just only a word Maria used two or three times after she came back, a dreadful, dreadful curious word. It wasn't like any word I ever heard spoke or read in a book; 't wasn't anything I can shape out in my mind to bring back now. First time I heard it she was sitting on the doorstep at night, all by herself. It was a nice night with no moon, but thousands of shining little stars, and the sky so sort of dark bluish and way, way off. Maria didn't know I was nigh, but I was, and I was peeking at her as she sat there. She looked up right overhead at the sky, and the shining and the blue, and then she spoke that word, that curious, singular word. I say she spoke it, and that I heard it, but somehow that don't make it plain what I mean. Seem's if she only meant it, thought it, and I sort of catched it, felt it— Oh, that sounds like crazy talk, I know, but I can't do any better. Somehow I knew without using my ears that she was saying or thinking a word, the strangest, meaningest, oh, the curiousest word! And once she said it in her sleep when I went into her room in the night, and another time as she sat by her own grave in the little burying-ground, and I had followed her there unbeknownst. I tell you, that wasn't any word they use in Vermont, or in the United States, or anywheres in this whole living world. It was a word Maria brought back, I'm certain sure from—well, wherever she'd been that time.

"Well, it was wearing to see Maria those days, growing poorer and poorer, and bleacheder and bleacheder, and failing up steady as the days went by. And one day just at dusk, when she and me were sitting by ourselves, I mustered up courage to speak out. 'Maria,' I says, 'you don't appear to be satisfied these times.'

"'Satisfied!' she says, 'course I ain't. Was I ever satisfied in all my born days? Wasn't that the trouble with me from the beginning? Ain't it that got me into all this dreadful trouble? Deary, deary me, if I'd only a stayed where'— She shut up quick and sudden, looking so mournful and sorry and wore out that I couldn't hold in another minute, and I burst out, 'Maria, if you feel that way about it, and I can see myself it's just killing you, why in the world don't you—go back again?' I was scared as soon as I'd said it, but Maria took it real quiet. 'Don't you suppose I've thought of that myself?' she says. 'I ain't thought of much else lately, I tell you. But as far's I know, and I know a lot more than you do about it, there ain't but just one way to go there, and that,' she says, speaking kind of low and solemn, 'that is—the way—I went before. And I own up, Lyddy,' says she, 'I'm scaret o' that way, and I scursely dast to do it again.' 'But,' I says, getting bolder when I saw she wasn't offended at my speaking, 'you say yourself you ain't sure. Maybe there is some other way of getting back; there's that way—well, that way you came from there, you know.'

"'That's different,' says Maria. But I saw she was thinking and studying over something all the evening, and after she went to her bedroom she was walking about, up and down, up and down, the biggest part of the night. In the morning when it got to be nigh on to seven o'clock, and she not come down, I felt something had happened, and went up to her room. She wasn't there. The bed was made up, and everything fixed neat and nice, and she had gone away.

"'Oh, dear,' I says to Mr. Weaver, 'that poor thing has started off all alone, weak as she is, to find her way back.' 'Back where?' says Pollos. Just as if I knew.

"But we both agreed on one point. We couldn't do anything. We felt to realize our own ignorance, and that this was a thing Maria must cipher out by herself, or with somebody that was way, way above us to help her. It was a dreadful long day, I tell you. I couldn't go about my work as if nothing had happened, and I couldn't get out of my head for one single minute that poor woman on her curious, lonesome travels. Would she find the road? I kept a-thinking to myself, and was it a hard, dark one like the one everybody else had to go on before they got to the afterwards-life, a valley full of shadows, according to Scripture, with a black, deep river to ford, a 'swelling flood,' as the hymn says?

"Well, the day went by somehow,—most days do, however slow they seem to drag along,—and the night came on. Though we didn't mean to meddle or interfere in this matter, Mr. Weaver and me, we had asked a few questions of folks who dropped in or went by that day. Maria had been seen by people all along the same road she had come home by that other time, and on both the roads that joined it. Two or three, seeing how beat out and white she looked, had offered her a ride, but whichever direction they were going she had always answered the same thing, that she wasn't going their way. It was nigh nine o'clock, and we were just shutting up the house for the night, when I heard steps outside and the gate screaked.

"I felt in a minute that it was Maria, and I opened the door as quick as I could. There she was trying to get up the steps, and looking just ready to drop and die right there and then. It took Pollos and me both to get her in and upstairs. It wasn't any time for questions, but when Mr. Weaver had gone, and I was getting her to bed, I says, as I saw her white face with that dreadful look of disappointedness, 'You poor thing, you're all beat out.' 'Yes,' she whispers, her voice most gone she was so wore out, 'and I couldn't find the road. There ain't but one,—leastways to go there by,—and that's the way I went first-off. I'd oughter known it. I'd oughter known it.'

"I couldn't bear to see her so sorrowful and troubled, and I said what I could to comfort her by using Scripture words and repeating the promises made there about that dark valley and the deep waters, and the help and company provided for the journey. But that mournful look never left her face, and she kept a-whispering, 'That's for *once;* not a word about the second time. Mebbe there ain't any provision for the second time.' And what could I say?

"I believe I haven't told you how much time the poor woman spent those days in the graveyard, sitting by her own grave. I can't get over that, even after all these years, that queer, uncommon sight of a person watching over their own burying place, weeding it and watering it as if their own nighest friend lay there. I don't see why, either. I don't even know whether her body was there. Folks don't have two, and she'd brought one back, and was in it now. And, as far as we could see, it was the very same body she wore when she died, and that we'd buried next to Mr. Bliven. Anyway, she appeared to like that place, and showed a lot of interest in taking care of it. There wasn't any headstone. We had ordered one, but it hadn't come home when she returned, and we had told Mr. Stevens to keep it a spell till we fixed what to do about it. I was glad it wasn't up. I can't think of anything that would be more trying than to see your own gravestone with your name and age and day you died, with a consoling verse, all cut out plain on it. I know, one time, I saw her putting a bunch of sweet-williams on that grave. She looked sort of ashamed when she saw I was watching her, and she says, a mite bashful, 'You know they was always her favorite posies.' 'Whose?' I asked, just to see what she'd say. But she was so busy fixing the sweet-williams she didn't take any notice.

"Maria failed up after this right along, and pretty soon she was that weak she couldn't get as far as the graveyard, hardly even down to the gate. And I says to Mr. Weaver that she needn't worry about finding the way back to where she belonged, for she'd just go as she went the other time if she didn't flesh up and get a little ruggeder. One day, when I went into her room, she says to me, 'Lyddy, I want help, and mebbe I can get it in the old way we used to try. You fetch me the big Bible and let me open it without looking, and put my finger on a verse and then you read it out. Mebbe they'll take that way of telling me what to do, just mebbe.'

"I never approved of that kind of getting help, it always seemed like tempting Providence, but I felt I must do most anything that would help satisfy that poor woman, and I got the Bible. She opened it, her lean hands shaking, and she laid one of her bony fingers on a passage. I must say it took my breath away when I saw how appropriate it was, how pat it came in.

'T was in Ezekiel, and it went this way: 'He shall not return by the gate whereby he came in.'

"Maria give a sort of cry and laid her head back against the pillow on the big chair she was sitting in. 'There, there,' she says, all shaking and weak, 'I most knew it afore, and now I'm certain sure. I've got to go—the—old—way.'

"And so she did. After all, I wasn't with her when she went, and it wasn't from our house she started. I got run down and pindling from taking care of her and studying how to help her out of her troubles. So Mr. Weaver wrote to John Nelson, and after a spell it was fixed that he should take Maria over to his house in Hanover, and he did. It was a hard journey for her, so weak as she was, and she didn't stand it very well. But she had one more journey to take, the one she'd been dreading so long, and trying to put off.

"It wasn't so dreadful hard, I guess, after all, for they said she fell asleep at the last like a baby. Just before she went, she says very quiet and calm, all the worry and fret gone out of her voice, she says to John and Harriet, who was standing by the bed, 'I'm dreadful tired, and I guess I'll drowse off a mite. And mebbe I'll be let go in my sleep.' Then in a minute she says slow and sleepy, her eyes shut up, 'And if I do, wherever they carry me this time, I guess when I wake up I shall—be—satisfied,' and she dropped off.

"I guess she was, for she went for good that time and stayed. She was buried there in Hanover in John's lot. We all thought 't was best. It would have been awk'ard about the old grave, you know, whether to open it or not, and what to do about the coffin. So we thought 't was better to start all over again as if 't was the first time, with everything bran-new, and nothing second-handed, and we did. But Maria Bliven's the only person I know that's got two graves. There's only one headstone, though, for we took the one we'd ordered before from Mr. Stevens, he altering the reading on it a little to suit the occasion. You see, the first time we'd had on it a line that was used a good deal on gravestones then, 'Gone forever.' That didn't turn out exactly appropriate, so we had it cut out, and this time we had on—Elder Fuller put it into our heads—that Scripture verse, a good deal like Maria's dying words, though I don't believe she knew she was quoting when she said it, 'I shall be satisfied.'"

"Well," said good Elder Lincoln one July day as we met on the Libson road, "have you heard Mrs. Weaver's account of Maria Bliven's unexpected return?"

The Elder had been at Streeter Pond fishing for pickerel, for he belonged to that class styled by dear old Jimmy Whitcher "fishin' ministers." He had not met with great success that day, but he had been all the morning in the open, and there was about him a breezy, woodsy, free look which seemed to dissipate shadows, doubts, and dreads. "Yes," I replied, "I have heard it all. What in the world do you make of it?"

"Well, I don't make anything of it," said the Elder. "There's no conspicuous moral to that story. Mrs. Weaver did not make the most of her opportunities, and we do not gain much new light from her account. Old Cephas Janeway, who wrote a ponderous work on *Probation* which nobody read, was largely responsible, I guess, for the feverish dream of the old woman. But to her it's all true, real, something that actually happened. And, do you know, somehow I almost believe it myself as I listen to the homely details, and it brings 'thoughts beyond the reaches of our souls.'"

He was silent a minute, then taking up his fishing basket, very light in weight that day, he raised the lid, looked with unseeing eyes at its contents, and said absently, "I can't help wishing I had met Maria after she came back. There is just one thing"— He did not complete the sentence, and I saw that his thoughts were far away. With a good-by word which I know he did not hear, I turned aside, leaving him there in the dusty road.

———◆———

GERTRUDE MORTON

(DATES UNKNOWN)

There is no information available about Gertrude Morton. "Mistress Marian's Light" was published in *New England Magazine* in September 1889.

Mistress Marian's Light

AR DOWN THE MAINE COAST, IN ONE OF THE MANY HAR-
bors of that good old State, is a picturesque little island inhabited by simple fisher folk. Generation after generation has been
born, lived, and died in this same island village, yet all the
people seem to retain the customs and quaint ways of fifty years ago; from
the old, weather-worn sailor, to the youngest child among them, they seem,
to an unusual degree, guileless and simple and kindly, while to the stranger
within their gates their goodness is unlimited. It is like a reminiscence of
bygone days to partake of their generous hospitality.

At a late hour one soft, sweet night in early summer, while sojourning for
a time among these people, I noticed, far down on a point of land, that rocky
and wave-worn, makes out into the sea, a strange light, that seemed to be
suspended a few feet from the earth. Soft and wavering it was, sometimes
dim; but so unmistakably a light, that I was somewhat perplexed, and the
next morning I asked my hostess the cause of the strange phenomenon.

The woman's countenance changed in an instant, and she assumed a
sympathetic, pitying look as she replied, with a wise, uncanny shake of her
head, "Why, that is Mistress Marian's light." And so she went on and told
me this story.

Away down on the point, where the brown soil of the interior of the
island begins to mingle with the white sand along the sea, there was, many
years ago, a small cottage, built by a seafaring man, who, with his family,
occupied it for a short time. They then removed to a neighboring shore, and
the house remained untenanted many months.

In the course of time two strangers came to the island,—an old man and his little daughter. Venerable indeed was the father, and with his snow-white hair and beard, and his dignified, scholarly bearing, he might have been a king among men. No one seemed to know just when or how they came; they appeared suddenly and unexpectedly, and seemed to find relief in the quietness of the place. As a wandering meteor, travelling through limit-less space, finds rest somewhere in God's great universe, so did these two strangers find a dwelling-place in this secluded spot.

To the little uninhabited cottage on the point they went, and the simple life of the islanders became their life. They became a part, and still not a part, of the fisher folk. The dignified old man was so unlike any one whom they had ever seen before that they were shy of him; and long though he lived among them, quietly assisting the needy, and lending a helping hand to all, they were never quite at ease with him, though they worshipped him from afar. It was as though he breathed a rarer atmosphere than they, and dwelt above them; and they were content to accept his kindness and to marvel at his greatness.

Not so the child, with her soft brown eyes and her gentle, winning man-ner. "A lady born and bred, she is," the good dames said, one to another, many times. But she was a child, strangely alone, so the motherly arms were opened to her, and the children made this little Marian their playmate.

They seemed to be people of means,—this father and daughter. The cottage was furnished comfortably, even luxuriously, and many books, some of them in quaint and curious bindings, were about. On the low walls hung several pictures, the like of which the islanders had never seen before; rich rugs covered the bare floors; a piece of rare Eastern embroidery was flung over a low couch; upon an oddly carved shelf were some bits of china, delicate and fragile, as though fashioned from rose leaves; while everywhere in the tiny house were evidences of refinement. From what faraway land the strangers came, or why they sought refuge on the little island, they them-selves never said, nor were they ever questioned. The people, with their simple faith and childlike credulity, accepted the fact of their coming as they did all the good things that befell them,—thankful, asking naught.

So these two lived on in an alien land, their lives replete with the satisfac-tion that comes from helping others, their desire to do good satisfied by the appreciation with which their efforts were met. Thus the little girl, the dainty Marian, grew to maidenhood, learning much from her father and his books, but more from Nature: of the sea with its wonderful treasures; of the rocks that she loved, gaunt and gray though they were; of flowers and fishes and birds. She learned, too, much of human nature—the kindly side—from the people about her; and their interests she made hers. Every mother on the island felt a deep affection for her, and her young mates were proud to be called her friends. She was a constant surprise to them. The dainty gowns that she fashioned for herself, out of strange fabrics, were marvels; even her language seemed somehow different from theirs; and when a stranger chanced to visit the little building where they gathered on Sundays for worship, "our young lady," brown-eyed "Mistress Marian," was always pointed out with secret pride. So she grew to pure and noble womanhood, winning respect and admiration from all.

The lads of the village were filled with unspeakable delight when she spoke to them in her sweet, low voice. Not one of them but that would have risked his limbs, almost his life, for anything that she wanted,—a wild-flower, a stone, or a bright bit of seaweed. Yet for none of them had she more than a word or a smile, except for tall, manly Phil Anderson. From her childhood she had seemed to set him apart from all others as a hero; and when he came to her out on the rocks one sweet summer night, when the moon was softly shining and the sea was bright with the phosphorescent gleam, and told her of his love for her, she accepted it quietly and trustfully.

It was a happy summer for the two, passing all too quickly. When autumn came, Phil was to sail with his father on one more voyage—to make his fortune, he said; then he was coming back to marry Marian and to take her away into the great world of which they were never tired of talking.

So the weeks slipped by. October came. The trees donned their gayest colors; each bush took its own particular, matchless tint, and the breakers dashed high in the cool breeze, as though to speed the parting, which was even then at hand. One bright, cool morning Phil went down to the little house to say good-by. Tremblingly the old man bade the brave young sailor farewell, then sent him out to the rocks—the place of their betrothal—where Marian was waiting. Silently he took her in his strong arms, kissed her soft hair, her forehead and her sweet red lips, then turned and strode quickly away, as though he could not trust his courage longer.

A year passed, bringing two letters to Marian from her lover, telling her of such success as even his fondest hopes had failed to picture. At the end of the third year, just after another letter had come, telling her that the *Watersprite* was homeward bound, and happiness seemed in store for her, her father died. For months the old man had been slowly failing, living only in his daughter's happiness. Now that she did not need him longer, he seemed to lose all power of holding on to his life, and one evening passed quietly away with the setting of the sun.

The grief of the young girl was well-nigh unbearable. The only bright thing that life seemed to hold for her was the fact that her lover was on his way to her. So she waited anxiously, longingly, expecting tidings every day. But after the third letter no news came.

As the days lengthened to weeks, and the weeks to months, the islanders were filled with apprehension and forebodings. A gloom settled over the people, which even the lingering Indian summer failed to brighten; and when, one bleak November day, beneath a darkening sky, a strange vessel came into the harbor with tidings that the gallant *Watersprite* had sunk and every soul on board had perished, it was almost a relief to the anxious watchers. Certainty, though hard to bear, was better than hope deferred.

Gently did sympathetic friends tell the mournful news to the lonely girl at the point; but dazed and bewildered, she did not seem to comprehend their meaning. For days she lay in a kind of stupor, unheeding everything, even the presence of the kind old dame who watched by her side night and day with tear-dimmed eyes. Only when the waves dashed loudest would the girl stir uneasily, raising her head as though listening for some one's command.

At last she awoke from her long sleep, coming back once more to life and to her senses; but the beautiful hair was as white as the foam that dashed against the rocks she used to love, and the dark eyes looked large and mournful beneath the snowy wealth. As strength slowly came back to her, so also came the firm conviction that her lover was not dead, but would one day return to her. So firm was her faith that she grew cheerful, almost happy. Once more she assumed her duties,—clothing little children, ministering to the sick and aged, helping weary housewives. There was not a person on the island who had not at one time or another felt her kindly influence or her strong, stimulating presence.

Every night at dusk, after her day's work was done, she would place a large bright light in the window of the little sitting-room that looked toward the harbor, leaving the curtain drawn aside, so that should he for whom she watched come at night, he would find her still waiting for him. Not a night did she fail in this most important of all her duties. Her light was a bright beacon. Sailors soon learned to know it and look for it, and they never looked in vain; it was always there, steady clear, unwavering.

Thus passed several years, when suddenly, mysteriously, without a shadow of warning, Mistress Marian disappeared. As silently as years ago she had entered the life of the fisher folk, so now did she leave it; and as they knew not then whence she came, neither did they know now whither she went.

There were many conjectures as to her strange disappearance. One old sailor affirmed that one night when he was out fishing he saw a little boat come from the point, bearing a solitary passenger with snow-white hair, who rowed out toward a large ship that could be dimly seen, as through a fog, and was taken on board; then the huge ship quickly vanished. But as this old man was well known to take his black bottle with him on his fishing expeditions, and as no other person could be found who saw the wonderful ship, his story did not gain the credence that its ingenuity deserved. The most of the people inclined to the belief that she had gone back to her father's relatives; but how, when, or where, not even the old woman who lived with her could tell.

A decade or two passed, and the old house in its exposed locality grew more and more weatherworn and dilapidated; and finally, one winter, doubtless feeling that its time of usefulness had passed, it succumbed to fate and, during a heavy gale, fell to the ground. Some of the timbers were washed away, others were used for fire-wood by campers and fishermen; so that after a time nothing remained to mark the spot where the cottage had been, save a few damp, moss-covered logs.

But still in this same place on quiet summer nights during the hot sultry time of July and August,—the time when the *Watersprite* was said to have perished,—this weird, white, uncertain, trembling light, a few feet from the ground, is at times plainly seen. Not all the scientific explanations of wiser heads can convince the simple villagers that this strange light is any other than Marian's beacon for her sailor lover, or shake their faith in the plausibility of a story handed down from successive generations.

The merriest sailing party, rounding the point of a sweet summer night, will become subdued at the sight of the light, while the timid maiden will nestle closer to the skipper at the helm, as she says in awe-struck tones, "See! Mistress Marian's light is still burning."

MARY E. WILKINS FREEMAN
(1852–1930)

Mary E. Wilkins Freeman was a prolific author of novels, essays, plays, and short stories. She attended school in Vermont, and then briefly at Mount Holyoke Seminary. Her literary career began with the publication of her poetry, but she was soon able to support herself by the short stories she wrote for national publications. She remained single until 1902, when she made what was by all accounts an unhappy marriage. Freeman wrote about close-knit, rural New England communities. In spite of the bleakness of their lives, her female characters often startle us into respect and admiration for their rebellion against oppression. The women in her fine ghost stories are no exception; they too are descendants of the Puritans, but they strike out in even more unusual ways than do her other characters. "Luella Miller" was published in the December 1902 issue of *Everybody's Magazine.*

Luella Miller

CLOSE TO THE VILLAGE STREET STOOD THE ONE-STORY house in which Luella Miller, who had an evil name in the village, had dwelt. She had been dead for years, yet there were those in the village who, in spite of the clearer light which comes on a vantage-point from a long-past danger, half believed in the tale which they had heard from their childhood. In their hearts, although they scarcely would have owned it, was a survival of the wild horror and frenzied fear of their ancestors who had dwelt in the same age with Luella Miller. Young people even would stare with a shudder at the old house as they passed, and children never played around it as was their wont around an untenanted building. Not a window in the old Miller house was broken: the panes reflected the morning sunlight in patches of emerald and blue, and the latch of the sagging front door was never lifted, although no bolt secured it. Since Luella Miller had been carried out of it, the house had had no tenant except one friendless old soul who had no choice between that and the far-off shelter of the open sky. This old woman, who had survived her kindred and friends, lived in the house one week, then one morning no smoke came out of the chimney, and a body of neighbours, a score strong, entered and found her dead in her bed. There were dark whispers as to the cause of her death, and there were those who testified to an expression of fear so exalted that it showed forth the state of the departing soul upon the dead face. The old woman had been hale and hearty when she entered the house, and in seven days she was dead; it seemed that she had fallen a victim to some uncanny power. The minister talked in the pulpit with covert severity against the sin of superstition; still the belief prevailed. Not a soul in the village but would have chosen the almshouse rather than that dwelling. No vagrant, if he heard the tale, would seek shelter beneath that old roof, unhallowed by nearly half a century of superstitious fear.

There was only one person in the village who had actually known Luella Miller. That person was a woman well over eighty, but a marvel of vitality and unextinct youth. Straight as an arrow, with the spring of one recently let loose from the bow of life, she moved about the streets, and she always went to church, rain or shine. She had never married, and had lived alone for years in a house across the road from Luella Miller's.

This woman had none of the garrulousness of age, but never in all her life had she ever held her tongue for any will save her own, and she never spared the truth when she essayed to present it. She it was who bore testimony to the life, evil, though possibly wittingly or designedly so, of Luella Miller, and to her personal appearance. When this old woman spoke—and she had the gift of description, although her thoughts were clothed in the rude vernacular of her native village—one could seem to see Luella Miller as she had really looked. According to this woman, Lydia Anderson by name, Luella Miller had been a beauty of a type rather unusual in New England. She had been a slight, pliant sort of creature, as ready with a strong yielding to fate and as unbreakable as a willow. She had glimmering lengths of straight, fair hair, which she wore softly looped round a long, lovely face. She had blue eyes full of soft pleading, little slender, clinging hands, and a wonderful grace of motion and attitude.

"Luella Miller used to sit in a way nobody else could if they sat up and studied a week of Sundays," said Lydia Anderson, "and it was a sight to see her walk. If one of them willows over there on the edge of the brook could start up and get its roots free of the ground, and move off, it would go just the way Luella Miller used to. She had a green shot silk she used to wear, too, and a hat with green ribbon streamers, and a lace veil blowing across her face and out sideways, and a green ribbon flyin' from her waist. That was what she came out bride in when she married Erastus Miller. Her name before she was married was Hill. There was always a sight of "l's" in her name, married or single. Erastus Miller was good lookin', too, better lookin' than Luella. Sometimes I used to think that Luella wa'n't so handsome after all. Erastus just about worshiped her. I used to know him pretty well. He lived next door to me, and we went to school together. Folks used to say he was waitin' on me, but he wa'n't. I never thought he was except once or twice when he said things that some girls might have suspected meant somethin'. That was before Luella came here to teach the district school. It was funny how she came to get it, for folks said she hadn't any education, and that one of the big girls, Lottie Henderson, used to do all the teachin' for her, while she sat back and did embroidery work on a cambric pocket-handkerchief. Lottie Henderson was a real smart girl, a splendid scholar, and she just set her eyes by Luella, as all the girls did. Lottie would have made a real smart woman, but she died when Luella had been here about a year—just faded away and died: nobody knew what aided her. She dragged herself to that schoolhouse and helped Luella teach till the very last minute. The committee all knew how Luella didn't do much of the work herself, but they winked at it. It wa'n't long after Lottie died that Erastus married her. I always thought he hurried it up because she wa'n't fit to teach. One of the big boys used to help her after Lottie died, but he hadn't much government, and the school didn't do very well, and Luella might have had to give it up, for the committee couldn't have shut their eyes to things much longer. The boy that helped her was a real honest, innocent sort of fellow, and he was a good scholar, too. Folks said he overstudied, and that was the reason he was took crazy the year after Luella married, but I don't know. And I don't know what made Erastus Miller go into consumption of the blood the year after he was married: consumption wa'n't in his family. He just grew weaker and weaker, and went almost bent double when he tried to wait on Luella, and he spoke feeble, like an old man. He worked terrible hard till the last trying to save up a little to leave Luella. I've seen him out in the worst storms on a wood-sled—he used to cut and sell wood—and he was hunched up on top lookin' more dead than alive. Once I couldn't stand it: I went over and helped him pitch some wood on the cart—I was always strong in my arms. I wouldn't stop for all he told me to, and I guess he was glad enough for the help. That was only a week before he died. He fell on the kitchen floor while he was gettin' breakfast. He always got the breakfast and let Luella lay abed. He did all the sweepin' and the washin' and the ironin' and most of the cookin'. He couldn't bear to have Luella lift her finger, and she let him do for her. She lived like a queen for all the work she did. She didn't even do her sewin'. She said it made her shoulder ache to sew, and poor Erastus's sister Lily used to do all her sewin'. She wa'n't able to, either; she was never strong in her back, but she did it beautifully. She had to, to suit Luella, she was so dreadful particular. I never saw anythin' like the fagottin' and hemstitchin' that Lily Miller did for Luella. She made all Luella's weddin' outfit, and that green silk dress, after Maria Babbit cut it. Maria she cut it for nothin', and she did a lot more cuttin' and fittin' for nothin' for Luella, too. Lily Miller went to live with Luella after Erastus died. She gave up her home, though she was real attached to it and wa'n't a mite afraid to stay alone. She rented it and she went to live with Luella right away after the funeral."

Then this old woman, Lydia Anderson, who remembered Luella Miller, would go on to relate the story of Lily Miller. It seemed that on the removal of Lily Miller to the house of her dead brother, to live with his widow, the village people first began to talk. This Lily Miller had been hardly past her first youth, and a most robust and blooming woman, rosy-cheeked, with curls of strong, black hair overshadowing round, candid temples and bright dark eyes. It was not six months after she had taken up her residence with her sister-in-law that her rosy colour faded and her pretty curves became wan hollows. White shadows began to show in the black rings of her hair, and the light died out of her eyes, her features sharpened, and there were pathetic lines at her mouth, which yet wore always an expression of utter sweetness and even happiness. She was devoted to her sister; there was no doubt that she loved her with her whole heart, and was perfectly content in her service. It was her sole anxiety lest she should die and leave her alone.

"The way Lily Miller used to talk about Luella was enough to make you mad and enough to make you cry," said Lydia Anderson. "I've been in there sometimes toward the last when she was too feeble to cook and carried her some blanc-mange or custard—somethin' I thought she might relish, and she'd thank me, and when I asked her how she was, say she felt better than she did yesterday, and asked me if I didn't think she looked better, dreadful pitiful, and say poor Luella had an awful time takin' care of her and doin' the work—she wa'n't strong enough to do anythin'—when all the time Luella wa'n't liftin' her finger and poor Lily didn't get any care except what the neighbours gave her, and Luella eat up everythin' that was carried in for Lily. I had it real straight that she did. Luella used to just sit and cry and do nothin'. She did act real fond of Lily, and she pined away considerable, too.

There was those that thought she'd go into a decline herself. But after Lily died, her Aunt Abby Mixter came, and then Luella picked up and grew as fat and rosy as ever. But poor Aunt Abby begun to droop just the way Lily had, and I guess somebody wrote to her married daughter, Mrs. Sam Abbot, who lived in Barre, for she wrote her mother that she must leave right away and come and make her a visit, but Aunt Abby wouldn't go. I can see her now. She was a real good-lookin' woman, tall and large, with a big, square face and a high forehead that looked of itself kind of benevolent and good. She just tended out on Luella as if she had been a baby, and when her married daughter sent for her she wouldn't stir one inch. She'd always thought a lot of her daughter, too, but she said Luella needed her and her married daughter didn't. Her daughter kept writin' and writin', but it didn't do any good. Finally she came, and when she saw how bad her mother looked, she broke down and cried and all but went on her knees to have her come away. She spoke her mind out to Luella, too. She told her that she'd killed her husband and everybody that had anythin' to do with her, and she'd thank her to leave her mother alone. Luella went into hysterics, and Aunt Abby was so frightened that she called me after her daughter went. Mrs. Sam Abbot she went away fairly cryin' out loud in the buggy, the neighbours heard her, and well she might, for she never saw her mother again alive. I went in that night when Aunt Abby called for me, standin' in the door with her little green-checked shawl over her head. I can see her now. 'Do come over here, Miss Anderson,' she sung out, kind of gasping for breath. I didn't stop for anythin'. I put over as fast as I could, and when I got there, there was Luella laughin' and cryin' all together, and Aunt Abby trying to hush her, and all the time she herself was white as a sheet and shakin' so she could hardly stand. 'For the land sakes, Mrs. Mixter,' says I, 'you look worse than she does. You ain't fit to be up out of your bed.'

"'Oh, there ain't anythin' the matter with me,' says she. Then she went on talkin' to Luella. 'There, there, don't, don't, poor little lamb,' says she. 'Aunt Abby is here. She ain't goin' away and leave you. Don't, poor little lamb.'

"'Do leave her with me, Mrs. Mixter, and you get back to bed,' says I, for Aunt Abby had been layin' down considerable lately, though somehow she contrived to do the work.

"'I'm well enough,' says she. 'Don't you think she had better have the doctor, Miss Anderson?'

"'The doctor,' says I, 'I think *you* had better have the doctor. I think you need him much worse than some folks I could mention.' And I looked right straight at Luella Miller laughin' and cryin' and goin' on as if she was the centre of all creation. All the time she was actin' so—seemed as if she was too sick to sense anythin'—she was keepin' a sharp lookout as to how we took it out of the corner of one eye. I see her. You could never cheat me about Luella Miller. Finally I got real mad and I run home and I got a bottle of valerian I had, and I poured some boilin' hot water on a handful of catnip, and I mixed up that catnip tea with most half a wineglass of valerian, and I went with it over to Luella's. I marched right up to Luella, a-holdin' out of that cup, all smokin'. 'Now,' says I, 'Luella Miller, *you swaller this!*'

"'What is—what is it, oh, what is it?' she sort of screeches out. Then she goes off a-laughin' enough to kill.

"'Poor lamb, poor little lamb,' says Aunt Abby, standin' over her, all kind of tottery, and tryin' to bathe her head with camphor.

"'*You swaller this right down,*' says I. And I didn't waste any ceremony. I just took hold of Luella Miller's chin and I tipped her head back, and I caught her mouth open with laughin', and I clapped that cup to her lips, and I fairly hollered at her: 'Swaller, swaller, swaller!' and she gulped it right down. She had to, and I guess it did her good. Anyhow, she stopped cryin' and laughin' and let me put her to bed, and she went to sleep like a baby inside of half an hour. That was more than poor Aunt Abby did. She lay awake all that night and I stayed with her, though she tried not to have me; said she wa'n't sick enough for watchers. But I stayed, and I made some good cornmeal gruel and I fed her a teaspoon every little while all night long. It seemed to me as if she was jest dyin' from bein' all wore out. In the mornin' as soon as it was light I run over to the Bisbees and sent Johnny Bisbee for the doctor. I told him to tell the doctor to hurry, and he come pretty quick. Poor Aunt Abby didn't seem to know much of anythin' when he got there. You couldn't hardly tell she breathed, she was so used up. When the doctor had gone, Luella came into the room lookin' like a baby in her ruffled nightgown. I can see her now. Her eyes were as blue and her face all pink and white like a blossom, and she looked at Aunt Abby in the bed sort of innocent and surprised. 'Why,' says she, 'Aunt Abby ain't got up yet?'

"'No, she ain't,' says I, pretty short.

"'I thought I didn't smell the coffee,' says Luella.

"'Coffee,' says I. 'I guess if you have coffee this mornin' you'll make it yourself.'

"'I never made the coffee in all my life,' says she, dreadful astonished. 'Erastus always made the coffee as long as he lived, and then Lily she made it, and then Aunt Abby made it. I don't believe I *can* make the coffee, Miss Anderson.'

"'You can make it or go without, jest as you please,' says I.

"'Ain't Aunt Abby goin' to get up?' says she.

"'I guess she won't get up,' says I, 'sick as she is.' I was gettin' madder and madder. There was somethin' about that little pink-and-white thing standin' there and talkin' about coffee, when she had killed so many better folks than she was, and had jest killed another, that made me feel 'most as if I wished somebody would up and kill her before she had a chance to do any more harm.

"'Is Aunt Abby sick?' says Luella, as if she was sort of aggrieved and injured.

"'Yes,' says I, 'she's sick, and she's goin' to die, and then you'll be left alone, and you'll have to do for yourself and wait on yourself, or do without things.' I don't know but I was sort of hard, but it was the truth, and if I was any harder than Luella Miller had been I'll give up. I ain't never been sorry that I said it. Well, Luella, she up and had hysterics again at that, and I jest let her have 'em. All I did was to bundle her into the room on the other side of the entry where Aunt Abby couldn't hear her, if she wa'n't past it—I don't know but she was—and set her down hard in a chair and told her not to come back into the other room, and she minded. She had her hysterics in there till she got tired. When she found out that nobody was comin' to coddle her and do for her she stopped. At least I suppose she did. I had all I could do with poor Aunt Abby tryin' to keep the breath of life in her. The doctor had told me that she was dreadful low, and give me some very strong medicine to give to her in drops real often, and told me real particular about the nourishment. Well, I did as he told me real faithful till she wa'n't able to swaller any longer. Then I had her daughter sent for. I had begun to realize that she wouldn't last any time at all. I hadn't realized it before, though I spoke to Luella the way I did. The doctor he came, and Mrs. Sam Abbot, but when she got there it was too late; her mother was dead. Aunt Abby's daughter just give one look at her mother layin' there, then she turned sort of sharp and sudden and looked at me.

"'Where is she?' says she, and I knew she meant Luella.

"'She's out in the kitchen,' says I. 'She's too nervous to see folks die. She's afraid it will make her sick.'

"The Doctor he speaks up then. He was a young man. Old Doctor Park had died the year before, and this was a young fellow just out of college. 'Mrs. Miller is not strong,' says he, kind of severe, 'and she is quite right in not agitating herself.'

"'You are another, young man; she's got her pretty claw on you,' thinks I, but I didn't say anythin' to him. I just said over to Mrs. Sam Abbot that Luella was in the kitchen, and Mrs. Sam Abbot she went out there, and I went, too, and I never heard anythin' like the way she talked to Luella Miller. I felt pretty hard to Luella myself, but this was more than I ever would have dared to say. Luella she was too scared to go into hysterics. She jest flopped. She seemed to jest shrink away to nothin' in that kitchen chair, with Mrs. Sam Abbot standin' over her and talkin' and tellin' her the truth. I guess the truth was most too much for her and no mistake, because Luella presently actually did faint away, and there wa'n't any sham about it, the way I always suspected there was about them hysterics. She fainted dead away and we had to lay her flat on the floor, and the Doctor he came runnin' out and he said somethin' about a weak heart dreadful fierce to Mrs. Sam Abbot, but she wa'n't a mite scared. She faced him jest as white as even Luella was layin' there lookin' like death and the Doctor feelin' of her pulse.

"'Weak heart,' says she, 'weak heart; weak fiddlesticks! There ain't nothin' weak about that woman. She's got strength enough to hang onto other folks till she kills 'em. Weak? It was my poor mother that was weak: this woman killed her as sure as if she had taken a knife to her.'

"But the Doctor he didn't pay much attention. He was bendin' over Luella layin' there with her yellow hair all streamin' and her pretty pink-and-white face all pale, and her blue eyes like stars gone out, and he was holdin' onto her hand and smoothin' her forehead, and tellin' me to get the brandy in Aunt Abby's room, and I was sure as I wanted to be that Luella had got somebody else to hang onto, now Aunt Abby was gone, and I thought of poor Erastus Miller, and I sort of pitied the poor young Doctor, led away by a pretty face, and I made up my mind I'd see what I could do.

"I waited till Aunt Abby had been dead and buried about a month, and the Doctor was goin' to see Luella steady and folks were beginnin' to talk; then one evenin', when I knew the Doctor had been called out of town and wouldn't be round, I went over to Luella's. I found her all dressed up in a blue muslin with white polka dots on it, and her hair curled jest as pretty, and there wa'n't a young girl in the place could compare with her. There was somethin' about Luella Miller seemed to draw the heart right out of you, but she didn't draw it out of *me*. She was settin' rocking in the chair by her sittin'-room window, and Maria Brown had gone home. Maria Brown had been in to help her, or rather to do the work, for Luella wa'n't helped when she didn't do anythin'. Maria Brown was real capable and she didn't have any ties; she wa'n't married, and lived alone, so she'd offered. I couldn't see why she should do the work any more than Luella; she wa'n't any too strong; but she seemed to think she could and Luella seemed to think so, too, so she went over and did all the work—washed, and ironed, and baked, while Luella sat and rocked. Maria didn't live long afterward. She began to fade away just the same fashion the others had. Well, she was warned, but she acted real mad when folks said anythin': said Luella was a poor, abused woman, too delicate to help herself, and they'd ought to be ashamed, and if she died helpin' them that couldn't help themselves she would—and she did.

"'I s'pose Maria has gone home,' says I to Luella, when I had gone in and sat down opposite her.

"'Yes, Maria went half an hour ago, after she had got supper and washed the dishes,' says Luella, in her pretty way.

"'I suppose she has got a lot of work to do in her own house to-night,' says I, kind of bitter, but that was all thrown away on Luella Miller. It seemed to her right that other folks that wa'n't any better able than she was herself should wait on her, and she couldn't get it through her head that anybody should think it *wa'n't* right.

"'Yes,' says Luella, real sweet and pretty, 'yes, she said she had to do her washin' to-night. She has let it go for a fortnight along of comin' over here.'

"'Why don't she stay home and do her washin' instead of comin' over here and doin' *your* work, when you are just as well able, and enough sight more so, than she is to do it?' says I.

"Then Luella she looked at me like a baby who has a rattle shook at it. She sort of laughed as innocent as you please. 'Oh, I can't do the work myself, Miss Anderson,' says she. 'I never did. Maria *has* to do it.'

"Then I spoke out: 'Has to do it!' says I. 'Has to do it!' She don't have to do it, either. Maria Brown has her own home and enough to live on. She ain't beholden to you to come over here and slave for you and kill herself.'

"Luella she jest set and stared at me for all the world like a doll-baby that was so abused that it was comin' to life.

"'Yes, says I, 'she's killin' herself. She's goin' to die just the way Erastus did, and Lily, and your Aunt Abby. You're killin' her jest as you did them. I don't know what there is about you, but you seem to bring a curse,' says I. 'You kill everybody that is fool enough to care anythin' about you and do for you.'

"She stared at me and she was pretty pale.

"'And Maria ain't the only one you're goin' to kill,' says I. 'You're goin' to kill Doctor Malcom before you're done with him.'

"Then a red colour came flamin' all over her face. 'I ain't goin' to kill him, either,' says she, and she begun to cry.

"'Yes, you *be*!' says I. Then I spoke as I had never spoke before. You see, I felt it on account of Erastus. I told her that she hadn't any business to think of another man after she'd been married to one that had died for her: that she was a dreadful woman; and she was, that's true enough, but sometimes I have wondered lately if she knew it—if she wa'n't like a baby with scissors in its hand cuttin' everybody without knowin' what it was doin'.

"Luella she kept gettin' paler and paler, and she never took her eyes off my face. There was somethin' awful about the way she looked at me and never spoke one word. After awhile I quit talkin' and I went home. I watched that night, but her lamp went out before nine o'clock, and when Doctor Malcom came drivin' past and sort of slowed up he see there wa'n't any light and he drove along. I saw her sort of shy out of meetin' the next Sunday, too, so he shouldn't go home with her, and I begun to think mebbe she did have some conscience after all. It was only a week after that that Maria Brown died— sort of sudden at the last, though everybody had seen it was comin'. Well, then there was a good deal of feelin' and pretty dark whispers. Folks said the days of witchcraft had come again, and they were pretty shy of Luella. She acted sort of offish to the Doctor and he didn't go there, and there wa'n't anybody to do anythin' for her. I don't know how she *did* get along. I wouldn't go in there and offer to help her—not because I was afraid of dyin' like the rest, but I thought she was just as well able to do her own work as I was to do it for her, and I thought it was about time that she did it and stopped killin' other folks. But it wa'n't very long before folks began to say that Luella herself was goin' into a decline jest the way her husband, and Lily, and Aunt Abby and the others had, and I saw myself that she looked pretty bad. I used to see her goin' past from the store with a bundle as if she could hardly crawl, but I remembered how Erastus used to wait and 'tend when he couldn't hardly put one foot before the other, and I didn't go out to help her.

"But at last one afternoon I saw the Doctor come drivin' up like mad with his medicine chest, and Mrs. Babbit came in after supper and said that Luella was real sick.

"'I'd offer to go in and nurse her,' says she, 'but I've got my children to consider, and mebbe it ain't true what they say, but it's queer how many folks that have done for her have died.'

"I didn't say anythin', but I considered how she had been Erastus's wife and how he had set his eyes by her, and I made up my mind to go in the next mornin', unless she was better, and see what I could do; but the next mornin' I see her at the window, and pretty soon she came steppin' out as spry as you please, and a little while afterward Mrs. Babbit came in and told me that the Doctor had got a girl from out of town, a Sarah Jones, to come there, and she said she was pretty sure that the Doctor was goin' to marry Luella.

"I saw him kiss her in the door that night myself, and I knew it was true. The woman came that afternoon, and the way she flew around was a caution. I don't believe Luella had swept since Maria died. She swept and dusted, and washed and ironed; wet clothes and dusters and carpets were flyin' over there all day, and every time Luella set her foot out when the Doctor wa'n't there there was that Sarah Jones helpin' of her up and down the steps, as if she hadn't learned to walk.

"Well, everybody knew that Luella and the Doctor were goin' to be married, but it wa'n't long before they began to talk about his lookin' so poorly, jest as they had about the others; and they talked about Sarah Jones, too.

"Well, the Doctor did die, and he wanted to be married first, so as to leave what little he had to Luella, but he died before the minister could get there, and Sarah Jones died a week afterward.

"Well, that wound up everything for Luella Miller. Not another soul in the whole town would lift a finger for her. There got to be a sort of panic. Then she began to droop in good earnest. She used to have to go to the store herself, for Mrs. Babbit was afraid to let Tommy go for her, and I've seen her goin' past and stoppin' every two or three steps to rest. Well, I stood it as long as I could, but one day I see her comin' with her arms full and stoppin' to lean against the Babbit fence, and I run out and took her bundles and carried them to her house. Then I went home and never spoke one word to her though she called after me dreadful kind of pitiful. Well, that night I was taken sick with a chill, and I was sick as I wanted to be for two weeks. Mrs. Babbit had seen me run out to help Luella and she came in and told me I was goin' to die on account of it. I didn't know whether I was or not, but I considered I had done right by Erastus's wife.

"That last two weeks Luella she had a dreadful hard time, I guess. She was pretty sick, and as near as I could make out nobody dared go near her. I don't know as she was really needin' anythin' very much, for there was enough to eat in her house and it was warm weather, and she made out to cook a little flour gruel every day, I know, but I guess she had a hard time, she that had been so petted and done for all her life.

"When I got so I could go out, I went over there one morning. Mrs. Babbit had just come in to say she hadn't seen any smoke and she didn't know but it was somebody's duty to go in, but she couldn't help thinkin' of her children, and I got right up, though I hadn't been out of the house for two weeks, and I went in there, and Luella she was layin' on the bed, and she was dyin'.

"She lasted all that day and into the night. But I sat there after the new doctor had gone away. Nobody else dared to go there. It was about midnight that I left her for a minute to run home and get some medicine I had been takin', for I begun to feel rather bad.

"It was a full moon that night, and just as I started out of my door to cross the street back to Luella's, I stopped short, for I saw something."

Lydia Anderson at this juncture always said with a certain defiance that she did not expect to be believed, and then proceeded in a hushed voice:

"I saw what I saw, and I know I saw it, and I will swear on my death bed that I saw it. I saw Luella Miller and Erastus Miller, and Lily, and Aunt Abby, and Maria, and the Doctor, and Sarah, all goin' out of her door, and all but Luella shone white in the moonlight, and they were all helpin' her along till she seemed to fairly fly in the midst of them. Then it all disappeared. I stood a minute with my heart poundin', then I went over there. I thought of goin' for Mrs. Babbit, but I thought she'd be afraid. So I went alone, though I knew what had happened. Luella was layin' real peaceful, dead on her bed."

This was the story that the old woman, Lydia Anderson, told, but the sequel was told by the people who survived her, and this is the tale which has become folklore in the village.

Lydia Anderson died when she was eighty-seven. She had continued wonderfully hale and hearty for every one of her years until about two weeks before her death.

One bright moonlight evening she was sitting beside a window in her parlour when she made a sudden exclamation, and was out of the house and across the street before the neighbour who was taking care of her could stop her. She followed as fast as possible and found Lydia Anderson stretched on the ground before the door of Luella Miller's deserted house, and she was quite dead.

The next night there was a red gleam of fire athwart the moonlight and the old house of Luella Miller was burned to the ground. Nothing is now left of it except a few old cellar stones and a lilac bush, and in summer a helpless trail of morning glories among the weeds, which might be considered emblematic of Luella herself.

———————•◆•———————